THE
SCANDAL

THE
SCANDAL

NICOLA MARSH

GRAND CENTRAL
PUBLISHING

New York   Boston

Copyright © 2019 by Nicola Marsh

Cover design by Flag. Cover images from Getty Images: photo of woman © PeopleImages, photo of nursery mobile © Henry Steadman. Cover copyright © 2021 by Hachette Book Group, Inc.

Grand Central Publishing
Hachette Book Group
1290 Avenue of the Americas, New York, NY 10104
grandcentralpublishing.com
twitter.com/grandcentralpub

Originally published in 2019 by Bookouture, an imprint of StoryFire Ltd.
First Grand Central Publishing edition published in trade paperback in October 2020

First Mass Market Edition: September 2021

Grand Central Publishing is a division of Hachette Book Group, Inc. The Grand Central Publishing name and logo is a trademark of Hachette Book Group, Inc.

The publisher is not responsible for websites (or their content) that are not owned by the publisher.

The Hachette Speakers Bureau provides a wide range of authors for speaking events. To find out more, go to www.hachettespeakersbureau.com or call (866) 376-6591.

LCCN: 2020938822

ISBN: 978-1-5387-3475-9 (mass market)

Printed in the United States of America

CW

10 9 8 7 6 5 4 3 2 1

For Millie and Ollie, I'm blessed to have parents like you.

THE
SCANDAL

PROLOGUE

Have you ever done something so terrible, so horrific, that it haunts you? A vile memory that clogs your throat and blurs your mind and sits like a heavy weight in your gut?

I have.

The memory of what I've recently done disturbs me. Every waking minute, every sleeping one too. The nightmares are bad; the kind that linger after I jolt awake, bathed in sweat, my hands trembling, my breathing ragged and harsh in the silence.

I pretend like I'm fine. I'm good at it. I've had a lifetime's practice. Fake it till you make it. But lately, it's increasingly hard to act like everything's fine. Because it's not. I'm unraveling.

I find myself drifting off at the oddest of times. I forget appointments. I order milk in my coffee when I always take it black. I jog into town when my daily route is along the beach. I can hide these oddities most of the time but those closest to me might start to suspect something's wrong and I can't have that.

I can't risk them knowing I harbor darkness inside, the kind that lashes out when I least expect it.

I killed someone.

Not accidentally. Not out of spite or revenge. Not out of deep-seated rage.

I killed because life is about choices and I choose me.

My secret is safe.

No one knows. Yet.

Because I choose *me*.

CHAPTER ONE

MARISA

Some women meet monthly for book clubs. But it's tedious being forced to read the latest literary masterpiece a friend has chosen when I'd rather have my nose stuck in a steamy romance, so I instigated a gardening club. Not the kind where Claire, Elly, and I weed or prune or plant. It's more the kind of club that takes place *in* a garden; with wine and cheese.

Besides, the thought of my glamorous friend Elly doing anything as menial as gardening is laughable, and Claire's far too busy chasing bad guys to mulch. I asked them once, if they'd like to actually garden when they came over. They'd declared me certifiably insane.

So, we sit under the towering oak in the far corner of my perfectly maintained garden sipping sublime Chardonnay, nibbling on imported Camembert, and discussing our lives in Gledhill.

People may envy us, living in the Hamptons: the beaches, the mansions, the restaurants, and enough celebrity sightings to keep things interesting. Considering my past I never take it for granted that I'm now residing in this idyllic location in my eight-bedroom, four-bathroom Colonial, complete with pool-house and tennis court. Avery and I worked hard to get where we are. We deserve to enjoy the spoils.

Not everyone feels the same way. I see how some of the less privileged townsfolk look at me: sly, covetous glances that judge me for living a privileged life. They choose not to see through my fragile façade to the uncertain woman beneath. They don't know how I've clawed my way to the life I now enjoy.

I don't like being found lacking by anybody, so I volunteer. A lot. I deliver meals to the elderly, I spend time at a youth center in Montauk, I man a stall at the monthly market, and I raise money for local charities. The generosity of my fellow Hampton inhabitants is legendary. They have money to spare.

But no matter how much I give back to my community I feel guilty somehow. Silly, because I work and I contribute. It's never enough.

"Sorry I'm late." Claire steps onto the back patio, a store-bought carrot cake in one hand and a Shiraz in the other. "Got caught up at work. I had to finish a stack of paperwork after that multi on the highway outside Greenport last night."

"Don't worry, Elly's not here yet."

She'll make a grand entrance as usual, craving attention, flaunting her freedom, making Claire and me feel like old married crones. And I do feel like a crone. Any woman would next to the perfection that is Avery Thurston. I chose this life. I knew what I was getting into when I married him. It doesn't make the reality any easier.

My life is like one of those cheap snow globes my twins collected when they were younger. Shiny and pretty on the outside, blurred beyond recognition when shaken.

Quashing my residual bitterness, I gesture at the table set up near the balustrade, covered in the usual nibbles I set out: crackers, cheese, antipasto, dips, and crudités. "I thought we could eat up here for a change?"

"Sure." Claire places the bottle of wine and cake on the table then gives me a peck on the cheek. "Let's go wild, shake things up a little."

I smile, shooting Claire a quick look. She sounds odd, her voice a tad high, like something's bothering her. Highly unusual, considering Claire is the calm one among us. Nothing

ever ruffles her. Her ability to stay detached from unpleasant-
ness makes her an excellent cop. As a friend, her cool logic has
defused many a tense moment. We've had a few of those after
what Elly went through last year.

"Everything okay?"

She nods, but I see a glimmer of wariness in her eyes.
"Nothing a good sugar fix won't cure."

All isn't right in my friend's ordered world. Claire is a health
freak: high protein, low carbs, minimal sugar. She always
brings cake but never eats it. The mother in me always wants
to fatten up her and Elly, to encourage them to indulge without
fear. I'd known that fear once but in my case it had been fear
of starvation. My mom had never cared what I ate; when she'd
been home, that is. Surviving on TV dinners and snacks I could
scrounge ensured I plied my own kids with food from the time
they could ingest solids.

No child of mine would ever know the gnawing hunger that
makes a belly ache, the feeling of emptiness that expanded
daily until it consumed you, the constant disappointment of a
parent not giving a damn.

I know Claire and Elly abstain from sugary treats because
of the inevitable terror women face when standing on the scales
and seeing those digital pounds tick over. So I don't shove food
down their throats like I want to. They'll discover soon enough
that with age comes curves, no matter how many choc chip
cookies they forego. Metabolism's a bitch.

"So cake before wine then?"

She holds up two fingers. "Give me a double of both."

Another sign Claire's rattled: she flops into a deckchair rather
than helping me. Claire's a doer, always at hand to assist when
needed.

Fate brought us together when she'd been transferred to
the Hamptons two years ago and attended a botched burglary
six months later at the halfway house where I volunteered. I'm
good at reading people and knew instantly Claire cared beyond

her job. She'd lingered longer than the other cops, had taken the time to ensure the battered women and the homeless street kids at the shelter felt safe by offering reassurance and exuding a quiet calm. She'd impressed me that night, exhibiting empathy beyond duty, and I instinctively knew that Claire working the Gledhill beat was the NYPD's loss.

On impulse I'd asked her out for coffee after her shift ended and we'd met Elly the same day. We'd both needed something stronger after the long hours calming terrified women at the shelter so we'd swapped coffee for martinis at a bar and Elly had been there, alone.

Elly wasn't the type of woman I'd normally befriend. Stunning on the surface, from her designer shoes to her flawless makeup, wearing her sexuality like a killer outfit. But the eyes never lie and I knew, with the instinct of dealing with fragile women for years, that Elly's overt beauty hid a brittleness she strove to hide. She'd flicked a disparaging glance at me and I'd glimpsed how forlorn she'd been, radiating a palpable loneliness, so I couldn't help myself. We've been friends ever since.

Avery teases me about my rescue complex. Helping others makes me feel good in a way I haven't felt since Trish and Terry left for college two years ago. The girls are my world and that world semi-imploded the day they'd shipped off to UCLA without a backward glance.

Empty nest syndrome my ass. Try empty house, empty heart. I'd pined for a week before Avery had snapped and even I'd grown sick of myself. I found a job the next day. Initially as a volunteer at the halfway house and six months later, as a paid social worker for the Gledhill Help Center. I never let my registration lapse even when I'd been a full-time mom, and returning to my profession gave me a renewed sense of purpose.

If my kids don't need me, other people do. I like being needed. I crave it, like addicts crave their next fix. Without it, I have too much time to think, to analyze.

I don't like doing that.

"Hey, ladies, what's happening?" Elly sashays onto the patio and places her usual offering—a bottle of French champagne—on the table.

She's wearing a magenta strapless sundress that's bold and glamorous. Her wild, curly, blonde hair is styled into a fancy chignon, her makeup is perfect, her cat-like green eyes are bright, and her nude wedges add another four inches onto her average height. She looks like she's stepped off the pages of a glossy mag and I experience the inevitable twinge of envy. If I didn't like her so much I'd hate her. But we've been through a lot together. When Elly needed me I was there for her, and while we never talk of that awful night, I remember when my friend fell apart and my heart broke for her.

"We're about to consume our body weight in alcohol." Claire stands and crosses to the table. "What are we drinking first, ladies?"

"Champagne," Elly says, at the same time I say, "Shiraz."

Elly wrinkles her nose. "You and your fancy-schmancy red wine."

Claire shoots her a glare and uncorks the wine. "Quit your moaning and pass your glass."

"Why are we up here anyway?" Elly glances around, her gaze drifting to our usual spot at the end of the garden. "I like being under that oak. It gives me a perfect view of that hot gardener next door."

Claire rolls her eyes and I laugh. Claire has a low tolerance for Elly's sexploits. Not that she dates a lot but when she does she regales us with exaggerated saucy tales. I don't mind. Being married for almost twenty-one years leaves no surprises. Not that Avery still isn't attractive: at fifty-two, he's sexier than most men his age, in that classic tall, dark, and handsome way. Women's heads turn when Avery strides past. Even after knowing him for twenty-two years, I wonder what he sees in me. I'm tall and slim with unusual hazel eyes but my particular shade of brunette comes from a bottle and I work like a maniac at maintaining my figure.

"Here you go." I hand Elly a glass of Napa's finest red. "It's the gardener's day off so I thought we'd stay up here for a change."

Elly pretends to pout. "Is Ryan home then? I need some eye candy."

Another thing about Avery that bugs me: his younger brother, Ryan, lives next door and despite the eighteen-months age difference they're like twins joined by some weird symbiotic bond. They're charming, charismatic, and self-absorbed, with a penchant for pushing boundaries.

Ever since I've known them Ryan has taken advantage of Avery: borrowing money and using him to get him out of scrapes initially, muscling his way into a managerial position in Avery's company later. I'm used to Ryan waltzing into our house any time of day or night, usually to ask Avery for another "favor." He's like an overgrown child and I treat him like the son I never had. Everyone loves Ryan. Pity I don't feel the same about his wife, Maggie.

"Ryan's always around. Though with Avery in Manhattan on business for a couple of days, maybe he'll make himself scarce."

I'd never admit it to anyone but I like the fact my industrious CEO husband travels a lot for work. I like having the house to myself. It takes the pressure off. Avery has a high libido and mine is nonexistent. On the rare occasion our schedules coincide for a quickie in the bedroom we're rote and lackluster. He's a busy man, I'm a tired woman. Like most parents our sex lives dwindled after the twins arrived and I'd dreaded picking up after the girls left for college.

These days, Avery touches me occasionally in the hope it leads to sex and I either laugh off his overtures or feign interest. If we actually do the deed, I inevitably fake it. He never notices. Avery rarely notices anything beyond his own insular world where he resides at the center.

"Damn. So all I have to look at is you two?" Elly snorts

in mock disgust and sips her wine, shooting me a wink that's endearing.

I chuckle but Claire doesn't join in. She stares into her wine like it holds some great secret.

"What's up with you?" Elly leans forward and taps Claire on the knee.

Surprisingly, it takes Claire a few seconds to realize we're both staring at her, and as I wait for her to answer, unease gnaws at my gut. Claire normally begins gardening club chatting about work; she loves regaling us with gory cop stories but she's hardly said a word, has drained her first glass of wine and is halfway through her second.

She swirls her wine absentmindedly. "You don't want to hear my sorry-ass news."

"Yes, we do." I pull my chair closer, leaving enough room so she won't feel crowded. "You haven't taunted either of us once so something's definitely up."

Claire sighs and Elly shoots me a confused look. I give a slight shake of my head, indicating we need to give her time.

After several more swirls of her wine glass, Claire finally looks up and I know what she's about to say is bad, really bad. She never cries and she's blinking rapidly.

I reach out but she scoots back as if my touch will unravel her completely. "Honey, what's wrong—"

"Dane and I can't have kids…" She trails off, her voice so soft that at first I wonder if I've misheard. But when she stifles a sob and murmurs, "He's infertile," I know the news is as bad as I first thought.

Claire is inherently a giver. Giving her dedication to the force, giving herself to Dane. She has a lot of love to give to a child and from a few hints she's dropped over the last year I assume they've been trying.

Now this. I can't imagine my world without my twins and to see how shattered Claire is over her inability to have kids with Dane is heartbreaking.

She dashes a hand across her eyes and lifts her chin in mock fierceness, but I see the devastation in her gaze. Claire is a master at being in control at all times but she's struggling and I wish I could take away her pain.

"I'm sorry, sweetie." Elly leans over and squeezes Claire's hand with the kind of caring I know she's capable of but rarely displays, too busy wearing her impenetrable armor. Claire and I know what's behind her bravado but we never call her on it. "Is there anything I can do?"

"Not really." Claire pinches the bridge of her nose and I know she's staving off tears.

Seeing Claire cry would be as monumentally shocking as witnessing Elly walk down the main street without makeup. Never going to happen. I know why Elly is always so immaculate, why she goes to great lengths to coordinate her outfits with her accessories, why her hair is lustrous and her makeup flawless. Presenting an impeccable front is at complete odds with the night we saw her completely unraveled, a physical and emotional mess.

"You've explored all options?" I sound callous, but at times like this I can't suppress my practical side. It's usually a strength, finding solutions to unsolvable problems. By the way Claire glares at me, it's not today.

"We only found out last week." Claire shakes her head, her brown ponytail skimming her shoulders, her eyes bright with unshed tears. "And the thought of considering options like sperm banks and donors and IVF and injections and adoption freaks me out..." She presses the pads of her fingers to her eyes and Elly makes a slashing action across her neck.

As if I could abandon this conversation without trying to ease Claire's pain.

"I've got contacts in several adoption agencies. And I know a top-notch attorney who facilitates private adoptions without charging a fortune."

When she doesn't respond, I add, "I have experience in this

field so could speed up the process for you if that's what you choose to do?"

Claire finally lowers her hands and looks at me. She's lost the death glare, thankfully. "It's kind of you to offer but leave it with me for a while, okay?"

Her gratitude is audible, like it's helped just talking about it and I know I have to do more.

"Sure," I say, ready to start investigating options for my friend first thing in the morning, just in case. Better to be prepared. A motto I've followed my entire life and it hasn't steered me wrong yet.

Elly holds up the wine bottle. "Refill?"

"To the brim." Claire drinks what's left in her glass then holds it out, her expression grim. "I've finally got a week off starting tomorrow, even though I needed it more when we first found out six days ago. But it's worked out well because I'm still not handling the infertility news and I plan on spending at least half that time drowning my sorrows."

Elly raises a perfectly shaped brow. Claire rarely drinks more than one glass at our monthly meetings and even less if we go out for dinner. I could lecture her on the futility of consuming alcohol to help solve problems. I don't. Who am I to talk when I've been guilty of the same vice late at night, alone, when the doubts creep in and I'm left wondering if my perfect life isn't so perfect after all?

I raise my glass and clink it against Claire's. "To you and Dane."

Elly winces at my faux cheerfulness but does the same.

Claire says nothing. The devastation in her big brown eyes says it all.

Of course, Ryan chooses that moment to waltz into the backyard like he owns the place. I resent the intrusion because our faux garden club meetings are a great way to de-stress. We usually swap pleasantries at the start—nothing like the bombshell Claire dropped on us today—then Claire talks about work but after a glass or two of wine we really get going. Laughing at inane jokes, gently jibing at each other in self-deprecation, complaining about the men in our lives, gossiping about people we know. We could've really done with the distraction today but Ryan's appearance has circumvented that and for a moment I contemplate sending him home. But I'm never that rude, especially not to family, considering I have none other than the one I married into.

"Hello, lovelies." He vaults the balustrade surrounding the patio and I'm pretty sure we all sigh in unison.

Ryan has that effect on women. He's not classically handsome, with that slight bump on his nose and his eyes spaced a tad too far apart, but there's something about him that draws attention. He's six-two, fit, with dark wavy hair and blue eyes the same shade as the Atlantic on a summer's day. Elly had once mentioned the comparison and he'd loved it.

"Can I join this party?" He doesn't wait for an answer and pulls up a chair. "Hey, gorgeous, can I have a drink? I'm parched."

I roll my eyes like I always do when he calls me this and gesture at the table. "Help yourself. But one drink and you're out of here."

"Heartless." He clutches his chest in mock indignation, his little-boy grin beyond charming.

"That's not very hospitable," Elly says, reaching for the Shiraz and pouring a healthy slosh into a glass while her coy smile makes Ryan's cheeky grin widen. "Here you go, handsome."

"Thanks." He raises his glass. "A toast to the three most beautiful women in the Hamptons."

Claire snorts but at least her eyes have lost that devastating, haunting darkness.

I say, "Don't let Maggie hear you say that."

He waves away my dry response. "Maggie's fine."

"Is she?" We lock gazes and he knows I'm asking for real answers and not making small talk. "I haven't seen her in a while."

For the first time since he arrived, his inherent cheeriness fades. "She's going through one of her phases."

I know what that means. She's hibernating, zealously cleaning the house and throwing out barely used items, frantically culling everything from clothes to kitchen utensils, skipping meals and dosing up on herbal tonics. I learned early on not to interfere when she's in one of her *phases*, as Ryan calls her obsession with detoxing. It's not a medical condition but I often think maybe it should be, she's that manic with regularly cleansing her life.

Maggie only tolerates me when she wants something and thankfully that's not very often. We're not close. Not from lack of trying on my part. I've cooked healthy meals for her during her phases, I've dropped off groceries, and I've included her in my social circle. But there's always an invisible barrier between us, like she's ashamed I've seen her at her most manic. She doesn't have to be. I've seen it all, and then some, working at the Help Center.

It must be tough living with her vagaries and I admire Ryan's patience in dealing with her eccentricities. Then again, Ryan enjoys a lavish lifestyle and thanks to his marriage to Maggie and her trust fund, he has it.

I eyeball Ryan. "Please give her my best and tell her to give me a call if she needs anything."

Elly, getting bored with our polite family conversation, interrupts. "Whenever Maggie pops into work she's fine, so let's stop discussing my boss and move on to more important things."

She does a cutesy finger wave at Ryan. "Personally, I think this man has excellent taste and if he thinks we're the most beautiful women in the Hamptons, I believe him."

Ryan laughs and the usual tension that discussing Maggie elicits dissolves. "What about you, Claire-Bear? You're awfully quiet."

Claire doesn't suffer fools lightly but for some reason she

puts up with Ryan's overt personality. He's loud, brash, and flirtatious but she's like me, tolerating him with a fondness that borders on indulgence and treating him like a younger brother.

"I'm trying to enjoy my wine by tuning out your bullshit."

He winces. "Ouch. You wound me, Claire-Bear."

"Yeah, I can see that." A small smile plays about her mouth and I'm glad that Ryan dropped in. He's the perfect antidote to the glumness pervading my friend. "You've got a hide like a freaking rhino."

He half lifts off the seat and pats his ass. "So you've been checking out my hide?"

We all laugh as he intends and I catch Ryan's eye. He has no hope of interpreting my grateful glance and his eyebrow rises. I shrug and he smiles, so much like Avery that for a moment my heart skips. I'm not attracted to Ryan, not in a sexual way, but his personality is so much bigger and brighter than my husband's that I envy his ease with people.

Whereas my girlfriends love Ryan, they tolerate Avery. Claire's always wary around him, like she doesn't quite trust him, and Elly's interaction with him is muted, which is a sure-fire sign she doesn't like him.

Avery picks up on their subtle dislike too. He's always polite but in that reserved way at complete odds with his usual charm with other women. I guess I should be grateful he's not like Ryan, always pretending to hit on my friends. But where Ryan's flirtations are harmless, I often wonder if Avery's flattery toward women holds more intent.

Claire drains her glass far too quickly and stands. She's unsteady for a moment, clutching at the back of the chair. "I have to go."

"So soon?" Ryan grabs her hand and I know my friend's tipsy when she lets him hold it.

"Thanks, Ris, it's been fun." She yanks her hand out of Ryan's and stumbles a little. Three glasses in quick succession is way too much for her.

"You're not driving home," I say, and Claire rolls her eyes.

"I'm not stupid. I'll leave my car here and walk home."

I nod in agreement and Claire waves at Elly. "Bye."

"Take care." Elly blows her a kiss.

"Thanks." Claire touches Elly's shoulder and bends to give me a brief hug. I squeeze tight, hoping to convey how much I'm hurting for her.

When she straightens, Ryan's arms are wide. "Where's my hug?"

"You're an idiot," she says, but hugs him just the same.

Despite his bluster Ryan's incredibly perceptive and waits until she leaves before asking, "What's up with Claire?"

"Women's business," Elly and I respond in unison, surprisingly in sync for once.

Ryan chuckles and holds up his hands. "Say no more. But she's sad and even my bullshit couldn't snap her out of it."

"It did for a while, so thanks." I pat his arm and he actually blushes.

"You actually don't mind me hanging out here despite the many times you tell me to leave?" He knows I'm a pushover for his hangdog expression because it works every time.

"That's because you practically live here."

I know why. It's difficult being in Maggie's company for more than thirty minutes; how Ryan puts up with her emotional fragility I have no idea. My minimal meaningful contact has nothing to do with a lack of understanding or compassion. I want to smother her with kindness she doesn't want and has told me in great detail during one of her particularly bad phases. She's borderline OCD and has to be in control all the time. I guess accepting my help equates with weakness for her, so she'd rather avoid me and I can't stand not being needed.

"I love you too, sis-in-law." He blows me a kiss and I roll my eyes.

"On that note, lovelies, I'll leave you to your inane gossip." Ryan places his glass on the table and pops a cube of cheese into his mouth. "Feel free to talk about me as much as you like when I leave."

"Good riddance," Elly says, but there's no bite behind her words and Ryan's wide grin indicates he knows it.

"See you later." He holds up his hand in farewell and vaults over the balustrade again before strolling around the side of the house in the direction of his.

"He's such an idiot." Elly sips at her wine, her expression pensive.

"But he's our idiot." I gesture at the food. "Please eat."

She shakes her head and points at her teeny waist. "And ruin this?"

"You're too thin."

"Yes, Mom." She rolls her eyes but her smile is kind. "Speaking of weight, I haven't seen you at Pilates lately?"

I grimace and flex my knee gingerly. "I'm too old to twist my body into a pretzel."

Elly snorts. "You're gorgeous and you know it."

"Actually, I don't."

Damn, where had that come from? I never air my insecurities with the girls, unless Claire and I are joking around and poking fun at our thigh cellulite, our muffin-tops, and our necessity to have more frequent waxing sessions as we age and hair sprouts faster.

I can blame the wine for my loose lips but I know it has more to do with my life; Avery taking me for granted and barely acknowledging I exist unless he wants me to host one of his work parties. A lifetime of pretense wears thin eventually.

Elly's eyebrows shoot up. "You're the most confident, poised, amazing woman I know so where's the insecurity coming from?"

I wave away her concern. "Don't mind me. Wine makes me maudlin sometimes."

Elly stares at me and I wait for her to call me on my BS; we both know wine makes me giggly rather than sad. But thankfully she raises her glass instead.

"I know that look, Ris. And whatever the jerk has done or not done, he's not worth it." She scowls. "No man is."

She's way too intuitive and I force a laugh before I blurt exactly how unhappy I am these days. "Hey, keep that up and you'll be taking over my job."

Her nose crinkles. "I could never be a social worker. I'm not that much of a goody-goody."

"Now who's kidding who?"

Our gazes lock and I'm struck once again by how special the bond is between the three of us. We're lucky to have found each other and I'll do anything to maintain our friendship.

As if sensing I'm about to get all deep and meaningful, Elly makes a grand show of glancing at her watch.

"Sorry, but I have to run. Do you think Claire's going to be okay?"

I nod, though I'm not confident at all. "I'll give her a call later. Maybe we can all get together in a few days, show our moral support?"

"Sounds like a plan." Elly kisses me on the cheek. "Thanks, Ris."

Her tone is wistful and when she eases away I glimpse something akin to regret in her eyes. But before I can ask if she's okay she's gone, traipsing down the patio stairs at an impossibly brisk pace for those towering wedges.

CHAPTER TWO

CLAIRE

It's almost sunset when I leave my car at Marisa's and walk home. Luckily, we both live on Sunnyside Drive and it's just a fifteen-minute stagger until I reach my front door. I've consumed enough alcohol to take the edge off my ongoing sadness. I'd fail a sobriety test if one of my colleagues pulled me over, which is why I don't drive home. I'm shattered but not stupid.

I usually consider Marisa's monthly gardening club gathering as something to tolerate. Ris, as she insists we call her, is the planner of our little threesome. She makes an effort to get us together regularly: dinners, movies, coffee dates, the occasional fundraiser, as well as the hokey gardening club. I should be grateful. If it weren't for Ris I'd have no friends in this town. She made me feel welcome at a time I needed it most, floundering in a new job in an affluent town, missing the vibe of the city and my old precinct.

So I attend out of obligation and try not to analyze why three women with so little in common are best friends. I think Elly feels the same. Elly's gratitude probably compels her to show up too. We're like some codependent sorority who bonded when we least expected it.

Deep down I know why we still cling to this unlikely friendship. We're similar: fiercely projecting our independence but with wounded cores we determinedly hide from the world.

Ris is a doer. She's so active in our local community that

everybody knows her name, from Dirk the trash collector to Phil the old guy who manually sweeps the boardwalk every night. She raises money for countless causes and is revered among the local charities. But I see behind her ruse. She keeps busy for fear of standing still. I don't know what's behind her funk—her marriage to that egotist Avery, missing her twins at college, or something more sinister—but I pity her. She appears to have it all but seems so...lost.

With Elly, her brashness hides a world of pain, some of which Ris and I have been witness to. I want to hug her every time I see her but knowing her she'd brush it off. She exudes fragility beneath her faux confidence and I hope that if she ever needs to talk about that horrendous night fourteen months ago I'll be there for her.

As for me, today I spilled too much. I blame Ris. Her nurturing always gets to me. Maybe that's why I like her. She's the sister I never had. One minute I'd been staring into my wine wishing things could be different, the next I'd almost started sobbing and had reluctantly divulged the truth.

Ris, the fixer, offered practical solutions. Elly, the emotionally repressed, appeared concerned. And I sat there, pretending I wasn't dying inside. Ryan's arrival had been timely. I'd been on the verge of bawling and his usual nonsense had been a welcome distraction.

I lurch to the front door and jab my key in the lock. Miss three times. Get it on the fourth. But before I can turn it, the latch clicks and the door swings open.

And *he's* there.

Bright blue eyes filled with compassion, mouth curved into an understanding smile, his expression serene. Like he's trying to calm me without saying a word.

My throat tightens like it does every time I see him. If I'm this much of a basket case, how much worse must it be for my loving husband who can't father the child we both want so badly?

Dane's empathy is all-encompassing. He's handling the news of our infertility so much better than I am. He's solicitous and understanding and way too nice when it takes everything within me not to scream at the injustice of it all.

Then again, he's not the one who has to prove his worthiness in a family of high achievers: a mother who held down two jobs in the garment industry while raising five kids, a father who made chief at thirty at the busiest precinct in NYC. Four brothers who balance their stressful cop careers with fatherhood, producing eleven kids between them.

I see their sideways glances when they think I can't. Condescending. Curious. Pitying. Like I'm a failure because I haven't contributed to the O'Grady clan yet. I've tolerated my brothers' lighthearted jibes for years, first about my lack of a man, then later my lack of kids, and my mom's subtle probing as to the reason behind my childlessness. They're incredibly insensitive, blasé, and unaware that there could be reasons why I haven't had kids yet. I want to snipe back often but it's not worth the drama. They're my family. I love them. But I wish they'd give me a break. Dad is the only one who never pries. I love him for it. Like all good Irish Catholic families, they see kids as God's gift. It makes me wonder. Am I being punished for my sins?

"How are the girls—"

"Sorry, babe, I need water." I push past him and stumble toward the kitchen, banging my elbow on the doorframe in the process and cursing under my breath.

"Take a seat and I'll get it." His hands, strong, capable, comforting, rest on my waist and guide me toward the table.

His solicitousness is sweet but my head is starting to pound and I scowl at my foolishness in trying to drown my sorrows when he places the glass in front of me, along with a couple of painkillers.

"You might need this for the hangover you'll have in a few hours."

"Thanks," I mutter, popping the pills and draining the glass.

"Did you girls have a fight or something?" He pulls up a chair, close enough our knees touch. Usually I welcome any contact from my husband. Today, I'm glum and out of sorts and want to be left alone.

"No." I sound snappish and immediately feel guilty because he doesn't deserve this crappy treatment. He's been so supportive and I've been wallowing, short-tempered and morose, blaming myself as much as him.

I slump in my chair and struggle to focus. It would be so easy to slip into oblivion, to sleep for the rest of the day and forget why the newly residing perpetual ache in my chest makes breathing difficult. But I can't forget. Nothing can help. Dane's tests may have come back negative, but I've done this to myself, waiting too long to start a family. Putting my career ahead of all else, including my considerate husband. Reaching forty and knowing it's too late to let things take a natural course.

If we'd started trying a few years ago, we may have more options now. Dane is incredible: he uprooted his life and followed me to Gledhill without question, he does anything I ask, he loves me unconditionally, and he has no clue how close I came to destroying our marriage years earlier.

I often think he deserves better than me, a woman living a lie every single day and doing her utmost to make up for the mistakes of the past.

"I've never seen you drunk after time with the girls so something must've happened—"

"I told them, okay?" I say quickly, taking some kind of warped pleasure from his shock. "They know all about our 'problems,'" I make cutesy inverted commas with my fingers, feeling like the biggest bitch in the world but unable to stop my vitriol from spilling out, "and they feel just as helpless as I do."

I hope he'll lose his temper. That for once he won't be so stoical. But he runs a hand across his stubble as if he's deep in thought before answering.

"You're lucky you've got best friends to talk to." He reaches across and snags my hand. "We're going through a rough patch, honey. We'll get through this. You know we will."

I know jack shit. The only things I know for sure: I know that I don't deserve my sweet Dane, I know that he'd leave me if he knew the truth, and I know that I've spent the last year going quietly insane because I thought our childlessness was my fault because of one stupid mistake I made before we married.

Guilt is a terrible thing. It eats away at all the good in life until you're left with nothing but resentment and anger. And I'm angry. Furious, and I deflect it onto Dane: I might be irritated with him for being the official cause of our situation, but I know I've had something to do with it too, and I'm incensed at the injustice of a good guy like him not being able to father kids.

I'm not the marrying kind. I'd been intent on proving myself on the job before settling down, if ever. Then I'd met Dane at twenty-nine, married him three years later when he finally wore me down, but put off having a family to establish myself at the NYPD. I'd had a plan. A plan now screwed every which way courtesy of the only guy I'd ever loved enough to have a relationship with.

My family will be gutted. I think of my eleven nephews and nieces. Mom never lets up about it being my turn next. I can't tell them. Not now, when it's raw. I'll wait; a decade or two.

"How are you so calm about all this?" I try to extract my hand from his and he tightens his grip.

"Because this is you and me, there's nothing we can't get through." The lopsided grin I adore chases the shadows from his eyes. "Honey, it took me years to get you up the aisle. Do you think something like this will split us up?"

I hate that my first instinctive response is "yes." Something—or someone—almost broke us up once before and he doesn't know. And while I haven't done anything bad this time around, technically I'm guilty of oversharing. Not with the girls, but with Griffin when we chat over sushi at lunch or meet for a beer after work.

Initially I'd justified my leaning on him because he's a colleague who's a psychologist, and who better to offer sage advice? I'm floundering and he's the only person who seems to get me. I talk and he listens. He doesn't offer advice unless I ask for it. It's so easy between us.

But Dane doesn't like him. They've met twice at work functions and Dane's indifferent and suspicious because he thinks Griffin *likes* me. Crazy, because Griffin is nothing but friendly, yet feeling guilty because he's my main sounding board at the moment is exacerbating my stress.

"Claire?" He touches my hand. "Talk to me, sweetheart."

So I put on a brave face, something I've done for the last week since the fertility specialist called us into her pristine office in the city and delivered the news.

"I have no idea how or why you put up with me." I lean into him and he slides his arms around me.

He's wearing an old cotton T that smells of manly deodorant, a musky, woody blend that's inherently him. I bury my face in his chest. He smells of something else too. Safety. Security. Dane.

I have to get past this.

I have to deal with everything before I ruin my life.

CHAPTER THREE

ELLY

I light the final candle and stand back to admire my handiwork. Fifty tea lights cast flickering shadows against the smooth marble of the bathroom wall. Rose petals float in the hot water filling the tub. Chocolate-dipped strawberries are arranged in neat rows on a silver platter next to a two-hundred-dollar bottle of champagne chilling in a matching silver bucket. My lover likes the finer things. He also appreciates my efforts to shake things up, so we'll start in here tonight.

I don't look at myself in the mirror. I despise the new teddy—sheer white lace, high cut, with a pop button where he'll need access fastest—because he'll love it. I slip on a silky robe, crimson, in stark contrast against the virginal white, and pad into the living room. I open a window, savor the view of the wild Atlantic Ocean as far as I can see, waves crashing on a windswept beach. Serenity.

He chose this cottage for its isolation and I appreciate it. No one knows about our affair and I intend on keeping it that way until it's time to inflict the most damage: on him, never the wife. I do this to help those poor, misguided, trusting souls who are duped, just like me.

I hate myself for doing this. Self-loathing fills me, expanding like a balloon until my organs compress and I can't breathe.

I remember the day my downward spiral started, initially as a way to make me feel *something* again after the numbness of the harsh truth. With my divorce finalized, severing ties with a monster, I left the courthouse in Chicago and stumbled into the first bar I came across.

A guy had approached me shortly after, though what he saw in a wild-eyed, tear-stained wreck I'll never know. He bought me a drink, another, several, and I poured my sordid story out. He'd been a good listener and had invited me back to his hotel room where we had rote, meaningless sex. Then his wife called—so much for him being single—while he was in the bathroom and I answered.

A red mist had swept over me, rage like I'd never known. I'd escaped one creep only to be duped by another. But my fury had morphed into something else when I told his poor wife the truth; that her husband had picked me up in a bar, lied about his marital status, and fucked me.

In helping her to see him for the liar and cheater he was I felt...free. Lighter. Empowered in a way I hadn't been since I discovered the awful truth about my husband. I had wrested back some semblance of control.

After that day I became some kind of cheating crusader. Stupid, I know, but I've exposed another four men since and my lover is the fifth. Not that I've slept with the others. I couldn't bring myself to go that far but I'd honeytrap them into taking me to a hotel, getting naked, then I'd do a big reveal to their wives.

My lover is different. He's the first man I've had any meaningful contact with since the disturbing night fourteen months ago and I've become more vulnerable.

That horrific night exposed every weakness I thought I'd conquered since the divorce. My partial breakdown in Chicago after I discovered my husband's duplicity had been dealt with via countless therapy sessions. I'd become confident in my invincibility and had tested it by exposing those other men.

But having no recollection of the rape early last year left me defenseless all over again, second-guessing my decisions, doubting everything I did. It also left me susceptible to kindness and that's why I allowed my lover to pierce my protective outer shell and I slept with him. He'd been nice to me before the sex, caring and sweet in a way I'd craved since my life in Chicago imploded, so when he put the moves on me when I was weak and needy, I succumbed. It had felt incredible to be held afterward, an intimacy I hadn't known I'd been yearning for. Having his arms around me had comforted the vulnerable, broken woman inside. But I'm not a fool. I know this can't go on. We can never have a real relationship. I may savor my brief moments of solace but he can only ever be an adjunct to revenge.

It's not good, because I know how badly it will hurt my friend when I reveal the truth. I want to stop. This isn't my fight anymore. I'm empty inside because despite helping those clueless women learn the truth, I feel bad for them. I remember the outrage, the hollowness, the sorrow I'd been through once, being in their shoes, and I hate myself for putting them through something similar.

But my friend is important to me so after this I'm done.

I have a good life in Gledhill, the small Hamptons town I'd moved to a few years ago after careful research. I loved the understated elegance of the place. The ecru and pale blue shop fronts on Main Street, the eclectic mix of high-end fashion boutiques with quaint cafés, the trendy bars frequented by locals and tourists alike.

Gledhill ages gracefully, unlike some of its counterparts, the larger towns farther along the highway that turn glitzy to attract attention. Here, I can proceed with my plan to get justice against the lying, cheating scum who break their wives' hearts, like how my ex-husband had broken mine.

It's warped, twisted psychology, my ongoing quest for vengeance. I know it. What I do is wrong on so many levels that I feel morally bereft most days. But this is about more than betrayal. It's about that devastating night when I'd first moved here, the night that shattered what was left of my meager trust completely.

I'm numb and confused and horrified. I have been through a lot in my life but not this. Never this.

There's a pounding at my door and I hear Ris, then Claire, yelling, "Elly, it's us. Open up."

I stand and limp toward the door. I'm sore. Inside. Further proof of the unthinkable. Shock renders my fingers useless and I fiddle with the lock three times before the door opens.

Ris and Claire stare at me for what seems like an eternity before Ris steps forward with open arms to hug me.

"Don't." Claire stops her, her expression inscrutable. "You can't contaminate evidence."

That's when the reality of what has happened to me sinks in. I can't do this. I can't go through questioning and statements. Not just because I can't remember what happened to me but because my past will become public knowledge and I can't have that.

My new life in Gledhill depends on secrecy.

"Hug me," I whisper, meeting Claire's eyes, and she knows. She knows I won't be prosecuting, even if I remember the horrors of last night.

After the slightest hesitation Claire steps forward and does exactly that. I see Ris, stricken, over her shoulder, tears in her eyes.

I can't cry. Not yet. I'm hollow, like the bastard who did this to me has scooped out my insides and left nothing behind.

Claire leads me to the sofa, Ris closes the door, then they sit either side of me, brackets of comfort. They wait, silent, supportive.

I try to speak and the first word comes out a croak so I clear my throat and start again. "I had two drinks last night. A martini and a margarita. One of them may have been spiked."

Claire's eyes widen. "GHB is a colorless liquid that has a salty taste, easily disguised in a margarita."

My insides heave. "The date rape drug?"

She nods. "You can't remember anything?"

I shake my head and it hurts. "It's hazy after the margarita, then nothing. I woke up here on top of the covers, dress up around my waist, no panties..." *I try to subdue a sob and fail.* "There are bruises all over my thighs and hips."

Claire's mouth hardens. "You sure you don't want to go to the hospital—"

"No!" *I yell and they recoil a tad.* "I—I can't go through it. I won't."

"Okay, honey, whatever you want." *Ris slides an arm around my waist and hugs tight.* "Whatever you need, we're here for you."

"I need a shower," *I say, a hiccup punctuating my increasing sobs.* "I feel so dirty."

"This isn't your fault." *Claire grips my shoulders and turns me to face her.* "I won't lie to you. If you can't remember what happened, there's a fair chance whoever did this gave you a good dose and losing consciousness followed by amnesia is common. And even if you do eventually remember, prosecuting men who do this ends up being a horror show for the victim, who's scrutinized extensively." *She blows out a breath.* "But I want you to think hard and make sure this is what you want to do. Because once you take that shower there's no turning back and the bastard who did this to you walks free." *She bites her bottom lip and glances away.* "Free to do it again."

I'm not callous. I do care about people despite the hard exterior I deliberately portray. But I can't do this. I can't feel guilty for letting this prick walk. My new life means too much to me.

"I'm sorry..." I shake my head and Claire nods. I glimpse understanding through the sheen of her tears.

I push into standing and my legs wobble. Ris and Claire are instantly beside me again, holding me up.

"Whatever you need," Ris says, enveloping me in a fierce hug while Claire does the same from the other side.

I don't know how long we stand there but I can't let go. I need their warmth to infuse me, to melt the ice that clogs my veins. I'm so, so cold...

These days, Ris, Claire, and I never talk about the incident; a misnomer for the catastrophic night fourteen months ago that still haunts me in my weaker moments.

I blink rapidly, dispelling the memories, willing them away. Thankfully, Ris and Claire respect my need to move on and pretend like it never happened. But it did happen, yet another shitty thing in a long line of shitty things that have plagued my life. I don't dwell. I get even. Even if the guys who are the objects of my payback have no idea why.

The girls are my rock. I value their friendship, though Ris's infernal nurturing of everyone around her is smothering and Claire's badass routine wears thin. I'm friends with Maggie too, though technically she's my boss. She owns the medical center where I work and she pops in weekly so we can catch up over coffee.

I like her. There's an inherent quietness about her that calms me. I can't fathom why Ris, her sister-in-law, doesn't spend much time with her despite the fact they're related and neighbors. Ris tolerates everyone but she's antsy around Maggie. I don't get it. But it's not my problem and I value my friendship with both of them so I never get in the middle.

Claire maintains impartiality around Ris and Maggie too, though considering how edgy she'd been earlier I'm almost glad Maggie didn't drop in with Ryan. I feel sorry for Claire. I'd seen real pain in her eyes when she revealed she can't have kids, the kind of pain I struggle to hide every damn day.

I am a master at hiding the truth.

From everyone.

I have reinvented myself here in Gledhill, a new life for a new person. I refuse to be vulnerable. I do everything in my power to mask the hurt. I have deliberately eradicated the agonizing aftermath of what happened to me in Chicago and last year, here in Gledhill.

Whoever said good girls finish last is a freaking genius. Being docile and acquiescent is for fools. Being strong and impenetrable is so much better.

I will never, ever, let a man take advantage of me again.

I hear a key in the door and a ripple of unease washes over me. It's always like this. I hate what I do in the name of vindication so I mentally recite my crazy mantra.

I am powerful.

I am in charge.

I am never going to be duped again.

The opposite of the woman I once was. I have to be. Look how that had turned out. This is better. Being in control. Never letting anyone get too close. Avoiding the inevitable pain when the people you love the most let you down, shatter you into a million itty-bitty pieces you think you'll never recover from.

I slip the robe from my shoulders and let it fall to the floor. My almost-naked body will be the first thing he sees as he enters the cottage. I glance at the floor, momentarily startled to see the robe looks like a blood slick against the ash floorboards. But then he opens the door and all I see is him: an egotistical asshole who doesn't care about anybody but himself.

"Wow." His tone is low, his libido high, going by the sizable bulge tenting his trousers. "I've been thinking about you all day but my fantasies don't come close to the reality."

"Thanks." I swivel on silver-heeled mules and head for the bathroom so he won't see my expression. I'm disgusted. At myself as much as at him.

He drops his briefcase, closes the door, and locks it. Not that anyone ever comes here. He's made sure of it. Finding the cottage online. Approaching the landlord directly to avoid a paper trail with the realtor. Paying cash for a year, with only two copies of the contract, under a fake name.

I pause at the bathroom door and glance over my shoulder. He's staring at my ass while toeing off his shoes and shrugging out of his jacket.

I watch him undress. He means nothing to me. And he'll soon mean the same to his wife. I need to keep telling myself this because lately I find myself looking forward to seeing him, to have him hold me, to savor his touch. These ridiculous feelings merely accentuate I need to tell his wife sooner rather than later but I'm so conflicted. She's going to hate me, it's inevitable. Maybe I should've thought of that before I started this?

He doesn't dally: tie, shirt, belt, pants, socks, almost torn off in his haste to get naked. He's an impatient man, except when it comes to giving pleasure. Not that I do this for the sex. It's the few moments afterward, when he holds me and talks to me, that I cherish because for those brief fragments of time I almost feel normal again.

He slips off boxers that are worth enough to feed a family of four for a week, takes himself in hand, runs his palm up and down the length, advances on me.

I back into the bathroom, my breathing shallow. I can never read his mood. It bothers me. Sometimes he's slow and sensual, other times he's hard and fast, bordering on rough. I don't do kink and he hasn't shown any predilection for it, thank goodness.

"Pretty," he says, glancing around the bathroom. "Not as pretty as you though."

Before I can move, his hand snakes out, grips the teddy between my breasts, and rips. Then he's upon me, his mouth devouring mine, his hands delving into crevices, his cock pulsating against my stomach.

Tonight will be hard and fast. He flips me around so I'm facing the mirror. Condoms are everywhere in the cottage and he sheaths himself quickly before nudging my knees apart.

I brace against the marble vanity and he looms over me. Enters me in one smooth thrust. Hard. Deep. Making me cry out a little.

Our gazes lock in the mirror: mine defiant, his demanding. He leans forward, reaches around, and fingers me. I make him believe he's the one in control when he never is.

His thrusts become more insistent, more brutal, as he slaps against me from behind. We don't speak for a few moments. We never do. I prefer it that way. No muss. No fuss.

After putting myself back together in Chicago I finally hold the upper hand. I will never be at the mercy of any man ever again.

Last year had been an aberration. A momentary lapse when I'd been duped without knowing it and the fallout had been devastating. It will never happen again.

Now I hold all the power, heady stuff for a broken girl like me.

"Champagne?" he asks, after he's taken care of business.

I nod. "Please."

Formal and polite, at complete odds with our frantic fucking.

What would my friends think of me if they knew the truth? About my lover, my life, all of it?

CHAPTER FOUR

JODI

I'm a magnet for losers.

Always have been always will be.

Which is why I'm five months pregnant, alone, surviving on noodles and little else in a crappy Manhattan studio apartment barely big enough for me, let alone a kid. My bank account is dwindling, my PA wage barely covers rent, and I'm too far along to consider other alternatives even if I could afford them.

That's the kicker of all this. I didn't discover I'm pregnant until last week. I had no freaking idea. I thought the nausea was a result of too much caffeine so I quit coffee and cola. As for my expanding waistline, I'd attributed that to bingeing on chocolate and pretzels most nights while glued to *Sex and the City* reruns like many single girls living in Manhattan. It wasn't until the annual physical at work seven days ago that I found out.

I've been a basket case ever since.

I know who the father is. I tried looking him up online and discovered the bastard had given me a false name. That's what I get for indulging in my first one-night stand. First and last, considering I'll be saddled with a brat for the next umpteen years.

Can I really do this? Doubtful, but what choice do I have? I have to give birth to him—the eager sonographer had let that gem slip yesterday—then consider my options. Adoption is the most logical but the thought of giving him away makes me feel queasy.

My mom gave up on me and I still carry the scars; emotional rather than physical, thank goodness, though it had been a close call over the years with her numerous boyfriends. I'd been smart enough to extricate myself from a dire home situation. How could I give up my baby, not knowing if I was dooming him to a similar life of uncertainty and potential abuse?

I'm perpetually worried and confused, my modus operandi these days. I flip the newspaper pages, scanning the print with little interest. Even my usual Saturday morning routine has lost appeal. I can't concentrate these days, my focus continually shifting from one thing to another, like the fetus is sucking all the intelligence out of me.

I turn the next page.

Freeze.

It's him.

The photo is small and grainy. It takes up half the size of a Post-it. He's in profile with a bunch of other dudes in suits. I wish I could see his eyes, see if they're as penetrating and mesmerizing as I remember, to see that sexy mouth that had done wicked things to me.

My heart rate quickens as I speed-read the article, greedy for details. A bunch of boring stuff about a business award... then I see it.

A name.

I quickly enter it into the search engine on my cell but I'm out of data and can't afford another upgrade until next month. Unfortunately, the name can be attributed to any of the suited dudes in the article so I reread the article, paying closer attention to details. It stipulates that all the suits work for the same company.

I have a starting point.

The glimmer of a plan teases me. I stare at the picture again and the threads of my plan start to weave together, coalesce. It's daring and unlike me in so many ways, but it could guarantee my future and that of my baby boy if I can pull it off.

Feeling increasingly confident for the first time in forever, I slip an arm around my belly and smile.

"Hey there, Jelly Bean, we're going to find your daddy."

Two hours later, I stand in the sleek yet understated reception foyer of the company named in the newspaper article. I've showered, put on my best black dress, applied makeup, and blow-dried my hair. Apart from the small baby bump, I look exactly the same as that night *he* had debauched me every which way.

I approach the receptionist, a cool blonde in her fifties, and summon my best schmoozing skills. They don't work. She won't let me see the guy named in the newspaper. Says he's not in. He's at home.

Annoyed I've been thwarted I leave the building. As I step onto Fifth Avenue, I realize I have another option. While my baby's father hadn't been forthcoming with the truth that night we'd screwed our brains out in a deserted warehouse where my employer had been hosting a party, the newspaper article has provided a wealth of information. Including another location...

I'm no rabbit-cooker but for this to work I'll have to chase him down.

CHAPTER FIVE

MARISA

I've dealt with my second teen runaway today at the Help Center when my cell rings. One glance at the screen and my throat tightens. I hit the answer button and the faces of my girls pop up on the screen as they jostle for position as usual.

"Hey, Mom, how are you?" Trish, the eldest by a minute, blows me a kiss, her dark hair in a single braid over one shoulder, a style she's favored since grade school.

I miss those days when she'd sit patiently at the island counter in the kitchen every morning, letting me plait her thick hair. She'd be chattering nonstop; about the five books she'd borrow from the library after school, about the latest boy band, about the many ways her twin tortured her.

Terry would always interrupt by poking her sister in the ribs, eliciting much teasing and name-calling that inevitably ended when I lost my cool. These days, my kitchen is quiet in the mornings. I hate it.

Fixing my usual all-is-right-with-the-world smile on my face, the one I've honed through many years of practice, I say, "I'm fine, baby girl. You?"

"All good." Trish gives a thumbs up, another endearing habit from childhood that makes the lump in my throat swell.

Terry nudges her aside. "Why do you always get to talk first? You're such a bossy boots." She smooches at the screen. "Love you, Mom."

I laugh, their antics never failing to ease the ache in my chest. I feel hollow inside these days, a strange emptiness that nothing but my girls can fill. I miss them way too much. Crossing off the days until Thanksgiving does little to alleviate the inherent loneliness that plagues me ever since they left.

The hollowness when they're not around reinforces what I've always known. My mother must've been a callous, robotic bitch for treating me so badly. I adore my girls, am filled with so much love I don't know what to do with it when they're not around. I can't fathom a mother not loving her own child.

Which is why I escaped mine as fast as humanly possible.

I resent Avery for many things. Providing me with an avenue to flee my past isn't one of them.

"How are your classes? Grades?"

"Mom," they groan in unison. "You always ask us that."

"That's because I'm interested."

Terry rolls her eyes. "We talk every week. Not much has changed since the last time you asked."

Actually, we talk every few weeks but I don't point it out. The twins—tall, slender brunettes with startling gray eyes the same color as their father's—are gorgeous. They lead busy social lives apart from their study load. I would never be a nagging mom, no matter how I wish we could talk more often.

Trish holds up her hand. "And before you ask, no, we're not seeing *anyone special*."

She draws out the last two words and Terry falls about laughing.

"Not that you'd tell me anyway," I say drily and Trish joins in her sister's laughter. "I wish you were closer."

I'd flown out to LA once since they'd left but had hated leaving them so hadn't done it again. They come home for the major holidays and that has to do. When they qualify as doctors I hope they'll return to the east coast. I'll have no compunction enlisting Avery's help in that regard when the time comes.

As if reading my mind, Trish asks, "How's Dad?"

"You know your father. Busy as usual, running the pharmaceutical company, lending a hand in research, trying to pretend he doesn't miss doing cosmetic surgery at all."

Terry smiles. "Sounds like Dad. Tell him we'll call next Friday night at eight."

My eyebrows rise. "You need to schedule a time to call him?"

Trish nods. "Of course, otherwise we can never get hold of him. Our schedules clash all the time."

I know they don't mean to make me feel bad but for a second I do. So it's okay for them to call me at work but not their precious father?

I dismiss the thought as quickly as it comes but I can't ignore the lingering resentment that Avery has everything easy. His life is ordered, structured, and perfectly run, down to the last minute. Thanks to me.

"Anyway, Mom, we have to go. There's an extra anatomy tutorial on dissecting the hand today." Terry wiggles her fingers for emphasis. "Did you know all sorts of conditions affect the metacarpophalangeal joint, and in turn the proximal interphalangeal joints?"

"Whoa. Quack terminology overload."

They grin, proud that they've got me again with their impressive knowledge of the human body. It has become a game to them, to see how long I'll tolerate their medico speak before I call a halt.

Terry glances at her watch and taps the face. "Not bad, Mom. You lasted a whole eight seconds today."

"Way to go, Mom," Trish adds, with a fond smile.

My boss sticks her head around the door to my office and makes a wind-it-up motion with her hand. I nod and return to the screen.

"Sorry, girls, I have to go. Work is calling."

"Sure thing, Mom." They blow kisses at the screen again and wave. "Chat soon."

Before I can respond, they hit the "call end" button, like they can't get off their obligatory call fast enough. I absentmindedly rub the ache beneath my breastbone. It flares like it always does when I see my girls.

I have to get past this; have to be grateful for the rosy life I lead. I created this picture-perfect life to obliterate the constant worthlessness that plagues me courtesy of Mommy dearest. I am a good person, no matter how invisible she made me feel. And I try to prove it every single day: at work, at home, at the charities I volunteer with, at the many social gatherings I organize and preside over.

My life is wonderful, just the way I want it.

Maybe if I recite it often enough in my head, I might start to believe it?

CHAPTER SIX

CLAIRE

After a week of going stir-crazy at home with Dane's molly-coddling, I'm glad to be back at work. The call comes through as I start my shift. Child abduction from Westhampton Beach. Usually, I'm detached. A good cop never lets emotions get in the way of crime solving.

Today, with a kid involved, I'm not so impartial.

If I had a kid I'd never let her out of my sight. It's always a girl in my dreams: a pretty princess with eyes as blue as her daddy's and a riot of dark brown curls. She loves trucks as well as dolls. She climbs and leaps and twirls. She's mischievous and adorable and smart.

She's fictitious.

And will remain that way courtesy of my *situation*.

I hated when the specialist had coolly announced our infertility then presented options for our "situation." Like we could solve it easily. Like it's a simple matter of choice. I have no choice. I have to accept it and move on.

"Hey, wake up." My partner, Ron Pensky, snaps his fingers in front of my face. "It's not like you to be daydreaming on a case."

"Didn't sleep well."

Ain't that the truth. I haven't slept more than two hours a night since we learned the news.

"There's a kid out there depending on us so whatever bug's

up your ass get rid of it and focus." Ron pulls the car over near the crime scene, already swarming with the usual crew. He turns to me, concern creasing the corners of his eyes. "Seriously, kid, you've had a week off for reasons you won't tell me when you haven't had time off in over a year. Now you're back and are spaced out. Want to talk about it?"

"I'm fine," I snap, instantly regretting it when his mouth compresses into a thin line. "Sorry. I've got some personal stuff going on. I'll be okay."

He nods but hasn't lost the wariness. "I'm here if you need me."

The thought of telling the fifty-something career cop my fertility problems is so unpalatable it makes me tumble from the car in haste.

We approach the scene, the somber expressions of the crew telling me all I need to know.

This is serious.

It isn't a simple case of a kid wandering off and getting lost.

This child has been snatched.

Ron and I get the preliminaries from one of the CSI team. Eight-year-old girl vanished twenty minutes ago. Parents saw her playing with some other kids near the dunes. The kids say she left with an older man.

My stomach roils. Panic floods me. My usual impartiality is shot to shit at the thought of what that girl will go through. I worked enough abduction cases in the city to know the probable outcomes, none of them good. Back then, I'd feel sadness initially, horror later, concern for my nephews and nieces who had to grow up in a terrifying world where no kid is safe. But I'd been single then and emotionally detached. Now, not so much and it bugs the crap out of me that my personal life is affecting my ability to perform on the job.

"Let's get to work," Ron says, shooting me a questioning glance when I don't move.

I can't. It's like my feet have sunk into quicksand, my legs too weak to lift them out. When the CSI crew cast me curious glances too, Ron moves. He grabs my arm and all but drags me toward the parents. I know we have to interview them. I don't want to. I don't want to see their anguish or hear their retributions. Gut-wrenching.

However, as my leaden feet approach the distraught pair clinging to each other, a miracle happens.

"She's been found," one of the crew yells and a collective sigh of relief is drowned out by the crash of waves. "Her senile grandpa showed up unexpectedly and took her for ice cream without asking the parents. They were spotted in Southampton just now."

I see the mother collapse and the father try to hold her up before he too sinks to his knees. Tears stream down their faces. I'm shocked to discover my eyes are damp too. We have a lot of work to do but Ron knows I've reached my limit before we've really begun.

"Go wait in the car," he says, a deep frown slashing his brows. "I'll take care of everything."

I don't take the easy option. Ever. But I'm eternally grateful as I stumble toward the squad car and collapse onto the passenger seat. This isn't working. Even after a week off, my grief at losing a baby I never had is too raw. Too agonizing.

My job is everything. If I can't even perform at that...I'm screwed. So I wait, knowing I'll have to tell Ron everything and dreading it. He'll say "man up" in that gruff way he has for anyone with a problem. He'll resort to lame-ass jokes to cheer me up. He may even hug me. I'm not ready for any of it. Until I've left my own pity party, I'm not ready for anyone else to RSVP.

Sympathy is for suckers. Which leaves me with a giant S stamped right in the middle of my forehead. I'd only let my personal life interfere with performance once before.

It had almost ruined me.

The solution had been easier back then. Remove myself

from the situation. Make it go away. Regain focus, move forward, and live with the guilt.

This time I can't do it.

I'm not prepared to walk away from my marriage. I love Dane. He loves me. We will get through this.

We have to.

CHAPTER SEVEN

ELLY

After another sojourn with my lover that leaves me more guilt-ridden than ever, I head to The Lookout, my favorite bar. I would rather go home and curl up on the couch with the latest thriller. Nothing in those novels scares me; I've been through worse. But I always do this after an encounter, when reality hits and I'm left questioning my dubious motives.

No shrink would accept my rationale for doing this. As for my friends, they would disown me no matter how hard I tried to explain. I hate the secrecy, the lies, but I'm doing it for my friend, the gullible wife like I'd once been; a wife who dotes on her husband, who's confident in her ability to keep him tethered, who doesn't dream that he'd cheat. I want better for her than I got. Screwing her husband may be an odd way of showing it but I care about her.

Women are stupid. We trust too easily. We take declarations on face value. We believe promises. I did. Until I discovered my gorgeous husband had another family, a wife and kids he'd had before me, and that my perfect life was nothing more than a charade.

I survived the fallout of that horror with the help of booze, pills, and an exorbitant therapist. Reinvention seemed the only option. So here I am, taking back control.

I'll tell my friend soon. This has run its course. But I know as soon as I reveal the truth my world will come crashing down and I'll be forced to leave this town I've grown to love.

Gledhill is quiet tonight. A few foolhardy patrons brave the brisk Atlantic breeze to sit outside the restaurants lining the boardwalk, enjoying cocktails and seafood under wide umbrellas that flap with every gust. I find a spot at the end of the boardwalk and park, vowing to have one quick drink before heading home.

The guilt is unbearable tonight. I can usually manage it with self-talk and vodka, but all the inner voices or shot glasses in the world won't help. The way I'm feeling I'm likely to do something stupid, like call my lover to head back to the cottage because I'm lonely, so it's best I have one drink to take the edge off and leave.

The Lookout is perched on a small bluff jutting out over the sand dunes. The exterior is shabby chic, wooden boards painted pale lemon and windows edged in salmon to give the appearance of a bygone era. Huge potted perennials line the path leading to the entrance: lespedeza in white and fuchsia, leonotis in vibrant orange, and plectranthus in muted lavender, a riot of color that soothes my artistic soul. I can identify every flower because I once had a garden that thrived under my care. Many had commented on it in Chicago and I'd preen, completely clueless I was about to take a massive fall.

I push open the glass door and enter the bar. The interior is minimalist and at complete odds with the outside. I love the contrast. It reminds me of me: falsely decorated on the outside, empty on the inside. The bar is all chrome and sleek lines. No mahogany in sight. I perch on one of the uncomfortable stools and order a martini from the bored waitress sporting surgically enhanced DDs probably paid for by tips. The mirror behind the bar is perfect for scoping out the patrons. Women are scarce and several men cast interested glances my way. I ignore them. I've had enough of men for the night.

When the waitress delivers my martini, I pick up the glass.

I'm about to take a sip when I spy Claire, alone, in the darkest corner of the bar, nursing her fourth scotch by the empty glasses scattered on the table.

I've never seen her like this: hair spiking in all directions like she's dragged her hand through it repeatedly, a deep frown grooving her brows, and a mismatched shirt and jacket. She's disheveled when I've never seen her anything other than organized and I'm devastated for her all over again.

Considering my mood when I entered, the smart thing to do would be to avoid her. But despite wearing my aloofness like a protective coat I have a conscience and find myself heading toward her table instead.

"Fancy some company?"

She startles and glances up, her expression sullen. "Not really."

"Too bad. I don't feel like drinking alone tonight." I sit and place my martini on the table. "Do you come here often?"

The corners of her mouth twitch in a semblance of a smile. "If you're trying to pick me up, I'm not interested."

I laugh. For someone who rarely smiles, Claire has a killer sense of humor. It's one of the things that makes her fun at Ris's gardening club gatherings. "I mean it. Do you often come into this bar to drink alone?"

I gesture at the empty glasses in front of her. "Because if you do, consuming that much alcohol alone on a regular basis may constitute a drinking problem."

She scowls and gives me the evil eye. "Fuck off, Elly."

I laugh harder, pick up my martini and raise it. "To us."

She doesn't lose the frown. If anything it deepens, before she finally says, "To alcohol," clinking her glass against mine. "Seriously, I'm not in the mood to make small talk so it's probably best you leave me alone."

"Then let's talk for real."

The offer pops out before I can censor it and I inwardly curse that I can't take it back. I'm not a listener. Not anymore. I used to be the type of woman who spent endless hours chatting with friends, interested in news of their husbands, their kids, their homes. Until my perfect life imploded, so these days I keep the deep and meaningful conversations to a minimum, which is easy to do around Ris, who chatters nonstop.

But Claire looks seriously shaken and she was there for me when I needed her most. I can't walk away. I care about her. Besides, deep down I know why I can't abandon her. I can identify with the emptiness Claire's experiencing but for very different reasons.

Claire can't have a baby.

I gave mine away.

Hating my traitorous heart for skipping a beat like it usually does when I think about how far I've gone to reinvent myself, I drain my martini. "This baby thing has hit you hard."

I state the obvious, hoping she'll open up. She glares at me and flips me the finger; a second before tears fill her eyes and spill over onto her cheeks. Crap. I haven't signed on for water-works but maybe it'll do her good to get it all out. It helped me, but I paid that therapist in Chicago thousands for the privilege.

"I'm a mess." She sniffles a bit, swirls her whiskey, then knocks back the rest neat.

After she takes a few deep breaths, the tears stop and she looks at me with surprising clarity. "I didn't know how badly I wanted a baby until I couldn't have one."

I can't think of anything worse, having a squalling brat to care for 24/7. Though that's not why I gave up my baby. I did it to get back at that bigamist bastard, who never knew he'd fathered a child with me, and thanks to the adoption process, he never will.

I'd never been maternal, even back then. I thought I'd hit the jackpot landing a husband who wasn't interested in having kids. Later I discovered why, considering he already had three with his first wife. His *legal* wife. Leaving me bereft and confused and yearning to castrate him.

It had been the ultimate irony, learning I was pregnant a week after discovering he had another family. Abortion had entered my mind fleetingly but it seemed like taking the easy way out. Because every day I carried that baby, every moment of that nine-month gestation, was a self-flagellating punishment for being so blind and so stupid.

There was no question I'd keep the baby. I couldn't live with a constant reminder of my foolishness. So when the time came I underwent a painless caesarian—I'd suffered enough agony at the hands of that prick formerly known as my husband—and let the adoption agency take my baby. A girl, as one nurse had accidentally let slip after delivery. Then I'd left the Windy City without looking back.

I rarely think about her. How old she would be. Is she happy? Is she healthy? It doesn't matter. That part of my life doesn't exist anymore. The woman I was back then doesn't exist. It's so much better being an emotionless drone these days.

"Why do you want a baby so much?"

Maybe if I keep her talking, she'll distract me from my unwelcome thoughts and remember that she has a life, a damn good one with that hot husband of hers. Dane is incredibly sexy in that rough-around-the-edges way some guys pull off to perfection.

She ponders my question for a moment, studying me, before a soft sigh alerts me that she's ready to talk. "I come from a big family, four siblings, countless nieces and nephews. It just feels…wrong, that I'll be the only one without a kid."

She's lying or holding something back. I see it in the quick look-away, the fiddling fingers. I know the signs because I've spent a while mastering them, hiding the evidence of deceit.

"Why does it have to be a competition?"

"It's not that." She sighs and nudges away her empty glass, adding it to the collection. "Don't you ever get the inevitable questions about why you're single at forty and why you don't have kids?"

I stiffen, hating that I'm instantly catapulted back to that day in the hospital when I heard a squall from behind the sheet shielding my lower half and wondered if I was doing the right thing.

I force a nonchalant shrug, feeling momentary empathy with Claire, even if she'll never know it. "All the time. But I don't care. My life is fine just the way it is."

Claire smiles for the first time since I sat down. "I've never met anyone as confident as you. No wonder you have men falling at your feet."

"Where?" I flex my ankle and glance down at my eight-hundred-dollar stilettos. "That's right, I had to cut a swath through them to get to you."

But I'm flattered she thinks I'm confident. Presenting a polished front to the world helps me keep the demons at bay, the relentless, clawing self-doubts that constantly plague me, the ones that scream I'm not fooling anyone, least of all myself.

"I don't get you." She cocks her head slightly, as if she can't quite figure me out. Join the club. "I assume you've come in here tonight to chill. Instead, you spot me and rather than leaving me to wallow you choose to talk."

She smirks and makes a cutesy heart shape with her thumbs and index fingers. "When did you grow one of these?"

"Ouch." I clutch my chest and sway a little. "I'll have you know I'm a very caring person when I want to be."

"And when's that, once a year?"

"Bitch," I say, without malice, and we grin at each other.

"It's actually kind of nice, us talking like this without Ris around," Claire says unexpectedly. "She tends to take over all the time."

"Yeah, it's tiresome after a while."

I tone it down when what I want to say is she drives me nuts with her perpetual nurturing. Because I know that if I let her get too close I'll fall apart under her overt caring. I see the way she looks at me, like she's torn between wanting to hug me or hover

over me like an avenging angel. It's sweet but I don't want to get used to it, in case I crack and blabber all my other awful secrets.

"She's a good person..." Claire trails off, as if she wants to say more.

"But?" I prompt.

"But if she tries to fix me one more time I'm going to scream." She crosses her arms, like she's subconsciously trying to fend off Ris. "I already feel like the scruffy lower-class citizen in our group, I don't need her reinforcing it at every turn."

"You're the most capable, practical person I know and there's nothing second-class about that." I slug her on the arm, a gesture I've never used on another woman—or man—in my life, but one I hope she understands is done in the name of friendship. "Don't let self-pity about the childless thing drag you down. You know how good you are."

She blinks rapidly, as if staving off tears again. "Thanks, I guess I needed to hear that."

"Another drink?" I quickly ask when my throat clogs with uncharacteristic emotion. This is what happens when I spend too much time around women. Men are so much less complicated. They like to watch sports, eat food, and fuck, simple creatures with simple needs; so much easier to control than women, with their unpredictability and emotional fragility.

She wrinkles her nose and glances at the glasses lined up in front of her. "I think I've had enough."

I hesitate, wanting to say more but unable to find the words. I'm not good at being a true friend. It doesn't come naturally. Not anymore.

So I settle for, "If you ever need to offload, I'm a phone call away."

"Thanks, Elly." She leans over and hugs me.

I stiffen, a reflex reaction, before forcing myself to relax and return the embrace.

She releases me and stands. "See you at the supper party tomorrow?"

I nod, my stomach sinking. "See you there."

I'm already dreading another of Ris's interminable parties, of which she has one every few weeks. I detest the small talk, the fake smiles, the schmoozing. That whole bogus Hamptons scene is tedious but I fit right in, considering I'm a phony too.

I love living in an affluent part of the world with its accompanying benefits but Ris takes her role as Hamptons hostess to extremes. Everything has to be perfect, from the canapés to the petit fours, which she plies on her guests too frequently.

Deep down, I know why I hate her parties so much. I'm jealous. I used to be her. Glamorous, capable, leading a charmed life, surrounded by equally gorgeous friends in a stunning house paid for by an incredible man. An illusion, all of it. A sham. And I hate that Ris is living the life I once had.

Ris is so capable, so self-assured, so effortless, in her role as wife, mother, and hostess, that I feel insecure.

And I don't like feeling second best, not ever again.

Claire waves and heads out, leaving me staring into my empty martini glass, and wishing I had made different choices with my life.

CHAPTER EIGHT

JODI

Gledhill is bigger than I expect. The tourist map I grabbed at the bus depot estimated the population at fifty thousand but I still expected some quaint old town filled with boutiques and cafés, not a thriving mini metropolis complete with an ultra-modern medical center, upscale restaurants, and a shopping strip that would put Fifth Avenue to shame.

Then again, the place reeks of old money. I see it in the designer fashion adorning well-behaved kids strolling down Main Street. I see it in the exclusive art galleries with their modern art adorning windows, without prices because that would be crass. And I see it in the unbelievable mansions in the realtor's window, the likes of which I've never seen before unless on TV.

I've made the right decision coming here. If my baby's daddy leads the kind of lifestyle I think he does, I'm willing to bet he'll pay a small fortune to keep his indiscretion secret.

I experienced doubt the entire trip on the jitney but when I felt the fluttering of a kick that's all the reassurance I needed that I'm doing the right thing. I'm having this baby. I want him to have the comfortable, secure life I never had. To do that, I need money.

I stroll the esplanade along the beach, admiring the undulating windswept dunes. Fancy restaurants with expansive back decks open out onto the boardwalk, where well-dressed people chat and laugh while drinking Long Island Iced Teas and sharing tapas. Soft jazz spills from the nearest restaurant and it's drowned out by the waves crashing against the sand. Families picnic on the beach, lolling on massive rugs, passing dainty finger food and bottled water, while kids cavort nearby. Smitten lovers, frequently casting longing looks at each other, walk hand in hand along the shoreline.

It's all too picture perfect and I want to bawl. I dash my hand across my eyes and take in a great lungful of Atlantic Ocean air. It calms me. This is my first visit to Long Island and I'm envious of the people who live here, who take all this pristine beauty for granted. I want to be them.

I will be, if my plan works.

My stomach rumbles and I realize I haven't eaten anything but dry crackers and ginger soda all day. So I make my way back along the esplanade and stop at the first café I find, aptly named Sea Breeze. Its French doors are open to capture the sea air blowing in off the ocean and it's filled with yuppies in their designer chinos, white button-down shirts and expensive leather satchels. They stare. Maybe because I'm a tourist and new in town, but my paranoia makes me want to yell "Don't young women get knocked up in the Hamptons?"

I perch on a stool near the open doors and scan the menu. Prices are expensive and the food looks sublime. Fresh shrimp sautéed in chili, garlic, and white wine, mozzarella balls with salsa verde, Camembert croquettes with a pistachio and cranberry dipping sauce, and freshly shucked oysters.

My mouth waters but with my bank balance I choose the cheapest thing on the menu, a four-dollar salad. Thankfully the service is quick and I'm prevented from fainting when a waitress brings my order in record time. The salad is delicious and the iced tea perfectly sweet.

I pay the bill, leaving an embarrassingly small tip I can ill afford, and exit quickly. I cross the street and enter the one building that can give me answers. Without any data left on my cell, I need to do an online search, pronto. Like everything else in this town, the library is bright and modern and airy, exuding a subtle class that money can't buy. Computer desks line floor-to-ceiling glass windows so people can take advantage of the stellar ocean view if they tire of the screen. The bookshelves are chrome and aligned in a star shape fanning out from the central help desk. Comfy armchairs are strategically scattered, beckoning borrowers to stay awhile.

I want to live here. I love books. Adore them. I always stroke the cover and sniff a new one before turning the pages slowly, taking great care not to crease the spine. I haven't been able to afford new books in a while so I frequent the library often.

Library books have a whole other smell: a little grimy, a lot shabby, like me, really. I haven't had an easy life but I've done what it takes to survive, which explains the worn-out feeling at twenty-five. I know it'll be tough bringing a baby into my world. A single mother in New York City working as some rich asshole's personal assistant and living in a studio isn't exactly "mother of the year" material. But I don't do drugs. I don't sleep around. I work hard for every cent I have. I guess my baby could do worse. And if we have enough money to make life comfortable...

This has to work.

I choose one of the empty computer desks and enter the free Wi-Fi password displayed next to it. The connection is swift and I open a search engine. I type in his name.

"Can I help you?"

I jump at the light touch on my shoulder and half spin in my chair to see an elderly librarian peering at me with obvious curiosity. I can't come up with a lie fast enough. Besides, all she has to do is glance at the computer screen to see who I'm researching. The name is stuck in the search engine, as I haven't had a chance to hit the enter key yet.

So I settle for a half-truth. "I'm new in town and doing some research for a project."

Her gaze darts to the screen and she nods. "He lives on Sunnyside Drive. Impressive house. You can't miss it. Lots of glass and sandstone."

I school my face into impassivity while dancing an excited jig on the inside. This helpful lady has saved me further snooping around town.

"Sounds lovely."

I must sound too hyper because she stares at me again, this time with a slight furrow between her brows.

"If you need any help finding what you're looking for, don't hesitate to ask." She points at her nametag. "Ask for Agnes."

"Thanks, I will." I beam at her, trying to put her at ease. She moves across to the next desk to offer assistance but she's hovering and I can't hit the enter key like I want to.

I need to see if the guy named in that article is my baby's father but with Agnes practically peering over my shoulder, I decide on another course of action.

I now know this guy lives on Sunnyside Drive.

It's a good place to start.

CHAPTER NINE

MARISA

I can't help myself. Whenever I see someone I care about hurting I try to fix it. My coworkers praise me for it but I'm more altruistic than that. I feel good when I see others happy. Avery calls it my Pollyanna complex, always seeing the bright side in everything and everyone. I don't like seeing my friends in pain and Claire is seriously hurting so I throw one of my famous supper parties to distract her and hopefully lighten her mood.

Since our monthly gardening club meeting ten days ago, she's avoided me. Screened my calls, texted back with lame excuses, citing she's busy at work. But she hasn't been at work. I called the station once. They said she'd extended her leave so, short of marching up the road and knocking on her door, I'm helpless.

I don't want to interfere. I don't want to leave her alone. I don't know what the hell to do. So I do what I do best. Throw a party. Invite friends. Supply quality alcohol and delicious food. Claire needs me. Besides, helping her will make me forget the reason my insomnia is escalating.

When I see a forty-something woman walk down the street in her designer cruise wear, clutching a handbag worth a small deposit on a house, I want to rush up to her and ask, "Is this all there is?" I want to ask does she ever feel so lonely, even when surrounded by people, that she could curl up in a corner and howl for a week? I want to ask does she ever feel invisible, even when standing right in front of her husband?

These questions and more reverberate around my head on a nightly basis when I lie on my eight-hundred-thread count Egyptian cotton sheets and stare at the ceiling, so exhausted I could cry but unable to sleep.

It's probably the onset of menopause: the mood swings, the fatigue, the dissatisfaction with everything. But deep down I know it's more than that: pretending to be the perfect woman with the perfect life comes at a cost.

Avery is clueless to my brittle emotional state. It makes me more depressed. My mother had been like that, living in the same house as me but never really seeing me. She worked hard, I'll give her that. But she never cooked or cleaned or acknowledged I existed, coming home from a long shift at the clothing factory where she worked and flopping in front of the TV. I'd serve her a microwaved dinner, bought by me from the grocery money she left in a cookie jar on the shelf over the fridge. I'd make an effort every night, sitting beside her on our threadbare chintz sofa, making small talk about my day at school. She'd grunt in all the right places, manage the occasional nod and smile. It was never enough.

That's why I married Avery. Because he'd been the first person in my life to really look at me, to *see* me. That has waned but I stay in my marriage because as long as I'm with one of the most powerful men in the Hamptons, others see me. People respect me. People look up to me. People thank me for doing so much.

I will do anything to protect my carefully constructed life.

I skirt the sixteen-seat table on the back patio, making last-minute adjustments: straightening serviettes, smoothing the tablecloth, aligning cutlery. Everything is gorgeous, from the platters of cheese and cold meat to the baby quiches and salmon croquettes, the dainty finger sandwiches to the barbecued shrimp. I could've used the usual caterers but I needed to keep busy the last few days so did everything myself. Menu-planned. Grocery-shopped. Cooked. It has been cathartic.

Avery wanders out onto the patio, the epitome of casual chic in khaki chinos, white polo, and boat shoes. The polo sets off his year-round tan and makes his peculiar gray eyes even more startling.

"Wow, great spread." He comes around the table to wrap his arms around me. "You sure know how to entertain, sweetheart."

I snuggle into his arms but something feels off as usual because my heart's not in it. I need to be careful. I can't alert Avery to the fact I'm struggling. He doesn't do well with weakness in any form. It's something Ryan knows and often takes advantage of.

Avery hates mess so whenever Ryan approaches him with a problem, Avery must solve it. We're similar that way. From the outlandish stories they tell, he's been Ryan's Mr. Fix-It from a young age. Lying to their parents when Ryan broke a window with a baseball, blaming it on a group of roving kids. Saying he dented the family car when Ryan had backed into a pole. Covering for him when Ryan double-booked dates on the same night.

I used to find these tales amusing but Ryan's dependence on his big brother all these years later wears thin. I want to tell him to grow a pair and take responsibility for his own actions but I won't. For the simple fact Ryan is one of the good guys and I've grown to love him almost as much as Avery does.

As for me, I have to be the strong, capable wife Avery admires. Anything less and he'll become suspicious. I may be imploding on the inside but I'll be damned if anyone else guesses how bad things really are for me.

"You smell nice," I say, nuzzling the skin under his jaw, inhaling the familiar sandalwood scent of his signature body wash and aftershave. It calms me, the feeling of belonging this man provides. He helped me forget the past and forge a future. He gave me the girls and for that alone I owe him.

I know it's unhealthy, having much of my identity wrapped up in my children, but they give my life purpose. Without them... well, I wouldn't have stuck out my marriage this long. I deserve a medal. Heck, I deserve a whole cabinet of trophies for tolerating Avery's foibles for so long.

What would Gledhill's elite think of that? That I stay in my marriage out of obligation and gratitude rather than real love?

I've come close to blurting the truth twice, in the most unlikely of scenarios. The first time I'd been at the retirement home in nearby Westhampton, where I volunteer on a monthly basis. I play board games with the elderly, watch soap operas with them and simply sit and chat most of the time. One of my favorites, Doris, an octogenarian with advanced Alzheimer's, had been waxing lyrical about her perfect husband who'd died a decade earlier. Her glowing praise had brought tears to my eyes and a startling urge to unburden myself about my less than perfect husband.

The second time I'd been stocking care packages for women in need, with everyday essentials from tampons to tissues. Once I'd finished I'd personally delivered a few packages and one of the women, Callie, had almost brought me undone. She'd revealed the hardships of her life, saying I was lucky. In that moment, with her eyeing me with open envy, I'd come close to telling her that creating a façade was easy and if something looked too good to be true, it usually was.

"You smell great too." He buries his nose in my hair and presses his pelvis against me. He's hard. It never takes long. He's always up for it, any time, day or night. I pretend to like it. I don't.

Thankfully, the doorbell rings and I slip out of his arms with a bashful smile, like I hate the interruption. He shrugs and winks, adjusting his chinos while I walk to the door.

The next ten minutes pass in a blur of guests arriving, drinks being dispensed, and introductions made. I've invited two new people into our circle tonight: a psychologist from work I hope

Elly will like, and the owner of the new gallery in town, a distinguished fifty-something. Knowing my bombshell friend, she'll probably have both men wrapped around her little finger by the end of the evening.

I'd like to see Elly settle down in a happy relationship. She deserves it after what she went through last year. It's why despite her external polish and pizazz she always appears brittle, like she's maintaining a fragile façade liable to crack. She pretends to love her single life. Flaunts it like she's healed and put the trauma behind her.

So I play along. It's what she asked of Claire and me. But I'll never forget the bone-deep dread that one of my girls had been injured or worse when I picked up the phone at some ungodly hour of the morning fourteen months ago, only to have that dread morph into panic when I heard Elly's wobbly voice say, "I'm at home, I think I've been raped."

Elly's devastation, her scary stillness as Claire and I bracketed her on the sofa trying to offer comfort that seemed inadequate at best, is something that makes me want to hug my friend every time I see her. Instead, we acquiesce to her wish to pretend like it never happened. We do it because we care.

Elly sidles up to me. "Who's the tall guy in denim?"

"Griffin Rally. Nice guy, lives up the road. He's a psychologist. Shall I introduce you?"

I know she's interested like I hoped, but she hesitates, casts a quick glance over my shoulder, before flashing a fake smile, the one I know hides her pain. "Sure. I'm all for meeting new people."

As we approach Griffin, I murmur, "He's new in town, mainly consults in the city but has worked here regularly over the last six months, for the police and the center. He only moved into our street recently though."

She rubs her hands together with exaggerated enthusiasm. "Fresh meat, just the way I like it."

I elbow her. "You're incorrigible."

"And you love me for it." She bumps me with her hip and I realize it's times like this I really value our friendship.

Elly can be brash and abrasive and self-opinionated, but she's also warm and quick-witted with a wicked sense of humor. We're not as close as Claire and I but that's understandable given our very different social lives.

When Claire and I swap the occasional recipe at our gardening club meetings, Elly covers her ears and yells "la-la-la" off-key. Elly survives on gourmet healthy takeout that's home-delivered, which explains her figure. When we discuss our gardens and the chances of rain to spruce up our flower beds, Elly rolls her eyes. The closest she comes to having a garden in her immaculate, trendy apartment is the pot of basil I gave her as a housewarming gift.

We're so different, Elly and I, but that hint of vulnerability she tries so hard to hide beneath makeup and designer clothes makes me want to break through to the woman beneath. I know little about her past, despite trying to probe a few times. She's fed me the occasional tidbit, like she originally hails from Chicago and had some high-powered job as an executive vice president at a medical conglomerate. But I know nothing about her family or if she's come close to marriage before.

I often wonder if her brazenness with guys is a direct result of the assault. Considering it happened only a few months after she moved to Gledhill and I know little about her past, I can't say for sure, but it makes sense. It's a coping mechanism. Go on the attack to avoid being attacked. I'd seen it in abused women at the center. Some retreated and avoided men while others became sexually aggressive, projecting a tough image to avoid becoming a victim again.

I tried to subtly suggest counseling once; but she'd frozen me out. I know the casual dating can't be healthy for her self-esteem but if it helps her get through the trauma, who am I to judge?

I've told Griffin about a potential meeting with a gorgeous

friend of mine and his eyes almost pop when he spies Elly strutting alongside me.

"Great party, Ris. Thanks for inviting me," he says, his gaze firmly fixed on Elly.

"My pleasure." I nudge Elly forward a tad. "I'd like you to meet Elly Knight, one of my best friends."

Griffin's hand shoots out before I barely finish the introductions. "Pleased to meet you, Elly."

"Likewise." Her voice is a sultry purr and I bite back a grin as Griffin shakes her hand but seems incapable of releasing it.

"I'll leave you two to get acquainted," I say, pleased that my matchmaking might result in these two getting together.

Neither of them hear me, already engrossed in making small talk. Flirting. I can never understand the single people of today hooking up with random strangers via social media, but at times like this, watching the sparks fly between Griffin and Elly, I can see the attraction.

When's the last time I experienced that hollow belly feeling? That heady sensation accompanied by the jitters when you first meet someone you know you'll end up naked with? Too long ago to remember and I immediately feel disloyal to Avery. I love him, in a strange obligatory way, but lately I'm feeling restless. Lost.

Like I've given up too much to be Mrs. Marisa Thurston.

Annoyed my thoughts are wandering to maudlin again I pop another tray of quiches into the oven, arrange more barbecued shrimp on a platter, then head back outside to the makeshift bar at the bottom of the patio steps for a refill. Nothing a good Chardonnay can't solve. However, as I take my first sip I spot something that sours the crisp grape tang on my tongue.

Griffin and Dane in some kind of altercation.

He must've left Elly to get her a drink and bumped into Dane along the way. They're not arguing per se, but even at a distance I can tell things are tense between them.

Griffin's back is ramrod straight, like someone stuck a poker up his polo. I've seen his wary posture at work several times, when he's dealing with domestic violence perpetrators. He's not moving a muscle. Usually I admire his self-control but tonight there's something almost aggressive about his demeanor. It makes me wonder if I've done the wrong thing inviting him into our circle.

I know he's acquainted with Claire because he works at the police department too. But Claire has never mentioned him and the way Dane is glaring at him I hazard a guess they're not best buddies. Dane's hands clench into fists before he rams them into his pockets. He's scowling as Griffin walks away and Claire is flushed, already on her third wine in thirty minutes, her posture rigid.

They exchange heated words. They're arguing about something—I hope it's not Griffin—and I stride across the lawn, determined to smooth things over for my fraught friend. But before I reach them Dane pulls his cell out of his pocket, glances at the screen, says something I assume is about taking a call, and ambles off around the side of the house.

Claire waits a few moments, glaring at his retreating back, before she strides after him. The kernel of worry I subdue on a daily basis flares to life. My friend's infertility issues have caused tension in her marriage and I'm clueless as to how to help.

I down the rest of my Chardonnay in a few gulps. Griffin is at the bar where he picks up two wine glasses before zeroing in on Elly again. He appears relaxed and laughs at something she says. Maybe I misinterpreted the vibe between him and Dane...besides, Claire's my main focus tonight.

My friend needs me. Everyone else can fend for themselves.

CHAPTER TEN

CLAIRE

Ris's soirées tend to make me uncomfortable. A mishmash of her closest friends and work colleagues that she assumes will like each other if plied with enough quality alcohol and fed exquisite food. Dane and I usually don't stay long. I give the work excuse. I can't do that tonight, not without lying and I'm already doing enough of that.

She's been trying to contact me ever since gardening club and I've been ignoring her. I can't cope with her pity. Not now, when I'm barely holding my life together. But when she'd texted me the invitation for tonight, implying she'd thrown this party for me, I couldn't say no. What do I hate more than being pitied? Being obligated.

But I'm here, pretending to enjoy myself. I'm not succeeding. Another wine might help but I'm cutting back on the alcohol tonight. Dane is a patient man but that's twice I've come home drunk and he's concerned. Our infertility issues are making me crazy but I can't seem to snap out of the downward spiral I'm in.

He's seen me like this once before, just before our marriage. Back then he'd given me time and space to get my head together, attributing my funk to pre-wedding jitters. Little did he know that what I'd done before I traipsed up the aisle haunts me to this day. It's the reason my frustration escalates, mixing with my guilt until I want to scream.

I want to have a baby with Dane so badly because I owe him. He never knew how badly I fucked up and he never will. A baby would've been my way of making it up to him. An apology he never knew he needed. It's driving me insane, keeping a secret from the man I truly love.

Thanks to Ron, I have another week off work. Once I told him the truth he insisted. Not that I blame him. I wouldn't want a partner alongside me who can't focus and is liable to burst into tears any moment. I'm embarrassed, because for the first time in my career I'm acting like a girl.

I glance around the garden, wondering if I can hide behind one of Ris's perfectly manicured bushes to avoid people. That's when I see Griffin stride toward Dane.

Dane has never thawed toward Griffin but he tolerates him for me; because we're work colleagues of sorts. He knows Ris is one of my closest friends and he won't do anything to muck up tonight, especially when I told him she's probably throwing this stupid party to cheer me up. Unfortunately, Griffin has picked up on Dane's animosity; he asked me about it after they met the first time and I laughed it off. But he's a psychologist and trying to fool him is tough.

I make a beeline for the men, wishing they could be friends.

"Hey, boys." I slide an arm around Dane's waist and to my surprise Griffin leans down to kiss my cheek.

He's never done that before and I'm uncomfortable. Sure, we're work colleagues but that kiss, even in greeting at a social setting, seems wrong. Dane thinks so too, his muscles tensing beneath my arm.

"Good to see you here." He straightens quickly but my skin prickles with unease.

"How's the medical rep business treating you, Dane?" He offers his hand to my husband and Dane shakes it reluctantly.

"Great."

Dane's monosyllabic around Griffin and my heart sinks. I'm delusional if I think these two will ever be buddies.

"If you're keen to move beyond a sales rep position, I know some people?"

What the hell is Griffin doing? Him offering Dane career advice is bizarre. I search his face for any clue to his motivation but I only see guilelessness. Maybe I'm overreacting.

"Thanks, but I'm good," Dane says and I squeeze his waist. He shoots me a look I know well: what the hell is this guy on?

Griffin shrugs. "I just thought you might like to know there are better opportunities at other companies." He jerks a thumb in Avery's direction. "I work with Marisa and she tells me her husband's company is going gangbusters and they're always hiring. Isn't he a friend of yours?"

If Dane is standoffish with Griffin, he hates Avery. We all know he's a brilliant cosmetic surgeon who's now CEO of a national pharmaceutical company because he never lets us forget it. Dane can't abide arrogance and whenever Avery approaches us at Ris's gatherings Dane makes himself scarce.

"Kissing ass isn't my forte so I doubt I'd be a good fit for Avery's company."

Griffin laughs but Dane's laconic smile doesn't fool me. My husband rarely loses his temper but I sense an undercurrent that has me worried.

"And for what it's worth I like my job. I like selling reputable medical equipment to doctors. Not peddling dodgy advice from psychobabble textbooks—"

"Dane, that's enough." I drop my arm, appalled that he's reacted this way. I don't think Griffin had been deliberately baiting him but his less than subtle jibe has escalated the situation.

Thankfully, Griffin doesn't take offense. He grins, holds up his hands, and takes a step back. "Just offering some friendly advice. No harm no foul."

He turns his back and walks away before either of us can respond and I immediately turn to Dane.

"What was that all about?"

"You're taking *his* side?" Dane glares at me, incredulous, like I've betrayed him.

"Don't be ridiculous," I snap, forcing myself to take a calming breath when he recoils a little. "What you said was a low blow when all he was doing was trying to be helpful."

He scowls and swipes a hand across his face. "He was trying to be an asshole. What's my job got to do with him?"

"Fair point. But he's a psychologist. He dishes out advice all day long. Maybe it's hard for him to turn it off?"

"Maybe." The frown creasing his brow eases and I sigh in relief. "If he doles out unwanted advice at work, I don't know how you put up with that dickhead."

"I only see him occasionally, as he works a few sessions a week at the station, and he's good at what he does," I say, knowing Dane would be livid if he knew Griffin had been freely dishing out advice to me because I'd confided in him.

"What's he doing here anyway?"

I glance over my shoulder, where Griffin is currently entranced by Elly. "Ris playing matchmaker, I think."

"Elly can do a lot better than him."

I clamp down on my first instinct to defend Griffin. Maybe Griffin would be perfect for her. He's never mentioned a significant other at work and doesn't elaborate on his dating exploits on the few occasions we've caught up outside of the station. Elly is the same: single and loving it. In the few years I've known her she hasn't been serious about any guy and tells us nothing beyond a few funny stories about her dates. Though she'd never admit it she strikes me as lonely. The more I think about it, the more I like the idea of Elly and Griffin together.

Dane's cell rings. He fishes it out of his pocket, glances at the screen, and the frown reappears. "I have to take this."

"Okay—" I lean in to kiss him on the cheek but he stalks away, leaving me floundering.

The tension between Dane and Griffin is a problem. This may not be the best setting but I think I need to come clean about my friendship with Griffin. It's silly that I'm even remotely worried about revealing that we're friends more than coworkers because it should be a nonissue. But after what just happened...he needs to know.

I round the west wing of the house and spy Dane with his back to me. He's angry. I can see it in the rigid set of his shoulders, the way his neck muscles bulge.

"Look, she can't ever find out about the fake test." He speaks in a low, lethal tone that raises the hairs on my arms. "So don't even think about it."

I have no idea what he's talking about but it sounds dodgy. I step forward, stand on a twig and it snaps. He spins around, wild-eyed, before he blinks and the man I love is back: serene, logical, calm.

"I'll see you later," he says, and ends the call, shoving the cell back into his pocket.

"What was that all about?"

He hesitates for the barest of seconds before responding. "We had our annual physicals at work last week. One of the guys supplied a fake urine sample and I advised him our boss better not find out, she'll fire him on the spot."

My nose crinkles. "I'm not even going to ask about the logistics of supplying fake urine."

"You're better off not knowing." He takes my hand, like all is forgiven for him ditching me earlier.

"Why did you walk away like that?"

"I told you, I had to take that call." His shoulders slump and he gives himself a little shake. "Guess you're not the only one feeling the pressure these days."

I feel like the biggest bitch in the world. While I've been wallowing in self-pity since we heard the devastating news I haven't spared a thought for how he's feeling. Primarily guilt, I assume. Maybe even less of a man, though virility has nothing to do with fertility in my eyes.

I want to reassure him that I still feel the same way I did

when he first approached me in that tiny Italian diner near the Brooklyn precinct and asked to pass the Parmesan years ago, that I love him unequivocally. That I'll do whatever it takes to ensure our marriage stays solid. That he's the love of my life, despite a momentary lapse in judgment made out of fear threatening it to this day.

But a small part of me also resents him for not being able to give me the baby I so desperately want, the baby I had to have to make up for my sins of the past, so until I get a grip on my feelings I can't talk about this; especially not here and now.

"I have to say this, Claire. I don't like that jerk Griffin and I think you should avoid him."

"Don't be ridiculous, he's a friend." My voice is raised and I immediately regret what I've said when he recoils.

"He's a *friend*? I thought you were just coworkers."

Crap. This is not how I envisaged telling him and I take a few deep breaths to calm down. "We are. But we talk."

His stillness is frightening. "Tell me, Claire, what do you talk about?"

Before I can respond, he spits out, "If you've told him that I'm shooting blanks...fuck."

When I don't answer he backs away, holding up his hands. "I'm out of here. I'll see you at home."

"Fine," I shout, but it isn't. Nothing is fine between us since that damn day at the fertility specialist's office.

I should go after him; try to explain. But what can I say? That I'm so discombobulated most days that it takes every ounce of energy to drag my ass out of bed? That I can't talk to Ris and Elly about how useless I'm feeling because their overachieving already makes me feel second-rate? That I doubted they'd understand considering our lives are so different? That Griffin is the only impartial friend I have and offloading to him is cathartic?

I'm an idiot to think Dane and Griffin can ever be buddies; tonight's debacle cements it. But I don't like being told to avoid him, like I'm a dumbass kid who needs guidance choosing friends. I'll talk to Dane when he calms down and try to explain in a rational manner.

I give him a two-minute head start before going in search of Ris to thank her for hosting. When I find her she's buzzing about the kitchen, mopping up spills and arranging platters and chopping herbs for garnish.

"Honey, could you do me a favor and grab some more Pinot Noir from the cellar?" She slips her hands into an oven mitt. "I've got baby quiches about to burn."

I really want to have that talk with Dane but she looks seriously frazzled and I take pity on her. I'll get her wine, then leave.

"Sure," I say to her retreating back as she's already opening the oven door to peek inside at her precious quiches.

I know my way around because Ris insisted on giving me the grand tour of her house when we first became friends. Back then, she seemed desperate for me to like her and was trying her best to impress me. Houses don't impress me, people do, and being a cop means I have good intuition. While I didn't give a flying fig about Ris's Colonial mansion that day two years ago, I liked her. She seemed genuine and a tad lonely.

I follow the long hallway from the kitchen to the den. It's lined with artistic black-and-white framed photos of the twins at various ages and one gigantic family shot taken at Disneyland about a decade ago. It's the only family photo among the lot and I know why Ris had it framed. They're all looking at each other and laughing, genuine joy radiating from the photo. Ris looks so much younger and I have to admit that in the two years I've known her I've never seen her that happy.

I know she projects an image of a perfect life but seeing her in this photo makes me wonder what has happened to sap the joy from my friend? I see her expression at times, part wistful, part sad. It's an occupational hazard, picking up on people's feelings, but when it comes to my friends I don't push them to reveal too much. Maybe I should? Maybe I should ask Ris if she's all right and ask Elly if she's really as tough as she likes to portray?

Leaving the photos behind, I find the cellar door and open it. Wall-ensconced lights immediately flare to life, illuminating a clear path. I traverse the steep stairs with care and make my way to the Pinot. Along with exquisite taste in interior design, Ris sure knows how to stock a cellar. I'm not a connoisseur but my dad loves a fine drop and I know the wines in this room could put ten kids through college.

I'm selecting a few bottles when I hear a footfall behind me. I hate people sneaking up on me and I spin around, immediately on guard.

Griffin holds up his hands and chuckles. "Hey, it's only me. Don't shoot."

"Very funny."

"I thought you might need some help?"

"Sure."

He takes a step forward and I realize he's standing too close. My gaze flickers to the door over his shoulder. It's closed. I left it open so I wouldn't have to juggle bottles and a door handle.

Trepidation crawls across the back of my neck. I'm probably overreacting as I've never felt unsafe around Griffin before and haven't picked up any unsavory vibes.

But Dane has.

I'd dismissed my husband's warning weeks ago that Griffin likes me and I'd been vindicated, as he's never shown a glimmer of anything untoward during the times we've hung out, talking. Besides, I would know. I'm a cop. I sense things beyond the obvious.

And I'm sensing something now.

"Ris said she'd be down soon to give me a hand," I lie, gesturing to the bottles I've already lined up.

He laughs. "Considering how flustered she is fussing over those food platters, I seriously doubt it."

He takes another step closer, less than two feet away. "Which is why I came down here. I knew you'd need help."

Maybe I'm reading too much into this and he is trying to be helpful, but then I glimpse a hint of excitement in his eyes and I know.

I'm a moron.

All those times we chatted over lunch or a beer after work, he's misread my friendship for something more. I don't know what makes me madder: that Dane is right or that my famous cop intuition has let me down. Worse, the fact that I've put myself in this position annoys the hell out of me.

"Great, thanks for the help." I keep my voice calm as I semi-turn toward the bottles. I don't want to turn my back on him completely but he takes advantage of my movement by shifting closer.

Before I can spin around, his body is pressed up against me.

"Let me get those," he murmurs, his warm breath fanning my ear. His boner digs into my hip and my fingers curl into a fist. Man, have I misread this situation.

"Back off, Griffin." I try to elbow him but he grabs my arms and spins me to face him.

"Is that what you really want?"

His grip on my arms tightens and his fingertips skate across my skin in a light, slow caress. He's looking at me, his stare inscrutable.

I tilt my chin up to stare him down. "Back the hell off, now."

He doesn't move and our gazes remain locked. I'm on a precipice, scrabbling to hold on to sanity but in grave danger of falling.

I've been in this situation before, knowing it's wrong, desperate to stop. Back then I'd been terrified of making a long-term commitment to Dane. At least, that's how I'd justified cheating on him eight weeks before our wedding. I'd conjured a whole string of excuses to explain my lapse. He didn't understand the pressures of being a cop. He didn't see the worst of humanity on a daily basis, making it imperative to blow off steam. What he didn't know wouldn't hurt him.

The first time it happened, my partner and I had survived a drive-by shooting. Adrenaline had been high. We'd done tequila shots at the bar near his apartment. We'd staggered back to his place together, intending to sleep it off. We didn't get much sleep.

The second and last time had been after my bachelorette party. Neither of us was drunk. No excuses that time, just two people who'd worked together for three years giving in to baser instincts. The sex had been uninspiring but that wasn't the point. I'd been hell-bent on deliberately sabotaging the best thing to ever happen to me before Dane could hurt me first. Warped logic. Crazy. But that's how I felt at the time.

I didn't believe a man like Dane could want me forever. That he'd put up with my neuroses and long hours. I thought he'd eventually tire of me. I hadn't given him enough credit.

My partner had transferred out to Washington the next week, leaving me with a guilty conscience and an STD. I'd been so goddamn mad for the last year while we'd been trying to conceive, wondering if I was infertile courtesy of the after-effects of my transgression. The doctor who'd initially treated me for the STD had lectured me about practicing safe sex and warned me about the possibility of infertility.

I'd been punishing myself so badly that it had almost been a relief to learn about Dane. Until reality set in and I realized I couldn't give him the one thing that would ultimately bind him to me forever. Instead, he'd have me for a consolation prize and my old doubts resurfaced all over again.

Would I be enough?

"You're so beautiful," Griffin murmurs, and then his mouth is on mine.

Fuck, my hesitation has cost me. I want to push him away, to knee him in the balls, to call out to my husband who walked away from me earlier.

My husband...

The second Dane pops into my head I place my hands on Griffin's chest and shove him away.

"Get off me." I swipe the back of my hand across my mouth to wipe away that two-second transgression but my lips are still tingling, an awful reminder that I'd let this jerk kiss me when I should've stopped him.

"You sure that's what you want?" He's unruffled, almost nonchalant. "I thought you liked me, Claire—"

"You're delusional."

Disgust makes my stomach clench. How could I have misread this guy? I should've decked him a few moments ago when I had the chance. My stupid hesitation has cost me, big time.

Confusion clouds his eyes. "But I thought...I mean..." He shakes his head, as if trying to clear it. "The way we talk, we seem to click...I really thought we had something."

The guy's a lunatic. But when I see genuine bewilderment creasing his brow, uncertainty makes me pause. Is he as crazy as half his patients or is he a sad, pathetic guy who can't tell the difference between talking and something more?

"There's never been anything between us beyond friendship," I say firmly. "If you've misconstrued, that's on you."

"I'm not stupid." His tone is low and oddly devoid of emotion. "Don't imply that I am."

He's staring at me with obvious perplexity, like he's completely mystified why I don't return his interest. It creeps me out.

"This is inappropriate." I square my shoulders, feigning defiance I don't feel. "Don't mention this again."

Confusion gives way to a manic gleam in his eyes and I'm instantly on guard again, my pity giving way to panic.

"Fine. I'll keep my mouth shut." His doleful half-smile makes me want to rub the goosebumps off my arms. "And we both know you won't say a word because Dane will go apeshit and he's already feeling emasculated enough as it is."

Damn him for being right. I can't say anything. I would hate for my husband to feel worse than he already does because I'm a slow-witted idiot who should've backed away the moment I picked up on Griffin's intent.

I scoop up an armful of bottles, hold them tight to my chest, and stalk past him. "I'll be civil at work when we're on a case, but that's it. Don't come near me any other time."

"Maybe you'll be the one finding me? Wanting to talk?" His ingenuity infuriates me. "Seeking my advice. Being *friendly*."

He makes "friendly" sound ugly and dirty so I ignore him. Either that or fling a thousand dollars' worth of Pinot at him and he's not worth it.

"Just leave me alone," I say, taking the steps two at a time despite the load in my arms. When I reach the top of the stairs I struggle with the door for a moment and then I'm through, back into the hallway. Free.

I drag in several lungfuls of air because my chest feels tight and I blink, willing the burn of tears away. I can't believe I trusted that jerk, let alone been stupid enough to hesitate, giving him a few seconds to take advantage. I'm reeling from our infertility news but that doesn't excuse my idiocy.

I didn't want that kiss. I didn't instigate that kiss. He misconstrued my hesitation and for that, I'll have to pay. As if I didn't feel guilty enough because of my past, now I'll have this unwanted memory plaguing me.

I've fucked up. Again.

Giving myself a shake I head toward the back of the house, avoiding the kitchen. If Ris takes one look at me she'll know something's wrong so I skirt around the conservatory and walk down the back steps to deposit the wine bottles on the makeshift bar. That's when I see him.

Dane.

He's come back for me.

CHAPTER ELEVEN

ELLY

My lover is here tonight.

I hate seeing him in social settings. It makes me uncomfortable and feel worse than I already do for perpetuating my revenge scenario. He's with his wife, of course. I want to rush to her, grab her by the shoulders and shake her hard until her teeth rattle. Can't she see what he is? Doesn't she have the faintest clue?

I hadn't. I'd been clueless until I'd seen the evidence of my husband's treachery with my own eyes. A sucker punch that left me broken and I still haven't recovered.

They seem on edge, tense when together, almost combative, then spending lots of time apart, a typical marriage. He vanishes for periods throughout the night, then reappears. I feel him watching me. Coveting me when he has no right.

So I flirt with Griffin, who took an eternity getting me another drink but has finally returned. He's sweet and attentive with a great sense of humor. Best of all, he's uncomplicated and that's something I crave in my otherwise convoluted life.

"At the risk of driving you away because you'll think this is a corny line, you're absolutely stunning," Griffin says, his smile genuine. "You've got this inner glow that makes you stand out in a crowd."

"You're right, I'm out of here." I half turn away, pretending to leave and his hand snakes out to grab mine.

"Stay. Please."

I bat my eyelashes at him. "Only because you asked nicely."

He laughs and I marvel at how easy it is to be with him. I barely know this guy but he has an ability to make me relax. I don't have that with my lover.

Griffin releases my hand when I give it a gentle tug. "Do you have family in Gledhill?"

I hate small talk and hate talking about my family more. But my lover is staring again so I flash a dazzling smile, like Griffin has asked me the most interesting question ever.

"I'm an only child. My folks are in LA. I moved here for college and never went back."

An easy lie that tumbles from my lips, one I've used many times before.

"They must miss you."

Dad does. I've always been his princess. Mom's not maternal. I must get that gene from her. They don't know the truth about my marriage. I told them my ex had been physically abusive and I'd walked away. They believed me, and it ensured they never wanted to see or talk to my husband ever again.

I'd gone home briefly after Chicago, before I was showing. I'd let them fuss over me for two weeks before escaping to New York to begin my new life. The only pang I'd experienced watching my swaddled baby being taken away had been for them. My folks were good people and they'd never know they were grandparents.

"We see each other at Christmas." I shrug, like it means nothing, when in fact there are times I miss the only people in this world who genuinely care about me. I can count those on one hand, which is rather sad. "How about you?"

"Big Irish family in Brooklyn. I came out here to escape them." He swipes his brow in mock relief.

"Gledhill's not that far from the city."

"Far enough they can't do constant drop-ins." He grins again and I'm infused with warmth, soon dispelled when I make the mistake of glancing at my lover over Griffin's shoulder and he's frowning while crooking his finger at me like I'm a dog at his beck and call. As if he expects me to come running. Good luck with that, buddy.

Griffin says something and I miss it. "Pardon?"

"Can I have your number?"

I bite back my instant response of "no." I rarely date but with my lover looking on possessively, I'm increasingly tired of my ridiculous revenge fiasco.

"Why don't you give me yours instead?" I slip my cell from my clutch.

He rattles it off quickly, like he thinks I may not want it after all. When I'm done, I look up and see my lover advancing on us, his glower formidable.

I touch Griffin's arm. "If you'll excuse me for a moment, I see an old friend who's waving me over."

"Sure." In his sweetest gesture yet, he leans down and pecks my cheek. "Great meeting you."

"You too."

My lover is glaring at me. His wife comes down the back steps and he talks to her for a moment, enveloping her in a hug.

That poor, deluded woman; he has her completely fooled. How can she tolerate a demanding, egotistical and fickle man? The urge to tell her the truth right this very moment is strong but it's too public so I swivel on my heels and head for the shrubs at the back of the property. In less than five minutes he's there. Pulling me roughly into his arms, his mouth slamming against mine, his tongue thrusting and taunting as he pushes me up against the nearest tree.

"Is this what you want?" he murmurs in my ear as his hand finds its way into my panties.

"Go back to your wife." I shove him away.

He laughs and nips the tender skin above my collarbone.

"Trying to make me jealous is beneath you, my darling."

He slides one finger inside me, another, as his thumb finds my sweet spot.

"Yet you are." I bite his earlobe and he growls, his fingers picking up tempo, thrusting into me with the kind of force he thinks gets me off but only serves to exacerbate the emptiness inside.

"It's a petty, wasted emotion." His thumb rubs harder. "We're so much better than that."

As if to prove it he claims my mouth again, his tongue mimicking what his fingers are doing until the friction is unbearable and I fake it so he'll leave me the hell alone. I sag against the tree as he wrenches his mouth away and lifts his fingers to his lips where he licks me off them. His stare is triumphant, like he's proved how much I want him and no other man. Asshole.

His smile is far from friendly and holds just enough malice to make me regret taunting him earlier. "What you did back there? Don't do it again."

It's a threat and I don't react kindly to it.

"Don't tell me what to do." I tilt my chin up in defiance, staring him down, refusing to cower like he wants me to. "I'm not your wife."

He hides his irritation beneath that chilling smile. "Thank God for that."

He reaches for me again but I push past him and head back to the party.

I'm an idiot.

Trying to wreak havoc on this self-centered bastard can only end badly.

CHAPTER TWELVE

JODI

It turns out Agnes the librarian isn't so helpful after all. I've trawled the length of Sunnyside Drive. It's long, takes me thirty minutes from the highway to the end of the street, and most of the houses have sandstone and lots of glass. Pity I didn't get a number from her.

I'm hungry, thirsty, and my feet ache from walking. I should turn around and head back into town but I've come this far. I see a house, brightly lit, with cars out front. Music and laughter carry on the breeze. A party.

The smell of something savory baking hits my nostrils and my stomach gripes. I'm really starving now. A wave of dizziness swamps me and I lean against an ornate wrought-iron gate. Rather than doing another reconnaissance of the street I should ask someone where he lives and this seems as good a place as any. Besides, I'm so woozy I can't walk another step.

I drag my feet up the driveway, stumble up the front steps, and ring the doorbell. No one comes. I try again. This time, a forty-something woman wearing a pristine white silk strapless dress and matching high-heeled strappy sandals opens the door. Her makeup is immaculate and her hair is a sleek and shiny brown. She could be a poster girl for the rich and pampered Hamptons wife.

"Hi, I'm looking for—"

"I don't see clients here." She sounds kind rather than mad

as her gaze dips to my belly. "I'd love to help but I'm busy right now. How about we meet at the center first thing in the morning?"

She thinks I'm here to see her. Ironically, I do need help but I need to find my meal ticket more.

I want to ask again where he lives, but my head feels foggy and when she asks, "Are you all right?" it comes from a great distance. I sway and lean against the side of the door.

"You poor girl, come in." She slips an arm around my waist and I'm grateful. If she hadn't done that I'd be on the floor. My legs have given out. I feel like puking.

She guides me into an alcove off the kitchen and pulls out one of the dining chairs with her foot. "Sit here and I'll get you something to drink."

I collapse into the chair and lean against the table when she releases me. I'm woozy so I rest my forearms on the table and drop my head forward. I feel like an idiot intruding on a stranger like this, but I'm grateful she's nice. I haven't had anyone look after me in forever.

"Here you go. Drink this." I lift my head and she places a frosty glass of orange juice in front of me, with a smaller glass of water. "The sugar hit will do you good."

My hand shakes as I lift the glass to my mouth and I gulp it gratefully, the sweetness sliding down my throat a welcome relief. I follow the juice with the water, feeling better by the minute.

"When was the last time you ate?"

I frown, trying to remember. "I'm sorry for all this trouble—"

"You need to eat," she says, a thread of disapproval underlying her tone as she glances at my baby bump again. "And you're dehydrated. It's not good for the cargo you're carrying."

I bite back my reply, *I didn't come here to be lectured.* Instead, I nod and she heads back into the kitchen.

The dining alcove is enclosed in floor-to-ceiling glass. It

must be beautiful in the morning with the sun streaming in, the perfect place to eat breakfast. I glance outside, at the people milling about on the lawn, the table laden with food, a makeshift bar at the bottom of the steps. A garden party, how quaint. Being in the Hamptons is like entering an alternate universe; so close to New York City in location but a world away otherwise.

The woman returns and places a plate in front of me. "I brought you a little of everything."

I stare at the assortment of dainty cucumber sandwiches, baby quiches, and strawberry tartlets, and my mouth waters. I manage to say thanks before devouring the food like I haven't eaten in a month.

She chuckles and her laughter is like the rest of her: refined and sweet. "Seconds?"

I nod and hand her the empty plate. "Yes, please."

As I start to feel almost human again, I take another glance outside and the fine hairs on my arms snap to attention.

It's *him*.

My baby's father.

He's mingling, chatting, and laughing like he doesn't have a care in the world.

I half-rise before slumping back into the chair. Can I seriously barge out there, in the middle of this nice lady's party, and confront him? I want to but I can't do it to her. She's been nothing but lovely and I don't want to make a scene.

"Here you go." She returns with another plate and I accept it gratefully. She sits and waits while I eat, watching me with open curiosity.

"I rarely have anyone from the center turn up on my doorstep," she says, studying me. "It's unorthodox but from the way you almost passed out I'm assuming they sent you here?"

It's easier to agree than explain so I nod, stuffing another mini quiche in my mouth.

"You're staying at the center?"

I have nowhere to stay. I hadn't planned on sticking around

in town longer than a day. But with dusk now falling I'll have to find the cheapest motel in town.

"You've checked in, right?"

Her questions are starting to bug me. I shake my head.

She looks appalled, like I've made some grand faux pas. "I'll drive you there now, get you settled, then we can meet in the morning, okay?"

Once again I nod, swept along in her wave of helpfulness, silently grateful I'd chosen her door to knock on tonight. I've found the man I've been searching for when I least expected it and I've found a place to stay for the night. I'll meet the woman again in the morning, discover exactly where he lives, and confront him.

Easy.

CHAPTER THIRTEEN

MARISA

I'm on my way to find Avery, to tell him I'll have to leave the party for a short time, when Ryan and Maggie waylay me.

"Great gig," Ryan says, while Maggie forces a polite smile.

"Yes, thanks for having us." Maggie sounds like she's a recalcitrant teen who's been dragged to a social event and is being forced to express gratitude.

"My pleasure."

"An eclectic crowd as usual." Ryan pinches my cheek like I'm a kid. "You sure are the hostess with the mostest."

"Ryan, leave Marisa alone." Maggie sounds like she's swallowed cut glass.

I don't think she's jealous of me, but tolerating Ryan practically fawning over me must be tough. I know what it's like because I frequently have to do the same with Avery.

"Yeah, Ryan, listen to your wife," I say, and to my relief Maggie and I share a conspiratorial smile.

She looks good tonight: her eyes clear, her expression calm, her posture relaxed. Her blonde bob is sleek, her makeup understated, and her sleeveless black shift skims her hips and falls in a classic drape to her knees. She always makes an effort when she appears in public with her husband, which is increasingly rare these days. I don't think she's obsessive-compulsive—I've dealt with clients like that at the Help Center—but her regular bouts with manic cleansing, both physically and in her house, border on bizarre. Ryan says she sees a therapist but I'm not sure it's helping. If anything, her last detox went on for two weeks and she ended up so emaciated I almost force-fed her my famous protein shakes.

"Have you both had enough to eat?"

Ryan pats his stomach. "Must watch my figure."

Maggie rolls her eyes and says, "The food is delicious. I must get the caterer's number from you."

"Actually, I made everything."

I try not to boast because I know Maggie doesn't cook and they have most meals delivered so they don't have to exist on takeout. I sent across the occasional casserole and lasagna when they first moved next door, but after I'd glimpsed one of my prized pies in the trash, I'd stopped.

Maggie's eyebrows rise. "You're very talented in the kitchen."

I search her face for some sign she's mocking me but I see nothing but admiration. Some of the tension I hold during our rare interactions dissolves.

"And in other rooms of the house according to Avery," Ryan murmurs, with a wink.

"You're disgusting." Maggie elbows him hard and he doubles over with a mock oomph.

"I don't know how you put up with this overgrown child." I offer another smile to Maggie but this time she doesn't return it. Too late, I realize I've said the wrong thing. Maggie has never wanted kids and took surgical steps early in their relationship to ensure it. Ryan is happy with the arrangement because I think he wouldn't like having any attention taken off him.

Their marriage has always fascinated me. What does Ryan bring to it? Maybe Maggie likes his charm and lightheartedness, and his tolerance for her odd obsession? As for Ryan, I think Maggie being an heiress and having a sizable trust fund has a lot to do with his love for her. An awful, cynical assumption and I hate myself for making it.

Thankfully, Maggie's expression softens and she leans into Ryan again. "We put up with each other. You know how it is."

"Yeah, I do."

Once again we smile and I hope our tentative connection can be built on. To her credit, she always makes an effort to come to my gatherings when invited. She doesn't have to. She can avoid me like she does the rest of the time. I've come to not expect too much from my sister-in-law but I love Ryan and they're a package deal.

"I don't mean to be rude but a client has turned up here and I need to take her to the center." I touch both their arms. "I'll be back soon, so please keep eating."

"Yes, Mom," Ryan drawls and this time Maggie shoots him a fond smile.

"Play nice." I waggle a finger at Ryan, who swats it away, and Maggie laughs. "See you later."

Eager to get Jodi settled at the center, I find Avery near the bar. He's brazenly chatting up one of his business partner's wives. The partner wears the long-suffering expression I do when the same happens to me: half-amused, half-uncomfortable, like we'd like to tell him to stop and grow the hell up but don't want to cause a scene.

"Can you excuse us for a moment?" I touch Avery's arm. His partner nods in relief, his wife looks disappointed. I want to say "stupid, gullible woman, don't you know it's a game to him? A power trip?" Narcissists like my husband get off on being admired. Avery is at his best when he's the center of attention, when men defer to him and women fawn over him. I've watched him for so many years I'm immune.

"What's up, sweetheart?" He cuddles me and I endure it for a moment before stepping back.

"A girl has turned up here and I need to give her a ride back to the center. I won't be gone long so keep everyone entertained, please."

"Who is this girl? She turns up at our house and you feel responsible for her?"

"She's young and pregnant and practically collapsed on our doorstep from dehydration. I have no idea why the night staff didn't let her in at the center so she must've looked up my emergency contact details, but I'll drive her there now and be back before anyone misses me."

"*I'll* miss you." He tries to snuggle me again but I'm not impressed by his callous disregard of someone in need.

I'd been like Jodi once: using every instinct to survive in a world that didn't live up to expectations. This girl had walked all the way from town in search of help, showing resourcefulness she'll need to cope as a single mother. I'd been ingenuous once too, though in my case I'd seen Avery as a way out of my life and had gone for it.

The other couple is watching us with open curiosity so I fix a bright smile on my face, the one I regularly pull out for social occasions while I'm feeling dead on the inside. "There's plenty of food on the table, just keep the glasses filled."

"You're too nice, sweetheart. Go rescue the needy." He shoos me away and I resist flipping him the finger for being patronizing as I go in search of the girl.

After initially not saying much, she's given me relevant information so I've called ahead and given the center a heads up. Jodi Van Gelder is twenty-five, a PA for an advertising firm in the city, is five months pregnant and alone. She won't tell me why she's in Gledhill but I can guess.

Her baby's father must live here.

I have to admit that part of my concern for her stems from my love of Trish and Terry. Young girls are impressionable and naïve. Either of my girls could be seduced by some charmer who gets them pregnant, then abandons them. If that happened I'd like to think some good soul would be there for them, like I'm here for Jodi.

I find her sitting on the third step of the staircase, chin

resting in her hands. She's a waif. Thin, pale, with blonde hair layered in a pixie cut, her face dominated by big blue eyes. I can't imagine her caring for herself, let alone a baby.

"Ready to go?"

She nods and grabs the banister to stand. "You sure I'm not dragging you away from your party?"

"Everything's under control. Let's go."

She sways a little, holds the banister tighter.

"Are you dizzy again?" I step forward to help and she waves me away.

"I've been woozy on and off since I discovered I was pregnant." She takes a deep breath and lets it out. "There. That usually fixes it. I'm ready."

She doesn't say much as I drive into town. I try to make small talk but she's not interested so I respect her need for silence until we reach the center where I work. It's on the outskirts of Gledhill, a low, redbrick building with a tin roof. It's nondescript and unassuming, perfect for the victims who seek refuge here. When it's packed to capacity, it can house thirty women and children in small, self-contained rooms that provide the barest necessities.

When I walk through the sliding doors every morning, I'm enveloped in a peace I rarely get at home. Even though my day may be filled with tales of abuse and too many tears, I derive comfort from helping those who need me.

I kill the engine and turn to face her. "You'll have a place to stay here overnight, then we'll talk in the morning." I pause, choosing my next words carefully. "Jodi, I assume you're in town to speak to the baby's father? Does he know yet?"

Her eyes widen in surprise, huge blue pools in her pale face. "No. But I want to tell him."

"And then what?"

Her face falls. "I—I don't know. I hadn't thought much beyond telling him."

She's hiding something. She can't look me in the eye and

her fingers are plucking at the hem of her skirt. Considering her baby's father lives in the Hamptons, it isn't a stretch to assume he has money; a good incentive for a desperate single mother to make the trip here, hoping for a handout.

"Is he rich? Do you expect money? Are you here to blackmail him?"

"No." She doesn't meet my eyes and her fingers continue fiddling. "I just thought he should know."

"Fair enough," I say, not convinced. "It'll be okay."

She mutters, "Easy for you to say," before she opens the door and steps out of the car, as if in a hurry to escape any further interrogation.

I check her into the center, give the night staff a brief rundown of how she turned up at my house, and bid Jodi farewell, promising we'll talk more about her options in the morning.

On the drive home, there are two things I can't get out of my head.

The staff hadn't closed the center for any period of time so why did Jodi appear on my doorstep?

And if she doesn't want her baby, I may know a couple that might.

CHAPTER FOURTEEN

CLAIRE

I feel like crap. Like the lowest of the low as I walk toward my husband after misjudging a guy I'd mistaken for a friend.

"You came back." I fling myself into his arms and hug him tight, silently conveying how sorry I am for everything.

"Sorry for acting like a dick," he murmurs in my ear, squeezing me so tight I yelp. "That was poor form, walking out on you like that."

"It's okay."

We ease back, still holding each other, close enough that I can see the genuine regret in his eyes.

It makes me feel worse. "I've been a bitch the last few weeks and I'm sorry. I shouldn't take it out on you."

"Why not? It's my fault we can't have a baby." He shrugs, expressing so much in that one small gesture.

"If I've made you feel that way..." I shake my head but hang on to him. "I'm so, so sorry. I should've talked to you about it, not...blamed you."

If he's surprised by my bluntness he doesn't show it. That's my husband, stoic and inscrutable. "We're talking now."

"And it's a good thing." I slide my arms farther around his waist and snuggle into him again, needing his warmth to infuse me, desperate to dispel the iciness gripping my heart.

I made a massive misjudgment in trusting Griffin and ended up doing something foolish to top it off. Not catastrophic like the last time, thank goodness, but bad enough to plague me on top of everything else.

He holds me, not saying a word. It's all I need. Dane has always been this way, giving me silent support when I need it, giving advice when I ask for it. He's a good guy, a good husband, and I almost screwed it all up yet again. I'm an idiot.

This time when we disengage, I've got tears in my eyes. "I'm ready to talk about other options now."

His eyebrows shoot up. "Right now?"

Considering I've been avoiding this conversation since we got the test results and he's been keen to have it, I understand his surprise. "I mean why don't we head home and talk."

A tear spills onto my cheek and he gently swipes it away with his thumb before kissing the damp spot. He really is the best.

"Let's go."

He grips my hand and intertwines his fingers with mine. In that simple gesture he makes me feel safe, like I've found my way back to a sheltered harbor after foundering in a storm for too long.

"Let's find Ris and say bye." But we scan the guests on the lawn and only see Avery. We both can't be bothered saying anything to him.

She's not in the kitchen either so I motion to Elly, who's standing near the bar looking shell-shocked. She saunters over to us, a tad unsteady. "What's up?"

"Can you say bye to Ris for us? I can't find her anywhere."

"Sure," Elly says. "You two lovebirds heading home already?"

"Yeah," Dane says, curt and dismissive, and I shoot him a puzzled glance. He's never rude to my friends, only Griffin, and he sure as hell isn't a friend anymore.

"Off you go then." Elly hugs me and waves at Dane before turning her back on us and sauntering toward Griffin, whose eyes light up as she gets closer.

I want to warn my friend to be careful, that he's prone to misreading situations...in a big way. But I can't say anything without alerting Dane and now isn't the time to tell him he's been right about Griffin all along, not when we're about to talk about our options to have children.

"I know you two are friends and I respect that, but that woman is a serious man-eater." He shudders for emphasis and I chuckle.

"Don't worry, she'd never set her sights on you." I pretend to whip a gun out of a holster. "I'd shoot her before she laid a finger on you."

His goofy grin makes my heart skip a beat, like it always does, as he traces my cheek with a fingertip. "I like it when you go all scary cop on me."

He lifts my hand to his lips and kisses the back of it. "Come on, let's go."

We walk home in companionable silence, our clasped hands swinging between us. The breeze off the Atlantic has cooled, raising goosebumps on my bare arms. The crisp brine scent fills my nostrils with familiarity. I like living in Gledhill after spending most of my life as a city girl. It's a great place to raise a family.

And just like that, I'm back in that dark place again, wondering "why me?" and blaming myself, convinced that I'm being punished for the sins of my past.

When we reach home, we pause at the front gate and Dane gestures at our house with his free hand. "I like living here but have you noticed how all the houses look the same? Even though Marisa's is huge and most are miniature copies, like ours, it's spooky."

"What's spooky about it? Just shows we all have great taste."

"Hamptons taste," he says, in a fake posh voice that makes me giggle. "Would you like a cup of proper Hamptons coffee, madam?"

"I'd love one."

It'll make a nice change from the bourbon nightcaps I've been having every night to wind down.

I sit at our kitchen table while he makes the coffee, as confident in a domestic capacity as he is at everything else. I sure lucked out when this guy convinced me to marry him.

Except...

In that instant, I crave bourbon more than ever. It's like I can fool myself into accepting our situation for a period of time and then boom, reality intrudes and I'm back to feeling sorry for myself.

"Here you go." He hands me a cup of steaming espresso, handle out, always thoughtful.

"Thanks." I take a sip and the caffeine jolts me back to the present and the conversation we need to have. "So about those options."

"Yeah?" He sits next to me, close enough I can feel the heat radiating off his thigh.

"I don't think I'm up for IVF, with the endless appointments and injections, finding a suitable donor, the stress of it all. And the cost would be exorbitant." I'm rambling and huff out a breath. "I think you're right. You've mentioned adoption before and I've been hesitant but I've thought about it and I reckon it's our best bet. And we can afford to go the private route so we could have a child so much faster that way."

His shoulders slump in relief and his gaze meets mine, his eyes bright. "I want a child with you. More than one if we're lucky. So however you want to do this, I'm one hundred percent in."

"So we're choosing to adopt?"

"Absolutely." He places his coffee cup on the table, takes mine out of my hands and does the same, before enveloping me in a hug that expels the air from my lungs in a whoosh. "I love you. Always have. Always will."

I hug him back, relieved we're on the same page and that we can finally move forward from the pain. But as he continues to squeeze me like he'll never let go, I can't help but wonder how he really feels.

I'm the one calling all the shots. I've been irrationally hostile, he accepted it. I withdrew from him, he accepted that too. When he initially pushed for adoption, I was against it, but now that I've changed my mind, he's equally fine. It makes me wonder.

Why is my strong, opinionated husband suddenly so agreeable?

CHAPTER FIFTEEN

ELLY

As I return to the party I feel dirty. Like I've waded through a swamp and it's clinging to my skin, cold and clammy and impossible to shake off. My lover has this effect on me. I should never have acquiesced to him. I'm not a woman who's at a man's beck and call. Not anymore.

A shiver wracks my body from head to foot and I rub my bare arms. It does little for the chill invading me. I feel cold inside. Empty. Worthless. I know the feeling well.

I'd felt the same way that fateful morning I'd seen my husband embrace another woman before kissing each of her three adorable kids. They'd all piled into an SUV, a *family* car, and I'd followed to the nearest school, where my husband walked the kids in, ruffling the boy's hair, picking up the girls and swinging them around. When he'd returned to the car, he'd kissed the woman with more passion than he'd ever shown me.

I'd known in that instant that my perfect marriage wasn't so perfect after all.

If I hadn't been sent to Elmwood Park that day to pick up my boss's laptop, I never would've known. I'd still be married, blissfully unaware that my husband had another wife and the kids he swore to me he never wanted.

Our confrontation an hour later at home had been ugly. He'd said he married me because he needed a professional, gorgeous trophy wife to advance his business. That the love of his life and his kids would drag him down in the cutthroat corporate arena he inhabited. So he put them in a little family box and shelved them, visiting them daily unbeknownst to me and the rest of the world.

Like our vows on the shores of Lake Michigan meant nothing, vows where he'd promised to adore and cherish me. Vows obliterated when he said he could never love a self-indulgent, shallow bitch like me.

He had ruined me that day and no matter how hard I strive to reinvent myself, I can never shake the worthlessness that plagues me.

Thanks to my lover, I feel the same way now. Insignificant. Hollow. Useless.

Unexpected tears sting my eyes and I blink them away. I'll never cry. Not over him. He's not worth it. I want to leave but as I'm skirting the garden Griffin spots me and waves. Damn, so much for a quick getaway. I could wave and still leave, we've already said goodbye, but he's been nothing but sweet to me tonight and I don't want to treat him like that, despite barely knowing him. I don't want to make him feel how I feel right now.

I force a smile and head his way. A quick word, then I'm out of here.

"Hey, have you eaten yet?" He points at the buffet. "I can grab us some plates?"

He's considerate too; another brownie point in his favor. They've stacked up pretty quick.

I shake my head. "Thanks, but I'm not hungry." I make a grand show of glancing at my watch. "Actually, I'm leaving."

Concern creases his brow. "Are you okay?"

For some reason, I'm compelled to tell the truth. "I've been better."

"Let me take you home," he says, his gaze guileless, without a hint of sleaze in sight.

"That's fine, I have my car here."

"Do you need me to follow you, to make sure you arrive home safely?"

I shake my head again. When I tuck a strand of hair behind my ear I'm appalled to discover my hand is shaky. "No, I'm good."

At least, I will be, once I get the hell away from here and my lover's covetous stares that even now burn a hole in my back.

"Okay then, I'll wait for your call."

He must realize how desperate that sounds because he quickly adds, "Not that I'll be holding my cell actually waiting for you to call, but I'm hoping you'll call." He grimaces and scrubs a hand across his face. "That sounds even worse."

I smile at his endearing goofiness. There's something inherently appealing about a guy who tries to say the right thing but messes up anyway. Amazingly, he's lightened my mood without trying. In that moment, I want to feel good so I give in to impulse.

"Would you like to go out for a coffee?"

"Now?" His gaze is hopeful, like an eager puppy.

"Yeah." I shrug, like his answer means little, when I'm hoping he'll come. I need the distraction. I need to lose the feeling of degradation.

"Sure, that sounds good. Where did you have in mind?"

"How about that all-night café on Main Street, Margot's?"

To his credit, he doesn't look disappointed that "coffee" doesn't mean more. "I'll meet you there."

"Great." And it is, to enjoy a guy's company with a view to nothing else but chatter.

However, fifteen minutes later, ensconced in one of Margot's crimson leather booths with only a coconut-and-lime-scented candle for illumination, I wonder what I'm doing here. I don't do small talk well, especially with a virtual stranger who I'd normally be tempted to flirt with. And while Griffin may be cute and polite, I have little interest in taking our mild attraction further. I've got too much on my mind: like how to tell my friend the truth without everything imploding.

"Did I say something wrong?" Griffin lowers his coffee cup to the table and reaches for my hand before thinking better of it. "We hit it off at the party and now you seem...different somehow. Distant?"

"It's not you." I gulp my coffee and it burns my tongue. "I bumped into someone at the party that rubs me the wrong way and I'm in a bit of a mood."

He's puzzled. I don't blame him. "Then why did you ask me here if you want to be alone?"

"That's the thing. I don't want to be alone and you seem like a nice guy."

He winces, like I've wounded him. "The dating kiss of death. The *nice* guy."

"But we're not dating." I sound sharp, shrewish, and he visibly recoils.

"I know that, but I thought..." He gestures around the place, filled with couples like us enjoying a late-night supper. Candles are lit, lights are low, and soft acid jazz filters through the café. Mahogany lines the walls and the monstrous fireplace that divides the room is lit, the slow-burning wood emitting the occasional crackle. Margot's vibe is cozy, chic, and way too romantic. I'm a fool for asking him here tonight.

"It's not you. I think you're a great guy but I rarely date. I wanted some company tonight and thought you might like to join me, that's it." I show him my open palms, like I have nothing to hide. "If you want to leave, fine."

Confusion makes his forehead crinkle, like he can't figure me out. He's not the only one. "Do you do this often?" There's a glint of anger in his stare. "Reel men in, then push them away?"

I hear the censure in his voice and I'm instantly transported back fourteen months ago to having a drink with another guy I thought I could trust, a guy who hadn't taken no for an answer and taken what he wanted regardless. At least, that's what I assume happened, because I still can't remember a thing.

"Is that your professional opinion?"

My sarcasm makes his eyes narrow, like he can't work me out. Join the club, buddy. I'm a warped, twisted mystery even to myself.

"Considering I've made some dubious decisions over the last few hours, my professional opinion isn't what it's cracked up to be."

His self-deprecation gets to me a little. Most guys would've called me out for being a sarcastic bitch. I'm right. He's nice and would be the perfect guy to get to know if I was so inclined, which I'm not.

"We all make questionable decisions at times."

Like me, sitting here pretending that I'm interested in what he has to say when I'm dying a little on the inside.

With every encounter with my lover, I lose another piece of myself. My self-respect shattered a long time ago but I've never felt this soul-destroying remorse before. I know why. This time I've taken it too far. I've slept with the guy and have let him into my hardened heart a little. But worst of all, a friend is involved and even when I tear the blinkers from her eyes I'll never recover from this.

He eyes me with respect. "I know you're not interested in hearing this but whatever's bugging you, it really does help to talk about it."

I rear back like he's poked me in the eye, but before I can tell him to fuck off, he holds up his hands and offers a rueful grin. "I'm not volunteering to hear you out, by the way. That was a general observation."

He's candid and I appreciate it. The subterfuge perpetuated by my ex, my lover, and all the other guys who dupe, taints my view of all men. Griffin isn't a bad guy. He's a dork, the kind of guy who says what he thinks and reads situations wrong despite the college degree. He's harmless but I'm not in the mood to continue being psychoanalyzed against my will.

"Thanks for the free advice but I'd rather be alone."

"My bill's in the mail." His smile is candid as he stands, slips a few dollars out of his wallet, and lays them on the table. "For what it's worth, I think you're great, and if you want to give me a call when you're in a better place, I'd love to hear from you."

I don't want to hurt his feelings so I remain silent. With a rueful shrug of his shoulders and a hopeful half smile, he's gone.

I made a mess of that yet I don't care. Even if he hadn't turned out to be sweet, what did I expect to happen? How would Griffin have been any different from the other guys I've been with? Guys I use in the hope I'll feel wanted in a way my husband never wanted me, even for the briefest speck of time.

If I hadn't driven him away tonight with my whacky behavior I may have asked him out on a date. Dinner maybe. Then when he called the next day, or the next, or even the week after that, I wouldn't have returned his call. Meaningless flirtations serve a purpose for a short time. It distracts from my self-doubt. It helps me escape if only during a brief interlude. So when the fleeting date is over, I don't want to see the guy again. I don't want to get close. I don't want to ever risk putting myself out there again.

Besides, Griffin is nothing like my lover, and against my better judgment I can't help but compare the two. I like a confident, take-charge man because it makes me feel more powerful when I get the better of him. At least, that's what I keep telling myself, because if I'd learned one thing tonight at Ris's party, it's that seeing him with his wife made me feel almost... jealous.

Crazy, because I'm only using him as an adjunct to make my friend wake the hell up. But every time I see him lately he's worming his way under my skin and making me *feel*, when

I'd vowed to never feel anything for a man ever again. It terrifies me.

I need to stick with the program and not deviate, like tonight.

Nice guys aren't my type. Nasty guys who lie and cheat are. I need to stay ahead of the game. Regain control.

Starting now, with a terse text to my lover.

CHAPTER SIXTEEN

JODI

I've had a good night's sleep at the center, which is basically a halfway house for lost souls like me. They fed me, gave me a change of clothes, and plied me with a pile of brochures outlining various scenarios, including adoption. It's not like I haven't thought about it. When I first discovered I was pregnant I couldn't envisage being a single mom so giving my baby up seemed like a logical choice. But now that I'm in Gledhill and close to my baby's father, I'm reassessing the wisdom of that. When I find him, I hope he'll be open to child support. If not, having a loving couple care for my baby wouldn't be the worst thing in the world. But the ache in my chest at the thought of giving him up suggests otherwise.

The receptionist ushers me into Marisa's office precisely at nine. Marisa looks the same as last night: polished, elegant, classy, this time in tailored black pants and a red silk blouse. She looks too posh to be a social worker and going by her fancy house I'm puzzled as to why she needs to work.

"So you've had a chance to read the brochures?"

I nod and mumble, "Uh-huh."

She rests her forearms on her immaculate desk. "Do you have any questions about adoption?"

I'm not surprised she's homed in on adoption as that's what most of the brochures referred to and it's the most rational step if I don't want to raise my baby. But before I can answer, she launches into a spiel.

"There are many couples in this area who have the money to facilitate a private adoption if that's what you choose to do. They would pay for an attorney who would handle all the legalities, negotiate payments to you, and protect the rights of all involved." She beams like it's the most natural thing in the world to give up one's baby. "Medical and social histories are obtained on the adoptive parents and a qualified home-study counselor will assess the parents' suitability. And if it's okay with you, the adoptive parents can be present at the birth and take the baby home directly from the hospital."

I tune out as she continues outlining the process: that my consent isn't binding before the birth of my baby, that because I'm unmarried there's no paternity test, and if it's unlikely the father will commit to parenting I can decide everything, that I can revoke consent even after signing the documents post-birth, and on and on until my head is spinning.

"So what do you think, Jodi?" She leans forward, pinning me with a hopeful stare I have no chance of interpreting because everything she's said is a jumble.

"Think?"

"About letting a childless couple in Gledhill adopt your baby."

I bite back my instant refusal. I'm nowhere near making a decision like that, especially as I don't know if I'll have money to support us yet. I'm about to tell her that when I spy a photo on top of a bookcase behind her.

There are eleven people in the photo.

One of them is my baby's father.

My breath stalls and my throat tightens. I remember those eyes, piercing and persuasive, the strong jaw, the handsome features, the wicked grin that undid me as much as his smooth lines. To my mortification I feel a flicker of heat shoot through me.

Trying to appear nonchalant, I point at the photo. "That looks like a happy group."

If she's surprised by my abrupt change of topic she doesn't show it. Instead, she picks up the photo and smiles. "A bunch of us took this in Montauk about eighteen months ago. A good day."

I want to ask how she knows my baby's father but I need to be subtle. "Friends? Family?"

"A mix of both, plus a few taggers-on."

He doesn't have his arm draped over any of the women but I wonder if he's Marisa's husband: he'd been at her house last night and now in this picture.

I want to jab at my baby's father and ask, "How do you know him?" but I don't. I need to be circumspect until I find him and if I demand information from Marisa she'll figure out why I'm so curious about this guy.

"So would you be interested in adoption?" She replaces the photo and turns back to face me. "Because if you're not keeping the baby I think it could be the best option."

There she went again, using that word, *option*. Like I have any choice in this. Ever since I discovered I'm pregnant I've felt like all my choices have been taken away and I'm caught up in some endless swirl of helplessness. A vortex I can't escape, no matter how desperately I claw at the sides to climb out.

"I'm not sure," I say, and I'm not. I have no idea what to do if I can't get my hands on some serious money to raise this kid.

When I'd first come up with my plan it had all seemed clear: find the father, demand the dollars. But what if he doesn't care if I divulge the truth about the baby? What if he denies it? What if he doesn't give me what I want?

I haven't thought this through enough. I rushed to Gledhill on a whim, with a vague plan that hasn't come to fruition yet. And if it doesn't...I'm screwed. But my baby won't be. I'll make sure of that. Adoption is a viable option but I'm all talked out for today.

"The thing is, this childless couple are locals and if you agree for them to adopt your baby I think you should stay in town. We could help you with whatever you need." She leans forward on her desk, sounding too eager. "If you have no one back in the city, this could be good for you and the baby."

She doesn't care about me. All she wants is for me to present this couple with a baby.

"Unless you've told the father and he's agreed to co-parent?"

I shake my head too quickly, the familiar wooziness overcoming me. "I will tell him but I doubt he'll want any involvement."

She doesn't appear sad. She looks positively gleeful. "In that case, why don't you take a few days to think it over then let me know what you decide?"

I don't have the funds to stay in a motel for a few days and I don't want to. I want to find my baby's father, get my money, and head back to the city. I've only been granted three weeks' paid leave and I can't risk losing my job if the baby's father won't pay up.

As if reading my mind, she adds, "You can stay here. We'll take good care of you."

I force a smile, her effusiveness increasingly annoying now that I know she's like everyone else and has a hidden agenda. "Thanks. You've been very kind."

"It's my job," she says, with a diffident shrug, but I know it's more than that now.

She stands and shows me to the door. "How about we meet again in two days and see where you're at?"

"Okay."

I have forty-eight hours to find him. If I don't, staying in town on the pretext of giving my child up for adoption might not be such a bad idea until I have what I've come here for: money.

Even after I locate my baby's father it may not be easy to instigate a one-on-one meeting. And in turn it may take longer for everything to fall into place. Yes, staying here while I "consider" adopting out my baby is a good idea.

My plan is evolving and it's solid.

I should know better than anyone that the best-laid plans eventually end up astray.

CHAPTER SEVENTEEN

MARISA

The next day, I'm waiting for Claire on the boardwalk at lunchtime. I've done well to hold out this long to tell her my news. Technically her news, if she approves of the idea. It's outlandish and may not happen because I sense Jodi is fickle but I have to tell her before I burst.

Rosie, one of the cooks at Sea Breeze, spies me sitting on a bench and saunters over.

"Hey, Marisa. How are things?"

"Good. You?"

She wavers her hand side to side. "I've been better."

"What's wrong?"

Rosie darts a nervous glance over her shoulder before continuing. "My sister's in trouble. I hope you don't mind but I asked her to go see you at the Help Center?"

"You did the right thing." I reach out and clasp her hand briefly. "Toxic relationship?"

Rosie's eyes fill with tears as she nods. "The guy she's with is no good for her and I feel so fucking helpless."

My heart aches for this cheerful, generous girl who has helped me serve food at a shelter in nearby Westhampton on countless occasions. It's rare these days to find a young woman in her twenties willing to give up her time to help those less fortunate but Rosie never balks when I ask her to lend a hand.

"Taking the first step is the hardest." I hate how trite I sound. "If she wants to distance herself from a bad relationship I'll do everything I can to help, okay?"

"Thanks, Marisa, you're the best." She leans down and gives me an impulsive hug, making welcome warmth spread through me. This is what I like doing: solving problems, helping people, the buzz far better than anything I get from socializing with Avery's wealthy friends. "Next time you're in Sea Breeze, the Thai chia salad is on me."

As she walks away I see Claire approaching so I wave. When she reaches the bench she sits, places two soda cans between us, and hands me a tuna and pickle on rye before unwrapping her pastrami sandwich.

"What's this all about? You sounded hyper on the phone earlier."

"Let's eat first." I chicken out at the last minute, afraid she'll hate me for interfering in her life. Not that sandwiches and soda will make this task any easier but it gives me time to formulate some kind of rational presentation rather than blurting, "I think I've found you a baby."

"What do you think of my domestic skills?" Claire brandishes the crust of her sandwich.

"You made these?" I sound incredulous, intent on making her laugh and she does.

"Who knew that if you have time on your hands at home you can do all sorts of extra stuff like make lunch?" She places the crusts back into a paper bag and dusts off her hands. "Beats the unhealthy donuts and awful quinoa salads at the station."

"I thought that whole donut-eating-cop thing was a fallacy?"

"Have you seen the size of Ron's gut?"

We laugh in unison and it feels good. With the sun on our faces and the wind ruffling our hair I can momentarily pretend that all is right in my world. But it's not and the faster I focus on fixing Claire's life than dwelling on my own, the better.

"When do you go back to work?"

"Next week." She sips at her soda, staring at the ocean through narrowed eyes. "I'm ready. Things are better at home."

She turns to me, clarity in her eyes I haven't seen for weeks. "I've been so angry, mostly at Dane, and he doesn't deserve it. But we're talking now and working through stuff."

"Good for you." Having their relationship on solid ground will make what I have to tell her all the more exciting. "You two are one of the best couples I know."

She manages a lopsided grin. "We are pretty great, aren't we?"

"Absolutely."

"The thing is, I expected to feel sad and disappointed about our infertility, but I never expected the resentment." She shakes her head, pain glinting in her eyes. "When we first found out, I resented Dane, and that's not good." Her nose wrinkles. "Drinking alone late at night and using alcohol as a crutch is so not me."

"Considering you barely finish a glass of wine at our gardening club meetings, I tend to agree."

"Anyway, rather than wallowing I've taken a more proactive approach." Her face eases into a smile. "We've discussed it and we're going the adoption route."

"That's fantastic, sweetie." I hug her, squashing my sandwich in the process but not giving a damn. She's given me the perfect segue.

When I pull back, I grin like an idiot and she stares at me, one eyebrow quirked. "What's going on?"

"Did you see that girl who turned up on my doorstep the night of the supper party?"

She shakes her head, a faint blush staining her cheeks.

I call her on it. "Were you and Dane off doing naughty things down by my pool?"

"Something like that," she mutters, a cloud passing over her eyes before she blinks and it's gone.

"Well, her name's Jodi, and she's pregnant. She's considering giving her baby up for adoption. I thought..." I hesitate for a moment "...you might be interested?"

She startles, like I've electrocuted her. "Are you serious?"

I nod, glad to be the bearer of good news. I've been involved in several adoptions over the years and seeing a childless couple hold their baby for the first time is something that makes my job incredibly worthwhile. To think I might be able to bring that joy to Claire and Dane...helping my friends would mean everything to me.

"I've broached the idea with her that I have a couple in mind who are keen for a baby. And if you agree, she can stay in town until the birth and you can be there if you both want and—"

"Whoa, slow down." Claire's overwhelmed, her expression stunned and her mouth opening and closing like a goldfish, and I don't blame her. This has happened so fast but it seems like fate. "It can't be that simple, surely? Wouldn't there be waiting lists and forms and interviews and all the rest? Not to mention the expense."

My always-practical friend asks all the right questions and luckily I have the answers. "It would need to be an independent adoption, so it's done privately by an attorney. It can be costly, anywhere between ten and forty grand, but if she chooses you as the adoptive parents everything can be streamlined."

"But...oh my God." She slumps against the bench, shock making her mouth slack and her hands tremble before she clasps them in her lap. "How far along is she?"

"Five months. I'll make an obstetrics appointment for her at the medical center to make sure her pregnancy is progressing well and the baby's okay."

Technically, I should've done this first without raising Claire's hopes. But I wanted to garner her level of interest before I proceeded too far. We have a doctor who visits the center weekly and he has experience with our single mothers. But if Jodi agrees to give her baby to Claire, I'll pull out all the stops, including private health care to ensure my friend gets the baby she deserves.

"I can't believe this." Claire shakes her head, absentmindedly peeling the label off her soda. "I want a child so badly but I never thought...I mean, I thought adoption takes years and even then we might not get a baby, maybe a toddler or an older child..."

She bursts into tears and it startles me. In the few years I've known Claire I've never seen her cry. She's too stoical for that.

"Oh, sweetie." I envelop her in another hug and let her cry it out, smoothing her back and making soft comforting nonsensical noises that I used to when the twins were little.

My throat tightens at the memory and I hold her tighter. I can't imagine my life without the twins and if my friend wants to experience the joy of motherhood I'll do whatever it takes to help her.

When her sobs ease to sniffles, she pulls away and swipes a hand across her eyes. "I must look a fright."

I rest a hand on her shoulder and squeeze before lowering it. "You look like a woman who's received some surprising news and is probably confused and elated and terrified."

She stares at me, her smile crooked. "How do you do that? Home in on exactly how I'm feeling?"

"I'm a mom, I've had years of mind-reading practice with the girls."

More memories spring to mind: Terry breaking an expensive fruit bowl and Trish lying to cover for her, Trish sneaking my favorite cashmere sweater and accidentally staining it with ink that Terry swore she'd done, both girls hiding the truth about the after-party following their prom until their dates had brought them home drunk. Precious fragments of time with my kids that I sift through at will, poignant snapshots I use as reminders to stay in my increasingly grim marriage.

"Your girls must adore you."

Her praise makes me want to bawl. I don't get much of it at home these days.

"I adore them." It's a simple statement that leaves a lot unsaid and Claire doesn't push me on it.

Until she has a child of her own I don't think she'll understand the overwhelming love I feel for my girls. How I still tidy their rooms every day. How I flick through their yearbooks, pride for their achievements bringing tears to my eyes. How I sit in front of the computer for hours, scrolling through photos chronicling their growth from babies to toddlers to school-age to young adults, wishing I could turn back time.

I'm not a helicopter mom, never have been. I dote on my girls but I'm not overprotective. Heck, I encouraged their move to LA for college because that's what they wanted. But I miss them so badly, clinging to the memories of motherhood to sustain me. They enable me to keep going through the daily charade that is my marriage.

"So what happens from here?" She lobs the soda in the nearby trash. "I mean, I'll need to discuss this with Dane, but I'm sure he'll be as excited as I am."

"If he's fine with the idea, I'll orchestrate a meeting between you and Jodi so you can discuss the process."

Claire presses the pads of her fingers to her eyes. "Is this really happening?"

"It might be, so stay strong and keep the faith. And if this doesn't work out, trust me when I say I'll do everything to help you get the child you deserve." I lay a comforting hand on her forearm and she covers it with hers. "You'll make a great mom."

She tears up again and I feel the burn of tears too. "Truly, Ris, I can't thank you enough for thinking of us." Her voice hitches and ends on a sob. Claire is rarely speechless so I can see how much my gesture means to her.

"You're welcome."

I've done the right thing in telling her and it feels good. Until I remember what's happening in my own life and my happiness fades fast.

If only I can fix my problems as easily.

CHAPTER EIGHTEEN

CLAIRE

I'm in a daze. Ris wants to talk more but I can't. I need to get home and tell Dane the news. She understands my flightiness, hugs me yet again, and says we'll talk soon. As if we'll be discussing something mundane like the next party Ris is hosting or what we'll be drinking at Gardening Club.

A baby.

In four months I could be a mom.

With diapers and night feeds and strollers and fluffy toys.

How amazing is that?

It's not quite the scenario I envisaged—being pregnant, going through hormone swings and bloated ankles and nausea as some sort of penance for what I'd done to Dane all those years ago—but having a child of our own by any means will solidify our bond and go some way to easing my guilt.

I love my husband. I want us to be happy. I want to focus on the future and forget about the past.

A sliver of regret pierces my euphoria. I'd watched my sisters-in-law get pregnant repeatedly over the years and had swallowed my envy each time. Not that I would've welcomed a baby back then; I'd been striving to cement my career in the force. But I'd been jealous of the shared confidences over the best diapers, formulas, clothes and that special glow each of them had sported while resting a protective hand over their bulging bellies.

Since Dane and I started trying, I'd find myself doing online searches for strollers and cribs, lusting after the cutest rompers and scouring endless lists of baby names, envisaging our very own Emma or Josh.

I'd imagined myself going shopping for maternity clothes and attending ultrasound appointments and dosing up on vitamins. Even the heartburn and swollen ankles would've been welcome, now that I know I'll never experience any of it. I feel...robbed somehow. I know I'll love any child we adopt with all my heart but I'll never know what it feels like to nurture a baby in my belly for nine months and ridiculously I miss it.

Tears sting my eyes and I blink them away. Probably just as well I can't get pregnant. I'd be a mess with the riotous hormones.

I glance at the speedometer regularly all the way home so I don't go over the limit like I want to. In fact, I'm tempted to break every land speed record to get home and tell Dane the news.

When I finally pull into our winding drive, tumble from the car, and run into the house, he's not there. I should've known because his car isn't under the carport but I'm so damn excited I can't compute anything beyond *baby*.

Momentarily deflated, I wander into the kitchen and spy the note he's left me on the counter. I snatch it up and read the usual work excuse.

HEY GORGEOUS,
CALLED INTO WORK.
HOPEFULLY WON'T BE LONG.
LOVE YOU. X

I crumple it into a ball and lob it in the trash. I miss. This has been happening for most of our marriage, Dane being called away for work. Clients wanting to see the latest in medical equipment, doctors demanding to hear his sales spiel after-hours, bosses insisting he travel to keep up to date with the latest technological advances.

I should be used to it. I should understand, especially as I can be called out to a job any time of day and night even when I'm supposedly off-duty. And Dane has never, ever complained about that. But today is different. I have news that impacts our future and a small part of me resents him for not being here.

Irrational, but I'm consumed with the possibility of us being parents and I can't wait to tell him. With Dane not around, I'm tempted to call Mom before thinking better of it. I haven't told her about our fertility issues, how can I call out of the blue and lump a possible adoption on her?

I could've called Griffin: if he hadn't turned out to be a misguided asshole. Being away from work has been timely because I'm not ready to face him again. Every time I see him I'll remember those two seconds I let him kiss me, how badly I misjudged our situation, and be mortified all over again.

Gripping the phone tight I call Dane but he doesn't answer. Another thing that bugs me, the number of times I talk to his message service. Sure, I understand he's meeting with clients so he can't answer but it happens most of the time and today I really need to get hold of him.

Frustrated, I kick a leg of the kitchen table. It doesn't help. Then the phone rings and I glance at caller ID. It's Beau, Dane's brother. He's a sweetie and I'd usually answer but the way I'm dying to spill the exciting news I'll probably blurt out the possible adoption and Beau will know before Dane. Not an option so I let the call go through to our message service and wait the appropriate few minutes before dialing in to hear the message.

"Hey, bro, it's me. Look, we need to talk. I've tried your cell five times today, where the fuck are you? It's your day off so you should be picking up at home. Anyway, I'm not in a good place after you gave me the brush-off while you were at that party. So call me ASAP. We need to figure this out."

The dial tone sounds and I hang up, bewildered. Day off?

First thing this morning Dane had told me he'd probably be called into work because of a new MRI delivery and his note had reiterated that. And that night at the supper party Dane had told me he'd been speaking to a work colleague yet it turns out it was Beau? Why did he lie?

I can always count on Dane's honesty. At times he borders on bluntness but I love that about him. Now, as the doubts creep in, I wonder if I'm too trusting.

Does my husband have secrets?

Like I do?

CHAPTER NINETEEN

ELLY

Maggie is waiting in my office first thing on Monday morning as usual. As the owner of the medical center she doesn't need to show up, she's that rich, and she doesn't take an active role in the everyday running—she leaves that to me—but she still stops by every week with two lattes and gluten-free blueberry muffins. I like that we've become friends, and discounting Ris' and Claire I don't have many of those. I hope that's why she turns up each week, because she values this friendship as much as I do.

"Hey, Mags, how are you?" I slip out of my jacket and hang it in the wardrobe, along with my handbag.

"Good. You?"

"You know me." I sit and she hands me a takeout coffee cup. "Living life. Loving it."

"Good for you." She raises her coffee cup in a toast. "You're one of the most upbeat people I know."

"That's because you only live once." I sip at my coffee and sigh: extra dash of cream and a half sugar, perfect. "Sorry I didn't have a chance to talk to you at Ris's supper party the other night."

"Don't worry." Her eyes light up. "You seemed otherwise occupied."

I inadvertently squeeze my cup and a bubble of coffee appears on the rim. "That guy isn't my type."

Her eyebrows rise. "I hear he's a good psychologist."

I snort. "Yeah, who apparently thinks I'm a head case who needs a shrink."

She smiles but there's fragility behind it and I inwardly curse. I know she borders on fanatical with her cleansing obsession and has probably had her fair share of visits to a therapist.

"Anyway, do you want to take a look at the new staffing rosters?"

Thankfully she buys my change of subject. "Sure. And I wouldn't mind going over last month's billing."

It's a ruse we both indulge in every week. Maggie pretending like she's interested in the center while I play the diligent manager.

"I'll pull up the figures for you." I tap on my keyboard and in a second I've brought up the spreadsheets. As I turn the screen to face her, my cell rings. It's Ris.

"Do you mind if I get this?"

"Go ahead." Her gaze is on the screen, already glazing over. She'll make a few cursory remarks, make small talk about life in Gledhill, trade fashion advice, and then leave, until next week when we'll do it all over again.

It staggers me, how a charming extrovert like Ryan hooked up with this eccentric woman. Then again, a twenty-million-dollar trust fund explains a lot.

I stab at the answer button on my cell. "Hey, Ris, how are you?"

"Fine. You?"

"Couldn't be better." I mime chatting with my hand and Maggie manages a tense smile. She's not close to Ris, despite Ryan practically living at Ris's house. Then again, I can imagine Ris doting on Maggie because of her issues to the point of suffocation and there's only so much TLC a person can take.

"I have a favor to ask you." She's using her work voice, an added posh tinge to her vowels. "I need an urgent appointment with your best ob-gyn for a client here, Jodi Van Gelder."

Ris rarely asks me for a favor so this call is a surprise. "Sure, give me a minute."

I point at the screen and Maggie swivels it toward me while I type with one hand, pulling up appointments. "I can fit your Jodi Van Gelder in at eight tomorrow morning? We try to keep that time free for emergencies so it shouldn't be a problem."

"Thanks, Elly, I'll email her details through to you now. I owe you one."

We both know it's not true. After the way she supported me following the rape, I owe her, big time.

"Jodi's the girl who arrived unannounced at my place the night of the supper party."

"I remember."

I didn't see the girl but Ris explained later when I queried where she'd disappeared to. I didn't think much of it at the time. Ris is a do-gooder. She thrives on it in her job on a daily basis. So it doesn't surprise me if one of her strays shows up on her doorstep.

But now I know the girl is pregnant I'm curious. Ris said it's a first, having a client arrive at her house. This Jodi could've easily waited until the next morning to see Ris at work. So why did this girl do something so unorthodox and show up on her doorstep? And why would the center—or in this case Ris—pay for one of our top ob-gyns to see her?

"Anyway, I have to dash. Thanks again, Elly."

"Anytime."

I hang up, relieved that Maggie is already standing. She never stays long. It's one of the reasons I like her visits. We both have limited patience for faux cheerfulness. She's blunt and I like her all the more for it. I'm also drawn to her air of serenity, an inner quietness that shines through despite the turmoil she must face during her manic detox episodes. I admire her resilience. Another quality we both share.

"How's Marisa?"

Maggie never calls her Ris. For sisters-in-law and neighbors, they're not close. Not from Ris's lack of trying. She's always trying to draw people into her social circle. But if Maggie's anything like me, I know why she's standoffish with Ris. My friend can make the most accomplished woman feel inadequate. Not deliberately, but just because of who she is.

She works full-time, runs a busy household for Avery, who constantly entertains his work cronies, serves on countless charities where she raises money like a fiend, and volunteers at several organizations. Ris is a dynamo but in my weaker moments I want to throttle her for being so damn accomplished.

Then I remember her softer side, the woman beneath the mask, and I want to hug her tight for being there for me when I needed her most.

"She's fine."

"I can't believe she cooked all that food for her supper party." Maggie hesitates, gnawing on her bottom lip, as if she wants to say more. "I know she's your friend and I like her, but if I spend more than thirty minutes in her company I need to double my herbal detox teas."

I laugh. "Yeah, she's pretty full-on. But her heart's in the right place."

Maggie nods but her eyes shift, like she doesn't quite believe in Ris's sainthood. "See you same time next week?"

"Only if you bring coffee and muffins."

"I can do that." Maggie pauses at the door, her expression uncertain. "I enjoy our chats."

A sliver of guilt worms its way through me. She obviously values our friendship but technically she's my boss and I have to be nice to her. Would we be friends if we'd met another way, out of the workplace?

"Me too." I force a smile and raise my hand in a casual wave.

When she leaves I check my inbox and sure enough, Ris has emailed Jodi's details. Jodi Van Gelder, twenty-five, Manhattanite, employed as a PA for an advertising firm I haven't heard of in New York City, five months pregnant and the father is unknown.

I enter the data into a patient file, wondering what it is about this girl that has Ris calling in favors. She's never done it for other clients at the center before. I'm curious but I can't ask Ris. She'll get suspicious and will clam up using some bogus client-therapist-confidentiality crap.

I know who I'll ask.

My lover will know.

He knows everyone and everything in this town and for some reason there's something about Ris's interest in this girl that has me wondering what's really going on.

CHAPTER TWENTY

CLAIRE

"Are you serious?" Dane picks me up and swings me around, his enthusiasm infectious. When he puts me down, his eyes are glistening with unshed tears. "Why would you even have to ask me this? Of course I think this is a great idea. A baby in four months..." He shakes his head like he can't believe it. Join the club. "It's incredible. I know you mentioned private adoption before but I actually thought we'd have to jump through hoops for years to adopt."

"Me too, that's why Ris thought of us." I cup his face in my hands, thrilled he's so excited. "I still can't believe it."

"She's sweet." He brushes a kiss across my lips, the first real intimate contact we've had in weeks. When I release his face he drags a hand across his eyes and sniffs. My big, rugged husband never cries so it melts my heart that he's tearing up. "So what happens from here?"

"Ris said if you're agreeable she'll organize a meeting between the mother and us. That way, we can get the ball rolling with all the legal stuff. Maybe talk about where she'll stay for the next four months." I hesitate, not sure how he'll take the rest of the news. "As part of the private adoption arrangement we would pay for her accommodation, that sort of thing. Help support her?"

He ruffles the hair at the nape of his neck in a gesture I find endearing. I always have to remind him to get a haircut. I don't mind because when it reaches this length, skimming his collar, I love running my fingers through it when we lay sated together in bed.

When's the last time that happened? Since the moment we'd met we'd been crazy for each other in the bedroom. I'd held him at arm's length for months emotionally but physically we'd had an all night sex-athon after our second date and hadn't stopped since.

Except for that period before my wedding when I cited old-fashioned values to abstain so our first night as husband and wife would be all the more special. He'd thought I was kooky but agreed. He never suspected I had an ulterior motive, like ensuring the STD got treated and I was clean in time for our honeymoon.

Guilt lies heavy in my gut like a stone I can't budge no matter how hard I try. I hate myself for that lapse, hate that I'm still feeling the repercussions hanging over me all these years later.

When was the last time we had sex? With all the tension after the fertility testing, then waiting for the results...damn, had it really been that long? Six weeks?

"We can afford it but..." He screws up his nose like he's smelled something bad. "Doesn't it seem like we're buying her off somehow?"

The thought has crossed my mind but I'll do anything to make this process go smoothly, including lie to myself.

"Ris said it's an accepted part of a private adoption and Jodi's not flush with funds so she can't stay in town until the baby's born unless we pay for it."

Some of the tension bracketing his mouth softens. "Jodi? That's her name?"

"Yeah." I save the best news for last. "She's having a boy."

His eyes light up as he reaches for me. "Don't you mean we're having a boy?"

We grab at each other's arms, holding on like drowning

people grasp at lifebuoys, staring at each other in bewilderment. "Are we really doing this? Having a baby?"

I nod, finally allowing myself to get swept up in the excitement when Dane lets out a whoop and crushes me to his chest. My cheek is pressed against his heart. It's racing. Suddenly, I want to make it race for a different reason.

"Honey?" I snuggle into him tighter.

"Hmm?"

"It's been a long time since we . . . you know."

He stiffens. All over. Eases away to look at me. "We've been under a lot of pressure. I didn't think you wanted to."

"I guess I haven't felt very sexy lately."

It's the truth. I've been so miserable, wallowing in self-pity, that I haven't felt like myself, let alone a desirable woman.

He frames my face with his strong hands and stares into my eyes. "You're always sexy to me."

We usually make love leisurely, taking our time with foreplay. Dane's diligent in everything he does and I'm grateful for that. He loves going down on me. He's a master with his tongue. He draws it out for as long as possible, making me teeter on the edge so my orgasm is explosive. Only then will he chase his own satisfaction.

Today is different. He pushes me down onto the carpet, pushes up my denim skirt, and tears off my panties, another first. I expect him to lower his head. He doesn't. He unzips. When he's inside me, he'll hit all the right spots.

I wriggle a little, impatient to get to the good stuff. I never knew how much I missed this until now. Maybe it's been too long or maybe Dane's mad at me deep down for being so moody these last few weeks but he's different today. Less focused on me.

I reach for him and he slaps my hand away. "Playing hard to get, huh?"

I push up on my elbows, watching him pleasure himself.

"Making sure you know what you've been missing out on." He winks as he swoops in for a kiss that leaves me breathless.

"Turn over," he murmurs in my ear, his hands already flipping me.

Another surprise. Dane always likes looking me in the eye when he first enters me. Sure, he enjoys taking me from behind but we always start face to face. I'm excited. I like this new, take-charge lover. I'm barely on my front before he spreads my legs and thrusts deep.

The carpet muffles my moan and I almost bang my head on the coffee table when he slides a hand under me and finds my clit. I'm so sensitive after so long, craving a quick release.

Thankfully, Dane's in sync because he's not drawing this out. He rubs my clit as he thrusts in and out, harder and faster than I expect. It's exciting and exhilarating, having my husband want me this much. The exquisite friction borders on painful as he pounds into me, pushing us both over the edge into the kind of mind-blowing orgasm I only have with him.

"You okay?" He gently nips the back of my neck and I arch a little, my hypersensitive nerve endings already craving more.

"Never better." His weight is pinning me to the carpet and I wriggle against him to prove it.

"I've missed us," he says, kissing his way across to my shoulder before sliding out of me. "Back in a minute."

I don't move. I'm too sated, too relaxed, for the first time in a long time. I feel like we've taken a giant step forward in our relationship. We've battled a monumental hardship in dealing with our infertility and have come out on the other side. Well, almost. Hopefully it will only be formalities from here on out and in four months' time I'll be holding our child.

Our baby boy.

Maybe I'm being too sentimental, focusing on the baby and not all the other stuff that can go wrong before we get him. But for now it makes me happy and I haven't felt this way in a long time.

I hear Dane re-enter the living room and his feet stop in front of my face. "Come on, lazy bones."

"Too tired," I mumble but raise myself up onto my forearms.

"In that case, it's bed for you." He helps me to my feet then sweeps me into his arms.

I whack his chest but I laugh. I've missed our playfulness so much. He marches into the bedroom and lays me on the bed. We crawl under the covers and stay wrapped in each other's arms for ages, murmuring general stuff, the way we used to.

It isn't until later, when Dane's soft snores lull me to sleep, do I remember.

I forgot to ask him about the message on our answering service.

CHAPTER TWENTY-ONE

MARISA

This is it.

The day I can make my best friend's dreams come true.

In an effort to distract myself until our meeting at midday I took a few hours off from the Help Center and spent the morning in Montauk, volunteering with a bunch of kids. My 9–5 work hours at the center are flexible and they never begrudge me taking time out to work offsite occasionally. Though technically it's not work when I value the interaction more than the youth do. I rent out a room at a rec hall and most of the kids are drop-ins who know they can tell me anything and not be judged for it. They come from rich Hamptons families but experience the same issues teens do the world over: an inability to fit in, feeling invisible and disempowered, the vagaries of social media, bullying, and problems with the opposite sex. Word has spread that I'm not an uptight adult doling out trite advice and I saw eight kids this morning, six girls and two boys, reluctantly keen to ask me anything from contraception to deferring college.

Time had flown and I'd been buzzed. I consider it an honor to be a trusted adult in their topsy-turvy lives and I hope my girls have similar faith in their guidance counselors at college.

As I cruise the highway back to Gledhill, I mentally rehearse the professional spiel I'll need to give Jodi, Claire, and Dane so I can maintain my impartiality; even though I'm anything but impartial. The sky is gray today, reflected in the murky Atlantic, and while I've never believed in omens I hope the oppressive weather isn't a sign of trouble ahead with this adoption.

I've gone over the paperwork countless times, even though I've done this before. I refuse to allow even the smallest margin for error where my friends' lives are concerned. Besides, if the paperwork's in order, once Jodi gives the go-ahead—and I'm hoping that's soon—the adoption can proceed quickly.

An hour later I hit the outskirts of Gledhill and my nerves take flight. Caffeine is the last thing I need but I pull over outside Java Groove, the coffee shop near work, and order a double shot grande to go.

Pedro, the twenty-something Spanish barista who has a lot to do with the queues here every morning, flashes his signature grin that works well with the younger ladies. I feel heat creep into my cheeks, meaning this old girl isn't immune to a handsome charmer either.

"Late start at work today, Marisa?"

"Something like that."

He pours the café's signature roasted blend into the machine, grinds it, before adding the fragrant beans to the elaborate coffee machine. "If you haven't had lunch, I recommend the pecan muffins." He kisses his fingertips before releasing them with a flourish. "They are to die for."

I chuckle at his salesmanship. "You're good for business, Pedro."

He wiggles his eyebrows suggestively. "But am I good for you?"

I roll my eyes but laugh all the same. "Is that coffee nearly ready? I've got an important meeting to get to."

He clutches his heart. "Always out to save the world, my Marisa."

"Your Marisa is thirsty and in a hurry, so hop to it." I snap my fingers and he laughs, working his magic on the machine to produce the perfect coffee.

"One of these days I will convince you my intentions are honorable." He hands over my takeout cup with a bow.

"And one of these days you'll figure out that shameless flirting will only get you so far." I pat myself on the chest. "And it's totally wasted on this old duck."

He appears suitably outraged. "Old duck? Never."

I laugh and hand over my money. "See you tomorrow."

"I'll be waiting." He presses a hand to his heart again. "Have a good day."

I smile. "You too."

Feeing ridiculously lighter like I always do after Pedro's over-the-top antics, I walk the rest of the way to the Help Center. The coffee hits the spot and by the time I enter the building I'm alert and ready to face what promises to be one of the most important client meetings of my life.

Our reception area, more a casual meeting room with a few chairs, several beanbags, and a stack of ancient magazines, is surprisingly empty.

I cross to the desk, manned by the ever-efficient Lisa. "Where are—"

"I saw you coming up the path so I've taken them to the waiting area near your office."

"Thanks, you're a gem."

She beams under my praise, a far cry from the terrified teen who'd stumbled in here three years ago, desperate to escape a violent stepfather. We live in an affluent part of the world but that doesn't stop the darker aspects of life from creeping in. Most of our runaways and domestic violence victims come from rich families in the area but money can't solve all problems, and often facilitates them. Drug addictions and alcoholism are commonplace when money can buy the best of both vices.

My office is the last down a long, narrow corridor and I spy Claire and Dane sitting beside a huge bay window with distant views of the ocean. Lisa will guide Jodi to my office when I buzz her. We never let prospective adoptive parents and single mothers bump into each other unexpectedly: their first meeting is fraught enough.

"Hey, you two. All set?"

Claire leaps to her feet and hugs me, and Dane does the same. They're speechless and I don't blame them. I can't believe that if all parties agree to it I can get legal proceedings underway today. This time in four months Claire and Dane may have a baby boy. It makes me want to bawl.

"Let's go into my office." I open the door and gesture them in. "Any questions before Jodi arrives?"

Dane shakes his head, mute, as Claire asks, "Has she agreed to the adoption yet?"

"No, not yet, but I'm hopeful." I perch on the edge of my desk, hating their matching crestfallen expressions. "The adoption process is filled with uncertainty and I understand how hard this must be for you, but keep the faith, okay?"

They nod and Claire says in a tight voice, "Should we ask her anything in particular? Show how enthusiastic we are?"

"Just be yourselves." I reach out and pat Claire on the shoulder. "I've facilitated private adoptions before so if you're uncertain about anything at any time, don't hesitate to ask."

"Thanks, Ris." Claire's relief is audible but Dane's tense, the muscles in his neck standing out.

"Ready to meet Jodi?"

They nod so I stab at the intercom button on my phone twice, a signal to Lisa to bring Jodi in. A few moments later there's a brief knock at the door before it opens to reveal a nervous Jodi.

"Thanks, Lisa," I say, opening the door wider to welcome Jodi in. "Come in, Jodi."

When she enters I clear my throat, assuming my best professional persona. "Jodi, I'd like you to meet Claire and Dane Casey."

Despite being briefed on all aspects of this meeting Jodi appears ready to flee.

"Hi." She tentatively shakes the hand Claire offers, then

Dane's, but drops his quickly like she can't abide his touch. Considering the predicament she's in I'm guessing she's not too enamored of the entire male species at the moment.

"Nice to meet you." Claire's calm but I hear the quiver in her voice. Claire's a strong woman. She never sounds weak but in that moment I want to embrace her, to offer hollow reassurance and tell her everything's going to be okay.

There are no guarantees. I've seen private adoptions like this fall apart in the past when I've tried to broker a good solution for everyone concerned. I'm worried for my friend, that if this goes wrong she'll blame me. I'm hoping it won't come to that and Jodi will stick around and hand over her baby when the time comes.

"Thanks for agreeing to meet with us," Dane says, waiting until all of us are seated before he sits. He's such a gentle giant, one of those men who is inherently good and will do whatever it takes to make the woman he loves happy. I liked him from the moment we met. I like how he idolizes Claire and supports her in everything.

I should be so lucky.

"So you want my baby?" Jodi blurts, her gaze switching from Claire to Dane, who she glares at with ill-concealed hostility. Her arms are folded protectively over her belly, like the last thing she wants is to give it up. She's wiggled into the farthest corner of the sofa, as if trying to put as much distance as possible between her and my friends. And her glare continues to swing from Claire to Dane and back again, accusatory and mutinous, like she blames them for her predicament. This isn't looking good.

Before I can mediate, Claire responds. "If you want us to, we'd love to raise your child and look after him like he's our own." She presses her palm to her chest. "We'll love him so much. You never need to be concerned about that. And if you want him to know who his biological mother is, we're okay with that too."

She smiles, soft and reassuring. "I come from a big family. Four brothers, two who are years younger than me, who are all pains in the ass but I love dearly. So I know a bit about raising boys and what makes them tick."

She jerks a thumb in Dane's direction. "Not to mention living with this one for the last decade. I've learned a lot about guys."

I'm glad Claire's taking the initiative and trying to put Jodi at ease. If this is how she lulls suspects into confessions, she must get a lot of convictions.

"I guess what I'm trying to say is, we'll try to make this as easy on you as possible and hope you'll understand how much this baby will be loved."

Claire's declaration, along with a heartfelt smile, seems to work. Some of Jodi's animosity fades, but not all. She stares at Dane through narrowed eyes, bristling and defiant. "What about you? What do you think?"

I see a vein pulse in Dane's temple but he's calm. "I wouldn't be here if I'm not willing to love this kid with everything I've got."

"Hmm." Jodi's noncommittal answer scares Claire. I see it in the slight widening of her eyes and the way her fingers dig into her thighs.

But to my friend's credit, she won't give up.

"What can we do to make this easier for you?" Claire clasps her hands in her lap and leans toward Jodi. "I can't imagine how difficult this decision must be, giving up your baby, so tell us what we can do to help."

I swallow the lump in my throat. Claire is so sincere, so sweet, I know I've made the right decision in putting these people together. It has to work out. It just has to.

"You seem nice..." Jodi clears her throat and I'm on the verge of stepping in to take the pressure off her when she continues. "If I agree to this I want to stay in town." She reddens and hugs her middle tighter. "But I can't afford to and the stuff I've read said it's all covered as part of the adoption?"

Claire shoots me an uncertain glance, like she's not sure whether to reiterate this or not. We've already talked about the costs for private adoptions and Claire reassured me they're more than happy to pay.

But I sense Jodi is overwhelmed by this meeting and I don't want to scare her by forging ahead to the nitty-gritty details. She's fragile, and jumpy, which compounds my sense of something else going on here, more than she's told me.

I clamp down on my spidey sense and aim for reassurance.

"You're right, Jodi, a private adoption takes care of you financially but we can discuss the details later." I gesture toward my friends. "This meeting is about you getting a feel for Claire and Dane as parents."

A frown dents her brow as she scoots forward to the edge of the sofa as if she's about to bolt. "But how can I do that in a short space of time? It's impossible."

Dane looks helpless, like he's floundering for the right thing to say but not willing to risk it. Claire looks plain terrified now. I need to intervene quickly before the whole meeting implodes.

"Do you trust me, Jodi?"

Jodi stares at me for a long time, before she eventually nods. "Yeah."

"Then you know I'm telling the truth when I say I've facilitated private adoptions like this before and that prospective parents like Claire and Dane are vetted extensively. Experienced counselors visit their home and intensive background checks are done. They're interviewed about everything and their suitability as parents is assessed by experts." I offer her a reassuring smile. "Trust in the process and they'll do right by your baby. I wouldn't have facilitated this so quickly otherwise."

My little speech has the desired result when the tension drains from Jodi's rigid spine and she eases back into the sofa.

"I don't think you can ever really know a person." Jodi shrugs, like she's unsure which ice-cream flavor to choose, not making a decision regarding her baby's future. "But okay."

I see Claire and Dane sit forward slightly but I need to clarify what Jodi means before my friends are potentially devastated.

"By okay, you mean you agree to this adoption proceeding?" I'm clasping my hands so tight my nails leave tiny indentations in the skin.

Jodi nods and I exhale a breath I'm unaware I've been holding. "Yeah, I think so."

She glances at Claire and Dane and flashes a tentative smile. "Let's hope this works out for everyone."

Claire's eyes fill with tears and Dane blinks rapidly, his jaw clenched in that way men do if they don't want to appear vulnerable or emotional.

I should be ecstatic but I still can't shake the feeling something is wrong. Jodi's responses have been evasive and what does she mean by "let's hope this works out for everyone"?

But it's a start down this potentially potholed road and I need to capitalize on it.

"This can't have been easy for you, Jodi, I'm proud of you." I touch her shoulder, pleased when she doesn't flinch away like she did the first few times. "Why don't we go through some of the logistics now, if you're up to it?"

Jodi wrinkles her nose. "Actually, I'm exhausted. Do you mind if we do it later? I need a nap."

Claire gives an imperceptible nod so I say, "Sure. Rest up. We'll meet again later this afternoon."

Jodi pushes herself into a standing position and I see Dane has to sit on his hands to resist helping. "See you guys later."

Claire and Dane mumble goodbyes, wearing matching thunderstruck expressions, like they can't quite believe Jodi has agreed to let them adopt her baby.

I wait until Jodi has left my office before speaking. "I know you're both overwhelmed right now, but what do you think?"

"I think you're incredible for doing this." Claire flings herself at me, knocking me sideways, and we bump into a filing cabinet.

Paperwork tumbles to the floor. We don't care. I hug my friend as she cries a little, while Dane picks up the mess we've made.

My eyes are damp when she releases me and we resume our seats. "Look, I just want to say that while I think this will go through, be aware there can always be hiccups."

Claire deflates a little. Her bottom lip trembles, as if she's on the verge of tears again. "You get that feeling about her too, huh?"

I nod, glad my intuitive friend has picked up on Jodi's flighty vibe. "She's opened up to me a lot but I can't help but feel she's hiding something. Though it's perfectly normal for expectant mothers to be jittery. Thankfully, as we mitigate more meetings, they tend to become more comfortable and show faith in the process as time goes on. I think she came to town to tell the baby's father about the pregnancy but she's changed her mind for some reason. Yet she wants to stick around regardless. Seems contradictory."

Dane fixes me with a speculative stare. "I've been researching private adoptions online and it can be tricky, right? Are you saying that once we get proceedings underway, she can still back out?"

I hate reining in their enthusiasm but I'd be an awful friend if I didn't prepare them for the worst. "Unfortunately, yes, it's the mother's prerogative. Even the private adoption route can be complicated and there's always a risk involved. The first step is at a court hearing where a judge issues a decree that permanently ends Jodi's parental rights. Though even when she consents to an adoption there's a period where she can change her mind and revoke consent."

Claire pales but I must give them all the facts in case Jodi reneges. I'm not sure how committed she is to the process despite her vague verbal agreement.

"I've done a bit of reading too," Claire says, her fingers fiddling with the seam on her skirt. "How intrusive is the home study? I mean, we have nothing to hide but..." She shrugs. "It sounds nerve-wracking."

"It's not. Because it's an independent adoption, the court will appoint someone to check out if you're suitable parents. Do background checks, that kind of thing. But you won't need to undergo counseling, which happens if you're going through an agency. And I'd consider this a low risk adoption, where rights haven't been terminated yet but we expect they soon will, and there's little likelihood of the child returning to Jodi."

Claire and Dane continue to stare at me with abject horror but I want to educate them on the process as best I can.

"The last step is the finalization of the adoption in court, making you the child's permanent, legal parents." I blow out a breath. "I'll be honest and say lots can go wrong along the way, especially if Jodi is fickle. But in saying that, independently adopting a newborn this way is the fastest way to have your baby."

Claire reaches for Dane's hand and holds on tight. I stare at their clasped hands, envying the kind of bond they share, the kind of unequivocal support through good times and bad. "We need to keep the faith."

Dane raises her hand to his lips and kisses it. "You're right, as usual."

The way he gazes at Claire, the obvious adoration, makes me want to bawl again. "I'm extremely hopeful all will be well but I wouldn't be doing my job unless I gave you every possible scenario."

Claire's smile is understanding. "Thanks, Ris, we appreciate it. You've done so much for us and we can't ever thank you enough."

"Letting me be a part of your child's life will be reward enough."

Trite, but true. My friends will make exceptional parents and I'll get to be around a gorgeous baby again. I remember the early days with the girls like it was yesterday. Sure, feeding and bathing and transporting twins had been a handful, but I'd thrived on caring for them. I'd never felt so alive as I had when I'd been their mom.

Kissing their cute little toes, blowing raspberries on their tummies, tickling them under the chin, savoring their unique baby smell...Avery never understood my obsession. He'd called me a martyr for wanting to do everything for the girls myself. I hadn't wanted a nanny or a housekeeper even though we could afford both. I'd relented when he insisted on having a part-time cook, because caring for the twins left little time to whip up the kind of meals he expected.

It had been a hectic whirlwind and I cherished every moment. Even when babyhood gave way to the toddler years and they needed me more than ever, I thrived. And as tweens they'd always been after me to do stuff for them.

Like all teens, they'd been trying, but I never begrudged them. I'd wanted them to have the wonderful childhood I'd never had. That's the ultimate reason I tolerated Avery's frequent late nights and absences.

How many times had I pestered my mom for details about the father I never knew? How many evenings I'd be doing my homework at the kitchen table, glancing at the back door in the hope a kind, distinguished man would walk through it, take one look at me, and say, "I've missed you so much"? How many science fairs and first days of school had I watched the front gates, willing my mythical father to appear?

Mom never told me who he was and as the years passed I gave up begging her to know. But every time Avery walked through our front door and the girls flung themselves into his arms, I knew I'd done the right thing in turning a blind eye to my husband's transgressions.

I don't know how long I'm lost in memories of motherhood but when I refocus, Claire and Dane are both watching me with matching odd expressions.

"Sorry, just visualizing what kind of first gift I'll buy your baby boy."

Their expressions are even stranger now and I make a grand show of glancing at my watch. "I have another client meeting shortly. Is there anything else you wanted to ask before we finish up?"

"Yeah." Dane's adorable little-boy grin conveys just how excited he is by the prospect of becoming a father. "How often can you babysit and what do you charge?"

We laugh and exchange hugs again before they leave my office. As I gather the paperwork together and slip it into Jodi's file, I can't shake a niggle of worry. Usually I distance myself from clients but this time I'm too invested. Claire and Dane are my friends. I don't want anything to go wrong. They'll make great parents and I want them to experience the joy I had. Watching my friend go through the wonderful years of motherhood, helping out whenever she needs me, is something I can't help but look forward to.

I shouldn't worry. Every time I meet with Jodi she trusts me more but I'll feel a lot better when we get the paperwork started.

Sooner rather than later.

CHAPTER TWENTY-TWO

ELLY

My lover is satisfied and slumberous. It's the perfect time to interrogate him.

"I didn't like how you treated me at the supper party." My voice is soft and hurt, not confrontational and accusatory. I know how to play this. He doesn't take kindly to pushy women.

"How's that?" His drawl is amused, as if he finds my question funny.

"You know." I roll toward him, lying on my side so we're staring at each other. I can only just see his face in the dim light. Darkness fell hours ago and only a single lamp is on in the cottage bedroom. I prefer the darkness but I need to see his face, to see how he reacts when I drop my bombshell.

His hand, resting on my hip, drifts lower. "I thought you always like when I do this."

He sweeps a finger between my folds and when I don't react, he laughs. "Too late to play hard to get now. We both know you're always begging for it."

I hate when he talks to me like this but I bite back my first expletive, along the lines of "go and procreate with yourself." Because I have an agenda tonight and if all goes according to plan I'll be the one smirking at the end, not him.

"Do you know the girl who arrived unannounced at the party?"

He scowls and snatches his hand away. "What is it with you and that night? It was weeks ago now."

"It's strange, that's all. Ris told me this girl Jodi arrived at the party, then she took her to the center."

He rolls his eyes and makes a disparaging sound akin to a snort. "We all know Ris and her rescue complex. Probably another of her strays seeking guidance."

He made it sound like Ris killed puppies rather than helped people. Bastard.

He fixes me with a speculative stare. "Why are you so interested in this girl anyway?"

I school my face into an impassive mask, not wanting to reveal too much before I get to the zinger. "I got curious when Ris asked me to get her an appointment with our best ob-gyn at the center."

I see something in his eyes then. A flicker. It's enough to inform me he knows more about this girl than he's letting on.

"Apparently she's staying in town, until the baby's born, in one of those studio apartments on The Rise."

I shrug and the sheet falls. He doesn't look at my breasts, which speaks volumes. He's a sex maniac. One glimpse of me naked is enough to make him pounce. So the fact he hasn't even glanced at my breasts means he has something on his mind.

I drop a few more morsels into the conversation. "As manager of the swankiest medical center on Long Island, I don't do menial tasks for anyone but Ris has personally asked me to ensure this girl is well looked after so it got me thinking."

"Don't do that," he said, his gaze finally lowering to my bare chest. His pupils dilate and his mouth curves into the smug bastard grin I know so well. "Thinking is highly overrated when you look like that."

Misogynist creep. I fake disinterest and tug the sheet lower, exposing my tanned torso. "So you know nothing about this Jodi Van Gelder?"

He hesitates for the barest fraction of a second but it's there and I know he'll lie before he speaks. Lying is what he does best. "Nothing."

He reaches for me and yanks away the rest of the sheet. "Why are we wasting time talking about this knocked-up tramp anyway?"

He lowers his mouth to my nipple. "I've got way more important things to do and they sure as hell don't involve talking."

His mouth fastens over my nipple, his tongue laving and licking in the way he thinks I like. My mind is ticking over. My lover knows a lot more than he's telling me.

He nips my nipple, a bite bordering on painful, and I involuntarily arch. He takes it as an invitation. He shoves my legs apart with characteristic roughness. Sex is always on the verge of brutal with him, like he wants to go further but is restraining himself.

He parts me with the fingers on one hand while stroking me with the thumb on the other. His gaze glazed and fixed, like he's never seen me before.

It's this ability to make me feel like I'm the only woman in the world that gets to me every time. It's not his skills as a lover that I like as much as his intent to make me feel good.

He's eager to be inside me again, his weight heavy on top of me as his thrusts start. He's focused, single-minded in his quest for pleasure, and while I like it when he clasps my face between his hands and stares deep into my eyes, making me feel at one with him, I can't help but wonder what my lover knows about Jodi but isn't telling.

When it's over, he folds me into his arms and I finally relax. My cheek rests over his heart, the steady rhythm an odd comfort. Back in Chicago, this would be the best part of my day, when my husband would hold me and tell me snippets about his job and retell funny anecdotes with clients. We'd laugh together and I'd be secure in the crook of his arm, my head resting on his chest, smug in my perfect life.

What a crock.

I'm aware not remembering the rape has messed with my mind to the point I look forward to being in my lover's arms. It's probably some warped, twisted way to make up for what I once had with my husband: the solid comfort of having a man hold me.

It's unhealthy, becoming dependent on this man for comfort. It won't end well. It can't.

But for now, I allow his shallow breathing to lull me toward sleep. It's the only time I don't have nightmares, a few snatched hours of slumber in his arms.

I better not get used to it.

CHAPTER TWENTY-THREE

CLAIRE

The evening our second meeting with Jodi got canceled I serve my famous ten-minute pasta, fast-cooked spaghetti with a stir-in tomato sauce and sprinkled with Parmesan and parsley, and sit at the dining table opposite Dane.

With our manic work schedules we rarely get to sit down to dinner together, so while I hated not being on active duty the last few weeks I enjoyed a stint at playing domestic goddess. Not that I'm fooling anyone; we both know I'm an atrocious cook. But it's the effort that counts.

I'm waiting for him to ask me how my first day back at work has been. He doesn't. In fact, he's almost salivating as he stares at the pasta, waiting for me to serve so we can eat.

Not that I feel like it. I've lost my appetite since we still haven't had confirmation from Ris that Jodi is keen on us parenting her baby.

Ris reports that today's cancelation means nothing and that Jodi is saying all the right things, but she hasn't started the legal proceedings. It doesn't inspire me with confidence that this girl holds our parenting future in her hands. I know if we don't get Jodi's baby we'll get another but it could take years and now that I've got my hopes up I'm anxious to embrace parenthood sooner rather than later.

I've been foolish. Searching cribs online, checking out cute outfits in boutique windows, trolling the grocery aisles to investigate the various brands of formula. Crazy, when we have no guarantee we'll get this baby but I can't help myself. For the last year since I ditched my contraception and we started trying I've been obsessed with all things baby.

Not that anyone knows. I hadn't told Ris and Elly we'd been trying because knowing Ris she'd buy me a bassinet before I could say "baby shower" and Elly would've feigned polite interest. Even Dane has no idea how thoroughly baby-focused I've been.

When I hadn't fallen pregnant after ten months of vigorous trying—a benefit my husband had enjoyed immensely but had almost turned into a chore for me after a while—we'd made the decision to check our fertility. I've been on an emotional rollercoaster ever since. For every one of those ten months when I'd pee on a stick and will those two blue lines to show, I'd make deals with a God I barely believed in.

"If I'm pregnant, I'll do whatever it takes to keep our baby safe and happy."

"If I'm pregnant, I'll make our baby a priority and put my precious career on hold."

"If I'm pregnant, I'll consider telling Dane the truth about my slip before our wedding."

The last one terrified me and God probably knew it, which is why I didn't fall pregnant no matter how hard we tried. Telling Dane about my infidelity before our wedding would crush him and I love him too much to risk losing him. We've been happy for a decade, why ruin it? Instead, I let guilt ruin my self-esteem, eroding it slowly but surely when I got my period every month like clockwork.

I'd done this to us.

Contracting that STD, I'd been warned by the doc at the time it could result in problems conceiving. But another doc had given me the all-clear so I hadn't worried. Until I wondered if not being able to give Dane a child was my punishment for withholding the truth from him. I convinced myself it was.

I'd been shattered when the fertility specialist had announced Dane couldn't father a child, but I couldn't deny I also felt a tremendous relief.

I wasn't to blame.

But I continue to pay for my sins every single day because the last year has taken its toll. Once I resurrected the old guilt through constant self-flagellation, I can't put it back in its box. It gnaws away at me, prickling and niggling at the oddest of times.

I'm hoping a baby will take all my focus and catapult me into a future of diapers and feeds, without time to dwell on anything but playing happy families with Dane. So until I hear from Ris that Jodi has started signing adoption papers, we're in limbo. I hate it.

Dane, on the other hand, digs into his pasta like he hasn't eaten in a week, oblivious to the worry churning my gut and making eating impossible. I'm puzzled by his apparent indifference, like he doesn't care either way if we get to start our family sooner rather than later.

He's been so supportive of this idea from the start, but ever since we got the call from Ris that the meeting with Jodi was canceled, he hasn't seemed fazed. I've been a mess but pretending to hide it considering it had been my first day back on the job today and I can't afford to screw up. No more time off. No losing it at a crime scene. I love being a cop. It's part of my identity. And I've lost my way recently, like a tiny part of me broke when I acknowledged I'll never be pregnant.

Ron nursed me through today, even though I didn't need it. We had an easy eight-hour shift. Two call-outs: one to a domestic involving a jealous boyfriend having the house locks changed on him, the other to a DUI, a soccer mom who enjoyed one too many wines at a long lunch. Thankfully I didn't run into Griffin, who was consulting in the city. I wish he'd stay there. But I know I'll face an inevitable confrontation at some stage; I'm just glad it wasn't on my first day back.

After the call-outs I spent the rest of my day tied to my desk doing endless paperwork, drinking coffee, and glancing at my cell, hoping Ris would call with good news. She didn't. Being back at work is good for me, now that I have something to look forward to and I'm not wallowing in my misery anymore. I've been grieving for something I never had and it has taken its toll, the ever-present, bone-deep sorrow that I won't be pregnant and won't have a chance to raise my biological child.

Working through that grief has taken time, several weeks, which my husband seems to have coped with admirably. While Dane has seen the fallout from my grieving, he doesn't seem to realize how much of a big deal it is that I'm back at work. All he's asked since I walked in the door half an hour ago is "How was work?" A generic greeting that has me stewing since. We rarely fight but his blasé attitude makes me want to get some kind of reaction out of him.

I push my spaghetti around on the plate with a fork while he shovels pasta into his mouth as fast as humanly possible. When he's done, he dabs his mouth with a napkin and pats his belly.

"That was good, babe, thanks." He glances at my untouched plate and frowns. "Not hungry?"

"No." I nudge the plate away and lay down my fork. "Aren't you the slightest bit bothered that Jodi canceled the meeting today and hasn't given us the go-ahead yet?"

A flicker of unease darkens his eyes to indigo. "Ris warned us about this. It might not be smooth sailing so no point getting worked up because Jodi's taking extra time making up her mind."

I huff out a breath, his eternal optimism one of the things I love about him, but tonight I want a wallowing buddy, someone to offload my fears to, namely what if Jodi changes her mind?

"I adore you but your ability to constantly see the positive side of every situation is infuriating."

He chuckles but I don't join in, poking my tongue out at him. "What's really bugging you?"

I can't tell him the truth so I settle for a lame half-truth. "Being back at work today was a big deal for me and you barely asked me anything about it."

He fixes me with a baleful stare. "I asked you how was work, you said fine. I didn't want to push. From past experience if you've got something to say you'll usually say it." He reaches out to touch me. "I'm not a mind reader and I know there's something more going on up here," he taps his temple, "that you're not telling me."

I want to tell him. I've wanted to tell him for years but can never summon the courage for fear of losing him. We've never kept secrets from one another.

Except the doozy that would signal the end of our marriage.

Secrets are poison. I know it. I've coped all these years, and if I don't get a grip now, my entire world could implode.

Thinking about secrets reminds me about the phone message weeks ago from Beau, along with another two terse "Call me" messages since, which have all been deleted. I'd intended on asking him about why he's avoiding Beau's calls but with all the baby business it has slipped my mind until now.

"Maybe I'm not the only one with something on my mind?" I point to the phone. "Why did you lie to me that night at the supper party?"

Shock widens his eyes for a second before he quickly masks it with indifference. "What are you talking about?"

"I heard the phone message, the one from your brother, who's freaking out over that conversation you had at the supper party. And he's called a few times since." I rest my forearms on the table and lean forward, my classic cop interrogation posture.

It doesn't sit well with me, that I have to ask my husband questions about something he's hidden, when we usually share everything. Then again, I realize how hypocritical that is when I haven't shared the worst with him.

"That night, you said it was someone from work. Why did you lie?"

His glance shifts away, so unlike Dane I'm taken aback. "Beau's going through some really personal stuff and he doesn't want anyone to know about it but me."

My stomach sinks. He still can't look me in the eye, which means he's lying again.

I call him on it. "That's crap and you know it."

Foreboding churns my gut as I wonder what is so terrible that Dane can't tell me the truth, let alone look at me. "If you told me you were talking to Beau on the phone that night and that it was personal I wouldn't have asked anything beyond how he is."

"Just leave it alone, okay?" He leaps from his chair so fast it slams against the wall behind him.

This time I'm the one in shock as he makes a grab for his plate and knocks over the Parmesan grater, scattering cheese all over the floor.

"Fuck," he mutters, grabbing a dishcloth and getting down on his hands and knees to clean it up.

I have no idea what's going on but I realize something. Secrets breed discontent, and if I can't tell him about my slipup all those years ago, maybe I should come clean about Griffin. I've pushed it to the back of my mind once this adoption business started. Ris has been so kind and caring I've focused on that, not that meaningless kiss from a misguided colleague I had valued as a friend.

But I wonder. I've been discombobulated lately, attributing it to guilt from the past, when in reality it could be my latest slipup that's bothering me the most. Even with the potential good news regarding the baby, me being back at work, and our lives as parents about to start if all goes well, I can't get past what I did.

Maybe that's why I'm picking a fight. My latent antagonism probably has nothing to do with him and that phone call, the hold up with the baby, or me being back at work.

I'm angry at myself.

The guilt is consuming me. It's an ever-present burr digging at me when I least expect it since that incident in the cellar with Griffin. I want to forget. I want to pretend it never happened. But I can't ignore this any longer. The repercussions of that one, stupid, impulsive act threaten to overwhelm me when I least expect it.

How can I be outraged with Dane for not telling the truth when I'm guilty of the same? And who knows, depending how he reacts to this, I may pluck up the courage one day to tell him the rest?

I have to tell him.

I wait until he's finished cleaning, then I stand and approach him near the sink. "I have to tell you something and I don't want you to freak out, because it lasted less than two seconds and meant nothing."

He's rinsing the dishcloth and his hands still. He turns off the taps, hangs the cloth up, and swivels to face me. I've never seen him look so somber. Tiny worry lines appear at the corners of his eyes and his lips are compressed.

"What meant nothing?" His voice is cold, chilling, and he sounds nothing like the man I know and love.

I clamp down on my irrational fear, take a deep breath, and release it. "That night at the supper party, when you stormed out? I was coming after you when Ris asked me to get some wine for her. She was flustered so I agreed. I thought it'd only take a second, then I could follow you home. But in the wine cellar Griffin came up behind me."

Regret sits heavy in my chest. "You were right about him."

He inhales so sharply his nostrils pinch, making an odd whistling sound. "What did he do?"

Hell, this is harder than I thought. I don't want to cause Dane pain when the incident with Griffin is now a blip of disgust in the recent past. That's the thing about honesty. I have good intentions but now I'm partially through the execution I know this is a really bad idea.

"He...he kissed me. It didn't last long. And I stopped it when I realized what I was doing—"

"What *you* were doing..." He grips the bench behind him so tightly his knuckles stand out. "Are you trying to tell me you responded? That you kissed him back?"

I swallow down the bile burning a path up my throat. "No, but I hesitated—"

"No fucking way!" He pushes off the bench so fast I startle and almost trip in my haste to get out of his way. "You kissed that asshole?"

He stalks the kitchen, kicking out at random cupboards, muttering expletives I've never heard spill from his mouth before. My calm husband who never loses control has morphed into a monster.

What the hell have I done?

"How could you fucking do that to me?" He pauses at the dining table we've just vacated long enough to sweep his arm across it, sending plates and pasta and cutlery flying across the kitchen.

I gape, stunned by the ferocity of his rage; I expected anger, not this...this...torrent of fury that blinds him to everything but how much I've hurt him.

In that moment I know I can never tell him the rest.

It would ruin us.

I have to try to calm him. "I know this is a betrayal, Dane, and I'm not proud of what I did, but I'd been going crazy over our infertility, grieving really—"

"Don't you mean *my* infertility?" he spat, hatred making his eyes glow like a feral cat. "That's what this is all about. You don't think I'm man enough because I can't give you a kid so you turn to the first prick who puts the moves on you..."

He punches the wall so hard his fist goes through the plaster, leaving a hole. He barely notices. "Fuck! Why him? That asshole has lorded his damn superiority over me ever since we met, and now, when we're at our most vulnerable..."

He shakes his head and stares at the gaping hole in the wall, then the mess all over the floor, like he's seeing it for the first time.

I've done this. Not with telling the truth but by not avoiding that kiss in the first place. The kicker is, Dane's right. I'd been suppressing so much resentment toward him that I'd let that kiss happen.

I could've pushed Griffin away faster. I could've cut him down with my usual sarcastic jibes. Instead, I'd stood there, knowing what could happen but not stopping him quick enough. It doesn't matter that my brain eventually kicked in and I stopped it a second later. It doesn't matter that the guilt has been eating me alive. I did wrong and I need my husband to understand I get that.

"It lasted less than two seconds and I was so repulsed I could've killed him. But I hesitated, trying to stare him down and act all tough, rather than moving away, and I'll have to live with that for the rest of my life."

I take a step toward him but he holds up his hands, as if warning me off. "I love you, Dane. Nothing or no one can ever come between us—"

"Wanna make a bet?"

He punches the wall again, leaving a matching hole beside the first, before he grabs his keys and cell, and storms out.

I can't summon the energy to go after him. I'm in shock. The potency of his wrath...I didn't know he was capable of it.

So I slide to the floor, hug my knees to my chest, and cry.

CHAPTER TWENTY-FOUR

JODI

I've made a decision.

I glance down at my small bump. "Thanks to you, our lives are about to get easier."

Until I saw that picture in the paper I'd been adrift, swept up in a force bigger than me. I don't like it.

I hate feeling out of control. I'd suffered enough helplessness as a kid: Dad dying young, Mom drifting from one loser to another, and me fading into the background trying to draw as little attention to myself as possible.

Then I hit my teens and it became harder to hide. Mom's boyfriends would leer behind her back no matter how hard I tried to avoid them. I didn't want to hurt her and I didn't want to get hurt, so I left. Became the clichéd teenage runaway. I headed to the busiest city in the world, New York, intent on losing myself for real. Mom couldn't find me there and I regained control of my life. I survived, too. Waitressing initially, working in admin later. I thought I'd been doing okay.

Until this.

I rub my belly, liking the smoothness of it. It has become a comforting gesture, something I do regularly to reassure myself I'm not alone.

If my plan succeeds, I'll never be alone again.

Thanks to Ris, I have resigned from my PA job and now have a one-room studio on a hill outside town called The Rise.

It overlooks the ocean and I hear the waves crashing on the shore, I'm that close. I leave the windows open, something I never did in the city, allowing the refreshing tang of brine to waft in.

This is my first night here and I love it. I love the pristine white walls, the honey-colored floorboards, the tidy kitchenette. I've never lived in a new place before and I like that fresh-paint smell. It sure beats the pungent aroma of stale curry that permeates the studio I rent in the city, considering I live over an Indian diner.

I particularly liked curling up in the window seat today and staring at the ocean. There's something inherently soothing in watching the waves come in. Evenly spaced. Regular. Dependable.

I really love this place and I never want to leave. For now, I won't. I'm going to string this process out and not sign the adoption papers. Ris's friends will have to find some other baby to buy because I have plans for mine. Now that I'm settled in a place of my own, I don't have to expedite my blackmail. I can take my time.

I've instigated what needs to be done. I sent a letter addressed to the guy in the newspaper via his company rather than tiptoeing around Gledhill trying to discover his whereabouts, whether he's my baby's father or not. Either way, the father works at that company so he'll get the letter.

Besides, I'm a coward, and even if I find him, confronting him face to face would be a challenge. A civilized letter outlining my situation and demands is much more my style. Now I just need to sit back and wait for the money to flow in.

Simple.

The stupid thing is, for a brief moment after I set my plan in motion, I had second thoughts. What if I didn't do this for the money? Then reality had set in and I knew I'd given up on pipe dreams a long time ago, around the time I turned fourteen and told Mom the creep she'd been dating for three months had put his hand on my ass. She hadn't believed me and I'd got a slap across the face for my honesty.

I've been a fighter ever since and I refuse to walk away from this baby without giving it a chance to have the secure life I never had. That means I need money.

I'm almost asleep when there's a soft knock at the front door. The studios, tiny cottages really, are spaced out on The Rise so it can't be one of my neighbors unless they fancy late-night walks in the dark.

Another thing I like about living here, the lack of street lights. The darkness enables me to lie in bed and stare out the window at the million stars dotting the sky. Beautiful.

The knock comes again, sharper and more insistent this time.

"Hold on," I call out, slipping a long T-shirt over the cami-sole and boy boxers I'm wearing.

By the time I make it across the small living room the knocking is relentless and I wish I had a peephole like I did back in my apartment. Then again, this is the Hamptons. What's the worst that can happen to me? I get mugged for...what? I don't own anything of value. Considering the wealth in this town, I should be the one doing the mugging.

I open the door and see a tall shadow. For a second I think it's my baby's father. He must've received my letter, discovered my whereabouts via Marisa, and come to discuss everything. But this person is wearing a large, shapeless, hooded jacket. In fact, in the darkness of the tiny porch, I can't tell if my visitor is male or female.

"Can I help you?"

The figure nods and steps forward, as if to embrace me.

I take a step back but I'm too late. He or she wraps me in a hug. I struggle to escape, opening my mouth to scream.

A prick stings my neck, like a mosquito intent on gorging on my blood. I start to struggle in earnest, pushing and shoving and kicking.

But my limbs grow heavy. Weighed down by an invisible load that presses on my head at the same time.

The room spins as my head lolls back. I still can't see who has me in their arms as they drag me to the sofa and lay me down.

My vision is blurred, contorted images of shadow and light fading in and out.

"Listen to me, you money-hungry bitch. Pack your bags and leave, now."

The voice is distorted, like one of those box thingies that kidnappers use to demand ransom on the phone.

"You'll get a pittance, not a cent more. And if you persist with this blackmail, you'll be sorry."

I'm being threatened. I should be scared. But all I feel is relaxed, like I'm floating on clouds: gossamer-thin, wispy clouds that cradle me.

"Are you listening? Can you hear me?" Hands grab my shoulders and shake me but my eyelids are heavy, so deliciously heavy. "Leave Gledhill and don't come back."

The shaking increases. "Answer me, dammit."

I ignore the distorted voice; I'm too comfortable and my head is stuffed with cotton. The clouds are thickening around me. What feels like thousands of fluffy white clouds, so soft, so comforting. I'm floating.

The rough hands release me and I drift off again. I'm surrounded by white light, then dark, like a weird hypnotic kaleidoscope. My mind's blank . . . I like not having to think . . . pretty white light . . .

"Hey, wake up." The hands are back, shaking me so hard the fog in my head momentarily dissipates before thickening again, making rational thought impossible. "This isn't supposed to happen. Wake up!"

The voice is angry. I don't care. I haven't felt this weightless before. I'm flying.

Fingers jab at my neck, then my wrist, checking for a pulse.

The hands release me and moments later I hear a door slam.

I'm glad. The crazy person has left me alone. I want to sleep so badly.

The door creaks open again and I want to protest but I can't move, can't speak. I hear footsteps. *Go away,* I think, wishing my lips could form the words.

The clouds are thicker now, surrounding me, cradling me. So nice...

Until a cloud covers my face. Stifling. Suffocating.

I can't breathe.

I struggle to resurface. Gasp for air.

I need to stay awake for my baby.

But the cloud continues to fill my nose, my mouth. I can't fight it any longer.

I drift off.

It's not so bad.

Clouds are harmless and pretty.

CHAPTER TWENTY-FIVE

CLAIRE

Dane didn't come home last night.

I should know. I haven't slept. I lay in bed and alternated between staring at the clock, trying to read, resisting the urge to check the police scanner, and calling him unsavory names. I gave up around four-thirty and transferred to the kitchen table, where I began those inane rituals all over again.

I've had four espressos so I'm buzzing. Drained, exhausted, and worried, but hyped, ready to face whatever the day brings, good or bad. I'm on the verge of listening to the police scanner when he stumbles in around six a.m., disheveled and dazed. I want to yell at him but I don't. I wait.

He hovers at the back door, staring at the kitchen floor, which I cleaned. It took me fifteen minutes to get every crumb of Parmesan out of the tile grouting. Then his contrite gaze drifts to the two holes in the wall and his shoulders slump, like he's been hit from behind.

"I'm sorry," he says, reluctantly looking me in the eye after he finally tears his gaze away from the wall. "I drove around for an hour or two last night, ended up doing a lot of thinking."

When he doesn't elaborate I'm forced to ask, "And?"

"I acted like a douche. Overreacted big time." He swipes a hand over his face to hide his embarrassment. "I'm sorry for the way I behaved."

I want to forgive him. After all, it's my appalling behavior that precipitated his freak out. And I know if our roles had been reversed and he admitted to allowing a woman to kiss him I'd be catatonic right now.

But I need to let him know his behavior scared me, without causing another fight. "I've never seen you so angry." I point at the holes in the wall. "You frightened me."

"I'm sorry, the guy who did that, he's not me."

He's so forlorn I want to go to him, but I'm still reeling from seeing my gentle husband morph into a furious, out of control Neanderthal that punches holes in walls.

"Where were you last night?"

Guilt shifts across his face like a shadow, gone before I can pinpoint it, and I wonder if I imagined it.

"Already told you, I drove around."

His deliberate evasiveness isn't helping. "You said that was for a few hours. What about the rest of the night?"

"Dozed in my car at the beach." He shrugs, like staying out all night means nothing.

I want to interrogate him further. It's not the cop in me; it's the wife. I want to ask which beach and for how long. I want to ask what made him think it was okay to take his temper out by smashing things and punching holes in our wall. I want to ask what it will take to get past this.

Before I can formulate the words, my cell rings next to me on the counter. I glance at the screen. It's Ron.

"I need to get this."

He nods and I pick up the phone as he slouches off toward the bathroom.

Weary to the bone, and my workday hasn't even started, I hit the answer button. "Hey, Ron, early call-out?"

"Yeah, we've got an anonymous call tipping us off about a body in a studio out by the back beach. Not sure if it's suicide or not yet. They want us out there pronto."

"Okay, I'll be there in ten." I glance down at my gray

sweatshirt stained from cleaning up Dane's pasta mess last night and my grimy yoga pants. "Make that fifteen."

"I'll text you the address. See you soon."

I hang up and rush into the bedroom. Dane's in the shower so there's no chance I'll have time to take one before I leave. So I tie my hair into a ponytail and change into a clean uniform.

He's still in the shower when I have to leave so I stick my head around the bathroom door. "Got an urgent call-out from work, I have to go in early."

I expect him to open the glass door and respond. He doesn't. He merely raises his hand in a wave and proceeds to rinse the shampoo out of his hair.

We're in a bad place after last night. And I want to bring a baby into this crappy environment? Kids are like mood stones. I've seen it with my nieces and nephews. They can sniff out the faintest hint of discord between their parents at twenty paces. They call them out on it too, which only seems to escalate the tension.

While a baby won't be so intuitive, I don't want anything to taint his early years. I want a stable, loving environment. Then again, plenty of babies are raised by single parents so maybe I'm projecting my own need for stability and love onto a helpless baby?

I haven't got time for the doubts to swamp me so shoving my concerns aside I check the address Ron has texted me. It sounds vaguely familiar but I don't know anyone who lives in that part of town.

The Rise. A windswept, backwater, beachside suburb on the outskirts of Gledhill, with tiny cottage-like studios offered for short-term rentals, mostly to vacationers or people having affairs.

I plug the address into my GPS and a quarter of an hour later I reach it with a minute to spare and Ron is already waiting for me. He opens my car door, his lined face grim.

"Forensics thinks it's a murder."

I figured. Police don't get an early call-out unless foul play is suspected.

"You mentioned suicide on the phone?" I follow him to the front door, slip the plastic covers over my shoes, and slide on gloves.

"It's definitely murder. Looks like she suffocated, pillow over the face. Forensics have already taken it away for testing." He shakes his head, the groove between his brows deepening. "There's also a pinprick at the base of her neck which means she was probably drugged first."

He waits for me to step inside before following. "We won't know what drugged her until the tox screen comes back but Matt thinks it's probably the usual, something like GHB."

"The date rape drug." I hate it, have seen more than my fair share of crimes committed against women in the city because of it. And right here in Gledhill, with Elly. She'd fallen victim to having her drink laced and had woken up hours later, violated, without any memory of the assault. Foul stuff. "So what's the early presumption? She was out with some guy, he spiked her drink to take her home?"

"Unlikely." Sadness downturns Ron's mouth, accentuating the creases bracketing it like a roadmap. "She's pregnant."

My heart stops. Then restarts with a jolt I feel all the way to my toes. I can't breathe, my lungs seizing. My palms grow clammy and a prickle of premonition strums my spine.

No way. There could be any number of pregnant women living in Gledhill at the moment. I see many of them waddling down the main street. Icons of proud expectant mommas, something I'll never be. I guess that's why I notice them.

But it's odd that one of them would be living out here alone. It's isolated and these tiny studios only have one bedroom, meaning she's probably a single mother.

Hell. Not helping the wild, unsavory assumptions pinging in my head.

"Hey, are you okay?" Ron touches my arm but I'm already past him and into the studio.

No point jumping to conclusions. I'm a cop. I deal with facts.

The first thing I see is a woman lying on a sofa, surrounded by examiners.

The second thing I see is her small baby bump.

The third, her face, peaceful and serene, like she's napping.

It's Jodi.

CHAPTER TWENTY-SIX

MARISA

It's a beautiful Hamptons morning. One of those crisp days with a brisk wind off the ocean that brings a chill quickly banished by the sun. I actually managed a few hours' sleep last night so I'm feeling half human and won't let anything ruin my uncharacteristic perkiness. Including my husband, who only came home at one a.m.

I don't care anymore. I don't care about his whereabouts or who he's spending his time with. I gave up buying the work excuse a long time ago though it's easier to go along with it.

I have my job, my home, and my girls. It's all I need. Besides, I have an inherent fear of ending up like my mom, alone in a tiny two-bedroom apartment working my ass off to make ends meet, cynical and bitter and depressed.

It's why I stay when every instinct insists I leave.

That's the good thing about putting up with Avery's bullshit. I get to live in a mansion, I can afford the best of everything, and I'm a respected member of the community. I'll do anything to maintain the status quo.

I'm an excellent actress.

"You got in late last night." I add spirulina to his smoothie, making sure to avoid mine. I hate the stuff.

"Working hard, you know how it is." He has the gall to meet my eyes.

"Work, yeah."

He hates sarcasm and sure enough, he frowns. Our gazes lock in a staring contest until I realize he's spoiling my good mood so I turn away. He comes up behind me and slips his arms around me. Typical. He always thinks he can soften me up with physical attention. Little does he know his touch repulses me most days and it takes every ounce of willpower not to elbow him away.

"Yeah, things have been busy at the center too." I screw the cap on the blender and flick the switch, glad the noise will drown out any more of his trite, meaningless responses.

I always do this, back down to avoid the ultimate confrontation, where I may be tempted to tell him exactly how I feel. He drops a peck on the back of my head and releases me. I can breathe again.

When his smoothie's done, I pour it into his glass-to-go. "What's the next few days looking like for you?"

"I'll be in the city for the rest of the week."

I hand him the smoothie and he does his usual raise it in the air in a silent cheers. "So you won't be coming home?"

He shrugs, his gaze evasive. "Not sure, depends on the hours." He takes a sip of the smoothie and smacks his lips. "Delicious as always. What would I do without you?"

"I have a feeling you'd cope just fine."

Either my dry response doesn't register or he doesn't care. "Fancy a vacation?"

I can barely tolerate spending a few hours with him these days—as my age increases, my acceptance of his smarmy BS decreases—I can't imagine being stuck with him on some tropical paradise 24/7. If our past vacations since the twins left for college have been any indication, he'll spend the time alternating between drinking too much, flirting with random women, getting turned on, and dragging me back to our room for sex. I hate being used.

Then again, I'm hypocritical, for that's exactly what I'm doing staying in this dead-end marriage. I'm using Avery as an adjunct to my perfect life. Sure, I have my own money that I work hard for but it's nothing on the lavish lifestyle and the Hamptons prestige we enjoy courtesy of him.

I wonder what he'd think if he knew the truth, that I'd used him way back when we first met. He'd been a confident pursuer. No woman ever said no to Avery Thurston. To this day he thinks he spotted me first and had to have me.

It's my little secret that I played him like the fool he is.

"Where did you have in mind?" I keep my voice steady, despite the disgust simmering beneath the surface.

"Somewhere warm, of course, so I can see your great bod in that blue bikini I love so much." He winks and blows me a kiss. "Leave it with me. I'll check out a few options and let you know."

Translated: he doesn't give a crap about my opinion, he'll book it and tell me where we're going.

"Just make sure it's not over the next four months, okay?"

"Why?" He doesn't like being thwarted. His mouth compresses into a thin, unimpressed line.

"Because there's a pregnant single mother at the center and I want to be around to ensure her adoption proceeds smoothly."

"You're kidding, right?" He slams his cup down on the table and I jump. "Our lives have to revolve around some slut who got herself knocked-up?"

My fingers curl into fists. "Most of our clients come from families like ours and you're not the only one who values his job. I want to be around for this. I will be."

It's an ultimatum of sorts and he knows it. I rarely stand up to him. It's easier to go along with his plans, to keep the great Avery Thurston happy, because when Avery's happy he tends to leave me alone and I value my alone time.

I know what he thinks of my job. He thinks I'm wasting my time helping a bunch of misfits who should help themselves. He much prefers me to be a kept woman at home, playing hostess to his rich cronies. He had an excuse to keep me tied here when I had the kids but now that the girls are at college and I'm back working he has less control over me. That's what bugs him the most.

As for my volunteer work, he grudgingly tolerates it because of the praise it garners. We've been stopped in town many times, while having dinner at The Lookout or picking up fresh seafood from Cray-Cray, by grateful people wanting to thank me for my time.

I don't need their gratitude—seeing the joy on their faces when I help them is enough—but it's nice to be appreciated and when this happens I see Avery staring at me like he can't fathom what makes me tick.

Just the way I like it.

He has no idea that my rescue complex stems from guilt for duping him. That I knew exactly who he was during those hospital rounds and I'd deliberately insinuated my way into his path. I knew about his penchant for leggy brunettes so I'd shortened my skirts and dyed my hair. I knew he was a control freak so I deferred to him on every patient. And I knew he loved having his ego stroked so I pandered to him on our first date, our second, and every one that followed until I had him exactly where I wanted him.

Down on his knees and proposing.

I needed a way out of my crappy life and Avery had been the means. I don't regret what I did but guilt is a terrible thing and I can't help my never-ending quest to help people as a result.

I'd brought a stray teen home once, not long after the twins had left for college. Gemma had been on the run from Michigan and the wily sixteen-year-old had made it to Long Island in one piece. But the Help Center had been packed to capacity—I'd been volunteering there then, not employed—and I'd offered to give her a bed for as long as she needed it.

Avery had gone berserk. He'd ranted behind our closed

bedroom door then sulked in silence before packing his bag and heading for the city. I'd been relieved until I checked the spare room to fine Gemma gone.

She'd come from an abusive family so had probably heard our shouting and left. I have forgiven Avery for many things over the years but his callous indifference to those in need is something I will never get over.

"Book the vacation for five months, you choose, anywhere you like." It's a half-assed apology to keep the peace and he knows it.

"Fine."

He sulks if he doesn't get his way and it isn't pretty. I'd rather play nice than suffer his middle-aged mood swings.

"Anyway, I'm off to visit that pregnant client to see how she's settling in so I'll see you later."

He scowls and grabs his drink. "I'll let you know what I'm doing work-wise for this week once I check my agenda."

I bite back the classic response the twins would use often in their teens: "whatever."

He raises his hand in farewell and I soon hear the purr of his V8 engine before he roars away.

I hope he chokes on that smoothie.

I blend mine, drink it down, and grab my keys. I deliberately stayed away from Jodi yesterday, wanting her to enjoy her first night alone in the studio. It's a quaint place and I saw how much she loved it when I first took her there. It had been a bold move on my part because I knew the center wouldn't fund accommodation like that, so I'm paying. No one knows but the relevant staff at work and I want to keep it that way. It's my pre-baby gift to Claire and Dane. They deserve it. I like doing nice stuff for good people. Bad people too, considering I still pander to my husband.

The drive is fifteen minutes to The Rise but it takes me twenty today when I stop at Java Groove on the way for bagels, homemade raspberry jam, and hot chocolates. I have a feeling Jodi hasn't had many treats in her life. I asked about her parents and she clammed up. Her father died when she was young, her mother has remarried but they lost contact years ago.

I know it's crazy but the moment I heard that, I felt vindicated in stepping in to help, almost like a surrogate mom. The further this pregnancy progresses, the more changes she'll face, the more uncertain she'll become. I can provide reassurance and support while ensuring she's ready to give up the baby once he's born.

I turn down the winding seaside road that leads to her studio, surprised when I see a bunch of cars in the distance. According to the realtor this road is quiet, only frequented by the few renters currently occupying studios. Oddly, the cars seem to be clustered near her place.

A sliver of foreboding slithers down my spine but I shake it off. I'm being silly. It's probably maintenance men doing repairs on the road or the power lines. But as I get closer, that foreboding gives way to panic. There are police cars and medical examiner vehicles parked along the road.

Outside Jodi's place.

My heart starts pounding, loud and erratic, as I pull over. I exit the car and my hands shake as I struggle not to drop the bagels and hot chocolates. A host of scenarios play out in my head as I walk the forty feet toward her door.

She could've heard a sound, assumed it was a burglar, and called the police. She could've gone for a walk and witnessed something she shouldn't. She could've found a fugitive hiding out on her back deck. All perfectly plausible reasons.

If it wasn't for the M.E.'s van parked directly outside her front door.

The medical examiner isn't called out unless there's a corpse to examine, as Claire has told me countless times while regaling tales of her job.

The shaking migrates from my hands, up my arms, along

my shoulders, and down my torso. When the quivering hits my legs I stumble up the path. I spy Claire, white-faced and grim, stalking out the front door.

Our gazes lock across the short distance.

And I know.

The bag of bagels and tray of hot chocolates slip from my nerveless fingers. The bagels roll into nearby bushes, the hot chocolate splashes my beige capris. I barely notice.

"What happened?" My voice sounds croaky, like I haven't spoken in fifty years.

Claire gives a brief shake of her head, like she can't tell me, or doesn't want to.

"Claire, tell me." I walk toward her, each step bringing me closer to an unpalatable truth: that the sweet girl I've been helping is probably dead.

I stop two feet in front of Claire, determinedly not looking past her and into the studio.

"Jodi's dead."

Her voice is calm, clear, like she's delivering news about a stranger.

"Oh God."

The enormity hits me and I sink to my haunches, backing toward the nearest rock so I can sit. Claire squats next to me and awkwardly pats my back. She's on duty. I get it. But I need to be held so badly.

"I thought she'd be happy here…" I stare at a row of ants meandering along the path, going about their business as if nothing remotely horrific has occurred in the new studio behind them. "I never would've brought her out here if I thought she needed to be on suicide watch."

Claire doesn't answer, and when I tear my gaze from the ants to look at her, I know something's drastically wrong even before she speaks.

"It's not suicide, Ris." She drags in a steadying breath. "It's a crime scene in there."

She blows out the breath in a long whoosh. "Someone murdered Jodi."

I hear the words but I can't compute. This can't be happening. Suicide is horrendous enough, but murder?

"You're wrong," I say, with little conviction, knowing Claire wouldn't tell me something like this unless she knew the facts.

"You know me better than that. I wouldn't make wild assumptions."

She sits on the rock beside me, stoic and strong, while I'm a mess inside. "I shouldn't be telling you this but someone drugged her, then suffocated her."

"But who..."

The moment I utter the words I have a suspicion. I don't keep it to myself. "You think she told the father of her baby and he killed her because of it?"

I glance sideways at Claire when she doesn't answer. It's like she's in a trance. I know the feeling.

"Claire?"

She nods, biting her bottom lip. "It's the first thing I thought of. But it's not that type of crime scene. If she told the guy and he snapped over this unwanted pregnancy, she would've been bashed over the head or strangled. A crime of passion, spontaneous and erratic. There'd be signs of a struggle."

I wince at the gory picture she paints and Claire pats my hand. "Sorry, just musing out loud."

I don't want to know what the scene is like in that studio. Details will only haunt me later. But if Jodi suffocated, why do they think she was drugged?

"So the suffocation is definitely not natural?"

Claire shakes her head and glances around to make sure there's no one within earshot. "A pillow was found over her face. Then there's a puncture mark at the base of her neck." She lowers her voice and points to the spot on herself. "It goes without saying this is confidential and I'm only telling you because of your connection with Jodi, but the perpetrator probably wanted her weak and helpless before they covered her face, so they injected her with something like GHB."

My eyebrows rise. "The date rape drug? Like what that creep used on Elly?"

We lock gazes, remembering our friend and her humiliation after she'd woken to find she'd been drugged and raped.

Claire looks away first. "Yeah, it's easy enough to obtain, kids take it in clubs all the time, or any idiot can find out how to make it on the Internet."

Her glower ages her, making the lines bracketing her mouth deepen and the dark circles beneath her eyes prominent, like she hasn't slept in a week. "The fact the killer arrived with a syringe of the stuff indicates premeditation. So it's unlikely the baby's father killed her in a fit of rage after learning the truth."

So much for my theories; I'd make a lousy cop. "Then who?"

Claire straightens, the grief in her eyes solidifying into something harder.

Determination.

"I don't know but I'm going to make damn sure I find out." She rests her forearms on her knees. "Any murder is difficult, but that poor defenseless baby..."

She shakes her head, her lips compressed like she's struggling to keep it together. That's when it hits me, how much harder this must be for her. Her hopes and dreams of having a child sooner rather than later have gone. Taken brutally. How could I have not realized? My first thought had been for Jodi. Had the murderer cared that they'd committed a double homicide, killing an innocent baby too?

Poor Claire must be grieving on the inside, struggling to present a brave front. I want to help. But one look at her rigid posture and the way she's staring determinedly into the distance means I won't. If she's barely holding it together I can't be the one responsible for tipping the balance.

"Are you sure you should be working this case?" I touch

her back and she flinches away, reinforcing my earlier supposition. "I mean, no one knows about the adoption yet because we didn't file paperwork. So unless they read my case notes no one knows but you, me, and Dane."

"I'll be the lead on this case, Ris, with Ron assisting, so I'll be delegating tasks accordingly." She looks at me then, her gaze pleading. "I need to discover the truth. For closure or something. Or I'll go crazy."

I believe her. She has a glint in her eyes. I don't like it.

"Okay. I won't say anything about the adoption unless one of your delegated officers asks me."

She opens her mouth to respond and I add, "I can't lie, Claire. It's not in my DNA. I'll protect you as best as I can so you can work this case but at some point the truth may come out."

"I can deal with that." She stands, a slow push up of a woman double her age. "I don't intend this investigation to take long. The team already know her identity because she had her social security card and other identification in her wallet, so I'm going to fast track this and devote every waking second to get answers."

She holds out a hand to me and I take it. She pulls me to my feet and finally envelops me in a hug.

We cling to each other. I've been holding back tears but I let them fall now; she's surprisingly dry-eyed. When we release each other, I say, "You're handling this well."

"I can't afford to fall apart on the outside, they'll take me off the case." She glances over her shoulder, worried, as if we'll be overheard. "This is only my second day back on the job after those weeks off and I can't screw up."

"I get it." I briefly squeeze her hands. "Keep me posted, okay?"

She nods but she's already half turned away, ready to head back into the house.

I swallow several times to subdue the sobs tightening my

throat and manage to say, "I'm sorry, Claire, about the baby. About everything."

I feel compelled to apologize, though this isn't my fault.

I've always done it: say sorry to smooth over an altercation or back down even when I'm right. It became ingrained growing up, so I wouldn't cop a backhander from Mom. With Avery, it helps keep our marriage on a track that won't end in divorce.

She raises her hand in farewell but doesn't turn back.

CHAPTER TWENTY-SEVEN

CLAIRE

Seeing Ris calms me. She's so shocked I have to play the responsible cop, slipping into my role with ease. Supportive and reassuring, strong and capable, qualities cited in my file on record at the police department. I'm a good cop and I know it, even if unexpected emotion has derailed me the last few weeks. My dad, a chief in Brooklyn, rarely gives praise so the day he called me one of the best officers he's ever seen, in front of my brothers, I knew I'd made it.

I wonder what Dad would think of me now? Foundering the moment my friend leaves, doubts about my capabilities to do a good job on a case I'm too close to plaguing me. A phone call to my parents is long overdue. We usually chat regularly, every week or two, but lately I've been avoiding contact because I'm emotionally fragile and will blab about our infertility issues. Then the whole family will know in a few hours and I'll be fielding calls from everyone.

During our brief calls where I've begged off early citing a huge workload, Mom hasn't pushed but Dad isn't so diplomatic. He asked point-blank what was bugging me and I cited women's problems, which shut him up completely.

Now, with Jodi dead, I'm glad I didn't tell them about the adoption. I'm gutted and they would've been too. My stomach is hollow, the little liquid that's in there sloshing around and making me want to puke. I wish I'd eaten this morning rather than drinking those four espressos.

I need to play this right, exactly how I outlined to Ris.

I have to be on this case and the only way to do that is to prove to Ron and the other cops surreptitiously watching me that I'm competent enough to be back on the job. I feel their eyes on me. Judging me. Ready to find me lacking. I won't give them the satisfaction.

Sadness is seeping all the way down to my soul, the type of sorrow that won't be shifted for a while. The only way I successfully dealt with our infertility issues was focusing on adopting Jodi's baby. Now that precious baby is dead, along with her mother, and I'm drifting again; powerless to stop the grief swamping me in relentless waves, crashing over me, drowning me.

I'm dying on the inside. On the outside, I'm Sergeant Claire Casey, ready for duty.

Ron pauses at the front door of the studio, staring at me. I know he's looking for the slightest sign of weakness. So I square my shoulders and stride up the path toward him.

"Any progress?"

He shakes his head. "It'll take a while to get the tox screen results and CSI are working the scene, so why don't we head back to the station and make a start on establishing motive?"

"Sure, I'll meet you there."

I'm glad I drove straight here and we're in separate cars. It gives me time to think. Process. Deny. Because ever since I saw Jodi lying there, lifeless, I can't get the vision of Dane last night out of my head.

It's why I won't share my connection to Jodi with the rest of the team: I can't put Dane in the firing line when I don't know enough yet. Besides, I'm terrified by what the memories of last night might mean. His explosive temper. His lack of control. His rage. What if that fury against me had morphed into a desire to punish?

He knows my sole focus is having a child. It's all I've talked about for months. Before we discovered the infertility. After. And now, during the adoption that will never happen.

What if he realized the worst way to punish me for my altercation with Griffin was to deprive me of the baby that was supposed to be ours?

It's a ludicrous, outlandish thought and I immediately feel guilty for even thinking it. But there's one thing . . .

He didn't come home last night.

Had he been guilty, unable to face me after what he'd done?

Though my theory is flawed. I'd told Ris this hadn't been a crime of passion and Dane killing Jodi to punish me would've been just that.

Except . . . Dane is inherently a gentle man. And this is a very civilized, gentle murder.

Dane's a medical sales representative. He has access to all kinds of pharmaceuticals. GHB wouldn't be hard to produce.

I can see him justifying it in his head. He puts Jodi to sleep first. It slows her breathing, then he covers her face with a pillow . . . She won't feel a thing. Gentle, indeed.

It's a theory I can't dislodge as I drive to the station. But I need to. I need to find another motive. Another angle. I guess I should be grateful that at least Dane can't be the father of Jodi's baby.

Because if that was a possibility . . .

I shudder as I park in my usual spot at the front of the station. I need to find another suspect.

ASAP.

CHAPTER TWENTY-EIGHT

ELLY

I have a headache, the persistent kind behind my eyes that no amount of pain reliever eases. Lack of sleep does this to me. I left the cottage around midnight, getting to bed around one, but I need time before I go to bed. I cleanse, tone, slather on serums and eye creams and moisturizers. It's a calming process. A ritual. I need to take my mask off because for those few hours when I've removed all traces of my outer persona and I'm in bed, alone, I can finally let my carefully erected barriers slip and be myself.

It's exhausting, projecting an image. I live in constant fear that somehow my past will find me and destroy everything I've worked so hard to build. Or worse, my present will implode if my secret gets out. I need to tell my friend my way. I can't imagine her finding out any other way. I'm not callous, I'm fucked up, and soon the people I value most will know it.

No prizes for guessing why I'm an insomniac. The lack of sleep combined with the headache makes me grouchy so when I see a group of receptionists clustered around the front desk I march across the marble tiles of our specialists' foyer, my heels making an angry clicking sound. When I reach the desk, I slam my hand on it. "Stop gossiping and get back to work immediately."

They turn to me in unison and the first thing that strikes me is the tear stains on some of their faces, the runs of mascara streaking their cheeks with black.

Feeling like a heartless bitch, I lower my voice. "What's wrong?"

"One of our patients was murdered last night." Sadie, the front desk receptionist, dabs at the corners of her eyes with a tissue. "That girl Jodi, the pregnant one?"

Spots dance before my eyes for a moment and I reach for the desk, needing the support.

"Are you sure?"

Sadie stares at me like I'm an idiot. "My boyfriend works at the M.E.'s office."

I can't believe this. While I never met this girl she'd insinuated her way into my life via Ris. I was helping facilitate her appointments, keeping an eye on her, making sure she received the top-notch ob-gyn care Ris wanted for her.

I blink away the spots, hating to appear weak in front of my staff. "Do they know what happened?"

Sadie shakes her head. "They found her at home this morning, that's all I know."

"Right," I say, but it isn't.

Crime in Gledhill is low-key. I know this via Claire. DUIs are commonplace. The odd break and enter. Teens vandalizing or dealing party drugs. Domestics.

Rape under the influence of GHB...

I quickly quash the memory. Besides, I didn't report what happened to me to the cops, despite Claire's insistence I should. What would've been the point? I'd been in Gledhill less than two months and had been intent on rebuilding my life. Having my past revealed in court, the stupid, gullible woman who'd fallen prey to a bigamist...I would've made a lousy victim and the perp would've been acquitted.

If I knew who raped me, that is.

All I have is a vague memory of him on top of me: his weight, his strength. Maybe it's a good thing I can't remember more. It's enabled me to put it behind me. But there are the rare times when I actually sleep that I wake in the middle of the night, drenched in sweat, my subconscious desperately grasping at an image, a shadow...

It's the not knowing that's the worst.

I'd had my revenge on my ex by giving up his child for adoption. I would relish the chance to make the monster that violated me pay for what he did.

"She seemed really nice when she came in here for her appointment the other day," Sadie says, to nobody in particular.

The rest of the girls titter in agreement but it's time to break up their gossiping session. I need time to think. "That is sad news but we've got a busy day ahead with booked out appointments for all doctors and specialists, so get back to work, please."

A few girls shoot me venomous looks they think I can't see while Sadie ushers them away. I'm not well liked here. I don't care. I'm a tough boss who expects perfection and young people today often don't work hard enough. They're an entitled generation of takers. They perpetually annoy me with their addiction to social media and dating apps and high expectations.

It's only when I reach the sanctity of my office that I allow the mask to slip. I sink into my chair and reach for an iced water. It does little for the pain behind my eyes. I pinch the bridge of my nose. That does little too.

Jodi Van Gelder is dead. Murdered.

An image flashes into my head, of lying next to my lover last night and asking him about her.

He feigned cluelessness.

Was it real?

My lover is a man who hides many secrets.

Is this another?

Only one way to find out.

I need to see Claire and discover what she knows.

CHAPTER TWENTY-NINE

CLAIRE

When I'm back at the station I pull up the new active file on Jodi Van Gelder, which has already been updated to include a plethora of relevant information. I type in any pertinent questions I can think of, then flip the page of my notepad to a blank one.

I scan the screen and jot down information that needs following up. Namely why this twenty-five-year-old woman who hadn't been out of Manhattan before arrived in Gledhill.

It's a no-brainer. She wanted to tell the baby's father her big news. Ris had virtually said as much. So I need to retrace her steps when she first came to town and discover if the father knows. Because if the father is aware of Jodi's pregnancy, and he didn't want the baby for a variety of reasons—namely he's married and it would ruin his reputation—that's one big motive for murder right there.

I like this theory. It distracts me from the possibility my otherwise stable, reliable husband, who lost it last night, did this out of anger and revenge.

I tap a few more keys and the relevant information pops up. Jodi arrived in Gledhill on the Hampton jitney a few weeks ago. The bus depot is where I'll start investigating.

After filling Ron in, I set off to walk the few blocks to the depot. I've walked this route many times, as I like being away from the office for lunch. The Atlantic wind is oddly balmy today, like we're in for a storm, but the gusts are refreshing and help clear my mind.

I pass the gourmet delicatessen with its pricey caviar and expensive cheeses from all around the world, the book-shop I can never resist popping into, the electronics store with the latest devices artfully displayed in the window, and an art-ist's gallery where the average painting sells for a hefty five figures.

I pick up the pace as I pass the last shop, determinedly avoid-ing looking in the window. But I can't help it; like the vehicular accidents I attend where I don't want to look but have to, I find my gaze drawn to it against my will.

My heart lurches as I glimpse the ornate Baby Bubs sign swinging in the breeze and hear the soft tinkle of wind chimes. I stare at the window display—the latest in sophisticated jog-ging strollers, a pristine white crib, an oak cradle, and a plethora of stuffed toys—and resist the urge to press my nose up against the glass.

I've been into this shop so many times since we started try-ing to have a family twelve months ago that I know the layout by heart. The entrance is adorned with blue and pink mobiles that flutter as customers pass into the quaint shop filled with everything expectant parents might need. Strollers, diapers, nursery furniture, toys, breast pumps, and the cutest clothes that I'd been drawn to repeatedly.

I'd sifted through rompers covered in delicate pink butter-flies and miniature denim jeans and blue T-shirts emblazoned with trucks, imagining my very own girl or boy to dress and raise and love.

My throat tightens with emotion and my eyes burn with tears so I wrench my gaze from Baby Bubs and continue toward the depot, lengthening my strides to put as much distance between me and baby heaven as possible.

Jodi's murder is bad enough but every time I think of that poor unborn baby boy who never had a chance I can't breathe.

It's inhumane, taking an innocent life, and even if I didn't have a vested interest in Jodi's baby I would feel just as shattered.

I'm one block away from the depot when Phil, the old guy who sweeps the boardwalk because he's lived here his entire life and sees it as his duty, waylays me.

"I'm doing my duty, Officer, honest." He winks and salutes me, his false teeth startlingly white in his tanned, wrinkled face as he grins.

This is our in-joke. Whenever he spots me out walking he'll make a beeline for me.

"Of course you are, Phil, you're an upstanding citizen." I salute back and force a smile, hoping it doesn't look like a wince. Not that it's his fault I'm on the verge of breaking down in tears. I should've taken a squad car to the depot rather than walking today, knowing I wouldn't be strong enough to avoid glancing at Baby Bubs.

He peers at me, eyes narrowed. "Something bothering you?"

I want to respond with "Where do I start?" but I settle for, "Policing is rough sometimes."

"Well, everyone around here knows you're doing a stellar job, so keep up the good work."

With another salute, he turns away and heads back to the boardwalk, his enormous frayed broom dragging behind him.

I wish I had as much confidence in my abilities as Phil does.

One of the upsides of walking is being interrupted by greetings along the way and I crave that today.

The disruptions in a small town when I'm on a case can be annoying but today I appreciate the distraction.

Focusing on Jodi's movements has dislodged the image of an irate Dane from my mind but not for long. It's back all too soon, front and center, making me doubt my husband when I shouldn't. It's absurd. People lose their temper all the time. It doesn't mean they channel that anger into murder out of some warped sense of revenge.

The bus depot sits on top of a small rise in the center of town. It has five docking stations for embarkation and disembarkation, and several external cameras for security purposes. Perfect. I speak to the manager and explain the situation. He gives me instant access to the cameras. While I hate computers generally I love how fast it is to pull security footage from a camera because of them.

I type in the relevant date when Jodi arrived and the bus number. It takes less than five seconds for the screen to come alive with passengers disembarking off the jitney. I scan the faces. Jodi's last. She probably bunkered down in the back of the bus, as most young people like to do.

She crosses the road; strolls along the boardwalk for a while, before entering the Sea Breeze café opposite. I fast-forward to the precise moment she exits the café and heads for the library.

The library...

I'd pulled her phone records already and seen she'd run out of data on her cell, meaning the library, with its plethora of computers, would be the perfect place to research information about her baby's father.

After thanking the depot's manager I walk the short distance to the library. I enter and inhale like any book-lover would do. There's nothing like the smell of books to get my nose twitching.

I haven't read anything lately. Haven't had the desire or the concentration. But I devour thrillers. Ris thinks it's odd, how I like reading crime when I'm submerged in it every day at work, but I find it fascinating, delving into the machinations of devious minds, fictional or otherwise.

I know the head librarian, Agnes. She's a wizened but spritely septuagenarian born and bred in Gledhill. She knows everyone, has a keen ear for gossip, and has been helpful in other cases.

She's the woman I need to speak to. She's not behind the

front desk so I search the aisles, spotting her on her knees, shelving returned books.

"Hey, Agnes, got a minute?"

Her eyes light up when she sees me in uniform. She knows I'm on "official business."

"Claire, lovely to see you." She holds on to a shelf and struggles to stand.

When I instinctively move to help, she holds up her hand. "I'm old but I'm not dead."

She winces and flexes her right leg. "Damn arthritic knees."

Her pained expression clears and she taps her temple. "Lucky I'm still as sharp up here. What can I do for you?"

I glance around and see a few borrowers lurking in the aisles. "Can we talk somewhere more private?"

Her eyes widen and positively gleam with excitement. "Sure. This must be important. Follow me."

She leads me to one of the small conference rooms. The door barely closes before she's asking questions. "I heard the police found a dead body this morning? Has this got anything to do with that?"

It never ceases to amaze me how fast bad news travels. "Where did you hear that?"

She taps the side of her nose. "The owner of the boutique next door is an avid reader. She came in first thing, said she'd been buying coffee at Sea Breeze when she overheard two of the receptionists from the medical center discussing it. Apparently one of them has a boyfriend who works at the M.E.'s office."

She clasps her rheumatic hands together and leans forward. "So it's true, then?"

"Don't be a ghoul, Agnes."

She puffs up in outrage, her frizzy gray hair bristling like a halo. "I'm a concerned citizen, that's all. If there's a murderer on the loose I need to know."

She winks and pats her hair into some semblance of normality. "I'm a single gal, you know. I need to protect myself."

Her sense of humor never fails to make me smile. "That's my job. I'm only a phone call away."

Thankfully, she doesn't point out the obvious. Where was I last night when Jodi needed protecting?

She rubs her hands together. "How can I help?"

I need to choose my words carefully, not wanting to give away too much. "Whatever we discuss is confidential, you understand that?"

Offended, she tilts her nose in the air. "Of course."

"I mean it, Agnes. This is a murder investigation and if you tell anyone it can compromise a conviction when we catch the perp."

Somber, she nods. "I understand."

"The victim arrived in Gledhill a few weeks ago via the jitney. I've checked footage and it shows her coming in here so I'm hoping you may have spoken to her, or seen what she was doing while she was in here. Tourists don't usually visit the library. They can't borrow books and the information kiosk is better for directions. So I think she was in here researching something or someone?"

Agnes's forehead creases in concentration. "We don't get many tourists in here."

"This girl was pregnant?"

Agnes's frown deepens as I will her to think, to remember. When her frown clears and her eyes glitter with triumph, I'm hopeful this dear lady can provide me with the clue I need.

"I remember that girl. Young thing, in her twenties." Agnes mimics a small bulge over her belly. "Thin, so her bump was more noticeable, even though she was barely showing."

"Did you talk to her? See what she was doing?" I mentally cross my fingers.

Agnes nods, her eyes bright, and I know I'm onto something.

"She used one of the computers. She was researching pharmaceutical companies." Agnes leans closer, as if about to impart some great secret, and I inwardly relax that Jodi hadn't been researching medical supply companies like the one my husband works for. "She spent an awful long time reading about the staff."

She pauses, whether for dramatic effect or not I'm not sure. "She seemed particularly interested in Avery Thurston so I told her he lived on Sunnyside Drive."

My heart leaps, then sinks. I have my first solid lead.

But it's my best friend's husband.

Is he responsible for getting Jodi knocked up? If he's the father of Jodi's baby and he learned the truth that makes him the prime suspect in my investigation.

Another fact slides into place. Ris told me Jodi turned up at her house the night of the supper party. Ris thought it had been a mistake, a client from the center searching for her.

But what if Jodi had been searching for Avery?

"Thanks, Agnes, you've been a great help." I make a zipping motion over my lips. "But remember, not a word about this to anybody."

Agnes holds up her hand like a Girl Scout. "I promise."

"Thanks."

Anticipation buzzes through me as I try not to run back to the station. I know what needs to happen next. Call Avery in to take a paternity test, then go home and hug my husband for suspecting him even if he'll never know it.

But first, I need to fill Ron in and follow up with forensics to see what they've discovered. If there's the slightest chance Avery is behind this I want to do everything exactly right so the resultant fallout on Ris is minimal. I can't imagine what she'll go through if she learns her husband got some girl young enough to be his daughter pregnant and then killed her because of it.

Ten minutes later I'm back at my desk, typing my notes. I don't hear my door close until it's too late, the soft snick drawing my attention as I glance up to see Griffin leaning against it.

"Got a minute?"

I clamp down on my first urge to tell him to go screw himself and nod. "Sure. What's up?"

"I heard about that pregnant girl being murdered. Anything I can do?"

I shake my head, wanting him to get the hell out of my office so I can get back to my notes while everything's still fresh in my mind. "No need for a psychologist. We're working through forensics at the moment, waiting for a few results to come in. We'll let you know if we need your assistance."

"Wow, I've never heard you give me the company spiel." He pushes off the door and lopes toward me. A flicker of unease makes me grip the underside of my desk. I'm not scared of him, per se, but I don't like his eerily serene expression. "I thought we were going to put that kiss behind us."

"We have," I say through gritted teeth, wanting to stick a pen in his eye for bringing it up again. "I really do have to get back to work—"

"While murder is never pleasant, and I feel sorry for that girl, personally I think you've had a lucky escape."

He perches on the edge of my desk. I used to like his ability to appear at ease in any situation; now his familiarity in my office makes my skin prickle with indignation. "Bringing a baby into your marriage would've been a mistake."

Disbelief renders me speechless. I stave off a shudder as a chill washes over me, like he's tipped a bucket of icy water on my head.

"How dare you—"

"You forget, I work with Marisa too, and when I saw you and Dane meeting with Jodi at the center, I figured it out."

His audible pity makes my palm itch to slap him and I curl my fingers into a fist.

"You were going to adopt her kid." He stands, looming over me. "For what it's worth, I'm sorry. But I think you bringing a child into a marriage fraught with problems is a short-term fix for deeper unresolved issues."

He braces his arms on my desk and leans forward, annoyingly nonchalant. "I'm just saying it how I see it, Claire, like all those times you asked me for advice."

Bile rises in my throat and I swallow it down, the burning trail it leaves behind as unpalatable as what I'm listening to. I don't want his unsolicited marital advice and I can't believe how blasé he is after the awkwardness of our last confrontation.

I *trusted* him. I let him into my life by confiding my fears about so much: my fear of never having a child, of not being enough for Dane, of our marriage imploding. And now the bastard is throwing it back in my face, all wrapped up in a solicitous, faux caring, bundle of *advice*.

"You can stick your advice up your ass." I stand so we're almost eye-to-eye. "We're done here."

His blasé mask slips for a moment and I glimpse a startling mania before he blinks and it's gone. In that second I wonder if I've misjudged Griffin more than I already have.

I've seen how he twisted our friendship into something more.

What if he's more warped than I think and has harmed Jodi in the hope my marriage will fall apart if we can't adopt?

It's a whacky theory. Then again, I've had a few of those in the last few hours.

"How much time have you spent with Jodi?"

He stiffens. "A little. I consulted with her once at the center."

"If you know something about her that can help—"

"You know I can't say anything because of patient confidentiality—"

"She was murdered!" I thump my desk. "If you know something, tell me."

He compresses his lips like a kid and shakes his head, so I decide to rattle him.

"Where were you last night?"

He rolls his eyes. "In New York City."

"How convenient—"

"Look, I don't know why you're asking me irrelevant questions when the most important one is when you're going to see sense and admit there's something between us—"

"Stop." I move so suddenly my chair slams the metal filing cabinet behind me. The resultant clang is loud and I wince, before squaring my shoulders. "You need to listen and listen good. If you approach me with any of this drivel again, I'll have you up on sexual harassment charges so fast your head will spin."

I stalk around the desk and open the door. "Now get the fuck out of my office."

I say it loud enough that several heads pop up from the dividers between desks. Sensing an audience, Griffin assumes his usual carefree mask and strolls out of my office with a casual wave, like our fraught exchange is nothing more than an overreaction on my part.

I slam the door, and determined to delve further because I won't get any answers from him, I get back to my computer and start investigating. In the name of thoroughness, I check his alibi. Traffic footage of his car on the highway and the tolls prove he's telling the truth. The guy is guilty of being an idiot but he didn't kill Jodi.

I need to focus on discovering who did.

CHAPTER THIRTY

MARISA

When I make it into the office, staff tell me to take the day off. I can't. I need to stay busy and check Jodi's paperwork is in order. I usually keep meticulous files because some cases end up in court, especially the domestic violence ones. With Jodi murdered, I know my files can be subpoenaed and I have to ensure I've followed procedure every step of the way.

I scroll through Jodi's details on the computer. All seems to be fine. Then I flick through her paper file and glimpse the unsigned adoption papers and the attorney's contact details. Sadness sits on my chest like an invisible giant, heavy and stifling until I can hardly breathe. I saw the devastation in Claire's eyes at The Rise. It was the pain of a woman who's lost a dream, not that of a policewoman investigating a murder. Would she start to spiral again?

I've hated watching my friend turn to alcohol for comfort, being forced to take leave from work because she wasn't coping. Claire is tough. She has to be in her line of work. But it's the people with the hardest exteriors that often hide secrets deep inside. I should know. I've put on a brave front for years.

Not that I'm tough. I'm a marshmallow. A pushover, my girls say. They could coerce me into giving them anything when they were younger. I justified it by thinking we had the money but we wouldn't have the twins forever so whatever they wanted I provided.

Now I wonder if I've done them a disservice. Will they expect to coast through life without facing hardships? Will they seek out men to marry like their father, a good provider but a lousy husband? I hope not. I wouldn't wish that on my girls.

I'd like them to have husbands like Dane: dependable, chivalrous, solid Dane, who has been so supportive of Claire through their fertility issues. Most men would've retreated, maybe felt guilty if they couldn't father a child. But the few times I'd seen Dane since Claire revealed their secret he's been the same. I admire that, the ability to take the bad that life dishes out and move forward without falling apart.

I think he's helped Claire through the adoption process too. She's been a different person since I gave her hope. A hope cruelly ripped away by a monster. Something we'll all have to live with.

I'm concerned that Claire may revert to self-pity. I worry about her more than Elly. Even after the rape Elly bounced back quickly. She's resilient and adept at putting the past behind her. She reminds me of me. Not that either of them know how much I worry. I'm used to hiding my true feelings. Claire is vulnerable beneath her hardy hide. Elly is too but to a lesser extent. My friends need me to look out for them.

They don't know it but when my girls left for college I transferred my mothering onto Claire and Elly. I don't feel whole unless I'm caring for someone. Avery gave up needing me a long time ago, unless it's to act as a trophy wife and a hostess.

I need the validation and my friends provide that. Without them, I'd be lost. My job feeds into my neediness too, not that my clients know it. Nurturing is what I do best, and as I gather the adoption papers into a bundle, tap them on the desk to neaten them, then slide them into the folder and paper clip the lot, I know Claire needs me more now than ever.

Thankfully, everything is in order with the paperwork. I wish I could say the same for the impending sense of doom I can't seem to shake.

Something is seriously off about this murder.

Jodi didn't have any friends in town. She knew nobody but me, Claire, and Dane.

And the baby's father.

I can't shake the thought that he might've had something to do with this. I wish I'd pushed her further for answers regarding his identity. I wish I had some clue.

A knock sounds on my door and Claire pops her head around it.

"Can I come in?"

"Sure." I quickly shove Jodi's file under the stack on my desk. The last thing Claire needs is to find me brooding over it.

I stand and come around my desk to give her a hug. "Is this official business?"

"Yes and no." We release each other and I gesture at the sofa. "Want something to drink?"

She shakes her head. "I'm fine."

We lapse into an awkward silence that isn't us. We always talk, even if we don't have much to say.

"Are you sure you should be on this case?" It sucks as an opener but it's something I've been thinking about since I saw Claire at The Rise this morning.

She immediately bristles, her gaze wary while her nod is emphatic. "I need to be."

I should keep my mouth shut. I can't. "But aren't you too close to it? I mean, you were hoping to adopt Jodi's baby. It's your dream to be a mom and now that's been taken away from you in the most unexpected, cruel way—"

"Ris, you're a good friend, but trust me when I say I have to be on this case."

Her gaze is evasive. She can't look me in the eye and she's fidgeting with the seam on her uniform trousers. Claire never fiddles. She's too controlled for that.

That's when I know something is seriously wrong.

"You have a suspect already?"

It sounds like a question but I'm making a statement. Because deep down I know, know without a doubt that she's here because she has to impart bad news and it has something to do with me.

She takes a long time to speak, as if searching for the right words, and that's when I guess the truth before she says anything.

"You think Avery's involved in this?"

Pain darkens her eyes as she finally meets my gaze. "I would never discuss any aspect of this case with you if I thought it could be compromised. But you're my best friend and after all you did for me with the adoption..." She shrugs, a simple gesture that is far from nonchalant. "I wouldn't feel right following up this lead without you knowing."

I want to know.

I don't want to know.

The story of my life with Avery.

"You shouldn't tell me." A wave of nausea rolls over me as I place my palms on my knees and breathe deeply. It does little for the fear making me want to cover my ears and not hear another word. "Because if he's responsible for what happened to that girl I want you to lock up that son of a bitch and I know that can't happen if this investigation is compromised in any way."

Her lips part in shock but she quickly masks it. "You're not angry? Or surprised?"

"Honey, I've got years of pent-up resentment against that man." My nausea eases, replaced by a determination to nail whoever killed Jodi, even if it's the man I've been married to for twenty years. I pat Claire's knee and she manages a wan smile. "As for surprise, I wouldn't put anything past him."

Speechless, Claire stares at me, the friend she thought she knew, realizing maybe she doesn't know me at all. I've always been a doormat around Avery: throwing the perfect parties, supporting him unquestionably, being the model wife.

I'm surprised that Claire doesn't understand that if something appears too perfect, it usually isn't. She's an expert at reading people. I've seen her in action at my parties when she meets my acquaintances for the first time. She's the epitome of polite, able to make small talk with anyone, but later she'll describe in detail what makes an individual tick. I envy her that ability. It would've saved me a lot of heartache if I'd been able to do that twenty-two years ago when Avery had strutted into my life.

As Claire continues to look at me with open curiosity, I can read her stare: she's still wondering how much to tell me.

"I'm not as clueless as I make out to be." I sound snappish when it isn't her fault I've portrayed exactly that to my friends. Appearing blissfully oblivious is often much easier than admitting my marriage is a sham and I'm desperately unhappy.

Claire doesn't know what to say in response to my honesty so she waits, looking at me expectantly. I've never admitted Avery's faults to anyone. I've spent my entire married life pretending: first for my kids, later for appearances. Probably for me too, because I never want to admit to myself that I made a horrific mistake the day I married Avery Thurston.

I'd been so smug back then, knowing my plan worked. I felt superior in every way, knowing I'd targeted a big fish like Avery and reeled him in without him having the faintest clue. My life had changed for the better. At least, that's what I kept telling myself, because as it turned out no amount of skiing holidays in Aspen or designer wardrobes or lavish degustation dinners could make up for the fact I'd married an egotistical, vain man-child that didn't give a crap about anything but his image.

"Let me give you a little background, then it might make it easier for you to understand." I steeple my fingers and rest them in my lap. "Avery's a classic narcissist. But he gives me the life I always wanted so I'm happy to tolerate his shortcomings."

Until now, because if that bastard has done anything to harm Jodi I'll castrate him myself.

"My father left when I was a toddler, I never knew him. Mom worked hard, never cooked or cleaned, so we lived in a hovel and had frozen TV dinners every day. She was never there for me so I vowed to never be like that when I had my own family."

Some of my outrage against Avery fades as I think of the twins. My gorgeous girls with their clear eyes and radiant smiles. They're so innocent, though I'm hoping they're not half as naïve as their mother at the same age. I can't hate Avery no matter how much I want to because he's the father of my beautiful children. "I met Avery in my first training hospital. He was doing post-surgical rounds, I was organizing temporary housing for a battered wife."

I remember the way he looked at me that day in the hospital corridor: it still gives me chills. Like he knew what he wanted—me—and nothing would stand in his way of getting it. An intense, commanding stare that brooked no argument, a smug smile like he knew he had me, the confident wide-legged stance of a man used to owning the world and everyone in it. Avery Thurston was king, on the lookout for his queen, and I'd been only too happy to accept his crown. Pity it had been thorned.

"I didn't stand a chance. He was charming and generous, swept me off my feet and into a life I'd always craved. Beautiful house, security, kids." I'm pressing my fingers too hard against each other and I forcibly relax. I can't tell Claire the whole truth, that I'd deliberately targeted Avery in the hope to escape my crappy life. He'd been my way out and thankfully he'd fallen for my ingenuous, deferent act. Still does. I guess it's not his fault I'm tired of acting and putting up with him. "My identity became wrapped up in my kids. They gave my life meaning. A purpose. I kept the perfect home, raised the perfect girls, played the perfect wife. And then they left for college."

I fall silent and Claire prompts, "That's two years ago, right? Just before I arrived in town?"

I nod. "You always had good timing. I was foundering without the girls. And being alone with Avery became...difficult."

Claire's expression is carefully neutral. "How?"

"He became more demanding. In all aspects of our life."

I don't need to elaborate. She'll read between the lines. Though it's not his insatiable sexual appetite that bothers me as much as his never-ending sense of entitlement. Avery Thurston expects the best in life and if he doesn't get it he's a nightmare to live with. The best clothes, the best restaurants, the best service...the best wife. Because that's how he sees me, as an adjunct to his perfect world. If I slip up, I'll be out. That's how he makes me feel. It's no way to live.

I tolerated being an accessory while the girls were home but now that they've gone it's becoming increasingly difficult to pretend I'm happy. I've been faking it for twenty-two years and it's wearing me down. Something has to give and I'm hoping it's not my sanity.

I press my palm to my chest. Like that will help the hollowness that resides beneath my breastbone every single day. "I accommodated him, I still do. I put up with his frequent absences for work, I tolerate him constantly having to bail Ryan out of situations, I act like I'm happy with it all, because my greatest fear is losing him."

There, I've said it and it sounds just as crazy articulated out loud as it does in my head. Because for all his faults, the small, insecure part of me that I thought I'd conquered a long time ago after escaping my past still rears its ugly head, making me want to cling to him despite abhorring him. We're like some strange codependent couple pretending like everything's fine when we know deep down that nothing could be further from the truth.

"I despise him most of the time but I'm afraid of being alone." Which is madness. I know this.

How many women have come through the Help Center after being through horrific traumas and go on to live full, independent lives? I catch myself at times, giving them a stupid trite lecture about conquering their fear of loneliness and being strong and comfortable in their own skin.

I need to practice what I preach. "I don't like quiet. I need to keep busy. I need to be needed, otherwise I'll be left with my thoughts and emotions and I can't face that."

Because there's only one outcome if I acknowledge my innermost thoughts and I don't think I'm ready to leave my life behind as I know it. Not yet. Someday. Possibly sooner rather than later. I don't know when and this self-enforced powerlessness isn't helping.

I'm exhausted by the time I finish talking and Claire radiates sympathy.

"So that's why you constantly throw parties and volunteer alongside work?"

"Yeah. If I stop being busy..." I inhale sharply, my throat tightening. "I might actually realize how utterly miserable I am and want to do something about it."

"I'm going to follow up with Avery but I need to ask you one thing. Was he home last night? And if he wasn't, and if he uses you as an alibi, will you lie for him?"

I've done many things to keep my husband happy, including lying to his smug face. But I'm done. No more.

"After what you've just heard I think you know the answer to that."

Foreboding tiptoes down my spine. I have a feeling my life is about to change irrevocably. For better or worse, I'm not sure.

"He wasn't home until one a.m." I meet her curious gaze dead on, relieved I won't be Avery's patsy any longer. "And I won't lie. Not anymore."

I've been lying to myself for years. Pretending I was okay being raised by a mother who'd checked out emotionally the day my father left us. Pretending I adored Avery for years when in fact he makes me feel second-rate. Pretending I lead the perfect life so I won't end up full circle, alone and poor and pitied.

That's the thing about lies. They eventually come back to bite you on the ass.

"Okay, thanks, you've helped." Claire stands and I do the same. She's about to hug me again when Elly opens the door to my office and enters without being invited.

Her imperious gaze sweeps us both, as if we're guilty of some unspoken crime. "What's all this about Jodi being murdered?"

CHAPTER THIRTY-ONE

ELLY

Ris and Claire gape at me like they've seen a ghost.

Ris is pale, her immaculate makeup doing little to hide the shadows lurking under her eyes. Her silky hair looks like she's dragged her hand through it a hundred times and her ebony pin-striped suit is creased. Claire appears formidable as usual in that police uniform but I glimpse sadness in her eyes, as if she's just imparted bad news to Ris.

When their gawking at me borders on uncomfortable, Claire finally recovers. "How do you know about the murder?"

I roll my eyes and close the door. I don't want other people privy to what I may or may not divulge in the next few minutes.

"The health center was abuzz with the news this morning." I cross the small room to perch on the edge of Ris's desk. It's as tidy and pristine as her house. "She was a patient of ours."

Claire frowns, the grooves between her brows appearing all too quickly. If she's not careful, she'll need Botox sooner rather than later. "But that doesn't mean anything. Details haven't been released yet."

I wave away her concern. I don't need vague cop-speak; I need the truth. "One of the receptionists' boyfriends works with the M.E. Anyway, I'm presuming it's true?"

Claire's lips compress. More lines appear, this time at the corners of her mouth. "I'm not at liberty to discuss the case."

"Then what are you doing here? Having a little catch-up without me?"

Ris flushes, her fingers fiddling with the hem on her skirt, plucking at a loose thread. "Contrary to popular belief, the world doesn't revolve around you, Elly."

I'm stunned at her comeback. Ris is nothing but pleasant and upbeat, always. Today, she looks like she hasn't slept and her eyes have a strange maniacal gleam, like she can't quite fathom that one of the women under her care has been murdered.

"What's going on, Ris? It worries me when you're not your usual Pollyanna self—"

"Fuck off." Ris collapses back onto the sofa, crosses her arms to hug her middle, and pins me with a glare that can freeze the Atlantic.

Claire's gaping mouth matches mine. Ris never swears, ever. Something's going on. I felt the undercurrent the moment I stepped into the room. I don't like being kept out of the loop. It makes me nervous. I don't like being oblivious to what's happening with those closest to me. I don't cope well with secrets other than my own.

"Let me guess, you feel responsible for that girl." I cross the room to sit on a chair at right angles to the sofa. Ris's eyes shift away from me, and focus on a point over my shoulder. "For what it's worth, one of the things I most admire about you is your dedication to helping others, but you can't save the world, Ris, no matter how much you want to."

Ris's head turns slowly toward me, the pain in her glare startling. "Thanks," she murmurs, shooting Claire a frightened glance I have no hope of interpreting.

"We're all in shock, Elly, Ris more than anyone, because Jodi was her client."

I'm used to Claire's short, sharp way of speaking. It's as natural to her as breathing. But she sounds softer today, like she's treading on eggshells around Ris.

"How did she die?"

Ris visibly flinches and Claire shakes her head, disapproval pursing her lips. "You'll read about it in the newspaper like everyone else."

I snort. "It's already online."

Claire huffs out an angry breath, her exasperation palpable. "Why are you here, Elly? Really?"

I can't tell them the truth, that I have my suspicions. So I fake it. I'm used to that.

"Because I care, okay? I may not act like it most of the time but I know Ris had a bond with this girl because of the favor she asked, so I wanted to make sure she was all right."

Claire's in full cop mode—she doesn't need the uniform to do this but when she's in it she's intimidating—and she fixates on my slip up instantly. "What favor?"

"Sorry," I mouth at Ris, who hasn't lost the scared look, before continuing. "Ris asked me to pull strings at the center to get Jodi in to see the best ob-gyn ASAP. So I did."

I still can't figure out why. What was so special about this girl?

"You did that for me?" Claire turns to Ris, her eyebrows raised, her eyes soft and filled with emotion. "Thanks."

"Means little now." Ris sounds bitter and so unlike herself I feel like I've stumbled into some alternate universe.

I'm confused but neither of my friends seems inclined to enlighten me. "Why would Ris organizing an appointment for Jodi have anything to do with you...oh."

I stare at Claire, who's blushing. I get it now and it makes me sadder, knowing that Jodi's death affected both my friends in its own way.

"I'm sorry." I step toward Claire, unsure if she'll accept my hug. She's not usually the touchy-feely type.

She must hear the sincerity in my tone because surprisingly, she allows me to embrace her for a few seconds before stepping back. Ris is staring at me like I've grown another head.

"Look, just because I'm a self-absorbed bitch most of

the time doesn't mean I don't feel bad for my friends," I say, annoyed I have to justify my good behavior.

Then again, I don't do it very often. Be nice, that is. I like playing the badass. I like holding my friends at bay, only letting them get as close as I allow. It helps me justify my appalling behavior when they eventually discover what I've done. Our friendship circle is close. We've been through a lot together and now this, yet another traumatic incident to bind us further.

But it doesn't matter how close we are, when I tell them what I've done, the judgment will come and our friendship will be over. I'm prepared for it. I expect it. It doesn't make it any easier.

I don't want to reinvent myself all over again. But I will have to and it's a risk I'm willing to take. If anyone deserves to know the truth, these women do. Trusting, kind-hearted souls easily taken advantage of.

I should know. I'd once been just like them.

"You're also insightful and incredibly supportive," Ris says, a soft smile curving her lips. "And we love you, even if you don't want us near you half the time."

Claire laughs and I'm glad to hear it. She's been so morose lately. Not that I blame her, with all she's had to deal with. But Ris's declaration gets to me where I fear it most: my impressionable, bruised heart. I love these women too and it's unbearable to contemplate the betrayal they'll feel when I tell them everything.

I swallow to ease the sudden tightening of my throat.

"Who are you and what have you done with my friend Ris? She's never as mouthy as you."

"About time I started, don't you think?" Ris stands and squares her shoulders like she's preparing for battle.

"Yeah," Claire and I answer in unison.

We all glance around, as if seeing each other for the first time.

"Group hug?" I venture, tongue in cheek, yet in less than a second I find myself enveloped by these two women.

We hug each other tight and tears sting my eyes, for all of us and for what is to come.

If only I didn't have to tear their worlds apart when they discover I'm not the person they think I am.

CHAPTER THIRTY-TWO

CLAIRE

Chas, the medical examiner, a career veteran of forty years, confirms what the early responders from forensics thought.

"She was drugged with GHB. Much higher than the standard dose that we normally see from date rapes. So whoever did it wanted to ensure she wouldn't wake up... or was so damn clueless they had no idea about dosages and accidentally gave her an OD."

He consults his clipboard while absentmindedly pushing his glasses up as they slide down the bridge of his nose. "Doesn't look like a manufactured blend. Probably an amateur mixing up batches at home after downloading the recipe off the Internet, so it's not a stretch to assume they didn't understand how to administer the dosage correctly."

I nod and avert my gaze from the huge glass window where Jodi is laid out behind it. I can't look at her, not now. I made that mistake the moment I entered the M.E.'s office and what I saw will haunt me for the rest of my life.

Her stomach is flat.

Jodi doesn't have a small baby bump anymore; the baby is gone, as if he never existed. I almost lose it but manage to fake a cough or two, buying me some time while Chas gets me a cup of water from the dispenser outside his office. I'm okay, as long as I don't look at that awful window and what lies behind it.

"Pressure patterns here and here," Chas says, pointing to

his nose and eye sockets, "indicate she suffocated by having a pillow forcibly held over her face." He tuts. "Thankfully, with the amount of GHB she had in her, she probably wouldn't have realized what was going on."

"So it was quick and painless?"

I have no idea why I ask such a stupid, pointless question but somehow, the idea of Jodi suffering—and in turn her baby—makes me even sadder if that's possible.

Chas nods, as solemn as always. "That amount of GHB would've kicked in pretty quickly. She would've been in a trance-like state and would've thought she was falling asleep."

I like that analogy. I'll remember it whenever the image of Jodi's flat belly pops into my mind. I've been privy to horrific details of torture inflicted by madmen and seen my fair share of gruesome crime scenes over my career, but I know that seeing Jodi lifeless on the M.E.'s slab will haunt me more than anything else.

I clear my throat, determined to gain as much useful information as possible so I can bring her killer to justice. "No defensive wounds? Nothing under her fingernails?"

Chas shakes his head and his glasses slip again. "Nothing. Then again, with that amount of GHB in her system she wouldn't have been able to put up a fight. The team scoured the scene for any traces of hair or fibers but came up blank. Sand on the carpet from the front door to the sofa and back don't tell us much. The composition of the grains matches the sandy path outside Jodi's door."

He pauses, his brow furrowed. "I have to say, I worked in Washington D.C. and New York City for most of my career, and I've never seen such a civilized murder. It's almost like..."

"What?"

"Like the murderer didn't really want to hurt the girl." His gaze drifts to the glass panel before refocusing on me. "In fact, it seems like this person cared. Drugging someone before suffocating them is a mild form of murder." He screws up his nose.

"You know as well as I do that a lot of the depravity we see is born of violence, horrific, bloody murders where the perp has either lost control or has no empathy for the victim. This crime..." he shakes his head "...it's subtle."

Chas's assessment surprises me. I can't see Avery caring about anyone but himself, least of all a girl he may have impregnated during one of his sordid affairs.

Chas taps his pen against his clipboard in an annoying staccato rhythm. "I'd even go as far as to say I think your suspect could be a woman."

I struggle to hide my surprise. Chas only deals in facts so his assumption comes from so far left field it's out of the ballpark.

I have my theory and my motive. Both revolve around Avery. But if what Chas says is true...this case just got a whole lot more complicated.

"Thanks for your help, Chas." I don't shake his hand. I never do, considering what that hand has been cutting into before I arrive and this time it's too close to home. "If you come up with anything else, let me know."

"Sure thing." He does a cutesy salute and turns back to re-enter the autopsy room.

My cue to bolt; I hate that room. I rarely enter it if I have a choice. The pungent smell of formaldehyde makes me light-headed and conjures up memories of every repugnant, macabre corpse I've had the displeasure of seeing.

With Chas's surprising assessment of Jodi's murder bouncing in my head, I'm back at the station in ten minutes. Avery should arrive in another five.

Gledhill citizens come into the police station for a variety of reasons, most of them not nefarious. Witnessing of legal documents. Reporting of minor misdemeanors. Neighborhood disputes. So Avery entering the station won't be big news. What I have to ask him will be, so I've reserved an interrogation room.

Thankfully, Ron is happy for me to run with my theory while he chases up Jodi's last movements in the city for possible leads there. I've convinced him I'm one hundred percent better and work focused.

If he only knew.

I'm grateful that Ris won't mention my possible adoption of Jodi's baby if anyone else from the department questions her. Not that they will. I'm the senior officer on the case and I'm grateful I can control the situation. But with the clock ticking I need answers and I'm convinced Avery can provide them.

He arrives seven minutes late, as if to prove that his time is more valuable than mine. Asshole.

I greet him at the front desk, eager to whisk him away and begin. "Thanks for coming in, Avery."

"Anything for you, C.C. You know that."

He has the kind of voice that most women would love: deep, resonant, with just a hint of naughtiness. It's that hint that riles me. Ris is a wonderful woman, and while I have no idea if Avery's unfaithful or not, she certainly hinted at it earlier. She doesn't deserve a philandering husband whose practiced charm tends to fool most people.

If he is responsible for getting Jodi pregnant, I can only imagine the lengths he would go to in order to protect his precious image.

I wait until the door is closed before gesturing at a chair. "Take a seat and we'll get started."

He appears completely unfazed by being called in for questioning. Either it's more of that supreme arrogance or he's a damn good actor.

"Are you going to handcuff me when we *get started*?"

His innuendo makes me feel sick. He's always like this with me, with Ris's friends, usually in front of her, as if trying to prove he's man enough to attract any woman he wants. I know now why she tolerates it, but for me, I've never liked the sleaze. I pity Ris, keeping up appearances of her perfect life, despising her husband but not willing to leave for fear of being alone. It's sad because she's accomplished and warm and the kindest woman I know. She would thrive on her own if she dumped this jerk.

He grins as he takes a seat and interlocks his hands behind his head. His legs are outstretched, ankles crossed. He's totally at ease and his confidence sows the first seed of doubt. If he were guilty would he be this relaxed, this nonchalant?

So I decide to rattle him.

"Cut the bullshit, Avery. You're here for one reason only." I brace my hands on the table in front of him and lean over, trying to intimidate. "I need you to take a paternity test."

I watch for the slightest tell. Widening of pupils. Beating of veins. Twitch of lips. Clenching of jaw.

Nothing.

The man's either an amazing actor or he's innocent.

"Why?" He smirks, his gaze sliding up and down my body in a slow, deliberate perusal that only angers me. "Wouldn't you and I have to do the good stuff first before we do a test like that?"

He never quits with the bullshit flirting. I thought he only did it at social gatherings to try and impress his friends or tease Ris. Now I know better. The guy's a liar and a cheat, if my theory about his connection to Jodi is right. He can't help himself. The flirting is his thing. He can't turn it off.

Annoyed that I can't fluster him, I aim for bluntness again. "Have you ever met Jodi Van Gelder?"

He frowns, like he can't place the name. "You mean that girl my wife rescued when she turned up at our house?"

"That's the one. Have you ever met her?"

"Never."

He doesn't hesitate and his emphatic response resonates. But I continue to push.

"Seems odd then, that the first thing she does when she gets to town is research you at the library."

One eyebrow raises a fraction at that. "Me? Are you sure?"

"I wouldn't waste my breath saying it if I wasn't."

He feigns bafflement. It has to be fake. I can't accept the possibility he may not have anything to do with this. As long as Avery is my primary suspect I don't have to remember my first theory, that Dane is somehow involved.

"Look, C.C.—"

"It's Claire, asshole," I snap, immediately regretting my outburst when a slow, self-righteous smile creeps across his face. He called me the stupid nickname the first time Ris introduced us and I voiced my disapproval. He's persisted with it ever since.

"Fine, *C.C.*" His grin widens as I resist the urge to slug him again. "I don't know this girl. Never met her."

"So you won't object to taking a paternity test then?"

"I object, but I assume it's pointless? That you'll file some trumped-up charge, get a court order, and I'll end up having to do it regardless?"

Now it's my turn to smirk. "Something like that."

"In that case, I'll do it." He shrugs, as if presenting DNA for implication in a possible murder means nothing. "I'm a busy man. I run one of the biggest pharmaceutical companies on the eastern seaboard. So let's get this over with."

He stands so quickly I jump, annoyed by his sudden move that I shove the table hard into his thighs. He doesn't even flinch.

I'm surprised and a little uneasy he's agreed so fast. "We'll do the test now and expedite results, so don't leave town."

The first chink in his indifferent armor appears; his fingers inadvertently flex, like he's trying to grab hold of something. "Are you actually trying to tie me to this unsavory business?"

I nod, glad his impenetrable façade is wavering. "I'm trying to solve a murder and considering we suspect Jodi only came to Gledhill to tell her baby's father the news, and the first person she searches for is you, we're exploring all possibilities."

He's shaken, finally. I see it in the nervous fiddle as his fingers adjust the cuff of his coat. "Let me get this straight. You think I didn't want the baby so I killed her?"

I shrug, like accusing my best friend's husband of murder is something I do every day. "Something like that."

His lips thin and his eyes turn mean. "Let's get this paternity test done."

He doesn't wait for me to open the door. He storms out without looking back.

I usually have a gut feeling about suspects but I didn't get a true read on Avery. It bothers me as much as his willingness to provide a saliva sample.

Something's not right here.

I'm hoping it's not my theory.

CHAPTER THIRTY-THREE

ELLY

As if this bizarre day can't get any stranger, my lover turns up at the medical center.

I've seen him around here before but we don't interact beyond a casual greeting. In private he deliberately teases me for working such a menial job, when he knows how much I love it. We're the number one center in the Hamptons. Excellent doctors, experienced specialists, with a separate cosmetic surgery wing for the many procedures booked months in advance. We're high profile and I manage the entire place. I'm proud of the way I have everything running smoothly.

I'm also suspicious. Why is he here? We're never seen in public together. He gets off on the illicitness, I can't afford to hurt my friend by us being sighted. Though if we were spotted out and about, no one would suspect a thing. We're friends, of sorts. So the fact he's hovering in the doorway of my office, looking edgy and glancing over his shoulder, is a big deal.

I muster my best dazzling smile, the one he likes because he thinks he's made my day just by being in it. Men are idiots. "What are you doing here?"

He doesn't return my smile. In fact, he hasn't done his usual leer after checking me out, the first thing he does whenever we meet. I like it. Not from a sexual viewpoint but because every time he treats me like some object he owns, I know I hold the power.

My ex had never objectified me. He'd been sweet and loving and attentive. He'd made me fall head over heels and trust him implicitly. Making his ruse all the harder to stomach when I discovered the truth. These days, I prefer cocky and charming. I can control men like that.

I don't ever want to be emotionally sucker-punched again.

His gaze is darting around and combined with the fact he's shown up here, something's not right. He steps into my office and closes the door. "I came to see you."

"Really?" I can't hide my surprise. He likes sassy so I fire a comeback to test him. "That's a first."

He doesn't respond with a smart-ass remark and I realize something even more startling. He's nervous. He's fidgeting with his cuffs, tugging on the end of his tie, smoothing his jacket. I can almost see the wheels turning in his head as he tries to find the right words to explain why he's here.

Finally, he halts in front of my desk, his expression apologetic. "I can't do this anymore."

I feel like he's driven a stake through my heart, the pain is that swift, that intense. In all the warped scenarios of how our affair ends, this isn't one of them. I'm the one in control. I hold all the power. I've envisioned dragging him along for another week, then dumping him. Revealing the truth and making him feel the pain he so carelessly inflicts on other people; especially his poor unsuspecting wife.

Since my golden life disintegrated I've had to reinvent myself. Once I'd taken care of the physical transformation— I'd had some nonintrusive cosmetic work done on my face and invested a sizable chunk of my settlement on a designer wardrobe—I'd assumed a role, becoming a honeytrap for cheating men.

When I messed with their heads, I felt like I was messing with my ex.

When I screwed them over then dumped them, I was dumping my ex.

When I forced their hands and insisted they tell their wives the truth, I felt like I was doing their wives a favor, giving them the gift of honesty that I never got.

With my lover, it has been different. I have allowed myself to feel *something* and while the end is inevitable, having the power yanked out of my hands is unpalatable.

I'd planned on giving my friend the greatest gift any woman can receive when living a lie she doesn't know: freedom. She deserves better than this asshole. She means too much to me.

The end has been coming because I can't go on like this. I'd planned on instigating steps shortly, so in all my imagined scenarios of how we'd end, this isn't one of them. This is plain wrong. I need to gain the ascendancy and take back control. I stand and move around the desk, close enough to touch him if I want. I don't.

"What do you mean?" I sound blasé, like I don't give a crap. But I do. I want to end this my way.

He doesn't react to my offhand tone. He stares straight ahead and I've never been so grateful not to have a glass-walled office. We don't need prying eyes for this final confrontation.

He rubs the back of his neck, another nervous tell that's uncharacteristic, before finally facing me. "What if I end my marriage so I can be with you?"

The bottom drops out of my stomach and my palms grow clammy. I feel light-headed, woozy, like all the air has been sucked from the room.

When we started up, this was never my endgame.

I remember our first time together so clearly. He asked me to meet him at his office in the city, giving some vague excuse that it would benefit both our careers. I knew it was BS. But I wanted to see how far he'd go, if his flirting to that point was all bluff.

Like the others, I had no intention of sleeping with him. So I'd worn a sedate mid-calf pale blue sheath and hit record on my cell before entering his office. But my lover was different from all the rest. Because of my friendship with his wife we'd social-ized together and I'd been privy to how charming he could be. I felt like I knew him and a small part of me liked him. When I'd gone to his office that day I'd hoped he wouldn't put the moves on me, proving himself different from all the rest.

For a brief time, I thought he was. He'd made me a drink and we'd chatted about our respective jobs, money, and where we'd like to be in five years. That's when it happened. He mentioned something about a hotshot investment banker in Chicago who turned everything to gold if I was interested, and I knew, I just knew, he was talking about my ex-husband.

Inexplicably, tears had filled my eyes, he'd comforted me and somehow we'd ended up having sex. It should never have happened, but when he held me afterward, it was the first time since the rape that I felt halfway human. I thought it would be a one-off considering my connection with his wife. A connection I would exploit when the time came for her to know the truth. However, as we became firmer friends I struggled with my con-science. With the other guys I'd targeted for vengeance I hadn't been close to their wives. It had been easier to tear their lives apart in the name of helping those unsuspecting women when I didn't know them.

But I had second thoughts with my lover, considering his wife was so nice. I held him at arm's length after that time in his office but he pursued me relentlessly and I eventually gave in. I justified my capitulation as doing my friend the ultimate favor. That she may even thank me when the time came. Totally warped logic, I know, because she'll hate me for lying to her just as much as she'll hate her husband.

But I can't help it. This is who I am these days, some kind of black widow who can't stop the crusade. I need to ruin the lives of all the cheating, lying bastards who lead duplicitous lives.

Now that my lover wants to make our arrangement public, I'm flabbergasted. I don't need a full-time man in my life. I don't want him. His lies and unfaithfulness toward his wife make my skin crawl while a small part of me wants to run into his arms and be held. I need to play this smart.

"You're serious?" I wave my hand between us, and the sapphire ring he gave me as a present for my last birthday catches the light. "You want us to be together?"

"Yes." His response is instant, no hesitation, bold and confident, so like him. "It's time."

None of this makes sense, but I find myself asking, "Why now?"

My heart's beating erratically, making me slightly breathless. Something's not right and I need to find out what the hell he's playing at.

"Because my marriage has been over for a long time." He shrugs, like exchanging vows means nothing. "Because I'm tired of the hiding and leading a double life."

He takes my hand and stares into my eyes. I've seen many emotions in those eyes before. Desire. Lust. Ownership. Passion. Candor is rare and it disarms me more than his words. "I've never done this before with anyone else so I knew that once we started up it would lead to this moment."

I gape, the implication behind his declaration so startling I can barely comprehend it. I want to laugh, it's so outlandish, but with him staring at me with absolute sincerity it's hard to doubt him.

"I don't want to be the guy that lies anymore." He squeezes my hand, like a simple touch will convince me. "I want to be your guy. If you'll have me."

A host of responses, both suitable and otherwise, whir through my head, pinging off my skull like corn kernels in hot oil: random and haphazard and potentially dangerous. I should cut him down in response but I don't. I'm flummoxed.

So I settle for honesty. "I don't know what to say."

I see the shutters lower, as if I've wounded him. "You've never thought about it? You and me as a real couple?"

As if. My motives may be warped but I'm not stupid.

Why the hell would I trade one deceitful, cheating asshole for another?

So I do what he's done often enough: I lie. "I may have thought about it but only in that vague, nebulous way of 'this will never happen.'"

The slightest frown does little to detract from his mesmerizing good looks. "Why not?"

"Because your wife is one of my friends, for a start," I snap, annoyed by his obtuseness. "How can we ever be together in Gledhill without people hating us? She's well known around here. Our names would be mud."

It's an excuse he'll accept because he needs to be liked. He walks into a room and commands attention like it's his God-given right. He couldn't imagine being hated.

"We wouldn't live here." He releases my hand, like I've hurt him with my logical questions. "We could live in the city, anywhere, really. Our jobs are transferable."

"You've thought this all out, haven't you?"

I sound shrewish, and he's not happy. He's lost the edginess but his gaze keeps darting around, as if looking for an escape route.

He paces a few steps, stops, and grabs my upper arms so I can't move. "I'm not good with words, never have been. But I love you, Elly. I want us to be together. Say yes."

He's insane and for an absurd moment I'm tempted to blurt the truth, to tell him why I'd allowed him to touch me in the first place, that I'm broken inside and seeking comfort, that this has been about revenge and tearing his life apart, once his wife learns the truth.

He doesn't care that I haven't responded and continues. "If you say yes, I'm leaving my wife at the end of the week. It'll take that long for me to pack my things and organize my finances so there's no mess."

He's delusional. Of course there'll be mess when he leaves his wife, most of it landing on my head.

When I don't answer, his fingers dig harder into my arms. "I love you. I want you. Please..."

The frantic edge to his plea shocks me more than his declaration. He never asks anyone for anything. He demands it. He gets it. So why is he here, trying to sway me with empty promises? He likes being married. I see it in the way he parades his wife around like arm candy, how he dotes on her, how proud he is of her. He would never leave her voluntarily. His declaration is unorthodox, suspicious, and an outright fabrication. Why? Why now?

As I ponder a way to extract myself from this bizarre situation he misreads my head tilt for a nod and swoops in for a searing kiss.

"Stop." I try to push him away but he ignores me, kissing his way along my jaw, toward my ear, where he whispers, "There's just one thing..."

CHAPTER THIRTY-FOUR

CLAIRE

As I wait for the results of Avery's paternity test the next morning I follow up on routine stuff that I'd already delegated to other officers but want to recheck in the name of thoroughness. I do this if I don't have a solid theory, like checking CCTV footage to see who left Gledhill in the early hours of the morning after Jodi was killed. With The Rise on the outskirts of town, whoever visited the area would've been picked up by the cameras dotted through town and along the highway.

The coroner has given me a rough timeline: time of death had been around eleven-thirty so I start scanning license plates from eleven onward, something a junior officer has already done but I want to see for myself. Not many people leave town in the middle of the night so it doesn't take me long to scan the footage. It's short, but not so sweet.

Because one license plate leaps out at me, exiting Gledhill just after midnight and re-entering town around five forty-five a.m.

My husband's car.

I blink, rub my eyes, and refocus. It doesn't change facts. Dane, who told me he slept in his car at the beach that night he never came home, lied.

And his movements fit the opportunistic window.

He could have a perfectly logical explanation. He'd wanted to drive around to work off his anger toward me after my slip up with Griffin. But if that was the case, why lie? He'd told me he'd driven around for a while after he stormed out, then he'd slept in his car. But the CCTV footage indicates otherwise and with that timeline he would've barely had enough time to reach the city, spend five minutes there, before turning back for home.

It doesn't make sense. Why would Dane have to make a sudden trip to the city yet not stick around?

I don't like mysteries and I hate them when they involve people I care about. I can't shake the feeling I may have stumbled upon something life-changing when I've had to deal with enough crap lately.

I check my computer for the umpteenth time in the last half hour. Paternity test results still aren't through.

"Damn." I thump my desk, garnering several raised eyebrows from the cops around me, and I hold my hand up in apology.

I need to do something. I can't sit here and feign concentration when all I can think about is Dane lying to me.

I need answers.

Starting now.

I fire off a quick text to him, asking him to meet me at home. Thankfully, he's working locally in East Hampton today.

It will be the first time I've seen him since Jodi's murder. When I'd called him after arriving back at the station direct from the scene he'd already been on the road, heading into the city. He sounded gutted when I told him about Jodi and the baby, asking inane questions like "But how? When? Where? Who would do such a thing?" but now I wonder: Had it been an act? Had he already known?

I can't believe I suspect my husband of being complicit in a murder. This is the man who nursed me after a nasty bout of the flu, who held my hair back from my face when I had a bad stomach bug, who cuddled me for hours when I sobbed after hearing the news of our infertility. He's been nothing but gentle and loving and supportive all the years I've known him.

Except recently... when he overreacted and punched holes in our wall...

I make it home in fifteen minutes. He walks in the door five minutes later.

"Hey, honey, how are you holding up?" He envelops me in a hug, the kind I crave. I'd usually snuggle in, marveling at how well we fit when my arms slide around his waist. Today, I'm stiff and unyielding. He notices.

"You're not okay," he says, releasing me and heading for the fridge. "Drink?"

"No, thanks."

He pulls out a beer and my eyebrows shoot skyward. He only glances at me after he takes the cap off, equal parts furtive and guilty.

"Don't judge me. I need this." He raises the bottle in my direction before taking a deep slug, his throat moving convulsively as he swallows like a thirsty man having his first drink in days.

Speechless at this uncharacteristic display, and increasingly worried by his erratic behavior, I wait. When the bottle's half empty, he lowers it.

"I need to tell you something and you're not going to like it." He crosses the kitchen, grabs a chair, and turns it around so he's sitting backward on it, facing me. "It's big, Claire, and I don't know whether you'll forgive me."

I've never had asthma but in that moment I feel the tubes in my chest constricting, the air wheezing through, as I struggle for my next breath.

"What did you do?"

Four simple words that could potentially lead to a complicated answer I'm terrified to hear.

"The other night, when I said I slept at the beach, I lied." He lowers his gaze to the beer bottle in his hand, where he's picking at the label. "I've lied about a lot of things lately."

Oh my God. My husband has just admitted to telling

countless lies. He's about to confess. I don't speak. I can't. My mouth is dry, like I have the hangover to end all hangovers, and my throat is so tight I can barely breathe. I'm shaking as I sit and brace for whatever horrors he's about to reveal.

"Remember when Beau called me at the garden party freaking out? And then kept calling and leaving messages on our answering machine?"

I nod, still not trusting myself to say a word.

"He helped me do something I'm not proud of, but I thought it was necessary at the time." He raised his eyes to meet mine, beseeching me to understand.

How can I, when I have no idea where this is going? Unless Dane had enlisted Beau's help to get rid of Jodi?

God, the stress is getting to me, my logical brain deserting me, replaced by an overactive imagination conjuring up all sorts of crazy.

"I need to show you something first, then I'll explain." He fishes a folded piece of paper out of his top pocket and hands it to me.

My hands are trembling so when I open it the paper rattles.

It's a sperm count test.

With my husband's name on it.

I have no idea why he's doing this. I already know the results and will have to live with the consequences.

"Why are you giving me this?"

"Read it," he says, his tone rough and tinged with fear.

Foreboding makes my stomach gripe as I scan the results, my heart flip-flopping and my pulse racing. My lungs constrict to the point I'm dragging in deeper breaths so I don't pass out. I'm woozy, gripping the paper so hard it crinkles.

"I don't get it." I blink several times and stare at the results but they don't change.

My previously infertile husband turns out to be extremely fertile.

Confusion wars with outrage as I wave the paper at him. "What the—?"

"I faked the test."

He sounds so anguished I should feel sorry for him.

All I feel is soul-destroying rage.

He *faked* the test? What does that even mean? I can't fathom the logistics of doing such a despicable thing, let alone contemplate his rationale. This nightmare we've been living through since we discovered his infertility has been manufactured, by him?

I'm dumbfounded. Completely bewildered and utterly destroyed.

Fury constricts my throat, but I manage to squeeze out, "Why?"

He flinches at the sound of that one word, more a screech, and clasps his hands together in front like he's about to deliver a sermon. Though I know there'll be nothing remotely pious about his revelation.

"Because my father had Huntington's and I don't ever want to pass that on to a kid of mine."

This is the start. The lies will start tumbling one after another like dominoes, until I realize the man I thought I knew implicitly I might not know at all.

I clutch the damning test results so hard it crumples into a ball and I fling it away in disgust. "You told me your father's dead."

"He is." His eyes beseech me to understand. I can't. I'm shocked to my core. "The Huntington's disease manifested in his late thirties, he died two decades later."

I do a quick calculation. "So he was alive when we first met?"

He nods, hangs his head in shame. "It's an autosomal dominant disorder, which means I may still manifest in my forties, and I didn't want that to stop us getting together."

"Oh my God." I stand so abruptly I bang my knee on the

table leg. I barely register the pain. "Is anything you've ever told me the truth?"

That's rich coming from me, considering I've never told him I cheated. I should. Maybe I will. But for now I can't comprehend he's lied to me about something so significant, something that impacts the rest of our lives.

"I love you. Always have, always will, that'll never change." The beer label is now shredded and his eyes are bright with unshed tears. "I saw what Huntington's did to my dad. I could never handle a child of mine going through that, knowing it was my fault."

My heart breaks a little but I continue. "Why didn't you tell me? Why lie?"

The reality of Beau's involvement in this farce crashes over me, making me sick to my stomach. "Beau's infertile, isn't he? You used his sperm for the fertility test."

Dane blinks rapidly but it can't disguise the disgust. I know the feeling. "Yes. He didn't want to do it but he understands the ramifications if I have a child. But he started freaking out, feeling guilty, and said I had to tell you the truth or he would."

"So that's why you were so focused on adoption from the start and pushing me when I wasn't so amenable," I spit out, my venom-laced words peppering him like shrapnel. I half expect to see him duck.

He stands too but is wise enough not to approach me. "I want a family with you, Claire, I always have. But I can't take the risk of fathering a child, so before we started trying I enrolled in a well-known program for the male contraceptive injection in the city. Its efficacy is amazing but the drug would've been detected in a test and I couldn't take that risk—"

"Do you have any fucking idea what I've gone through this past year, believing I was a failure somehow because I couldn't get pregnant? *Do you?*" I yell, my legs trembling to the point of giving way. "And all that time you could've fathered ten kids if you wanted to."

That's the moment the remainder of my shattered world implodes.

What if my lying husband had an affair? Or a one-night stand?

What if that girl got pregnant, then turned up here, and told him?

How far would he go to ensure that child was never born?

I run to the toilet and retch, my gut heaving until there's nothing left. Even then I can't stop. This time, he doesn't hold my hair back. I'm reeling in a world completely out of control. My head's spinning, my eyes are blurred, my mouth filled with acid.

I stumble to the bathroom, rinse my mouth out, and brush my teeth. When I straighten from the basin, he's holding out a glass of water. I take it. Drink it. Resist the urge to smash the glass in his face. I lean against the handbasin for support, scared my legs will give out for real this time.

My throat is dry, raspy, but I manage to get the words out.

"I need you to take a paternity test."

CHAPTER THIRTY-FIVE

MARISA

It's no secret to those who know me best that when the going gets tough, I organize a party. It's my coping mechanism, a way to instill happiness to chase away the pain. It's what I've always done.

I've thrown a hell of a lot of parties in my lifetime.

But the last thing I feel like doing after Jodi's death is socialize, but Avery leaves me no choice. He insists we have an intimate gathering for our twenty-first wedding anniversary. I know why. He has a mega deal in the pipeline so it's all for show. He'll post the evidence of his perfect life on social media and leak snippets to the gossip columns in the newspapers, solidifying his position for whatever deal is going down.

He may not have known Jodi but I did and he should be sympathizing with me. His callous disregard makes it entirely possible that my husband fathered a bastard and then killed the mother. It makes me sick to my stomach.

But I don't want to alert him anything's wrong, especially with Claire investigating, so I pretend to be the cooperative wife as always. I call the caterers, hire a drinks waiter, order premixed cocktails. Once that's done I contact a local party planner to do the decorations and I organize a local beauty consultant to come to the house and do my hair and makeup.

I want to look spectacular for my twenty-first wedding anniversary so he won't suspect a thing. With a little luck, it will be my last party.

I'm keeping the guest list deliberately small. Ryan and Maggie, and close friends only. Claire and Elly might think it's odd, me throwing a party so soon after Jodi's death, but they'll understand. They get me like few other people do.

I glance in the mirror, pleased with how I look. Fancy updo akin to a French roll, smoky eye makeup in a rich navy to complement my satin fifties-style dress in the same color. Crimson lips. Highlighted cheekbones. Sapphires, a gift from Avery for our anniversary last year, glittering at my ears and neck.

I look good: a woman in control. When nothing can be further from the truth. But no one knows. All they'll see tonight is a glamorous forty-something woman who's the perfect wife paying tribute to her handsome husband.

If they only knew.

Avery is already downstairs, greeting guests. I hear his booming laugh, his jovial effusiveness. Forever the actor, trying to convince everyone he's bigger and better in all aspects of his life. I inwardly cringe. But I join him, making a grand entrance down the stairs as Claire and Dane walk in.

There's something drastically wrong. She looks shell-shocked; he looks gutted. Claire is sporting a pallor no amount of foundation or blush can hide. She's wearing an old black pantsuit, channeling a tux, I've seen many times before. That in itself is a giveaway of her state of mind because for all her toughness, when she sheds her uniform she loves dressing up for my parties.

Dane isn't much better. He's wearing a crumpled beige suit, an open-necked ivory shirt, and mismatched brown shoes. But it's his expression, like he's been through a war zone and come out on the other side that makes me want to hug him.

Dealing with Jodi's death can't be easy on them. They lost the baby they never had and it must feel like they're grieving all over again.

"C.C., looking gorgeous as usual." Avery steps in close to

kiss Claire's cheek and she sidesteps, treading on his toes in the process.

Dane's fists are clenched. He looks ready to deck my husband. Is Avery so self-absorbed and dense he can't see these two are on the edge?

I rush forward, needing to defuse the situation before it gets worse. "Thanks for coming, you two."

I slip an arm around each of their shoulders and subtly guide them away from Avery.

Claire leans in to whisper in my ear, "I only made an effort to come tonight because I know how hard it must be for you to celebrate your anniversary after all that stuff you told me about your marriage."

My chest tightens at her thoughtfulness as I murmur, "Thanks, I appreciate it."

Dane stares straight ahead like he's oblivious to everything and when we reach the glass-enclosed conservatory where I'm having the party tonight, Claire says, "We can't stay long. I'm expecting test results at work and it's important."

Dane stiffens, and when I cast him a sideways glance, his jaw is clenched so tight it juts out.

"Stay as long as you like, we're not doing a formal sit-down, just finger food and drinks." I gesture at the waiter. "What would you like?"

Both order soda with a twist of lemon but I don't say a word. I sense they're brittle, like the slightest thing might shatter them, so I kiss each of them on the cheek and drift away.

Elly enters the conservatory at that moment and I'm struck yet again by how beautiful she is. Avery's hovering nearby, moving between guests, the consummate performer. He abandoned his plans to work in the city and has been home instead, driving me nuts. I even threatened to leave at one point—an idle threat, we both know it—and he flipped, saying he's been under great stress at work, about a possible merger with the biggest pharmaceutical company in the world and needs me more than ever.

Apparently we have to host some of the international delegates over the next few weeks, a big splashy dinner party for the CEOs from France, Germany, Singapore, and Sydney. I'm so pathetic that I can't help but feel flattered that he needs me, the trophy wife who throws the best parties. What's flattering about that?

I watch him brush a lingering kiss on Elly's cheek and she recoils slightly. Avery's like a cat: he seems to pick the women who don't like him and makes a beeline for them. He consistently makes it a point to talk to Elly at my parties because he senses she's oblivious to his charms. Smart girl. He strides to the makeshift stage where the quartet I hired has set up.

He picks up a microphone, turns it on, and taps it. No feedback. Like everything else he touches, it works fine; for a time.

"If I can have your attention, please?"

Thirteen pairs of eyes, including mine, focus on him. I have to admit he looks spectacular in a charcoal dinner suit and white shirt, his tie matching my dress. He's the epitome of a successful man and knows it.

"I'd like to invite my darling wife up here."

I freeze. I hate the spotlight and he knows it. But he continues to beam at me and beckon so I'm left no choice but to cross the conservatory and stand by his side.

"We'd like to thank you all for coming to celebrate our twenty-first wedding anniversary." He slips his arm around my waist, holding on tight, like he expects me to bolt. I wish. "All of you have touched our lives in some way and we couldn't be more grateful."

He stares down at me and I can almost believe there's genuine love radiating from his eyes.

"I love you, Ris. You've been my rock since we met." He grins and taps the end of my nose. "You are my world."

I'm stunned by his effusiveness and a tad embarrassed it's in front of others but manage a weak smile.

He returns my smile, his bold and confident as usual. "I know I'm a selfish, demanding asshole at times, so what I'm trying to say is you're the best thing that ever happened to me and I appreciate you, even if I have a funny way of showing it sometimes."

To my mortification, tears fill my eyes and a few trickle down my cheeks, when I once vowed to never cry over this man again.

"Ryan, come on up here too."

My brother-in-law, who has been hanging around Maggie and Elly as they chat, appears startled for a moment before bounding toward us. He's always like this, filled with exuberance and zest for life that often leaves me feeling exhausted.

When he reaches us, Avery grins and claps him on the back. "As most of you know, this guy has been the bane of my existence since he was born and stole the limelight from me. He's shadowed me, he's bugged me, sometimes I think he wants to be me."

A polite ripple of laughter filters through the room.

"I'm his go-to guy, always have been, which is why he asked me to make this announcement rather than him doing the honors."

Ryan elbows Avery and there's more laughter before my husband lifts the microphone to his mouth. "Maggie, apparently this doofus you married wants to renew his vows with you, so we're hosting a celebration for you next week, the biggest shindig this town has ever seen."

I'm furious Avery hasn't asked me if it's okay we host a party for Ryan and Maggie but I can't say anything now, not after his public declaration of love. The announcement is obviously a surprise for Maggie too but she appears pleased, her peach matte lips curving into a shy smile.

"Go give your wife a smooch," Avery says, bumping Ryan with his hip.

I hear applause as Avery sweeps me into his arms and plants

a resounding kiss on my lips. When he releases me, I see two things that capture my attention.

Claire and Dane are storming out.

Elly is standing stock-still, oblivious to the broken wine glass in her hand, the stem snapped clean in two.

CHAPTER THIRTY-SIX

CLAIRE

"I need to get this, it's urgent," I say, my cell vibrating in the pocket of my black satin jacket. It'll be the test results.

Avery's paternity test, that is. My husband refuses to take one.

"Can't you leave work alone for one frigging night?" He scowls as he follows me to the foyer.

"This is important." I glare at him, waiting until he steps away a few feet before checking the text from Ron.

I'm stunned as I read it. Because the primary theory I have regarding Jodi's murder has been blown to pieces.

Avery isn't the father of Jodi's baby.

"What's wrong?"

He's by my side in an instant, the solicitous husband once again and nothing like the madman who'd flung his beer bottle against the bathroom mirror when I'd asked him to take a paternity test.

I can't be around him anymore without seeing his rage, twice now. He explained the rationale behind his explosions. He's worried because mood instability and depression can be the first signs of Huntington's, so I pretend to forgive him.

But our marriage is in trouble and we both know it. His lies have ruined everything. And with Avery's paternity test coming back negative, if he's not the father of Jodi's baby, who is?

Dane can father a child.

Dane can't risk bringing a child into this world.

What is he capable of if he accidentally got a woman pregnant?

"We need to get out of here." Fear makes my voice rise as I slip my cell back into my pocket. "I can't sit through one of Ris's interminable parties while Jodi's case is unsolved."

I throw it out there, deliberately baiting him. He doesn't react. My fear escalates to a bone-deep dread that I won't like what I discover as I continue to delve into this murder.

"She's your best friend and it's her anniversary." He shakes his head, judging me when he has no right. "After all she's done for us...did for us," he quickly amends, seeing my stricken expression. "It's the least we can do."

"Ris tried to facilitate an adoption for us, it doesn't mean we owe her anything."

I don't mean it. I'm randomly flinging words out because I'm shaken. I need to escape, head home where I can have some quiet time to think and formulate some alternate scenarios to figure out Jodi's killer.

I was convinced Avery would be the father of Jodi's baby. It all fit so nicely. His propensity for affairs, his time spent in the city for work. He'd told me he had an alibi for the night in question but I'd wanted to wait for the paternity test results before blowing his alibi sky-high too.

Now, I have nothing. Nothing but a suspect I don't want to interrogate standing right in front of me.

"Have you ever cheated on me?"

It's the question I've been dying to ask since I discovered he could've fathered Jodi's baby, but have been too afraid of the answer.

He staggers back, his eyes wide, like I've stabbed him. "Never."

He doesn't add, "I'm not you," though we both know that aborted kiss with Griffin was an aberration rather than the norm for me. At least, it has been since we've been married.

My conscience screams "hypocrite!" considering what I'd done before we'd walked up the aisle.

"I'm not implying with Jodi, I mean any time."

That's not what I mean and he knows it.

"Claire, I've never loved any woman but you. I wouldn't have gone through so much to have you in my life otherwise." He drags a shaky hand through his hair and it spikes up in the endearing way I love. "I'm not proud of the lengths I went to with the fertility test. And I get that my lies have potentially ruined us. I understand that you hate me right now. That you think I'm some kind of monster."

He takes a few steps forward, bringing him within touching distance if I'm so inclined. I'm not.

"But this is *me*, the guy who adores you. I would never do anything to hurt you." He glances away, his expression pained, before he eyeballs me again. "And I certainly didn't hurt that girl the way you think I did."

I burst into tears, of relief or disbelief, I don't know. He's instantly there, enveloping me in his arms, holding me tight, comforting me.

It should be enough for now.

It's not.

CHAPTER THIRTY-SEVEN

ELLY

I'm a consummate actress. I nibble on delicious salmon sushi and shrimp wontons, sipping my champagne like it's nectar from the gods. While inside, I'm a seething mess.

My lover is here with his wife. She won't be for much longer, not after I tell her everything. He seems to be comforting her. Always hovering, always attentive. He touches the small of my back as he passes once, as if to say "trust me."

Yeah, right. He's a lying, cheating bastard and is about to get his comeuppance.

It's clear to me why he came to the medical center and gave me that spiel about how much he loves me and about leaving his wife. He thought I'd believe his crap. He thought I'd bend to his will.

When I didn't, he blackmailed me into a horrendous breach I could lose everything over.

The kicker is, for a scant second when he'd been painting our rosy future I'd contemplated laying aside my retribution at all mankind and having another kind of life. The life I'd once dreamed of, before I'd been duped so badly. I'd envisioned having it all. The luxurious house, the sports car, the massive portfolio, the handsome husband. I'd built up an entire dream scenario in my head. Me, the woman who never wants to get married ever again, who's abhorred the institution ever since I discovered mine had been a ludicrous farce.

I'd momentarily pictured myself in a white dress, a slinky satin number with a fishtail skirt, holding lilies tied with a crimson bow. My hair would be loose, curled to perfection, and my lover would be waiting for me at the end of an aisle, tears in his eyes.

Now, there'll be tears for sure.

Thankfully, I hadn't lost control of my faculties and had told him where he could stick his happily-ever-after fantasy. That's when he turned nasty, leaving me no option but to do his dirty work.

Ultimately, I did what he asked because he threatened me. Because this no-good son of a bitch said he'd tell everyone all about me.

He knew.

Everything.

About my marriage, my partial breakdown, my humiliation.

He'd hired a PI and uncovered my demons. So the bastard had blackmailed me and I'd had no choice. I don't mind everyone knowing about my affair: my life in Gledhill is over once they find that out anyway. But falling prey to bigamy, my resultant breakdown and giving up my baby is information I want to keep secret.

Because I don't need Ris and Claire's pity.

I'd rather they hate me for the affair, I don't want them grabbing at any excuse to forgive my shoddy behavior. I deserve to suffer.

As will my lover. Come the end of this party, I'm going to deliver my vengeance and it isn't going to be pretty.

I bide my time. Making small talk. Watching him. He stays close to his wife. She seems rattled. She ain't seen nothing yet. I wait until the last guests leave. By this time, my fury has swelled to monstrous proportions. But I channel it. No point giving him any idea of what's about to unfold.

He blindsided me at work today and for the first time in a long time I felt fear, the kind of soul-sucking anxiety that everything I've worked so hard for can be taken away. By *him*. I can't believe I'd been so foolish as to let him in a little, to actually feel something. He's just like all the rest, only out for what they can get, oblivious to the hurt and havoc they wreak. I'm glad he likes surprises, because he's about to get one he'll never forget.

Claire, Ris, and Maggie are chatting. Avery and Ryan are nowhere to be seen and Dane is getting the car.

I pray the barely restrained anger in my tone won't give me away. "I need you to come with me."

Claire, Ris, and Maggie all turn, wearing matching confused expressions.

"Which one of us?" Ris smiles, the polite hostess until the very end.

I reach out and touch one of my friends' arms. "You."

CHAPTER THIRTY-EIGHT

MARISA

My best friends are freaking out.

First Claire, now Elly. They've been flighty and tense all evening so I deliberately stay clear, giving them time to work through whatever's bugging them. Besides, I have my own issues, namely what Avery is up to, announcing to our closest friends how much I mean to him.

I know why. It's a business decision. Everything revolves around his precious company and with an international merger in the cards he needs his perfect hostess. I'm tempted to shock the hell out of him and call it quits anyway. But I'm not that woman. When I make a commitment, I mean it, even if I'm dying a little more on the inside with every passing day.

Only Maggie seems happy tonight, more relaxed than I've ever seen her. She's luminous in a white sundress that sets off her tan, her coral-painted fingernails and toes the perfect foil for the simplicity of her dress. Ryan may be an overgrown child that she indulges most of the time, but regardless of his faults, he makes her happy.

If my marriage is like traversing a minefield, I can't imagine what theirs is like. Maggie has a fortune and seems completely oblivious to the fact that's why Ryan probably married her. I'd overheard him talking with Avery once, virtually saying as much. It had angered me, until I witnessed the extent of Maggie's cleansing obsession and what Ryan went through.

My sympathy had shifted then, because it can't be easy living with someone so unpredictable. By the glow she sports tonight, Ryan is doing something right.

Claire approaches me to say goodbye. She looks shattered, like the slightest breeze will blow her over.

"Thanks for a lovely party but we have to leave—"

"You don't have to pretend with me." I slip an arm around her waist and she leans against me gratefully. "Jodi's death has taken its toll on all of us, but you most of all."

She bites her bottom lip, probably to stop it quivering.

"At the risk of sounding like a broken record and asking for the umpteenth time, do you really think you should be investigating? I mean, if it's too close to home..."

I trail off when her eyes fill with tears. "Oh, sweetie, I'm sorry. You're dealing with everything the best you can and I need to keep my big mouth shut."

"It's not you." She blinks rapidly several times, followed by a few steadying breaths. "I thought I had it all figured out but turns out it's not that simple."

I glance over my shoulder. Avery is nowhere to be seen. "Did you find out more about why Jodi was researching you-know-who at the library?"

Her eyes widen. "He hasn't told you?"

The ever-present panic simmering below the surface rises. "Told me what?"

Claire looks away and mutters, "Fuck," as Maggie joins us, and Elly marches toward us, her beautiful features tight with anger.

"I need you to come with me," she says, her mouth twisted with bitterness.

Claire, Maggie, and I stare at her in confusion.

"Which one of us?" I smile, my famous soothing smile that can placate the most disgruntled client or guest.

She reaches out and touches Maggie's arm. "You."

Claire looks only too happy to be let off the hook before she can divulge what Avery's been keeping from me. "I'll call you," she says, pecking my cheek with a brief kiss before doing the same to Elly. She touches Maggie on the arm.

Dane toots the horn outside and Claire bolts, leaving me with Maggie and Elly, waves of anger rolling off her and making me nervous. Elly's posture is stiff, like someone has rammed a rod up her back, a vein pulses at her temple and her eyes are wild.

A small frown creases Maggie's brow. "What's wrong?"

"I can't tell you here. You need to come with me." She snags Maggie's hand and tries to tug her toward the front door.

Maggie's gaze locks with mine. She's nervous and I see her balk, so I chime in. "I've got a party to clean up and it's late. Whatever it is you have to say, can it wait until morning and I'll come too?"

"No." Elly practically hisses, she's that irate. "Maggie needs to come with me now."

Her gaze darts every which way, as if searching for someone. "Right now."

Her urgency is contagious. She's starting to seriously worry me.

"Okay, I'll come too. Let me tell Ryan and Avery we're going—"

"No!" Her other hand shoots out to grab me and her manicured nails dig into my forearm so hard I yelp. "We have to go now."

Elly's desperate to the point of unhinged and I glimpse confusion mingling with fear in Maggie's eyes.

"Is everything all right—"

"Shut up, Maggie," Elly growls, tugging on our arms. I've only ever seen her this freaked out once before, the night she'd been drugged and raped, and I hate seeing my carefully controlled friend so rattled.

"Let's go." I grab my keys and cell off the hall table, expecting her to release my forearm and Maggie's hand. She doesn't, like she expects us to make a run for it if she does.

We reach her car but I don't want to be a passenger, not when she's this unstable.

"I'll drive—"

"Fine. You two follow me." She finally releases us and waits until I slip behind the wheel of my SUV and Maggie gets in the passenger side before making a run for her convertible, no mean feat in her towering stilettos.

I don't care that Avery will wonder where I've vanished to. He can call me if he's worried. I'm guessing he won't. He'll be too absorbed chatting up the caterers while they clear away to even notice I'm gone.

"Do you have any idea what's going on?"

Maggie shakes her head as I follow our circular driveway out onto Sunnyside Drive. "None. But it must be serious because I've never seen Elly act crazy before. She's always so calm when I visit her at the center."

She gives a short laugh. "I'm the one who's supposed to be nuts, not her."

I feel compelled to defend my friend, even though Maggie's not being mean. "Elly's been through some tough stuff."

"Haven't we all?"

Maggie's response is soft and yet again I'm struck by how badly I've misjudged her. Lately, she seems more approachable, less critical, like she doesn't mind spending time with me rather than attending family events out of obligation.

"Yeah, we all have trials to bear." I follow Elly toward the highway. "Did you know about the renewing vows thing?"

"No. Though Ryan's rather romantic when he wants to be."

I refrain from asking, if that's the case why did my husband make the announcement for him? Then again, Avery does a lot of things for Ryan so it's more of the same old, same old.

We lapse into silence but it's not awkward for once and to my surprise Elly drives at a sedate pace, at complete odds with her manic behavior at my house. She turns onto the main highway from Sunnyside Drive and keeps to the speed limit for fifteen minutes. When she indicates left, we're almost at a small gravel road that's nowhere near her place, where I assume she's been taking us.

I'm uneasy. This erratic behavior is out of character for Elly. She never lets the mask slip. She's the most put-together person I know. I see past her shallow persona when most people can't. Even Claire has a low tolerance for her at times. Which is why I make an effort to maintain our friendship. I know they think our monthly garden club is BS. But to their credit they turn up anyway, despite their constant bickering. Even though I'm only eight years older than them I feel like their mom sometimes, having to step in and referee.

I care about Claire and Elly. But Claire has Dane to look after her; Elly has nobody, which is why I follow her for several miles down the winding gravel road until I see a cottage. It's perched on a small rise on the edge of the Atlantic. Elly pulls into a carport attached to the cottage, I park behind.

"Pretty spot," Maggie says, unbuckling.

"Yeah," I say, no closer to understanding why we're here.

When I open the door, I hear the waves crashing so close I half expect ocean to lap at my ankles.

Elly gets out of the car and slams the door. She doesn't speak as she slips off her stilettos and marches through the sand to the front door, which she unlocks with a key on her key ring.

"What is this place?" I call out, as she pauses at the front door, holding it open for Maggie and me.

"I believe you'd call it a love nest." Her eyes are mean slits but her voice quivers slightly, as if she's torn.

Confused, I enter the cottage alongside Maggie, immediately struck by its simplistic beauty. I jump when Elly slams this door too. When I turn to face her, she's standing a foot behind us, trembling.

"Do you know what a love nest is, Maggie?"

Her toxic tone slithers over me, making me step back. Maggie's nervous gaze, eyes round with panic, darts between us.

I don't like where this is going and when Maggie takes a step closer to me I'm glad I came.

"Why don't you just say what you brought me all the way out here to say, El?"

I've never heard Maggie call her El. It alerts me to the fact they're closer friends than I thought. Elly has mentioned Maggie drops by the medical center once a week to chat but I assumed that was more business oriented. Now I'm not so sure.

Elly's face is blank, like she's wearing an expressionless mask, but her lips peel back in a sneer. "Your husband leases this cottage so we can come here to fuck."

Her crudeness shocks me more than her confession. It's like she deliberately wants to hurt Maggie. Her friend. The woman I've been musing over how much I've misjudged. The fact Ryan's screwing around behind Maggie's back doesn't surprise me. The old cliché springs to mind: monkey see, monkey do. He's always idolized Avery and will do anything for his approval. I've suspected Avery's affairs for years, considering his frequent absences and propensity to come on to women in front of me, so the fact Ryan does the same isn't a shock.

But the fact one of my best friends is his mistress cuts deep. It's a betrayal of the worst sort. Not because she's lied to me all this time but because I didn't see it coming.

Have I been that blind? Were there clues along the way? I scan my memory but come up empty. Ryan flirts with Elly the same way he flirts with every woman. As for Elly, she's never been uncomfortable around Maggie, has never acted like she's having an affair.

It makes me feel betrayed all over again, that I've been too stupid to see her for what she truly is: a lying, backstabbing bitch. I pride myself on getting an accurate read on people the first time I meet them. What a joke.

"Why are you doing this?" Maggie's voice is steady, forceful, at complete odds with her pallor. I reach out and touch the small of her back, a show of silent support.

I glare at Elly, my lips compressed so I won't blurt how disappointed I am and give her the satisfaction of seeing how truly devastated I am.

Pain glints in her eyes. "I knew you wouldn't believe me, Mags, you're far too trusting, which is why I brought you here to see for yourself."

She drops her stilettos beside a low-slung camel suede sofa and strolls into the bedroom. I don't want to follow her but Maggie does so I trail behind.

"I obviously shouldn't have trusted you." Maggie stops abruptly in the doorway and I almost slam into her back.

Elly opens a few drawers and lifts the contents. "These look familiar?"

Ties, at least three of them: neat navy with sienna stripes, ebony with white dots, burgundy silk. I recognize two of them; I'd seen Ryan wear them some mornings when he dropped in to ride into the city with Avery.

"He said he'd left those at the office in the city when I questioned him where they'd disappeared to." Maggie sounds so lost, so small, I want to grab her hand and drag her out of here.

"And these?" Elly picks up a pair of cuff links from the top of the dresser, rolling them in her palm like dice.

I recognize them. Avery loved those silver four-leaf clovers so much Ryan bought him his own pair last Christmas.

"You know I'm not making this up." Elly flings the cuff links on top of the ties and closes the drawer. "Though I sure as hell didn't want to tell you like this."

Her shoulders slump and for the first time a flicker of guilt replaces fury in her eyes. "I did want to tell you, many times, so you wouldn't end up like me. But then he came to my office…"

Her expression hardens. "He's going to leave you. Not for me, because I told him to stick his offer up his ass, but at some stage in the future, when some gullible rich bimbo believes his bullshit, he'll dump you so fast your head will spin—"

"Elly, that's enough," I say, as Maggie makes a garbled sound halfway between a moan and a choke.

She needs to sit down before she falls down and I slide my arm around her waist to hold her upright. Ice flows through my veins because what Maggie is going through can happen to me. I know what Avery is. The one thing I fear most, being on my own, left with my own thoughts, is a real possibility with a man like him. I can't be left alone. The darkness I keep at bay most days may manifest when I'm alone, taunting me, terrifying me, mocking me that no matter how hard I try and how far I've come, I'll still end up like my mother.

I guide Maggie toward the sofa in the living area, my legs stiff and wooden as she stumbles along beside me. My entire body feels numb, like it's deliberately blocking out the agony, so I can't imagine how Maggie must be feeling.

Elly has followed us into the living room and is standing near the coffee table, her arms crossed over her waist like she's hugging herself. Her anger has drained away, replaced by a sadness that makes me want to go to her: if I didn't want to hit her so much.

"Elly, I don't know what you're gaining by doing this—"

"Tell me all of it," Maggie interrupts me, glaring at Elly with surprising fierceness. "I want to know."

I touch Maggie's hand. "Are you sure you want to hear this? We can leave—"

"No," she spits out, snatching her hand away. "I have to know." The shock in her eyes breaks my heart. "Wouldn't you want to know?"

After a long pause, I eventually nod. My respect for her has increased tenfold because deep down I wouldn't want to know. I don't want to know. If I did, I would've already confronted Avery years ago.

I'm nothing like Maggie. She's braver than me. I can't face the truth with Avery the way she is with Ryan.

Elly isn't gloating. She looks as shattered as Maggie as she continues.

"Ryan came to work yesterday, professing his undying love, saying he's leaving you and we have to be together." She's pacing, increasingly agitated, plucking at the sheer chiffon sleeve of her gown. "I'm not that naïve. So I didn't buy into his whole happily-ever-after scenario."

Her sudden stop in front of us momentarily disorients me, especially when she sinks onto the sofa beside me. At least that leaves Maggie on the other side. I'm a buffer, and for the first time since I offered to accompany Maggie tonight, I wish I hadn't.

"Do you have any idea what it's like to be me?" Elly's question is soft and filled with a world of pain.

Maggie's head snaps up as she stares Elly down. "No, because I'm not a home-wrecking slut."

She flinches, obviously not expecting Maggie to fire back.

"What were you thinking?" I get into her face, our noses almost touching.

I'm yelling but she doesn't flinch. She doesn't move a muscle. She just sits there, staring at us with . . . pity. I hate pity. Kids at school used to do that when they learned about my crappy home life and I'd done everything in my power since to avoid it. It's been a potent motivator for me my entire life. The mere thought of the solicitous benevolence I'd receive if I ever had the gumption to leave Avery is enough to make me stay.

Now Maggie will be subjected to it. And unlike me, I have no idea if she can cope with the fallout from this affair or not. Elly pushes me away and focuses on Maggie, who's clinging to me like she's scared Elly will vault me any moment to get to her.

"You'll never believe me but I was thinking about you through all of this," she says, the first sign of contrition in her stare. "You don't know me, Maggie. Not really. Not where I've come from, not about my past." She gnaws on her bottom lip. "I did this for you."

Maggie's fingers dig into my arm hard enough to leave bruises. "You're insane—"

"Let me finish. I didn't mean for this to happen. I hate men who cheat on their wives, so after my ex-husband screwed me over, I went on this weird binge, entrapping them, then making them tell the truth. I wanted Ryan to do that with you. But then things spiraled out of control for me personally and he was supportive and I ended up liking him a little, and everything went to shit. I know what I did is bad, inexcusable, but in some warped way I wanted to help you."

She's rambling again, saying stuff that doesn't make any sense and I can't comprehend how Elly believes her own BS. She's certifiable.

Maggie releases my arm to lean across me and jab Elly in the shoulder. "Cut the crap. You get off on knowing every man in a room wants you. You like the power trip."

Maggie scores a point as Elly's eyes flare with awareness. "You're wrong. I was once like you. So goddamn perfect and smug and condescending, safe in my marriage, thinking nothing could touch me. But men are scum and when Ryan came on to me, I wanted you to see him for what he really is."

A faint color tinges Maggie's cheeks. "How fucking noble of you, screwing my husband to *help* me."

"I didn't expect to like you so much, and the longer we screwed around behind your back, the harder I found it to come clean." She blows out a breath. "I knew ending your marriage would be the hardest thing you've ever done. I wanted you to be free but I didn't want you to hurt."

Bewilderment replaces my anger. How could any rational person do this? Start an affair out of some warped sense of doing someone else a favor? I've met some self-absorbed, irrational women in my time living in the Hamptons but Elly has them beat.

As for the part about her being married, I have no idea why she hasn't mentioned it before. Or is she truly delusional, grasping at any excuse to justify her appalling behavior?

"The real reason he came by work to say he wants us to be

together is because he asked me to do something bad." She shakes her head. "When I wouldn't consider his proposition or do what he asked, he blackmailed me into it, and I knew he was using me as badly as he uses you..."

She's scared now, her pupils dilated, eyes wide. "What I'm about to tell you both implicates me in the worst way possible." Her voice hitches, like she's about to cry. "I could lose my job and in turn, lose everything that's important to me."

"You mean free Botox and fillers on company time?"

The classic bitchy comment coming from Maggie is outrageous and for an inane second I feel like laughing. But something in her eyes stops me. Like she's teetering on a precipice, terrified of falling.

Elly blows out a long breath. "He asked me to fiddle with a test result."

I don't get it and by the confusion creasing Maggie's brow, she's just as clueless.

"What kind of test?"

She looks away, her mouth drooping, and for the first time I glimpse her age beneath her beauty.

"A paternity test," she murmurs, so softly I think I misheard.

"But why..."

In an instant it all becomes clear.

After years of Avery being Ryan's Mr. Fix-it, his younger brother has returned the favor.

If Avery asked Ryan to approach Elly to switch a paternity test, it can only mean one thing and that suspicion I've had in my gut since the moment Jodi turned up on my doorstep weeks ago has solidified into one giant horrific certainty.

Avery is the father of Jodi's baby.

Which makes him the prime suspect for her murder.

CHAPTER THIRTY-NINE

CLAIRE

When we get home, Dane stomps into the living room to play a mindless violent game on the video console. We didn't talk on the five-minute car journey home and he doesn't seem inclined to continue our earlier conversation from the party. I'm glad. It gives me time to do some further investigating. I log on to the police database to check on some of the grunt work I assigned my officers. No updates. Great. With my original theory for Jodi's murderer blown sky-high, I know it's time to recuse myself from this case. I can't work on it anymore.

Because the only other possible suspect at this time is my husband.

It could be some random guy we don't know about, and probably won't until we delve deeper into Jodi's activities, but I'll feel better once Dane is cleared. And he needs to provide a saliva sample for me to do that.

I have a kit. I brought it home after I discovered he isn't infertile. He's refused to let me swab the inside of his mouth, saying if I love him I should trust him. But there's a massive difference between trust and burying my head in the sand hoping this huge weight that's hanging over us will miraculously vanish.

Hating the inevitable confrontation that will end in a screaming match, I grab the kit and head for the living room.

When I get there, he isn't playing a game. The TV is off and he's sitting on the sofa, head in his hands.

"What's wrong?"

It's a pretty dumb question considering everything seems wrong with us these days. He takes an eternity to raise his head. His eyes are red. He's been crying. I clamp down on the urge to go to him, hold him tight, and say everything's going to be okay: because even if we survive this I have no idea if we'll be okay ever again. I linger in the doorway, unsure how to proceed, when his gaze focuses on the kit in my hand.

He leaps to his feet like he's been shot. "After all I said to you at the party, about how much I love you, and after answering your disgusting question asking if I've ever cheated, you still want me to do that damn test?"

Dane's a practical guy. I need to appeal to that side of him.

"I believe you. But I wouldn't be doing my job unless I followed up on this."

He's unmoving so I cajole further. "You'll be doing me a big favor because the sooner I prove you're not the father, the sooner the department can move on to finding the real father of that baby."

"The department?" His demeanor changes, like an internal switch has been flicked. He changes from morose to manic in a second. "So your whole damn police department thinks I'm guilty? Why? Because it turns out I'm not shooting blanks after all and I wasn't home with my 'loving wife' that night?"

He makes air quotes when he says "loving wife," like nothing could be further from the truth. He's mocking me, mocking what we have. Had. I want to curl up in a corner and bawl but I can't let this go. There'll be time enough for me to grieve for the loss of us later.

"What I meant was that as the lead investigator on the case, I'm assigning the usual fact-finding tasks to my officers and it would be easier on the entire department if they were focusing all their time on tracking down the real killer."

He glares at me, anger radiating off him, so I try another tactic. "Look, we've both been under immense pressure the last few months. All that baby stuff messed with our heads. I don't believe you cheated on me with Jodi. But I don't want others thinking that if they learn about the adoption."

His eyes narrow, suspicious of my change in tone. "You said Ris wouldn't tell anyone about that."

"The Gledhill Help Center is a big place. They keep online and paper records. It won't take much for it to be discovered during the investigation and then we'll be in the spotlight and the police will wonder why we never said anything."

I say "we" when I really mean *him*. "I could lose my badge over this if they suspect I kept vital information from them."

He presses the pads of his palms into his eyes, as if to erase the nightmare our lives have become. When he lowers his hands, sadness clogs my throat. His stare is one of a defeated man, like he's given up.

"You know why I don't want to take this test?"

His question comes out of left field.

"Why?"

"Because the moment you stick that swab stick in my mouth is the moment I realize how much my wife doesn't trust me and I'm worried there's no coming back from that."

It's a legitimate concern but I fear we've already passed that point.

"I don't have any magic answer for you." I hold my hands out, palms up, like I've got nothing to hide. "This whole situation has been horrendous and I feel broken in here." I press a hand to my heart. "But I can't move forward until we put all this to rest and that's what I'm trying to do."

He's wavering. I see it in the way his mouth twists to one side. He always does that when he's mulling a problem.

But before he says anything, there's a loud pounding on our front door. When he doesn't move, I sigh. "I'll get it."

When I open the door Ris is standing there, looking like

she's been caught in a hurricane. Her updo falls about her face in limp straggles, her makeup is smudged, and her satin dress is crumpled. She isn't wearing shoes.

"I need to talk to you," she says, her tone choked. "It's urgent."

I stand back and usher her in. "Are you okay?"

"No."

How one syllable can sound so desperate I'll never know but I immediately realize Ris is a woman on the edge. I've seen the same shell-shocked expression on women who've been traumatized.

"Is Dane here?" Her gaze is darting everywhere, like she expects a boogeyman to jump out of a dark corner and accost her at any second.

"He's in the living room." I take her arm and lead her toward the kitchen. "We can talk in here."

"I don't know if I'm doing the right thing." She's wringing her hands and I notice they're pink, like she's been doing it awhile. "This may not mean anything but he's such a lying bastard I don't know what he's capable of."

My inner radar tingles, the one that has served me well during my years on the force. She can only be talking about one man. Avery.

I lead her to a chair and virtually have to push her into it to sit, she's that tense. "Want a drink?"

She stares at me, round-eyed, like I've offered her arsenic. "Water, please."

I quickly fill a glass, my concern escalating when the woman who's usually so in control starts shaking, like shock has set in.

I swap the water for lemon soda. Looks like she could use a sugar fix.

"Drink this, sweetie."

She downs the soda mechanically, some of it sloshing down the front of her dress. She doesn't notice, emptying the glass before placing it on the table. "I'm not this woman, the type who airs dirty laundry. I've always stood by him, supported him, done everything right, and after all he's done you'd think I'd hate him, but I still feel like I'm the one betraying him somehow."

I want to say "take your time" but Ris is rattled, and if she has something to say about Avery, I want to hear it.

"Do you know why I'm a great listener?" She's staring at the wall, her expression catatonic. "The helpful, generous nurturer who'll do anything to keep the peace?"

I'm not sure if it's a rhetorical question so I wait.

"Because being the good guy for others makes me forget the bad stuff I've done in my past and the guy I'm married to because of it. And I can justify it by mentally listing all the great things in my life if only I maintain the status quo."

I can't make sense of her cryptic comment and she's starting to ramble so I need to pin her down.

"What did you want to tell me, Ris?"

Her eyes refocus on me and she blinks, as if she's seeing me for the first time. "Elly showed us a secret cottage Ryan leases. They're having an affair."

I'm stunned. Not by Ryan's appalling behavior. I never bought into his whole Mr. Perfect act so nothing surprises me where he's concerned. But Elly? How could she pretend to be Maggie's friend if she was having sex with Ryan behind Maggie's back?

"Who, what…I mean, when did she tell you all this?"

"Just now. I came straight here from the cottage. Remember when she confronted us at the end of the party? She asked Maggie to follow her to show her something, but I could see something was wrong so I tagged along."

The corners of her mouth droop along with her shoulders, like an invisible weight is pressing on her back and she can't shift it. "There's more."

Poor Ris. Learning her best friend is a traitorous bitch must've been bad enough. How much worse can it get?

The first thing I think is that Elly's pregnant.

That would totally gut Maggie. Especially after all that crap Avery spouted at their anniversary party in front of everybody about Ryan and Maggie renewing vows.

"Elly told me about the paternity test."

My eyebrows rise at that. I guessed Avery wouldn't tell Ris unless he absolutely had to and I couldn't because of confidentiality legalities.

How the hell did Elly find out?

"Avery didn't mention it?"

"As if." Ris makes an odd scoffing sound akin to having a fish bone stuck in her gullet. "Who knows what else he's keeping from me?"

She says, "I take it you were behind the paternity test?"

I nod. "I couldn't tell you. It's part of our ongoing investigation into potential suspects for Jodi's murder and I didn't want to compromise that because of our friendship."

"I get it." Ris's brow furrows, like she's just thought of something. "So if he's the father of her baby, he'll be the number one suspect?"

I hate to disappoint her when she's had enough of those already this evening—learning the truth about her cheating brother-in-law who she idolizes and her deceitful friend—but I say, "Yes, but he's not the father so—"

"I think he is."

I understand where she's coming from. She's angry, shocked, thirsting for revenge. But as much as I wish Avery were the father of Jodi's baby, it's a scientific impossibility according to the test results.

"Look, Ris, it's been a long night for you—"

"Elly fiddled with the paternity test."

She pronounces it calmly but she realizes the impact as she stares at me, a glimmer of a smile playing about her mouth as she notes my reaction.

My jaw drops. The back of my neck prickles. A cold sensation trickles down my spine. I manage to utter, "What?"

"You heard me." Ris isn't shaking anymore. In fact, she's smug. "You know how Avery has bailed Ryan out of situations since they were kids?"

I nod and Ris continues. "What if Avery finally called in a favor himself and asked Ryan to be the intermediary?"

I'm still not following but I give her time.

"Elly said Ryan came to her at work, professing his undying love, saying he'll leave Maggie and they'll be together. Of course, she had to do one small favor for him." She sniggers, her eyes switching from devastated to maniacal in a second. "Switch paternity tests. Swap Avery's for someone else's."

I can't comprehend this. It's like something out of a B-grade crime movie on TV.

"Why the hell did she do it? I mean, it's illegal for a start. She's tampered with a police investigation. Perverted the course of justice. My God, I can't believe she'd do this for some dickhead she's been foolish enough to fall for." I'm rambling out loud and stop myself when I see Ris's stricken expression.

Ris's bottom lip wobbles so I reach for her hand and hold it between both of mine. "Hey, you've done the right thing in telling me and, thankfully, Elly finally came to her senses and told the truth."

"What happens from here?" She's reverted to timid and afraid. "I can't go back to the house tonight. I can't pretend that everything's okay in front of him."

She starts to cry, tears trickling down her cheeks in a constant stream. "Regardless of what happens I can never go back there."

My grip on her hand tightens as I try to convey some degree of comfort. "Stay here. For as long as you need."

I need to buy some time, at least until the morning, so I can get Avery's DNA sample retested. If Ris goes home Avery will take one look at her and know something's drastically wrong.

She's not that good an actress. She's too guileless, too nice for him.

She hangs on to my hand like she'll never let go. "What will I tell him?"

"I'll call him and say you and Elly came over because I was upset, we ended up having too many drinks, and you're staying over."

A plausible story that would give me enough time to put together the pieces of this scrambled jigsaw.

However, my plan hinges on Elly too. "What about Elly? Is she likely to contact Ryan or Avery tonight?"

Ris snorts and the tears start again. "Right now, Elly is a woman scorned." She swipes at her eyes with her free hand. "She told us Ryan blackmailed her into fiddling with the test. Then she had the audacity to try and justify her behavior by saying she'd been married too, and gullible like Maggie, so she had the affair to *help* her wake up."

"What the..." I shake my head, not needing Elly's drivel to mess with my head, not now when clarity was all-important. "That's bullshit. She probably only told you because Ryan announced he wants to renew his vows and lied to her and our prima donna needed revenge."

More tears trickle down Ris's cheeks and I inwardly curse my bluntness. "Damn it, I can't stop crying."

I feel my eyes moisten for what my kind friend has had to endure. I pull her to her feet and propel her toward the bathroom. "Go tidy up. Take a shower. Whatever you want to do. I'll leave a spare set of sweats outside the door and there are clean towels in the cabinet under the sink. Will you be okay?"

After what seems like an eternity, she nods. "Yeah, I have to be." Her chin comes up in defiance. "I want to see that bastard get his comeuppance. And if he had anything to do with Jodi's murder..." She shakes her head, but not before I glimpse an expression that makes me pause.

Ris's twist of rampant fury indicates she's a woman capable

of anything. In that moment, the medical examiner's words come back to me.

"...*the murderer didn't really want to hurt the girl...it seems like this person cared...I'd even go as far as to say I think your suspect could be a woman...*"

No. I'm reaching. In my desperation for answers, my over-worked, overtired mind is coming up with implausible scenarios. But if there's one thing I've learned in this job over the years it's to never discount the impossible.

Had Ris somehow discovered Avery was the father of Jodi's baby and in some warped attempt to hide the truth she'd killed the girl?

Had she worried that even if her plan had gone smoothly, and I adopted the baby, that one day Jodi or the child would come forward and demand compensation—or more—from Avery and that would disrupt her perfectly ordered life?

Had she simply killed the girl in a fit of jealousy?

If so, was her turning up here tonight, distraught, part of some elaborate act, a way to throw me off? To get me to focus on Avery as the prime suspect, letting her walk?

I hate these questions and how logical they are. I need to get answers. Tonight. And I need to start at the beginning.

Getting those paternity test results.

"Go take that shower, leave everything to me."

Her anger has vanished and she stares at me for a long, inter-minable minute, a mix of sorrow and regret, before she enters the bathroom and shuts the door.

Dane pops his head into the hallway. "What's going on?"

I want to say, "You're off the hook. For now."

I settle for, "Ris is staying the night. She needs our support right now."

"Okay. Let me know what I can do." His agreement is instant, no questions asked. My supportive husband, one of the things I love about him. It's good to remember these things. It gives me hope for the future.

"I need to make a few phone calls. Can you grab the clean sweats out of my top drawer and place them outside the bathroom?"

"Sure thing." He's already gone, only too happy to help.

It makes me feel guiltier for suspecting he could've had anything to do with Jodi's murder. It's going to take us a long time to recover from this. Especially when I tell him the truth about what I did all those years ago.

I know that if we're to have any chance moving forward, there has to be no secrets between us. That we have to confront the mistakes we've made, deal with them, and embrace forgiveness. At least, that's my hope, once I solve this crime.

For now, I have to move quickly. Starting with a phone call to Ron.

We need to expedite a new paternity test, on the correct sample this time.

CHAPTER FORTY

ELLY

After Ris and Maggie leave I'm hollow. Like all the blood has drained out of me, my muscles can't function and I'm weak to the point of passing out.

Earlier, at Ris's anniversary party, I'd envisaged feeling relieved when I told Maggie everything. That in revealing the truth about her lying husband I would've saved her from a life of being duped so she wouldn't end up a loser like me.

Now, I feel empty. A failure. My good intentions shot to shit because this time my great reveal has torn apart the life of someone I actually care about. I'd known this all along, that I'd end up hurting Maggie, but somewhere along the line of my revenge plot I'd lost my way.

The rape had destroyed my meager self-esteem, and when Ryan had reached out, I'd taken what comfort I could get. Stupid, because it had never been anything beyond the sex for him, but the longer the affair continued the more I became caught up in something bigger than the both of us.

I sink onto the sofa and hug my knees to my chest. I rock a little. I want to cry. I can't. I'm dead inside. I've lost everything. My job, my friends, my home. I despise what I've become, a woman so desperate for comfort that she'd tear apart the lives of her friends because of it.

After leaving Chicago and wreaking revenge on those

other cheaters, I'd convinced myself I was invincible, devoid of empathy. I could be impartial and help other women like me.

But the rape had changed all that, and in turning to Ryan, I'd shattered what was left of my soul.

I should've stopped after that first time together. I should've changed my MO this time and kept the cheated wife out of it. I should've ruined Ryan some other way. Instead, smug in my delusions of retribution and caught up in feeling something for a man for the first time in forever, I hurt my friend, one of the few people in this world who actually gives a damn about me.

It makes me sick to my stomach.

I stop rocking and curl up in the corner of the sofa. What am I trying to do? Make myself invisible? It's not going to change anything. I can still see myself in the mirror over the low mantel. I know what I've done.

I expect Ryan will call any minute. Maggie will go home, confront him, and he'll go berserk. Backtrack. Make excuses. They all do when challenged with their lies. The others had all capitulated after I'd threatened them with exposure. I had voice recordings on my cell proving their infidelity so they'd had no choice. I'd witnessed their confessions from afar, usually from my car parked outside their homes, to make sure they went through with it. I forwarded those recordings to their wives just in case.

As for losing my friendship with Ris... there'll be no coming back from this with her. She'll judge me and find me lacking. Not that I blame her. I deserve her ire. But she's always been so good to me, especially after the rape, that I feel like the lowest of the low for flinging her friendship back in her face. Not having her in my life anymore will leave a gaping hole, even if a lot of the time we spent together she made me feel worthless. Not deliberately, but because of who she is.

From the first moment we met I felt inferior. I'd been having a drink in one of the Main Street bars and she'd breezed in, wearing a nautical dress I knew cost a fortune, with navy pumps and a matching handbag that had been released a week earlier with an extensive waiting list for it. I should know; I was on it. She'd been laughing at something Claire said, revealing the kind of smile that elevated her from pretty to gorgeous.

But it was more than her well-put-together appearance that made me feel mediocre. I envied Marisa Thurston on sight because she exuded that invisible quality that no amount of money could buy.

Class.

She reveled in it, confident in her own skin in a way I could try to emulate but never could. Because my confidence was as fake as the new life I'd created for myself. Despite the fortune I spent on cosmetics, skincare, and fashion, I could never command a room like her.

It's not her fault. She has no clue that her competence in all areas of her life makes me feel useless. She has everything. The husband. The kids. The house. The job. The adulation of the local community. The lifestyle. The friends. I have two of those, a job and a lifestyle, though I'll be fired now too. As for friends, I'll be cast out of her cozy circle and vanquished. My life as I know it over, just like that.

That's what I was trying to show Maggie. That no matter how great you think life is there's always a shit-storm waiting to dump on you around the next corner. Now that she knows the truth, what does she have? Nothing. Her life is in tatters, like mine once was. I'd planned on doing things differently. I'd wanted to tell Maggie and give her a chance to get her affairs in order. I'd envisaged her cutting him off financially, which would've been the ultimate payback for Ryan. But the announcement tonight of their vow renewal, hot on the heels of him blackmailing me, pushed me over the edge and I blurted the truth to her in the worst way possible. Remorse fills me for the pain I inflicted on her.

My cell rings. It's on vibrate and it starts skittering across the coffee table. I glance at the screen.

Ryan.

I consider ignoring him but I know he'll keep bugging me until I pick up. Or worse, he'll turn up here with some sob story and I can't face him. Not tonight, when I'm raw and exposed. He'll either be fuming and seeking revenge for me ruining his life and I have no intention of facing down a madman with the way I'm feeling, or he'll be apologetic for the renewing vows fiasco and conciliatory if Maggie has kicked him out. Like I'd want anything to do with him now.

I pick up the phone and stab at the answer button.

"Sweetheart, I'm so sorry about tonight," he rushes in before I can utter a word. "I know how shocked you must've been hearing all that bullshit about renewing vows, but I didn't have a chance to tell you my big news beforehand."

I'm stunned.

He doesn't know.

If Maggie had made it home he wouldn't be calling to apologize for his shitty behavior tonight. He'd be wringing my neck.

So I play it cool. "What news?"

"An international merger is in the cards for Avery's company. It's worth billions, which means I'll get a massive bonus and won't be reliant on Mags for money. And some delegates from the overseas offices are visiting next week so I need to present a stable front." He has the audacity to laugh. "You know how good Maggie is for my reputation, so I need to keep her around until then. And once the deal is done..."

His voice lowers to a seductive purr I'm all too familiar with. He uses it often to get his own way. "After that, it's just you and me, baby. I can't wait."

I can. An eternity. Is the idiot delusional? Because after he blackmailed me, I'd shut down. I'd told him we were over. Yet in typical self-absorbed fashion he hadn't believed me. He'd said that once we got past "this little hiccup" we'd be together for sure.

The guy is an egotistical moron with no conscience

whatsoever. Thankfully one of the doctors had needed to see me and I'd escaped. When I'd returned to my office, he'd left. I hadn't expected to hear from him ever again because once I told Maggie everything he'd paint me in the worst light possible.

Ris will stand by her brother-in-law, as it should be: family first. Claire will side with Ris and I'll be an outcast, banished from their circle.

Why hasn't Maggie confronted him yet? I feel disarmed. As usual, he doesn't even notice I'm not responding. He keeps talking.

"And Avery said we can have the cottage—"

"What's Avery got to do with this?"

"He's the landlord." He chuckles. "Surprise."

These two make me sick but I don't have a chance to tell him as he continues.

"I'd love to see you but I've got a videoconference with the French and German CEOs of the company considering the merger starting soon. I have no idea how long it'll go on for but if I can get away I'll pop by your apartment later tonight, okay?"

I don't respond, knowing he'll never call me again, because once Maggie makes it home we're over, thank goodness.

It can't come quick enough.

"Bye, sweetheart." He hangs up and I'm so relieved I actually drop the phone.

It bounces off the floorboards and slides under the sofa. I don't care. I can't summon the energy to look for it. I'm bone-deep exhausted yet want to get out of town as soon as possible. But the fatigue is relentless so I slide lower, until I'm lying flat on the sofa. I turn onto my side and press my face into a cushion, comforted by its downiness.

Is this how Jodi felt when Avery smothered her?

Now that Ryan has revealed the company's precious merger, it all makes sense. Having a bastard child would've put a major crimp in his grand plans, he would've lost his hostess,

Ris, before the merger went through, and there's nothing more important to Avery than image, money, and prestige.

But how much does Ryan know? When I asked him about Jodi and whether he knew her, I thought he'd been lying. If so, is he involved somehow? I'd hate to think he'd be involved in a murder but he's a master manipulator and an excellent liar.

After living with a chronic liar in a fake marriage for years, I should know.

I move the cushion away from my nose and gasp in a breath. I'm weary, soul-deep tired. I can't risk going home and have Ryan turn up there like he mentioned. I'll sleep here tonight and face my future, whatever's left of it, in the morning.

All too soon, sunlight is warming my face and I wake with a start, momentarily disoriented. Then I remember and wish I didn't.

I stumble to the bathroom and splash water on my face. I reach for a towel and remember I took them home to wash the last time I was here. I open the small cabinet under the sink, hoping I've left at least one towel here. I pat around, searching for it. I'm in luck. My fingers close over something soft, a towel, but as I pull it out I dislodge something. I hear a crash and smell something odd.

I squat, and peer into the cabinet. The smell is stronger now, bleach, but more pungent. It sticks in my throat and makes me gag a little. I cough and place a hand over my nose while I straighten the bottle and use some toilet paper to mop up the spill then flush it away.

There are two bottles in the cupboard and a few syringes. Concerned, I wonder if the tenant before us has left this stuff and if I've inadvertently inhaled some toxic gas.

I wrap my hand in the towel and gingerly pick up the first bottle, bringing it out into the light so I can read the label. Drain cleaner. That explains the bleach smell; a perfectly logical item to have under a bathroom sink.

The other bottle is more puzzling. Floor stripper. There's a small measuring jug under the sink too and I lift it to my nose carefully. It reeks of bleach.

I thrust it away and count the number of syringes. Three in total, though one is missing and only the outer wrapping remains.

A chill sweeps over me as a glimmer of an idea takes root. I back away from the cabinet, scrabbling across the tiles like a crab.

I need to find my cell.

Now.

I think the drain cleaner fumes have affected my brain because I'm foggy. Disoriented. Or that could be the fear making me stumble on the way to the living room, twice, before I trip and sprawl next to the sofa.

A memory from last night resurfaces. My cell is under the sofa. I slide my hand under, patting the rug, before my fingers hit something hard. I drag it out and check the battery life. I'm in luck, for once. I pull up the search engine and type in "what does drain cleaner and floor stripper make?"

The answer pops up within seconds and my back sags against the sofa. I'm grateful for the support.

I never knew that any kind of degreasing solvent or floor stripper, combined with drain cleaner, makes gamma hydroxybutyrate.

GHB.

The date rape drug.

I don't know the exact details of Jodi's death beyond the rumors that had circulated at work about her being suffocated. But what if she were drugged first? I know the feeling of falling prey to GHB and it's not pretty. Even now, fifteen months later, I hate the fact I can't remember much of the attack and that I woke up without knowing who had violated me.

I glance at my cell again, then back to the bathroom. If Avery is the landlord of this cottage, is he responsible for this secret stash and what does he use it for?

A shiver shimmies down my spine. Avery and Ryan had been at the bar the night I'd been raped. They'd been with a group of guys; a business meeting. They both came over and said hello. They both flirted with me. At that point, I'd met Avery a few times through Ris and had met Ryan once. When the guy I'd arranged to meet from a dating app didn't show, they'd been sweet. They'd bought me drinks...

No.

It's inconceivable.

I remember seeing them leave while I was still in the bar. But I'd accepted a drink from Avery before that...

A wave of nausea crashes over me. It can't be him. I would've remembered *something*...

I shut down the search engine and call the one person who needs to know.

CHAPTER FORTY-ONE

MARISA

I don't sleep.

I lie in Claire's spare room all night, staring at the ceiling, counting the spirals around the designer light in the middle. I hear her cell ring several times. I hope it's the police telling her they've arrested Avery's lying, cheating ass.

Dane must be a patient man, tolerating phone calls at any time of the day or night. I imagine him supporting her, like he did that day in my office when I tried to facilitate Jodi's adoption. What would it be like to be married to a man like that?

I have no idea if Avery is capable of murder but I'm certain he fathered Jodi's baby. Why else would he get Ryan to ask Elly to swap the test?

Elly...

Another reason I haven't slept. I always knew she was flawed and hiding secrets behind her polished façade but I accepted her anyway. I befriended her. I made Claire befriend her. We made an odd threesome but it worked. She repays me by having an affair with my brother-in-law. It's strange how outraged I am on Maggie's behalf considering we've never been friends; even though we're not close I feel sorry for her.

The thing is I'm not half as broken up over losing Avery as I am about losing Elly. In a town this size I know rumors will circulate, especially when Claire and I ditch Elly from our threesome. People recognize us when we have girls' time: dinners at The Lookout, where we always order the tapas platter to share, brunches at Sea Breeze, shopping along Main Street, lusting over ridiculously priced imported leather shoes from Italy and handmade cashmere scarves. They'll see Elly banished, my marriage over, and they'll make incorrect assumptions: that Avery had an affair with her too.

It's silly, worrying about such trivialities when I'll be the ex-wife of a murderer and that's what everyone will be gossiping about for a long time to come. They'll point and stare and find me lacking somehow.

I should care but I don't. For once in my uptight, pristine, perfectly ordered life, I don't care what other people think. Last night, I'd been terrified of being pitied. I'd lain here for hours, coming up with various ways to minimize the damage to my reputation, before I realized something. Nothing I do or say will change facts. I married a murderer. He'll go to jail, I'll divorce him. Life moves on. And finally, *finally*, I'll be free.

I'll have money: lots of it. My greatest fear, of being alone, will be irrelevant because I'll have wealth to protect me. I still can't fathom that I had no idea Avery could be capable of murder. He's many things, but to harbor the kind of cruelty to kill a woman?

Guilt pierces my false bravado. I should've known. I should've seen or suspected something... but all the second-guessing in the world isn't going to change facts. I need to formulate a plan, a way to move forward. Starting with going home to pack.

Claire and Dane are nowhere to be seen when I venture out of the bedroom, wearing her oversized sweats. I pad into the kitchen and spy a note on the counter.

DEAR RIS,
*   HOPE   YOU'RE   FEELING   BETTER   THIS*
MORNING.

I'M AT THE STATION FOLLOWING UP ON THAT INFORMATION YOU KINDLY PROVIDED LAST NIGHT. DANE IS AT WORK.

HELP YOURSELF TO BREAKFAST. I'LL TRY TO CHECK IN ON YOU AT LUNCHTIME.

CALL ME IF YOU NEED ME.

CLAIRE XX

I need Claire more than she knows. In fact, I'll be leaning on her a lot over the next few weeks as my life as I know it unravels and I build myself a new one.

Last night was a turning point for me. I'd known the moment Elly told me about the paternity test I had to take a stand. I could either pretend my life was still perfect out of fear of abandonment or snitch on Avery and ensure he became the prime suspect in Jodi's murder. In the end, I had no choice. I'm sick of toeing the line, doing what's expected of me rather than what I want to do. So I'd told Claire, knowing there's no turning back.

I check the fridge, pour an OJ, and drink it quickly. I grab an apple for the short journey home. I'm not hungry but I need sustenance to keep me levelheaded. If Avery's home, I'll need it.

It's seven a.m. when I pull into our drive. I got to Claire's around midnight, which means I spent six and a half hours staring at her ceiling, mulling my plan of action, summoning the guts to go through with it. I need to pack necessities and move out because once the news of Avery's arrest breaks, reporters will be all over the house in search of a story. I can't face that kind of scrutiny. I don't want to, so moving to an unknown location seems the best course of action. Once I'm packed I'll head back to Claire's and start searching online for a new place to live.

The garage is closed so I can't see if Avery's home or not. At this point, I don't particularly care. It won't matter, as I'll wait until he leaves for work, then I'll pack. I let myself into the house and listen for the slightest sound. Nothing. I exhale in relief and head for the kitchen. If my suspicions are correct, police will be crawling over our place at some stage in the next few days. Searching for clues. Looking for evidence. Trying to nail Avery.

I keep a stash of money in a cookie jar at the back of the pantry so that's the first place I go.

"How are you feeling?"

I jump so high my head clunks against the shelf above me. I withdraw from the pantry, mustering my best nonchalant expression.

"Better."

If Avery hears the vitriol in my tone, it doesn't register. Why would it, when he usually only loves the sound of his own voice? He searches the kitchen counter for his smoothie cup. I'd usually have it ready for him.

He's puzzled, his glance flicking between the counter and the blender, as if he can't figure out why I haven't made his breakfast.

"I would've come and picked you up from Claire's last night but I had a conference call with the overseas delegates regarding the merger." He rubs his hands together, his eyes gleaming with avarice. "Looks like it's all systems go so I've invited them here for a dinner party next week. You'll really have to wow them."

I summon my best placating smile and clasp my hands in front of me. "There'll be no dinner party next week."

The fact he hasn't noticed I'm wearing oversized sweats and no makeup speaks volumes. It means he never really sees me anyway. That he looks through me, takes me for granted.

"What are you talking about, sweetheart? You know how important this is to me." He sidles around the island counter, making a move toward me. I move in the opposite direction.

"I know, Avery."

I watch for the slightest tell that he's worried. Nothing. He truly is a narcissistic psychopath. Maybe I should've seen the signs before? Compulsive liar, no empathy, complete lack of conscience, preying on others' weakness, and a grandiose self-importance. He'd exhibited these behaviors repeatedly in our marriage: lying about his infidelities, no empathy for the clients I helped, swooping in and taking over struggling pharmaceutical companies without remorse, acting like the world revolved around him in all social situations.

"Know what?"

I tap my bottom lip, pretending to think. "Hmm...how about we start with the affair and the police asking you to take a paternity test to see if you fathered Jodi's baby?"

His pallor matches the ivory cabinets behind his head. I know him. He'll bluster. Feign indignation. Lie for the ump-teenth time. It won't make any difference.

"Who told you that?"

"Elly." Even saying her name brings a lump to my throat but I ignore it.

Once the color returns to his cheeks, he leans against the island counter, nonchalant and confident as ever. "I never slept with that girl. As for the police, they're deluded. The paternity test is a misunderstanding—"

"Don't," I yell, losing patience quicker than anticipated. "Don't lie to me anymore. It's over, Avery."

I expect him to try and talk his way out of this. Try to cajole me with his usual charm. I'm not wrong.

"Sweetheart, she meant nothing to me." His expression switches from shock to hurt little boy. He's a master manipula-tor. "You know how she is. She's a tramp and I got caught up in something that was bigger than me. Maybe it was the pressure of work or a midlife crisis, but it only happened once. You have to know I meant every word I said last night about how much you mean to me—"

"Cut the bullshit. Jodi's probably one of many of the deluded women that you use and discard."

Confusion creases his brow. "I'm not talking about Jodi. I thought Elly told you—"

"Shut up." As suspected, there are more women and I don't want to know. I want to throttle him for his constant lies. They roll off his tongue without a second thought.

"As for the paternity test being a *misunderstanding*, Ryan asked Elly to switch the test for Jodi's baby!" I'm screaming at this point and he's staring at me in openmouthed shock. "Guess you thought it was time he did your dirty work rather than the other way around. So not only does that make you a lying, cheating bastard, it means you're now the number one suspect in her murder!"

I fling the accusation at him in glee, hoping the police will drag him away sooner rather than later. But I underestimate him. He's not beaten, not yet.

"So you choose to believe a lying slut like Elly over your own husband?" He tuts, his upper lip curling in derision. "Poor form, Ris. I married you and dragged you out of that shitty hospital. I provided for you, I gave you the life you wanted, I gave you children, and this is how you treat me after all we've been through."

The truth hovers on the tip of my tongue, that I dragged myself out of that hospital by targeting him, knowing he'd be too wrapped up in his self-importance to know. But I don't reveal it. What would be the point? It's done and my life will be easier without him in it moving forward.

"Don't you mean what *I've* been through?" I fling my arm wide, gesturing at the kitchen. "I've been your slave for twenty-one years. I've raised your kids, hosted your parties, made your bloody smoothies every fucking morning!"

I never swear and I can see that shocks him more than anything else I've said.

But the shock soon gives way to another sneer. "You've had the lifestyle and the prestige associated with being Mrs. Avery Thurston so don't act like it's a hardship being married to me.

You should be thanking me for every goddamn thing I've done for you."

I'm tired. The type of fatigue that seeps into my bones and makes me ache. Maybe it's the lack of sleep, maybe it's the drama of last night, but I want this to end. Now.

"I'm done." I take a deep breath, ready to utter the words I thought I'd never say. "We're finished, Avery."

He morphs before my eyes. His cheeks redden and his eyes glow with such rage I take a step back toward the knife block.

"We make a great team with me managing our financials and you backing me up socially and professionally. Everybody knows it. We *are* the Hamptons! Don't you know that we're envied because we have the perfect life?" His hands are clenched into fists and he slams them on the counter. Cups rattle and glasses topple. He sweeps his arm across the countertop, sending the fruit bowl, cutlery, and a platter from last night's party crashing to the floor. "I'll destroy Elly for messing with our life."

I cringe but I won't cower. Not anymore. "Like you killed Jodi?"

I shouldn't provoke him, not in this mood, but what's he going to do, kill me too? My life as I know it is over anyway.

He's livid, his shoulders drawn up so tight they almost touch his ears. He stabs a finger at me. "I want you out of this house by the time I come back."

I call his bluff. "You're full of crap. As you just said, you need to keep up appearances, especially with your upcoming precious merger."

"Get out!" He roars but I don't flinch.

"No. This is my house so you do what the hell you want but I'm staying."

A small part of me is scared of him but I force a condescending smile that makes his eyes glint with fury.

"Bitch," he mutters under his breath, and I'm not sure if he's referring to Elly or me as he grabs his car keys from the counter and storms out.

I should call Elly and warn her. Avery is guilty of a lot of things—mainly lying and cheating—but I doubt he's capable of murder and responsible for Jodi's death. Then again, I've never seen him this furious so who knows what he's capable of in this mood? I wouldn't wish harm on Elly despite the way she's betrayed us all.

I reach for my cell. Weigh it in my palm for a few seconds. My thumb hovers over the "contacts" button, ready to scroll through my favorites. She's second on the list behind Claire. I guess it speaks volumes that Avery is third.

I stare at her name on my cell. This will be the last time I call her, ever.

Then I remember Maggie's face last night when Elly had revealed the truth. She'd been stricken, pale, bereft. Elly knows how fragile Maggie is, how her weird episodes rule her life. Yet she'd gone ahead and messed with her husband anyway.

I quash every instinct to help my friend one last time.

This time, Elly's on her own.

I leave my cell on the island counter and head upstairs, intent on cleaning up the mess I've made of my life.

CHAPTER FORTY-TWO

ELLY

I wish Claire would hurry up and get here. I've put everything back in the bathroom cabinet and I'm pacing, hoping I'm wrong about all of this but instinctively knowing I'm not.

If Avery owns this place, he's behind that stash and if Jodi was drugged before she was murdered...I've never liked the prick but is he capable of killing a woman? My skin pebbles and I rub my hands over my arms trying to warm up. Claire needs to arrive, now.

Ryan asked me to switch the paternity test.

He blackmailed me into it because it was so damn important.

Which means Avery is the father of Jodi's baby and that's why he killed her.

But how much does Ryan know?

Was asking me to switch the paternity test the only thing Avery involved him in?

After finding that stash and learning that Avery owns this place, I never considered Ryan could be involved. But what if he is?

I hear a car pull up and I run to the door. My steps slow when I glimpse the car through the window.

It's not Claire.

Panic washes over me. I break out in a cold sweat. My stomach clenches. I don't want to confront Ryan alone. Not when I'm reeling from my suspicions. I know why he's here. He'll know

I told Maggie about us. And if he is somehow involved with Avery in covering up Jodi's death, what's he capable of?

I back away from the door and head for the kitchen. There's not much cutlery here. We never eat. I wish I had something, anything, I could use as a weapon. Even a measly cheese knife would do at this point but there's nothing.

I hear his key in the door.

I'm out of time.

I need to be smart. Outplay him. Bluff him and beat him at his own game.

The door opens and I swear my intestines tie themselves into knots.

"Hey, you," he calls out.

I take a deep breath and shake out my arms, like a prize-fighter about to step into the ring. I'm hoping I'm not about to fight for my life.

"Hey…" My casual greeting dies on my lips as I enter the living room and see him staring at the notepad on the coffee table.

"What's that?" He points at the notepad, where I've scrawled evidence of my research, and scowls.

"Nothing," I say, wishing I could come up with a plausible lie, scrambling hard to make this sound logical. "One of the girls at work called me, she was concerned because her friend may have been drugged on a date so I was looking up stuff for her."

He picks up the notepad and flicks the pages, returning to the first one. "You haven't got much beyond GHB."

"I was only starting my research…" I trail off as he stalks into the bathroom and crouches down in front of the cabinet.

In that moment, I'm terrified. I'd assumed Avery was behind all this but if Ryan knows where the GHB is stashed…have I read this all wrong?

I edge toward the door but he whirls around and stomps

back into the living room, flinging the notepad at my head. I duck.

"What did you do?"

The chill in his voice makes me want to rub the goosebumps off my arms. His gaze is frigid, his mouth twisted. I've never seen him like this. The affable charmer who's always submissive to his older brother has morphed into a monster.

"Nothing—"

"So telling my wife about us is nothing?" Fury stains his cheeks crimson and his eyes bulge. "Telling her I asked you to switch the paternity test with someone else's is nothing?"

His tone is icy, chilling, and the feral gleam in his glare freezes my blood. "Meddling with Avery's stuff in the bathroom is nothing?"

So I'm right. Avery is behind all this. But why does Ryan know about it? And what does Avery use GHB for?

A sliver of memory shimmers across my mind...a hint of sandalwood, the cloying smell clogging my throat, making me want to retch as he's inside me, his weight too heavy...he's hurting me...

Sandalwood...

The significance hovers like a nebulous cloud, just out of reach. I can't recall who raped me but I remember the fallout from that night and how goddamn soiled it made me feel. I'll never forget that.

Ryan slams his palm against the wall and I jump. I have to calm him down, have to keep him talking until Claire arrives. If she's held up...I can't think of the consequences.

"You hurt me yesterday. Deeply." I press my palm to my heart, imploring him to buy my pathetic act. "Hearing you talk about renewing your vows made me crazy. In here." I tap my temple, making loopy circles. "Even after you called, I wasn't sure if I could believe you—"

"Cut the crap, Elly." His tone is so harsh it could shatter glass. "You don't give a shit about anyone but yourself.

Maggie's supposed to be your friend and you fucked her over when you fucked me. So telling her everything has got nothing to do with you feeling *hurt*."

Rage makes his eyes glitter. "You're a ball-breaking bitch and when you couldn't have me you wanted to stick it to me good."

He looks me up and down, a slow perusal that makes my skin crawl. "As if I'd ever leave a class act like Maggie for a whore like you."

Something inside me snaps.

"Too bad you'll have to leave Maggie anyway, because you'll be in jail." I wiggle my fingers in a little wave, deliberately taunting him. "Let's see how far your fortune gets you in there when you're some guy's plaything."

His smile fades fast. Good, I've scored a point. I need to keep distracting and pray that Claire gets here soon.

"It's only a matter of time before Avery's paternity test—that I didn't lose by the way and conveniently locked up for safe keeping—is retested and shows genetic markers proving he's the father of that poor girl's baby."

I make a grand show of pointing at the bathroom. "Then there's that little stash of goodies in there *that you know about*. Were you in on it? Did you help your psycho brother?"

I snap my fingers, like I've come up with something new. "Plus your alibi for the night of Jodi's death won't hold up when I vouch for the fact you left here early—"

"Shut up. Shut the fuck up." He's riled, his fingers clenching and unclenching in a way that quashes my bravado damn quick. "You women are all the same. That other one came to town to tell me about her bastard. Stupid girl saw our company's latest award win in the newspaper and tried to find me through Avery. Sent some stupid goddamn letter outlining her terms to the company. She actually tried to blackmail me. Like I could risk Maggie finding out and divorcing me."

His grin chills me to the bone. "So I got Avery to take care of her, just like he's always done. Good, old, dependable big brother."

Oh my God.

Fear like I've never known slithers through me, cold and insidious.

Ryan fathered Jodi's baby.

Avery killed Jodi because Ryan asked him to?

"Not that he was supposed to kill her." A flicker of remorse darkens his eyes. "I wanted him to intimidate her, enough to get her the hell out of town. Pay her something for her silence. But the dumbass miscalculated something in the dosage and she ended up dying." His mouth downturns in sadness. "That wasn't supposed to happen."

If he's just admitted to being an accessory to murder—though it's technically manslaughter if I believe what he's saying about that idiot Avery—what's he going to do to me to keep me silent? Claire needs to get here, pronto.

"Fuck, this is such a mess." He drags his hand through his hair and stares at me, wild-eyed. "For what it's worth, I'm sorry."

The apology comes from left field. "Sorry for being a lying, cheating scumbag to your wife who doesn't deserve it? Sorry for getting Jodi knocked up? Sorry for being responsible for a girl's death?"

"For all of it..." His cell pings and he slides it out of his pocket. Something inexplicable passes over his face when he reads the message, before he taps a quick response with his thumb as he heads to the door.

Confused, I remain silent. He's leaving after confessing?

"I really am sorry," he says, sounding genuinely contrite as he opens the door.

Avery is standing on the other side.

CHAPTER FORTY-THREE

MARISA

I'll never forget how broken Elly sounded the morning she called me after the rape; like she had no one else in the world to depend on. I'd only known her a few months and for her to reach out to me meant she truly didn't have a close friend or family.

Having an affair with Ryan is deplorable but she's inherently good; I know it deep in my gut where my instincts have never let me down.

Decision made, I pick up my cell to call her but there's a loud pounding on my patio door. Nobody would come around the back, yet there's a face peering through the glass. Maggie.

Immediately feeling bad for not calling to check on her last night, I let her in. But before I can say anything she shoves me so hard I backpedal and slam into the nearest cupboard, the only thing that saves me from landing on my ass.

"I can't believe you," she yells, her face flushed and her mouth twisted in disgust. "You knew about Ryan and didn't tell me?"

Confused, I hold my hands up like I have nothing to hide and edge around the island counter out of reach. "I had no idea about him and Elly, I swear."

"Liar," she hisses, following me around the counter. "Ryan said you knew about the affair."

"Your husband is lying."

I keep my voice calm and devoid of the outrage I'm feeling.

How dare she barge in here and manhandle me when I've been nothing but concerned for her since we learned the truth last night?

Then again, from her point of view, I have a funny way of showing it. I haven't called her since I dropped her off, and Ryan being Ryan he's probably invented all kinds of lies to cover his screw-up.

"He's not all bad," she says, her shoulders slumping beneath the weight of truth no matter how much she wants to deny it. "I love him."

She'd have to, to tolerate his usurping ways. For as long as I've known him Ryan has been fawning and deferent to his wife for her money, as the whole world knows except Maggie.

But I see where she's coming from. I loved him too. He's like a bold, rambunctious kid you can't help but like. Everyone adores Ryan, including one of my best friends, apparently.

"I'm sorry for not calling to check up on you." I gesture to the kitchen table. "Why don't you take a seat and I'll make us some coffee?"

"No, thanks." She glances around, as if in a daze. "Where's Avery?"

"Confronting Elly about telling us the truth."

She reaches for the island counter, as if needing the support. Her hands tremble slightly and I glimpse fear in her quick look-away. "She'll be okay, won't she?"

Incredulous, I shake my head. "You're actually worried about the woman who had an affair with your husband?"

She gnaws on her bottom lip so hard I see a speck of blood. "Avery's not a good man."

"Tell me something I don't know."

She doesn't register my dry retort. "There are things you don't know about . . . things I only just discovered."

She swallows several times, her throat convulsing, as if she can't get the words out, and for the first time since she's barreled in here I'm worried.

What else has Avery done?

"Ryan said Avery has this thing for helpless women...he gets off on it."

She's speaking so softly I struggle to hear and she can't look me in the eye. "Avery boasted a few times recently that he had sex with women after he...uh, relaxed them."

"Relaxed? What does that mean?"

But the moment I ask the question, I know. Like pieces of a puzzle slotting together, I know with certainty that when my husband used GHB to murder Jodi it hadn't been the first time he used it.

But I need to be sure.

"Are you saying—"

"Yes. It's as bad as you think. Ryan discovered a stash at the cottage and asked Avery about it. That's when he told him—" A sob bursts from Maggie's mouth and she covers it with a hand that's still trembling. "I'm sorry, Ris. My husband may lie and cheat but he doesn't drug women to have sex with them."

The import of what I've discovered crashes over me in a sickening wave. Nausea churns in my gut and I dash to the guest toilet, reaching it just in time. I fall to my knees and bump my head against the corner of the vanity. The pain barely registers as the OJ I consumed this morning burns a path up my gullet and spews out in a rush.

I retch continually until there's nothing left. I'm drained, hollowed, like someone has disemboweled me.

When I stumble back into the kitchen, Maggie has gone.

CHAPTER FORTY-FOUR

ELLY

"Leave us," Avery snaps, and Ryan's only too happy to oblige.

He glances over his shoulder once, and if I'd been scared before, now I'm terrified. Ryan looks...sad. In all the time I've known him I've never seen him express any emotion resembling sorrow. Even earlier, when he'd told me how Jodi died, he hadn't looked like this: like he truly regrets what is about to happen.

Avery slams the door and advances on me, his smug smile making my skin prickle with distaste.

"I hear you've been saying things you shouldn't, Elly." His gaze drops to my lips. "You really could put that mouth to much better use, you know."

"Go fuck yourself." I sound bold and confident and nothing like the quivering mess of nerves inside that make me want to vomit.

"Why, when it's so much more fun fucking you?"

Fear tightens my throat but I swallow to ease it. "Ryan's an asshole for cheating on his wife and a vile pig if he's told you about us, but you're just as bad for listening to his boasting."

His smile widens into a leer as he continues to stalk me. "I'm not talking about Ryan fucking you."

I back away, small, mincing steps around the sofa. But it's too late. Even at this distance, I can smell him.

Sandalwood.

He laughs, a deep-throated, low chuckle that along with that foul stench triggers a tsunami of memories.

Him helping me up the stairs to my apartment, solicitous and kind.

Him guiding me into the bedroom.

Him taking off my shoes, sliding my panties down, lying on top of me, his weight pinning me.

Him grunting and thrusting repeatedly until it was over.

"So you finally remember, huh?" He strokes his chin, as if trying to solve some problem. "Too bad it took you this long. We could've had a hell of a lot more fun together than you settling for second best with my brother."

I can't breathe. I'm choking, like he's wrapped his hands around my throat. I drag in breath after breath but it isn't enough. Spots and squiggles shimmer before my eyes and I blink rapidly to dispel them.

"I knew you wouldn't report it, even if you could remember." His leering gaze travels over me. "Women like you never do."

Something inside me snaps. In that instant, I know I have to fight back. I won't be a victim, not like last time.

"What now, Avery?"

My voice is embarrassingly squeaky—I mustn't show fear—and I clear my throat before continuing. "Now that I know you're a rapist and a murderer, what are you going to do?"

I'm buying time, taunting him to keep speaking. Claire should be here any moment and the longer I can get him to gloat the more chance I have to live.

That's another thing I realized when I chose to fight a few moments ago. A wealthy man like him may be able to wriggle out of a murder charge by downgrading it to manslaughter, but if I can add rape to the mix things will get a whole lot tougher.

Which also means I know too much and I am expendable.

"Hmm...what am I going to do?" He taps his bottom lip, pretending to think. "Well, now that everyone knows you're a slut they won't find it unusual that you bring other guys here."

He sniggers, supremely confident as always. "A guy who likes to dose you up to enhance the pleasure, huh?"

His gaze darts to the bathroom cabinet, almost eager. "Yeah, a decent dose of GHB should do it, like before."

He shakes his head and his wild gaze darts to the sofa as if he's remembering Jodi lying on another sofa in another cottage. "Not that I meant to kill the other one. That was an accident. And you were knocked out way too quickly with what I gave you."

His upper lip curls in derision as his gaze flicks back to me and I see hatred. "But this time I intend to have a little fun. The last interlude between us was over too quickly." The maniacal glint in his eyes terrifies me. "This time I'll give you a better dose so we can have fun for hours."

"You're insane," I manage to get out, my throat tight with terror. "I'll report you for rape. You'll be arrested—"

"Everyone in town will think you sleep around after news of your affair with Ryan is leaked and they'll think you lured me here too."

He chuckles, a chilling sound that rasps across my nerve endings. "Maybe you want to keep it all in the family, huh? Pretty kinky sleeping with two brothers. Ris and Claire will hate your guts for the affair with Ryan and you seducing me will be the icing on the proverbial cake."

His eyebrow rises in sardonic challenge. "A cake I'll get to eat."

Bile rises and I swallow it down. "You'll never get away with it."

"But I will." He snaps his fingers. "You didn't report it last time, who's going to believe you now?"

He pins me with a stare that sends a shiver through me. "Ryan told me all about you. That's some past you've got. Bigamist husband, breakdown, baby adopted out." He laughs again. "So who's going to believe *you* if you cry rape? Everyone in this town reveres me." He thumps his chest. "I'm a moral, upstanding citizen. Whereas you..." He trails off, sniggering, and I hate that he's struck at my vulnerabilities.

All those reasons he cited are why I didn't report the rape in the first place. Not that I could remember who the perpetrator was. Now that I can, I won't let him get away with it again.

"There are so many loopholes in your theory to rape me, then blame me, you'll never get away with it. Plus Ryan will know—"

"Just like he knew about Jodi? Ryan is spineless and indebted to me. He won't breathe a word of this."

He leers again. "He made his choice the second he walked out of here after I texted him that I'll take care of everything, like I have his entire life."

I'm fast running out of options.

Determined not to let my panic show, I point to the cabinet. "Too bad Claire knows about your stash so that part of your theory is flawed because if I'm found drugged she'll do a blood test and—"

I scream as he vaults the coffee table, so fast I stumble backward and almost hit my head on the mantel. Being unconscious around this madman isn't the best plan so I reach for the first thing I can get my hands on. A vase.

"Come on, Elly, you know you want it. Stop playing hard to get." He advances on me from four feet away. "On second thought, no drugs this time, just you and me." His lips peel back in a sneer. "Is it my fault you like it rough?"

He wiggles his fingers. "A little breath play? Asphyxiation while I fuck you? I guarantee you'll love it."

My revulsion must show on my face because his sneer widens into a smug grin so I wait until he's close enough. Until his hands are around my neck.

Then I smash the vase on his head with all the strength I can muster.

It doesn't knock him out as I expect. He staggers momentarily before coming at me harder, enraged I have the audacity to fight back. The way I should've fought back if I'd been conscious when he raped me the first time around.

I scream and kick and claw, doing everything I can to stay upright. My muscles ache and my calf cramps, but I twist and writhe and fight with everything I've got.

It's useless. He hooks his leg around my ankle and I topple to the floor. He's on top of me. Pinning me with his weight. I can't let this happen again.

I fight harder, ineffectual punches that only land glancing blows on his arms and head as my hips try to buck him off but can't shift him. I bare my teeth and shift my head to the side, trying to bite him. He leans forward and his forearm presses down on my windpipe.

"Relax, go with it, you'll enjoy this. Sex is so much better when you can't catch your breath..."

A shimmering crimson creeps over my eyes in increments. The edges of my vision blur.

I try to writhe one last time. My hand hurts, a raw stinging as something sharp pierces my skin.

A glass shard from the vase.

I try to grasp it, to muster the strength to raise my arm.

His face is inches from mine and he's grinning, a gloating leer.

He's won.

Or so he thinks.

The door bursts open, and in that second when his head snaps up to see who's there, I know I can't let him get away with this.

CHAPTER FORTY-FIVE

CLAIRE

I arrive at Ris's house to ask Avery to come in for questioning when my cell rings.

It's Elly. I answer the call. "What do you want?"

"Claire, this is important. I know you must hate me as much as Maggie and Ris right now if she's told you everything but please don't hang up."

I'm on the verge of doing just that when she says, "I've discovered a stash of materials that make GHB, along with syringes, in the place Ryan leases from Avery for us to be together."

My stomach falls away, a familiar feeling when I know I'm about to wrap up a case.

"I don't know how Jodi died but after Ryan asked me to switch the paternity test I'm worried that—"

"You should be worried," I snap, unable to understand how she could do this and even more baffled why she'd do anything illegal for that prick. "You're in a world of trouble for interfering with a police investigation."

"I know." Her soft sigh almost makes me feel sorry for her. "But I think you should get here and check out this stuff."

"I'll be there shortly."

After I ensure Avery is cooperative.

"Hurry," she says, and hangs up.

We're obviously both strung out because she didn't give me the address and I forgot to ask.

"Damn it." I bang on Ris's front door, hating to ask her for directions but needing to follow up on another piece of the puzzle that can put Avery away for murder. I'll call her once Avery is at the station. Hopefully she's had a good night's sleep at my place, though I doubt it.

I hope he comes to the door fast so I can get him to the station ASAP then check out the GHB. But when the door finally opens, it's Ris.

"What are you doing here?"

There are dark circles under her eyes, she's pale, and she's still wearing my sweats. "I came home to pack some stuff but then Maggie showed up and everything's a mess."

As much as I'd like to comfort my friend with what she's going through, I don't have time now.

"Is Avery here?"

"He left."

She sounds scared.

"Where did he go?"

"To confront Elly." Tears well in her eyes, and before I can respond, she breaks down. "And I didn't call her to warn her. What kind of monster does that make me?"

"She called me a few minutes ago from the place she meets Ryan." Foreboding makes me terser than I would usually be with a woman who's gone through as much as Ris. "We need to get there, now. Can you give me directions?"

She nods, gnawing her bottom lip. "I'll have to show you the way."

"No." I don't want Ris anywhere near a nasty confrontation between Avery and Elly. "Just tell me."

"I can't. I only remember how we got there last night by following Elly."

Damn. I have no choice but to take her along.

"Come on. We need to hurry."

Ris senses my urgency and is in my car before I call the station to call for backup.

I have a very bad feeling about this.

Thankfully Ron answers on the first ring. "Hey, Claire, I was about to call you."

It's the news I've been waiting for. "It's him, isn't it?"

I don't have time for Ron's dramatic pause. "Unfortunately no, Avery Thurston isn't the father of Jodi Van Gelder's baby."

"What the—"

"But the genetic markers are close, indicating it could be a sibling—"

"Ryan." I thump the car hood.

Ris is staring at me, wide-eyed and fearful, and I remember why I called him. "Listen, Ron, I'm with Ris and we're on our way to a cottage Ryan rents. He's been having an affair with my friend Elly. She called me a few minutes ago, saying she's found evidence of GHB there. We think Avery's on his way there too."

"Fuck, what's the address?"

Frustrated, I kick a tire. "I don't know. Ris is going to direct me there from memory. I'll call you as soon as I arrive so have backup ready."

"Shall do, and I'll put an APB out on Avery's car."

"Good idea. See you soon."

I disconnect and get in the car. Ris is staring straight ahead, like she's in a trance. She hasn't asked me about Ryan and I'm glad. I think she's too shell-shocked to compute much at the moment, but I hope to God she can direct me to this cottage. I fire up the engine and touch her forearm. She jumps and looks at me like I'm a stranger.

"I know Elly isn't your favorite person right now but I think she's in danger and we need to get to that cottage ASAP. You ready?"

After what seems like an eternity, Ris nods. "Make a left onto the highway from Sunnyside."

I floor it, breaking the speed limit as I fly down the highway but with sirens off. I don't want to alert Avery when we arrive in case he's a man on the edge. And now that I know

Ryan fathered Jodi's baby, maybe he's there too. I'm surprised when Ris directs me to take a small gravel road off the highway. I would've missed it if she hadn't pointed it out. I grip the wheel tight as the car sheers off the dirt a little, willing myself to slow down when every cop instinct I have is to do the opposite.

"It's up ahead." Ris's hand is shaky when she points. "Around those trees."

I call in the location and give Ron precise directions. The squad isn't far away. Thank God.

"When we get there, you need to stay in the car, okay?"

Ris nods, reverting to catatonic as she stares out the windshield. The road narrows, and as I make the final turn past the trees, I'm blown away by the view. The cottage is perched on the ocean's edge but I'm not here for the breathtaking scenery. I spy two cars. Elly's and Avery's.

I pull over and kill the engine. "Stay here."

I exit the car and unclip my holster. I need to be prepared for anything.

That's when I hear a blood-curdling scream.

I sprint for the door. It's unlocked. I open it and draw my gun.

Avery has Elly pinned to the floor. Her face is a scary mottled purple color. His head lifts slowly, his stare terrifying.

I've seen that stare on psychopaths before.

He's past the point of no return.

But before I can react I see Elly's hand lift.

And I see the glitter of glass.

CHAPTER FORTY-SIX

ELLY

I'd never believed the myth that when people are on the verge of death, their life flashed before their eyes. But as Claire bursts through the door and distracts Avery, time slows. I see every second in intricate detail. Individual snapshots of fragmented time, captured and highlighted.

Walking up the aisle in an ivory sheath and fingertip veil, my heart swelling when I glimpse tears in my fiancé's eyes.

Honeymooning in Hawaii, frolicking in the surf on Maui, cruising the green hills in Kauai, trekking on the Big Island.

Weekends spent curled in front of the fire, wrapped in each other's arms, while the familiar Chicago wind rattled the windows.

The morning I saw him with his real family.

My collapse after he left.

Moving to Gledhill. My apartment—my sanctuary—until this monster invaded it and tore an irreparable hole in my already shattered life.

Faces of the men I'd targeted since my reinvention, blending into one another.

Finally coalescing into this moment, with this man.

My senses are heightened. The clarity is unbelievable. Who knew oxygen deprivation could be so enlightening?

I see Claire standing in the doorway, gun drawn and pointed at Avery.

I see Ris peering over her shoulder, her mouth open.

I see Avery lift his head and turn to see who's interrupted.

There's stubble along his jaw. I spy a tiny scar, probably a shaving nick, below his ear. It's tiny yet jagged. I see an unsightly hair poking from his ear, probably the first of many.

I grip the shard of glass tighter. I'm bleeding. As I summon the energy to raise my arm I notice a bead of blood hovering at my wrist.

Drip.

Drip.

Drip.

Tiny drops that plop onto his shoulder, a startling crimson against his white polo. Spreading outward in those weird patterns used by psychiatrists to analyze patients. He doesn't notice.

My hand is at his neck now, the glass a hair's breadth away from his carotid.

"Avery, it's over," Claire says, her tone comforting and well modulated when I would be yelling. "Raise your hands above your head and get up slowly."

The unbearable pressure on my windpipe eases as he lifts his forearm. Slowly. Reluctantly.

I drag in a breath, another. My throat hurts like the devil where he's been leaning all his weight on me.

He's going to surrender. Claire has given me an out. I should take it.

But I don't have the energy to be dragged through a lengthy trial, being persecuted on the witness stand more than the perpetrator of the crime.

I'll be labeled every filthy name Avery called me earlier and more. A nameless jury will judge me on more than this. They'll scoff at my lifestyle, my choice to remain childless, my penchant for revenge on married men. They'll discover my farcical marriage, my breakdown, and my decision to give away my baby. My past laid bare for mockery and ridicule.

I won't have a job, I won't have an income, I won't have a life.

So I choose my life over his.

"No!" Claire yells as I plunge the glass into Avery's neck.

I'm sprayed with blood.

It's everywhere.

I can't see. I can't breathe.

The unmistakable coppery taste of blood is on my lips.

I roll onto my side as he collapses and topples off me. I gasp for air and swipe my hands across my eyes so I can see.

When my eyelids flutter open I'm staring into Avery's fixed, glassy gaze.

It's over.

CHAPTER FORTY-SEVEN

MARISA

I watch my husband die.

It's like one of those horror films the girls used to goggle over in their early teens, the kind of scene I wouldn't be able to un-see as I brought them popcorn and lectured them about the inevitable nightmares they'd have.

I've never seen so much blood. It covers everything: the rug, the coffee table, Elly. She's lying on her back, one hand over her throat, the other wiping blood from her mouth. She's a mess and I feel sorry for her.

Sirens sound in the distance. I know I don't have long to fix this.

"Don't move, Elly." I rush past Claire, who's frozen to the spot. "You have to let the police see you like this."

I stand over Elly, whose blank stare indicates she's already in shock. But I have to get through to her. I won't let Avery ruin any more lives than he already has.

"Ris, stand back. You're contaminating a crime scene." Claire's at my shoulder now, hovering. She grabs my arm, tries to tug me away. I don't budge.

"There's no crime here." I turn to look her in the eye, beseeching her to understand. "This was self-defense."

Surprise flares in Claire's eyes. "Ris, we need to—"

"Listen to me." I grip Claire's arms and shake her a little. "Elly had no choice. He was strangling her, you burst in, he looked up, and when Elly tried to struggle one last time he fell on the glass. That's it. End of story."

I shake her again for emphasis. She has to believe me. Because as much as I dislike Elly for what she did to Maggie, I don't believe she should be on trial for murder.

Avery deserved everything he got.

"Look at her neck." I point to Elly's bruised, mottled neck where Avery's forearm had pressed down with all his weight behind it. "She couldn't breathe. She was suffering oxygen deprivation. She was so traumatized she thought she'd die so when you distracted him she used her last ounce of strength to try and shove him off. That's it."

I don't ask if Claire saw Elly's arm rise when Avery turned his head toward the door.

I don't ask if she saw Avery lift his forearm to release her.

I don't ask if she saw Elly edge the glass closer to his neck.

I don't ask anything.

"H-he raped me. It was him. He admitted it. And he was about to do it again." A lone tear trickles down Elly's cheek as I stagger back, sucker-punched yet again by the monster I married.

I open my mouth to speak but no words come out and for the second time in thirty minutes I need to vomit.

Claire's glance shifts between us, stunned, and I slowly nod. "Maggie told me earlier that Avery boasted to Ryan about drugging women so he could have sex with them, so stands to reason he was the one who raped Elly."

"Fuck," Claire mutters, her pallor matching Elly's.

We stare at each other in shock.

I look at Claire, willing her to do the right thing by her friends, not by the law.

The sirens are close now. They drown out the sound of the waves, which I only just notice.

After what seems like an eternity, Claire's shoulders slump, like she's deflated, defeated.

"It was self-defense." Claire's disbelieving gaze swings from Elly to me, like she can't quite comprehend how we all ended up here. "She had no choice."

I touch her arm. "Thank you."

Claire's wrong though. We all have choices. We're all guilty of making a wrong decision at times.

But in this cottage by the sea that's been privy to a multitude of secrets, I'm sure we've made the right one.

CHAPTER FORTY-EIGHT

CLAIRE

Being raised by a family of cops, joining the force myself, all I've ever known is truth.

I fight to uphold it on a daily basis.

I strive to be honest in my own life.

It's why I had to tell Dane about that stupid almost-aborted kiss with Griffin: I couldn't not tell him. And it's why I'll tell him about my transgression before we married because it's the only way to start afresh after all the crap we've been through recently.

So as I stare at Elly covered in Avery's blood, and I puzzle over Ris's insistence this is self-defense, I'm torn.

I know the truth.

Elly killed Avery.

Nobody but another cop can understand the way I approach a situation like this. Adrenaline surges through my body, making me hyperaware of every single detail. I see more clearly. My hearing is heightened. And I record the visual instinctively, so I can play it back like a movie in my head later.

I've picked up vital details because of this, clues that have put away more bad guys than I can count.

As I watched Ris rush past me and hover over Elly, that's what I did. Replayed the scene from the moment I burst through the door.

I saw him trying to kill Elly by pressing all his weight

against her neck using his forearm. She was a nasty color, almost violet from lack of oxygen.

I pointed my gun at Avery, yelled at him to raise his hands and get up slowly.

I saw him turn his head to look at me.

I saw him start to raise his arm, obeying my instruction.

I saw Elly's hand with the glass near his neck.

I saw the exact moment she plunged it in.

There'd been a time lapse: a fraction of a second, maybe two. Long enough for me to understand one vital detail.

Elly could've stopped.

She didn't.

Now I have to decide.

Make a friend suffer for killing a murderer and a rapist, or pretend my detailed memory is faulty and there hasn't been a time lapse after all.

I holster my gun and approach Ris and Elly. I don't bother checking Avery for a pulse. His eyes are open and fixed. She hit the carotid and he bled out quickly.

It's not right to think ill of the dead but all I feel as I stare down at his lifeless body is relief.

Maybe Elly did us all a favor? Avoiding a lengthy, costly trial where Avery would've hired the best lawyer his fortune could buy. Sure, the paternity test proved he isn't the father of Jodi's baby and Ryan probably is, but I bet he killed Jodi to clean up another one of his younger brother's messes, and he'd plead insanity or manslaughter to get his sentence reduced.

While I haven't seen the GHB-making stash Elly found yet, I know enough about juries that a smooth-talking attorney can explain away drain cleaner and floor stripper. All we have is circumstantial evidence. Would it have been enough to prosecute? Doubtful.

I'd hoped to break Avery under interrogation but the man had been a consummate liar. I doubt he would've cracked so he would've walked.

Not that anyone deserved to die, even slime like Avery.

But this is wrong.

I know what I saw.

Ris tries to convince me otherwise. I listen to her blather about self-defense. I stare at Elly, Avery's blood dripping down her cheek, into her hair. I remember the times over the last two years the three of us have spent together. Coffee dates at Sea Breeze on the oceanfront, checking out the hot lifeguards and giggling like teenage girls. Late-night suppers at The Lookout after a movie when we'd dissect the plot and wax lyrical about our favorite actors. Ris's many parties where I'd mingle with the locals, glad that I'd met women like them I can call friends. Elly being there for me that night I'd been drowning my sorrows alone at a bar. I remember all of it: special times with my closest friends. And I waver. Who am I to determine what is the truth?

The truth is, Avery would've raped Elly again, and we know he's capable of murder. The truth is, Elly will have to live with the guilt forever, it will taint her entire life. What kind of friend am I? Ris is standing by Elly despite everything Elly has done. Will I turn my back on Elly when she needs me most? Or will I tell a lie that will follow me for the rest of my life?

Sirens draw close and cut off. Backup is outside. This room will be swarming with cops shortly.

I have seconds to decide.

I look at Elly again and this time, when her agonized gaze locks with mine, I know.

If I'd been in her position, I would've done the same. Any woman would've. Avery had drugged her, abused her. He wouldn't have let Elly get away with besmirching his precious reputation.

He would've come after her.

That's what settles it for me. Avery would've walked despite killing Jodi and he wouldn't have left Elly alone.

He still won't; she'll have to live with the memories of this horrific scene. And I don't want to make it any more painful for her than it needs to be.

"It was self-defense," I announce, sounding as authoritative as I can. I see the relief in Elly's eyes, mirrored in Ris's. "She had no choice."

Ron bursts through the door, followed by two detectives and three police officers.

Ris and I back away, giving them access to the scene. Ron's a veteran but his eyes widen when he sees Elly covered in blood and the livid bruises on her neck.

When his gaze swings to Avery, I see disgust.

I usher Ris off to the side. "We'll all be questioned. You ready for that?"

Her eyes are bright with unshed tears and she nods. "Absolutely. I won't let any of you down."

I hug her, sensing she needs it. She clings to me, cries a little against my shoulder.

When she releases me, her expression is serene. "Thanks, Claire."

I know she's thanking me for more than the comforting hug.

I have to ask. "How do you do that? Stand by her, after all that's happened?"

She doesn't hesitate. "Because we all deserve a second chance."

I couldn't agree with her more.

CHAPTER FORTY-NINE

ELLY

I'm photographed and swabbed and examined, prodded and poked and stared at, with pity and curiosity and suspicion.

I don't care.

I'm free.

Once forensics scour the scene and the cottage, and copious samples are taken from me, I'm given a towel and clean clothing and allowed to shower. I stand under the spray, tilt my face to the showerhead, and savor the water washing away the last remnants of Avery off me.

It's like being reborn.

I soap and scrub until my skin feels raw. When I towel off and see my reflection in the mirror I look like a beet. I don't bother with makeup. I finally feel clean.

After paramedics check me over and give me the all-clear, Claire's partner, Ron, is solicitous. I assume Claire's asked him to take care of me because he's kind and polite on our drive back to the station. He doesn't treat me like a murder suspect. Then again, Claire's probably told him she witnessed the entire thing and it was self-defense.

I still can't believe Ris came through for me like that.

I underestimated her. Once a nurturer, always a nurturer. Even after the way I let her down, she still cares for me. I feel bad for not trusting her enough with the secrets of my past. For taking advantage of her friendship, for sleeping with Ryan, for outing her husband as a filthy rapist.

I feel horrible, but in killing Avery, I did Ris the ultimate favor, one friend to another.

I set her free.

She'd been trapped in a marriage with a depraved monster, being his trophy wife, hosting his parties, under his financial control, clueless to the vile pig she slept next to most nights.

Then there's Maggie and what I did to her...I'd wanted to reveal Ryan's despicable infidelity by bringing her to the cottage last night. I never would've imagined in a million years what else he'd done.

When we reach the station I'm ushered into an interrogation room. Before the heavy steel door closes, I glimpse Claire and Ris entering different rooms, individually.

I'm not afraid. My friends will stand by me.

They have before.

Friends comfort and protect, even in the worst possible circumstances, and these women are my friends. They proved it the night of the rape and now, by agreeing that what I did was in self-defense, and I'm confident they'll stick by our story and tell the cops exactly that.

As Ris had stood over me next to Avery's lifeless body, I'd seen the relief in her eyes. No hatred. No disgust. Just blatant gratitude, like I'd given her a reprieve.

I'd known then she wouldn't blame me for killing her husband.

Claire had been the surprise. Upstanding, uptight Claire, whose clean-living reputation can never be questioned. I'd observed the war she'd waged, her face so easy to read. Conscience versus friendship, truth versus lie, right versus wrong.

Lucky for me, she made the decision to stand by our friendship. I'll never forget it.

I answer the detectives' repetitive questions, my voice quivering as I recite what happened. Tears fall and I struggle to stem them. I hate being a victim.

The police are sympathetic. I see it in their pitying stares, in the way they dart uncomfortable glances at each other when I go into detail about how Avery and Ryan confessed their involvement in Jodi's murder, Avery revealing how he raped me and was going to do it again. They wonder why I didn't report it at the time and I tell them I didn't want to go through an investigation that tends to put the victim on trial. They nod compassionately and I refocus on Avery attacking me, and my self-defense.

I'm being watched from behind the one-way glass too. I can feel the unseen stares. The back of my neck prickles because of it. The questions continue. I don't think the detectives are trying to trip me up, as much as get facts straight. At least, that's what I'm hoping. Claire warned me her subordinates would interrogate me because even though she's the lead on the case she's a friend.

Once they're done they leave and two other officers enter the room. One is tall, good-looking, with curly dark hair and blue eyes. His suit fits him well. He looks like a TV cop, an actor paid to be on set. The other is shorter, older, with a paunch. But his eyes are kind and the corners of his mouth tilt up rather than down.

They question me all over again. Asking me to repeat my story and to outline exactly what happened in the cottage. After what seems like an eternity, I sense they're winding down when the hot cop glances at his watch beneath the table then gives his partner a nod. There's a knock on the door and I try to stay calm. I know what's about to happen. The cops who interviewed me first would've interrogated Claire and Ris to ensure our stories match.

He strides to the door, opens it, and talks in a low voice for what seems like forever. I'm holding my breath but the short cop is watching me and I force myself to exhale. The door closes and my heart leaps.

This is it.

He comes back to the table. I try to read his face.

"Thanks for your assistance in this matter, Ms. Knight, if we need further clarification or more information we'll be in touch. We're sorry for what you went through." The cop holds out his hand and I shake it. "You're free to go."

I'm glad he hasn't said, "For now, you're free to go." The omission is significant.

"Thanks for your help." The pudgy one shakes my hand too and this time, his mouth curves into a full-blown smile.

I'm free.

As I exit the room, I see the doors where Claire and Ris entered are closed but I have no idea if they've already left or they're still in there. I leave the station, half hoping to see my friends waiting for me. They're not.

What did I expect? For us to revert to the way we were?

People like me don't have friendships that stay the distance. I'll move on. Find new friends. Try not to repeat the mistakes of the past. It's what I do and I have to be okay with that.

A hand lands on my shoulder from behind and I spin around.

"Maggie..." I'm lost for words, my mind blank as to what to say to this woman I once called my friend.

"Come with me," she says, her voice soft and devoid of judgment, so I fall into step beside her as we head for the boardwalk.

A brisk Atlantic breeze whips my ponytail across my eyes and when I tuck it into my collar I see Maggie studying me with open curiosity.

"They've arrested Ryan for his part in that girl's death," she says, gesturing to a bench, where we sit.

She stares out to sea and I remain silent, preferring she talk. After the truth I divulged to her last night, I've said more than enough.

"They tested his DNA. He's a match." She shakes her head. "He fathered that baby."

She makes "that baby" sound like the devil's spawn.

"I'm sorry—"

"No you're not." She spins so fast to face me I almost topple off the end of the bench in my haste to shuffle away. "I knew about your affair with my husband. Why do you think I tolerated your half-assed chatter every Monday morning?"

Her laugh borders on crazy. "I sat in your office week after week, wondering if you'd ever have the guts to tell me the truth. But you didn't so I waited."

Confusion clouds my brain. I'm tired so I can't make sense of what she's saying. I have to ask. "Why? If you knew, why did you befriend me?"

"Because you're damaged, like me." She taps her temple and makes loopy circles. "Up here."

I'm nothing like her. She probably has an undiagnosed medical condition. I've become so bitter and twisted I can justify anything, including sleeping with a friend's husband.

"I'm not a good person. Don't make excuses for me."

She doesn't speak for a moment but her unwavering stare is really starting to bug me.

"Why did you want to see me, Maggie?"

"To tell you this. I won't be divorcing Ryan. The charges won't stick. I'll pay whatever it takes to get him out." She shrugs. "Besides, he didn't really do anything. He told me. How he asked Avery to speak to that girl, to intimidate her into leaving, but Avery screwed up. So, he's not really guilty."

I stare at her in disbelief but wisely stay silent.

"I need him. He makes me happy." Her snort is loud and unladylike. "I know what people say. That he married me for my money. That he's spineless, a kept man, that he's nothing without me and Avery."

Her lips compress into a thin line. "I don't care. We're a team and he puts up with my eccentricities when not many men would so I tolerate his faults." She pokes me in the arm, hard, and I wince. "Stay the hell away from my husband, because if I get the slightest inkling anything's going on again, you'll both be sorry."

It's an idle threat. What's she going to do? Money can only buy you so much and she's not the type to order a hit. If so, I would've been dead a long time ago.

"You don't have to worry. I meant what I said when I took you to the cottage. I did this to give you the wake-up call I got too late."

It sounds lame but I continue. "I fell in love with the wrong guy once. Idolized him. Married him. Only to discover he already had a wife and kids and I was the idiot bride who fell for a bigamist."

I glimpse sympathy in her eyes. I don't need it, but I'm glad she understands my motivation, no matter how warped.

But I'm done. I've messed with the last woman. I can't spend my life exacting revenge when the one person hurting the most is me.

Maggie stands and looks down on me with pity.

I don't say anything as she walks away.

CHAPTER FIFTY

MARISA

I need closure.

I have to see Elly before she leaves town. I know it's crazy but I feel guilty that my husband was the one who raped her. I feel like I should've suspected something, I should've picked up some sign that he was dangerous. But I had no idea and I'll never get any real answers as to why a successful, handsome man had to resort to drugging women to have sex with them.

We were vanilla all the way. He never made odd demands or choked me or suggested any kind of kink. Then again, he was a control freak. He exerted influence on Ryan his entire life and I allowed him to think he controlled me. It stands to reason he would get off on dominating women who couldn't fight back.

I can't think about the fact that he would attack these women then come home to me. It makes me want to claw my skin off and no amount of showering or dips in the frigid Atlantic will ever make me feel clean again.

I'm glad Elly's leaving Gledhill. I can get past her betrayal of Maggie but every time I see her I know I'll remember how my husband violated her and feel bad all over again.

I have to say something today. It feels odd, apologizing for something so horrendous that I had no control over, but then I remember how broken she'd been that night and I feel sick to my stomach for the damage my husband inflicted.

I glance around the table set in the far corner of the garden:

cheese platter, fruit, Chardonnay. I wonder if the irony will be lost on them; our last garden party mirroring the first time we got together a few years ago.

I fiddle with the napkins and readjust the cutlery. I'm nervous. Will they think I'm mad for doing this? One last hurrah before we go our separate ways?

It has been a week since I saw Avery die. I haven't seen either of them since that day at the police station. I haven't wanted to. Once Elly reported the rape, the police compared alleged attacks on other women so I've been busy conferring with them, organizing the funeral, dealing with extensive legal issues. Avery was a very rich man and I'll benefit, along with the girls. They're flying in tomorrow for the memorial service. I expected them to be more upset when I told them the news but they must get their stoic outlook from me. They'd shed tears, hugged each other, but had been more concerned about me.

I haven't told them the entire truth. I stuck to a few doctored facts. Avery had been helping Ryan get out of a sordid blackmail, Elly had discovered the truth, they had a massive fight, he tripped and cut himself on a broken vase in a freak accident and bled out.

That's all they need to know. His death will be hard enough on them. And if the police match the MO and evidence on other victims to Avery's raping Elly—and the extent of his crimes come to light—there's time enough for them to deal with the ugly truth.

Claire rounds the corner of the house and waves. She's wearing a simple white sundress that sets off her tan, and silver flip-flops. Her hair is loose and swinging around her shoulders. She's even slicked gloss over her lips. She looks carefree in a way I've never seen before.

"Hey, Ris." She hugs me, her strong arms wrapping around me and squeezing tight.

"I'm so glad you came..." I trail off as I see Elly. She halts near the house for a moment, as if questioning the wisdom of turning up here. Then she squares her shoulders and walks toward us, her steps confident as usual in her four-inch heels.

She looks fabulous in a tight-fitting yellow dress that ends mid-thigh. Her hair is blow-dried, her makeup flawless. I know what Ryan and my husband saw in her, though what Avery did was abominable.

My husband had been psychopathic as well as egotistical and stupid. I know I'll be secretly thanking Elly every single day for doing me a favor and getting rid of him.

I must stiffen inadvertently because when Claire releases me, she says, "I won't have to play referee between you two, will I?"

"I'll be fine."

Claire shoots me a dubious look so I add, "I wouldn't have asked her if I didn't want her here. Besides, I feel like I owe her . . . something."

Claire nods. "Closure. I get it."

"Exactly."

Elly reaches us, her smile uncertain. "Hi, ladies."

Claire mumbles a greeting, I wave toward the table. "Take a seat. I think we need wine for this."

Elly looks grateful that I haven't launched a verbal tirade and reaches for the wine bottle. "I'm glad you reached out to me, Ris."

"We need to talk." I wait until she's filled three glasses before handing one to Claire and picking up one myself. "When I first discovered what you did, Elly, I overreacted because I felt betrayed, even though you'd had the affair with Ryan. I felt like I let you into my life and you undermined my family. But now, after learning the extent of Avery's depravity and what he did to you . . ."

Emotion lodges in my throat and I take a gulp of wine to ease it. "I remember that morning you called me, every agonizing detail, so I can't imagine what it must be like for you learning that someone you socialized with, someone you sat down to dinner with many times, was the monster who raped you."

My chest aches and I press my hand to it. "I'm so, so sorry for what you went through."

I take a large sip of the most expensive white wine in my cellar. Avery had been keeping it for a special occasion, and for me, today, this is it. These two have meant everything to me the last few years. They got me through my empty nest syndrome and now we're bonded forever, keeping the secret of Avery's death.

"Do you resent me?"

She frowns in confusion. "Why?"

"Because maybe I should've known something about my husband being depraved. Because of what you had to go through in fighting him off and almost dying." I shake my head, the sting of tears making my eyes burn. "I'm sorry that I let you down."

Elly leaps to her feet and some of her wine sloshes onto the patio. "I can't believe I'm hearing this. You have nothing to feel guilty for."

She places her wine glass on the table and comes to sit beside me, before resting her hand on my forearm. "You didn't let me down. You *saved* me."

I don't know if she's referring to the night of the rape, the lie we told to keep her out of jail, or our friendship in general, but when a lone tear trickles down her cheek I cover her hand with mine.

"You know some of this already, Ris, but I'll tell you both the rest. Before I came to town I had the perfect life and perfect husband. In Chicago, several years ago." She slips her hand out from under mine and swipes away another tear. "Then I discovered the lying prick had another wife and three kids and I'd been the victim of bigamy."

I glance at Claire, who's stunned.

"I had a breakdown, spent a ton on a therapist, and on the day the divorce came through, had meaningless sex with a guy who turned out to be married." Her gaze slides away and embarrassment tinges her cheeks pink. "I didn't know and when his wife called I outed him. And for the first time in over a year, I felt back in control again."

Elly gestures at her outfit. "So I reinvented myself. And when married men came on to me, I encouraged them, knowing that by exposing those traitorous bastards I was helping a clueless woman like me."

She shrugs and holds out her hands, palm up, like she has nothing to hide. "I liked Maggie and for what it's worth this is the first time I feel real remorse for screwing over another woman." She makes circles at her temple. "I went a little crazy after the rape and when Ryan paid me attention...well, he was the first guy I slept with in my warped revenge scenario. Not for the sex, but because he comforted me somehow."

She gestures at Claire and me. "And I'm sorry for doing it, because the friendship we have, I've never had anything like it. I was struggling when I arrived in Gledhill and you literally saved me, so you should know that."

Her teary gaze swings between the both of us again. "As for what you both did for me that day in the cottage with Avery, I'll spend every single waking moment for the rest of my life being grateful that you lied for me."

She leans over and hugs me, then does the same to Claire, who's increasingly uncomfortable being reminded that a police officer undermined the law and her duty to uphold it by lying.

"What will you do now?"

"I've accepted a job at a cosmetic surgeon's glitzy practice in LA." Her mouth twists into a wry grimace. "I should fit right in with all the phonies."

"We do what we have to do to cope and it sounds like you've had to cope with more than most." Claire bumps Elly gently with her shoulder. "For what it's worth, I'll miss you."

"Me too." I sling my arm across Elly's bony shoulders and squeeze.

She leans into me momentarily before straightening and when her grateful gaze locks with mine I see she's not defeated. She's not that type of woman. She'll conjure a new life in a new city. Elly's a fighter.

I want to suggest she seeks counseling for what she went through with Avery but when she stands I can already feel the distance being established between us. We won't stay in touch. I don't want to be reminded of what my husband did to her and she probably feels the same.

"Take care, girls." Her smile doesn't quite reach her eyes, where I glimpse real sorrow. "I'll try to keep the garden club tradition alive by consuming my body weight in wine and cheese on a monthly basis."

We chuckle and Elly raises her hand in farewell as she walks away, her daffodil yellow silk dress clinging to the curves that must've captured my degenerate husband's attention in the first place.

"That was unbelievable," Claire says, sadness downturning her mouth as she watches Elly until she's out of sight. "I can't imagine how broken she must've been to discover the truth about her husband."

I nod. "Sounds horrible."

I can empathize, considering I recently discovered the awful truth about the man I'd been married to for two decades, but I'm not broken. I would never give the lying creep the satisfaction.

"Not that it justifies what she did but still..." Claire drifts off for a moment, as if contemplating what Elly has been through. "I feel sorry for her."

"She's been through so much and we didn't know the half of it." I shake my head. "I feel sorry for her too."

Claire twirls the stem of her wine glass between her fingers absentmindedly. "It makes my problems seem insignificant after what she's been through."

"I guess we never really know a person no matter how close."

She nods. "Do you feel better, getting closure?"

"I think so." I top up my wine glass, determined to enjoy this two-thousand-dollar bottle to the last drop. "I can't help but think Elly's strong and she'll get through this. She'll reinvent herself in LA like she did here. But what about all those other poor women my husband violated?"

"The police will deal with that. They've already matched several similar rape incidents within the Long Island area so let them do what they have to do."

She hesitates a moment, before continuing. "Ris, he's gone. You need to move on." She stares at me with concern. "Are you okay, really? You watched your husband die, you learned horrific things about him, and now you're losing your best friends."

"I'm not losing you, you're only a few hours away."

Claire wrinkles her nose. "Can't believe I'll be living in Atlantic City."

"You're doing it for Dane and that's honorable."

"I'm doing it for me too." A soft smile plays about her mouth. "I'm incredibly lucky that he forgave me for the affair I had when we were engaged and he wants to start afresh like I do."

I'd been surprised when Claire had told me about a dalliance with a fellow cop a few weeks before she married. She doesn't seem the type. Then again, do we ever know what anyone's capable of? Avery's a prime example.

She wraps her arms around her middle. "Once we get through the genetic counseling I'm hoping he'll want to have a child with me."

"Are you sure you're ready to take such a risk?"

When Claire told me the truth about what Dane had done to not have a child and why, I'd been stunned. And filled with admiration that a man would go to such lengths to protect his wife from possible heartache. Dane's a keeper, but I guess I've always known that.

Claire shrugs. "Life's a risk. I want to live it, not tiptoe through it waiting for more bad stuff to happen."

More. I guess what we'd witnessed in that cottage and the aftermath qualified as bad stuff.

"Will you miss the police force?"

Her mouth downturns for a moment before she shakes her head. "Dane's brother is showing signs of Huntington's and he wants to be there for him. I want to concentrate on us for a while. We need to heal before we even consider having kids, biological or not. So that will be my life for now."

She hasn't really answered my question but I let it go. Who am I to judge her life choices when I've made some questionable ones myself?

"And I'm glad Griffin has been suspended."

Claire snorts. "When a policewoman in the city came forward and accused him of sexual harassment, it didn't surprise me. He totally misconstrued our friendship and sounds like he did the same with her. Anyway, he's off work for three months then will come back on supervised probation."

I have a feeling that's part of the reason why she's leaving but I don't pry. I'm glad she's following her heart and doing what makes her happy.

"What about you, moving forward?" She takes a sip of wine, watching me carefully, like she expects me to fall apart any moment. "Are you really staying in this place?"

I glance at the house, standing proud on a slight rise. Its sandstone exterior and white trim windows, the sun reflecting off the conservatory's glass. It's a beautiful home, the only real home I've ever known. Filled with memories, most of them good, some bad.

That's why I have to stay. This house is testament to the way I denied my true self. It will act as a reminder to how foolish I once was and to never be that way again. It's tangible proof that I've left my past behind and am ready to embrace my future.

"This is my home."

Claire accepts my simple response. We sit in silence for a while, sipping our wine. When our glasses are empty, she says, "You know, maybe we should've done a book club instead. Would've been a lot easier."

"What do you mean?"

She smiles. "Because fact is stranger than fiction and maybe if we'd read about bad stuff we wouldn't have had to live it."

I laugh, really laugh, for the first time since before that fateful day at the cottage. Once I start I can't stop, great guffaws bubbling up from deep within.

When they peter out, I hear voices. Elly and Maggie. They're not arguing, per se, but there's something odd in Maggie's tone...

CHAPTER FIFTY-ONE

ELLY

As I round the corner of the house I almost run into Maggie.

"Sorry," I mutter, quickly shrugging off her grip. I should be glad she prevented me from falling by reaching out but all I feel is cold from her touch.

"How are you, El?"

She sounds ridiculously chipper and upbeat, like nothing has changed between us.

"Do you really want to swap mindless pleasantries?" I shake my head. "Because I don't."

A flicker of anger lights her eyes. "After all you've done, I would've thought the least you can do is be polite."

I grit my teeth to prevent from responding and she continues, oblivious to my discomfort.

"Ryan and I are leaving for Europe in the morning. Our marriage is back on track and I owe it all to you." Is she really thanking me for having an affair with her husband? "If I hadn't heard that girl's name in your office the day you made her first ob-gyn appointment, I never would've figured it out."

I stare at her in confusion but she isn't looking at me any longer, she's staring at her house with a weird, fixed gaze. "When I overheard Avery and Ryan arguing about that girl...well, it all became clear. Avery said he'd fix it. So I followed him."

Her expression is at odds with her eerie monotone and I let her ramble.

"She had to die, you know. To keep things clean. I couldn't risk Ryan leaving me for the one thing I can't give him, a child."

Her lips ease into a smile. "A baby may have changed everything. Men are fickle and stupid, as we both know. I couldn't guarantee that money would've bought her silence so after Avery left I did what I had to do to ensure Ryan never got tempted to leave me for diapers and pacifiers."

I'm speechless, Maggie just confessed to murdering Jodi.

"Why are you telling me this?"

She shrugs and drags her gaze back to me. Her eyes are empty, unnerving.

"I know you understand what it's like to remove a threat and feel truly free." She lays a hand on my shoulder and I flinch. "This way, we all get to move on with our lives."

"What's going on here?"

I've never been more relieved to hear Ris's voice and I spin out of Maggie's grasp as she and Claire walk up to us. "Nothing. I was just leaving—"

"Elly and I were having a little chat, clearing the air, so to speak," Maggie says, incredibly blasé for someone who admitted to murder. "Cleansing ourselves."

I stifle the urge to step away.

She told me she killed Jodi.

Ris locks gazes with me and in that instant I know.

She heard everything.

"Maggie, are you all right?" Ris steps forward while Claire hangs back, like they don't want to startle her into doing anything rash.

"Never better." Maggie waves away Ris's concern. "I used to be so jealous of you girls, you know."

She points to her house. "I would watch your monthly gatherings from my upstairs window."

A slight frown mars her brow. "I envied your perfect life, Marisa."

"We all know there's no such thing as perfect," Ris says, her voice low and soothing, like she's trying to stop Maggie from jumping off a cliff. "You take care on your trip, okay?"

Maggie blinks several times, as if coming out of a deep sleep, and nods. Her blank gaze lands on each one of us, trying to convey a message we have no hope of understanding, before she raises a hand in farewell and walks away.

We wait until she's out of earshot before turning to each other, our eyes wide, mirroring shock.

Our odd little threesome has yet another secret to keep. After what we've been through, it doesn't matter.

What's one more?

A LETTER FROM NICOLA

I want to say a huge thank you for choosing to read *The Scandal*. If you did enjoy it, and want to keep up-to-date with all my latest releases, just sign up at the following link. Your email address will never be shared and you can unsubscribe at any time.

https://www.nicolamarsh.com

One of the most common questions I'm asked as an author is "where do you get your ideas from?" In the case of *The Scandal* the premise of the story came from so far left field I still marvel at it.

Summer holidays with my kids are spent lounging around the pool, reading, playing board games, and entertaining. The lack of routine is glorious and late nights are common. But during the summer a few years ago, I couldn't sleep much because the idea of three women becoming reluctant friends and bonding over secrets shimmered into my imagination. From there, every single night I went to bed, another scene would unfurl until I could see this story so clearly, like a movie, and I couldn't sleep until I started writing.

The words poured out of me in six weeks, leaving me stunned and a tad excited. Some stories demand to be told and *The Scandal* is one of those.

I hope you loved *The Scandal* and if you did I would be very grateful if you could write a review. I'd love to hear what you think, and it makes such a difference helping new readers to discover one of my books for the first time.

I love hearing from my readers—you can get in touch on my Facebook page, through Twitter, Goodreads, Instagram, or my website.

Thanks,
Nicola

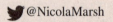 @NicolaMarsh

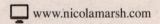 www.nicolamarsh.com

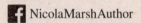 NicolaMarshAuthor

@nicolamarshauthor

ACKNOWLEDGMENTS

I knew I was onto a good thing when I saw Kim Lionetti's #MSWL tweet outlining how she would love to read an emotional, dark, twisty, domestic suspense novel. I'd recently completed *The Scandal* so seeing that tweet for her manuscript wish list seemed like fate. I've always been a huge fan of BookEnds Literary Agency and having Kim offer me representation after reading this story was just fabulous. So huge thanks, Kim, for seeing the potential in this story and helping me bring out the extra twisty elements. I love working with you!

Indebted thanks to Jennifer Hunt, my wonderful editor at Bookouture. From the moment she read *The Scandal* she championed it and her enthusiasm is truly infectious. Jennifer, you're a joy to work with. You make my writerly life that much easier with your clarity and speed. Thanks for loving my book and bringing out the best in it.

To the brilliant Bookouture team, with a special callout to Noelle Holton and Kim Nash, PR gurus extraordinaire. I marvel at your passion for every single book you publish. May this be the start of a beautiful relationship!

With thanks to Kirsiah McNamara and the team at Grand Central Publishing for loving my book baby and bringing it to US readers.

Soraya Lane and Natalie Anderson, you girls are my rocks. We've shared many ups and downs in this crazy rollercoaster ride that is publishing and I'm so lucky that you always have my back. Thank you!

To my loyal readers, I hope you enjoy reading my foray into the darker side of women's fiction.

To Martin, who supports me in everything I do, even when I initially researched how to kill a husband via poison in the first draft of this book! Thanks, babe, I heart you.

Last but not least, to my amazing boys, who light up my life every single day. Seeing me work on this book has taught you a lesson in persistence, that's for sure! I hope you follow your dreams and reach for the stars. You can do anything. I believe in you. Love you. Xx

ABOUT THE AUTHOR

USA Today bestselling author and multi-award winner Nicola Marsh writes feel-good fiction... with a twist. She has published seventy novels and sold over eight million copies worldwide. She's an Amazon, Apple iBooks, Waldenbooks, Bookscan, and Barnes & Noble bestseller, a RBY (Romantic Book of the Year) and National Readers' Choice Award winner, and a finalist for awards including the Romantic Times Reviewers' Choice Award, HOLT Medallion, Booksellers' Best, Golden Quill, Laurel Wreath, and More than Magic. A physiotherapist for thirteen years, she now adores writing full time, raising her two dashing heroes, sharing fine food with family and friends, and her favorite, curling up with a good book!

nicolamarsh.com

 @NicolaMarsh

 NicolaMarshAuthor

 @nicolamarshauthor